THE
BOY&GIRL
WHO
BROKE
THE
WORLD

amy reed

ATOM

ATOM

First published in the US in 2019 by Simon Pulse
First published in Great Britain in 2019 by Atom

1 3 5 7 9 10 8 6 4 2

A CIP catalogue record for this book
is available from the British Library.

ISBN: 978-0-349-00340-5

Printed and bound in Great Britain by
Clays Ltd, Elcograf S.p.A.

Papers used by Atom are from well-managed forests
and other responsible sources.

MIX
Paper from
responsible sources
FSC® C104740

Atom
An imprint of
Little, Brown Book Group
Carmelite House
50 Victoria Embankment
London EC4Y 0DZ

An Hachette UK Company
www.hachette.co.uk

www.atombooks.co.uk

For my Grays Harbor Reeds and my Cebu/Delano Padillos.
For my roots both known and hidden, my people
found and lost, my family inherited and conjured.

No matter how dreary and gray our homes are, we people of flesh and blood would rather live there than in any other country, be it ever so beautiful. There is no place like home.

—L. Frank Baum, *The Wonderful Wizard of Oz*

SURVIVAL

: the act or fact of living or continuing longer than
another person or thing

: the continuation of life or existence

: one that survives

INSTINCT

: a natural or inherent aptitude, impulse, or capacity

: a largely inheritable and unalterable tendency of an
organism to make a complex and specific response to
environmental stimuli without involving reason

: behavior that is mediated by reactions below the
conscious level

SURVIVAL INSTINCT

: ability to know what to do to stay alive[1]

---

1. "Survival Instinct." Merriam-Webster.com. Accessed April 17, 2018.
https://www.merriam-webster.com/dictionary/survival instinct.

PROLOGUE

Excerpt from

UNICORNS VS. DRAGONS: THE FOG APPROACHETH (BOOK ONE)

By Christie Romney

The blackberry vines are bare, and night comes early. Fog settles in a thick mantle over the land, and the unicorns know it is finally safe to come out of their summer hiding places. All across the flatlands, they stretch their sparkling white haunches as they breathe the cool, refreshing air of autumn.

But still, every owl cry and fern rustle makes them tense. They are always on guard, always vigilant, always ready to run. It's the only way to survive.

Moonracer's nose twitches as she sniffs the breeze. She can smell a trace of danger on the fog, a putrid scent that could only come from one place—the hot bellies of hibernating dragons.

She tosses her snowy mane as she worries to herself, *I hope the dragons don't wake up early this winter. They will be ravenous.* She has known this fear for as long as she can remember. It is in her blood.

"Moonracer!" her mother calls. "Time for mushroom hunting." Moonracer's stomach rumbles. She hasn't eaten since before the rhododendrons started getting their blossoms.

Ugh, Moonracer thinks to herself. *Another winter of foraging mushrooms, staying out of sight, and trying not to wake up the dragons. What if there's more to life than this?*

Just then, thunder rumbles noisily from the top of the mountain, and the fog thickens with the rotting stench of dragon snores. The unicorn herd trembles in unison and hides without a sound.

But not Moonracer. She stands tall, glistening in the mottled moonlight.

"Get in here!" her mother warns, peeking out from inside the dark, dripping, moss-lined cave, still stuffy from the family's months of summer sleep.

"I'm not scared of a dragon's nightmare," Moonracer says defiantly.

"You should be," whines her little sister, still a foal, from deep inside the cave.

"I want to know what's out there," says Moonracer.

"But curiosity leads to danger," her mother says. "This is who we are, Moonracer. This is our territory, and we must stay inside its boundaries. We're safe from dragons here."

But if we're safe, Moonracer thinks, *why are we always so scared?*

She's been hearing stories her whole life, about all the things to fear, all the things to hate, all the things *out there*.

But when was the last time a unicorn even stepped outside these woods? Does anyone really know what would happen if they climbed through the fog to the top of Mount Olympus? What does the world look like above the tree line, beyond the suffocating dark of the forest, where there are no towering firs or spruces or cedars, no hoof-tangling brambles and ferns?

What does the sky feel like outside the shadows?

BILLY

THIS ISN'T ANY OLD FIRST DAY OF SCHOOL. FIRST OF ALL,
it's my first day of *senior year*, which is supposed to be some kind of
Big Deal, like a rite of passage or something, except I don't really see
myself or most of my classmates changing much anytime soon, and
isn't that what a rite of passage is supposed to make you do? As far
as I can tell, most people in Fog Harbor stay the same until they die,
except instead of being in high school, they're working at BigMart
or the prison. So senior year isn't so much about growing up as it
is about doing a bunch of illegal things before you can get a permanent police record. But I have no interest in drinking and doing
drugs, and I don't know any other, cleaner options that sound any
good. I'm not cool enough to be straight-edge, and I'm not smart
enough to be a nerd, so mostly I'm just sober out of fear, which is
my motivation for most things when I think about it. Grandma's
been telling me since before I can remember that addiction is in
my blood and I'm a junkie waiting to happen, and I figure going
through withdrawal once as a baby is more than enough. Plus, I've
heard enough horror stories watching the AA channel on TV that
drinking and doing drugs don't really seem worth the trouble.

The whole Big Deal of senior year pales in comparison to

the *Really* Big Deal: that the high schools of Carthage and Rome will be combined this year. Things are tense, to say the least. Even before my uncle got famous, even before Carthage's Unicorns vs. Dragons connection, Rome and Carthage have had a rivalry as long as anyone can remember. This is one of Grandma's favorite topics of conversation, in addition to "environmental terrorists" and "fake news." The rivalry started sometime in the early 1900s, with a sordid story involving opium-crazed mill workers and a serial killer named Hilliard Cod, who was also the first mayor of Rome and was supposedly into witchcraft and put a curse on both the towns right before he was executed. For years, the biggest night of the year for both towns has been the annual Carthage High versus Rome High football game, which has the highest official violent crime rate of any night all year. But since Carthage High is closed down due to dwindling enrollment numbers and being condemned for a rabid raccoon infestation and literally the whole thing being a giant, crumbling box of asbestos, that particular night won't be a problem anymore. But now the whole school year might.

Until just a few years ago, most people only knew about us for having the highest per capita heroin deaths in the state and the most foggy days per year of anywhere in America and one of the worst rates of unemployment after all the logging jobs disappeared. We're also known as West Coast Appalachia, which sounds kind of fancy to me but apparently is not a compliment because the one time I asked Grandma what it meant, she yelled and chased me around the house (but slowly, due to her bum knee and arthritis and diabetes and a few dozen extra pounds) and threatened to smack my chin, even though these days, smacking chins is mostly considered child abuse, which she claims it wasn't back when her actual children— my mom (RIP) and uncle (estranged)—were kids. But look how they turned out (not good).

But Rome is famous now for something way bigger than fog and heroin and unemployment, and that big thing is my uncle, Caleb Sloat. The WELCOME TO ROME sign when you drive into town got replaced last year with a new sign that says WELCOME TO ROME—YOU CAN'T GO HOME AGAIN, which is the title of the song that catapulted Rainy Day Knife Fight (my uncle's band) into fame three years ago. If you ask me, it was a kind of hasty decision for Rome to make a whole new sign to commemorate a hometown hero, especially one who's only been famous for three years and isn't even dead yet, but I guess they were desperate for a hometown hero. The funny/tragic/ ironic thing is that "You Can't Go Home Again" is basically a song about how much Caleb hated growing up in Rome, which is what most of his songs are about and pretty much all he ever talks about in interviews, and if you think about it, the sentiment that "you can't go home again" is maybe not the most welcoming thought to have on a town's welcome sign.

So that's what Rome, Washington, is famous for—my uncle Caleb, who I haven't seen in five years, back when I was twelve and he was a twenty-two-year-old starving musician busing tables at Red Robin in Seattle and sharing a one-bedroom apartment with his bandmates. He came back to Rome for a couple of holidays but left both times screaming out the window of his junk car as he drove away, while Grandma stood at the front door screaming back, and I just sat in the house watching TV with the volume turned way up. Then Caleb got famous and stopped coming at all.

I feel weird even thinking about Caleb as my uncle these days. Sometimes I wonder if my real memories have been replaced by things I've seen on TV and online, and most of the things I think I know about him are based on stories he's told in interviews, which Grandma says are all lies. Then, of course, there's all the celebrity gossip about how he's a junkie and hasn't written a new song in two years, which I don't want to be true but I think probably is.

I don't know who to believe (Grandma and Caleb and celebrity gossip are all notoriously unreliable sources), so I try not to think about it too much. One thing I do know for sure is that old-timers like Grandma can't stop being nostalgic about a version of Rome none of the young people ever got a chance to live in. Not me. Not Caleb. Not my mom (RIP). None of us saw what it was like when, according to Grandma, our neighborhood was actually nice, back when everyone had good logging jobs. But then all the trees got cut down, and so did the people, and now our street is just one of many full of dilapidated houses with overgrown lawns and faded FOR SALE signs, in a part of town everyone calls "Criminal Fields."

But it's my home, so I have to love it. I love how everything is green all year and never dries out. I love how the air is fresh because it's always getting cleaned out by the ocean. I love how most everyone who lives here has lived here forever, so you always know what people are up to. I love how I can walk everywhere I need to go. I don't know much, but one thing I'm sure of is that happiness is all a matter of perspective.

So, in my humble opinion, Rome and Carthage have plenty to be happy about. Rome has my uncle, and Carthage has Unicorns vs. Dragons, which, if you ask me, makes the towns about even, but I guess no one's ever satisfied with what they have, even if what they have is the most famous rock star in the world and/or the most successful teen book and movie series in the world. One thing that really didn't help the rivalry was when Rome High changed its mascot to the Unicorns right after the first Unicorns vs. Dragons book came out, even though everyone knows the books mostly take place in Carthage. The city of Carthage actually sued the city of Rome for that, but some judge threw it out. Carthage High had to settle for the Dragons being their mascot, which they never quite got over, but when you think about it, aren't dragons way tougher than unicorns? And isn't it cooler to breathe fire than ice? But I guess when you think someone stole something from you, it makes you want it even more.

With the school merger, the mascot of the new Fog Harbor High is changing to the Lumberjacks, so now nobody's happy.

Honestly, I'm feeling pretty relaxed about everything, though

Grandma suggested I bring a steak knife to school today "just in case." One perk of being a loser is that I'm not all that attached to things staying the same. Where else were the Carthage kids supposed to go? Plus, Rome High has plenty of room because the town's population is about one-third the size it was when the school was built, since everyone who can moves away. I figure this is an opportunity for things to change a little, maybe end the town rivalry once and for all. Grandma says that's ridiculous, but she is against change in general as a principle, so I'm not putting a whole lot of stock in her opinions on the matter.

Besides practicing gratitude, another useful thing I've learned from therapy talk shows is to keep my expectations low and my acceptance high. That way, I won't get too disappointed. So I'm trying not to get my hopes up too much about this whole school merger thing, but I can't help thinking that maybe this year I'll find someone to eat lunch with besides Mrs. Ambrose, who spent all last semester telling me about her college year abroad in Prague a million years ago and harassing me to start a Gay-Straight Alliance club, and I couldn't break it to her that I'm not gay because I was afraid she'd be disappointed, like maybe my fictional gayness was the only thing she actually liked about me, and if I broke the news to her that I'm straight, she wouldn't want me eating lunch in her classroom anymore, and she'd throw me into the hall to fend for myself, which I am notoriously not good at, and that would definitely increase my getting-shoved-in-lockers numbers for this year.

Who knows? Maybe this year will be an opportunity to meet some new people. Not that I necessarily need to meet new people. I'm grateful for the people I have: Mrs. Ambrose, even though she mostly talks about herself the whole time; Grandma, even though 97 percent of the time she talks to me, she's saying something mean or ordering me around; that homeschooled girl across the street from my house whose family's in a cult who I think is my age and I say hi to the rare times she's allowed outside, and sometimes I even get a whole sentence out before she runs back into her house, and that's kind of like a conversation. But maybe it would be nice to know someone I can say more than hi to. Maybe it'd be nice if someone said something back that was more than just telling me what to do, or getting mad at me for something that's probably not my fault, or pressuring me to start a Gay-Straight Alliance club, or making fun of me, or asking if they can meet my rock star uncle. Maybe it'd be nice if I could find someone who actually wanted to listen. Maybe then I could figure out what I wanted to say.

LYDIA

I WASN'T EXPECTING A WHOLE LOT FROM THE PEOPLE OF Rome, but this is bad even for them. A handful of wrinkled old ladies are standing outside the high school with handmade signs that say GO BACK WHERE YOU CAME FROM and CARTHAGEANS NOT WELCOME IN ROME and KEEP TRASH AWAY FROM OUR KIDS. Clever. Someone painstakingly illustrated what appears to be a group of dark-skinned dragons being smashed by a giant sparkling white unicorn hoof. Besides being incredibly racist, it is also incredibly bad art. Someone's even holding up one of those PEOPLE BEFORE TREES! signs everyone has in their front yards to protest the fact that there are nearly a million acres of untouched old growth forest in Olympic National Park being wasted on nature when it could be creating jobs to cut them down. What that has to do with the school merger, I'm not quite sure.

These people have never met me, and already they hate me. I'm pretty sure they'd hate me after they met me too, but that's beside the point. What sucks is the powerlessness of the whole thing, how I have absolutely no choice about where I go to school, not to mention the fact that I don't even want to be here, but everyone still hates me, as if I am purposely trying to make their lives difficult, as if my very existence is an insult and threat to theirs. Plus, I'm brown, which has never been a particularly popular way to occupy space around here.

At least I'm getting to school early, before the explosion of arrivals officially starts. I recognize some Carthage kids on my way to the lunchroom, but they don't say hi. The unspoken rule about free breakfast is you do not talk about free breakfast, even though at least half of the kids in Fog Harbor are on some kind of reduced-price meal plan. There's also the fact that these people are all ass-holes and not my friends, and therefore not people I talk to.

A big banner says WELCOME, CARTHAGE STUDENTS! as I enter the lunchroom, but someone has already crossed out WELCOME and replaced it with FUCK YOU. I strap my skateboard to the back of my backpack and find my place at the end of the line to pick up today's offering of plastic-wrapped cinnamon roll, sugar cereal, and carton of chocolate milk. With free breakfasts like this, I'm pretty sure the government is purposely trying to kill poor kids with diabetes. My dad, Larry, said the King wants to get rid of food assistance programs altogether, so pretty soon all the poor kids will starve to death, which will be far more efficient. We already got kicked off of food stamps permanently four years ago because Larry accidentally ate a poppy seed muffin and the mandatory drug test everyone has to take tested positive for opiates. One more thing poor people can't do: eat poppy seed muffins.

I sit alone. I always sit alone. After three years at Carthage

High, three years at Carthage Middle, and six years at Carthage Elementary, it is just the most reasonable option. People in Carthage suck. By extension, I already know people in Rome suck. They are too close to be different. That's the big joke about the town rivalry that people around here refuse to recognize—Carthage and Rome are exactly the same. They're both washed-up old towns people either are desperately trying to escape or have resigned to stay trapped in, towns that no one cares about. The fame of Unicorns vs. Dragons and Rainy Day Knife Fight just adds insult to injury. Caleb Sloat got out. The author of those books has never even been here. Any interest people have in Carthage and Rome is for something imaginary.

What I'm not quite sure about is if this general suckiness of people is just a regional thing, or global. I wouldn't know, since I've never spent much time outside Fog Harbor. Apparently, there are rich kids who travel to places like Europe and the Caribbean on a semi-regular basis and go on African safaris. I've only been to Seattle three times that I can remember. My interactions with people there mostly involved restaurant staff, and those people were not promising. The majority of people are like restaurant staff when you think about it. If they're nice to you, it's probably fake and because they want something (like a good tip).

I have spent the last seventeen—almost eighteen—years perfecting my stay-away-from-me-or-you'll-get-stabbed look, but apparently this goofy-looking, mop-haired, skinny white boy currently taking a seat across from me is blind. I glare at him, and he just grins like he's some bad actor in a toothpaste commercial, except his teeth belong nowhere near a toothpaste commercial. Not that I'm judging. I've never been to a dentist either.

"Hi, I'm Billy," he says.

"What do you want?" I say.

"Are you new? Do you need someone to show you around?"

"Billy is the name of a little boy."

"Or a pet goat."

"Did you mean to be funny?"

"No."

"Then that means I'm laughing at you, not with you."

"What's your name?" he says without a beat, as if he didn't even hear my obvious insult.

"Lydia."

"I've never met anyone named Lydia," he says.

"That's because we're usually chain-smoking old women."

"I know a lot of chain-smoking old women."

"Good for you."

"Are you Quillalish?" he says. Predictable. Everyone asks me that. Like inquiring about the source of someone's skin color is an appropriate way to start a conversation.

"No, I'm Martian," I say. "Are you?"

"No, I'm from Earth. Are you from Carthage?"

"Yes."

"Welcome!"

This kid Billy is a certifiable weirdo. Hypothetically, I might like weirdos. But so far, I don't think I've ever met a real, true weirdo. Only the posers pretending to be weirdos because they think it's cool, those girls in pink sweatpants with fake rips and stains with that god-awful band's name printed on the butt from that god-awful Sizzling Subject store in the Fog Harbor Mall.

"What's your last name?" I say.

"Sloat."

"Your name is Billy Sloat?"

"Yep."

"What an unfortunate name. Do people ever call you—"

"Hey, Billy Goat!" shouts a large crew-cutted mouth breather as he slaps Billy hard on the back. The table shakes. Billy accidentally squeezes his juice box, and piss-colored apple juice erupts out of the straw.

"Hi, Grayson," says Billy as he mops up his spilled apple juice with a crumpled napkin. "How was your summer?"

"Whatever, doofus," the mouth breather grunts as he walks away. Then he shouts, "Unicorns rule!" and half of the lunchroom cheers.

"How long have you been putting up with that?" I say, surprised by a sudden, even-stronger-than-usual impulse to clobber the retreating baby-man.

"Pretty much since the day I was born," Billy says, attempting to clean apple juice off his shirt, but all he manages to do is spread ripped wads of napkin all over. He is some kind of rare alien species that appears to not get embarrassed. He may be worthy of further study.

"What's your deal, Billy Goat?"

He pauses his sad attempts at cleaning his shirt, looks up at me, and blinks earnestly. "I have an artistic temperament with no particular artistic talent," he says with no hint of sarcasm.

"Tragic," I say.

He just shrugs.

"Stop what you're doing," I say, reaching over the table with a clean napkin. "Dab—don't wipe." I position the napkin on the wet stain on his shirt, just over his heart, and apply pressure. I can feel his heart beating in my fingers. For a few seconds, he seems to stop breathing. And for some reason the thought pops into my head—I wonder, when was the last time he was touched?—and a weird warmness spreads through me.

I lean back quickly, suddenly wanting to get as far away from him as possible.

"Thank you," he says with a wide-eyed look on his face, like he might start crying any second. What have I done? I can't think of anything snarky to say back. Only the first day of school and already I'm losing my edge.

The thunder of students grows outside the lunchroom. It's almost time for the official start of what will undoubtedly be another miserable year. Same shit, different surroundings. The bell rings. All the kids make their annoying kid noises.

"It was nice meeting you," Billy says.

"I'm in the witness protection program," I say, gathering my things. "I can't have friends. I'm a danger to you and your family."

"Well, can I have your phone number anyway?" he says.

"Are you going to try to tell me about Jesus?"

"No."

"Fine. I'll text it to you."

"I don't have a cell phone."

"Your parents must not love you."

"My parents are dead."

"Mine too," I half-lie.

"You say even weirder stuff than I do," Billy says.

"Thanks," I say. I scribble my number on the one surviving napkin not drenched with apple juice. "Bye, Billy Goat," I say as I hand it to him, and I grab my backpack and walk away before he has the chance to say anything else. I feel wobbly and weak, like maybe I'm getting sick. I'm exhausted in a strange new way.

That may have been the longest conversation I've had in years.

BILLY

THAT GIRL LYDIA GAVE ME HER PHONE NUMBER, SO I'M
pretty sure that makes our friendship official. It's not even a fake
number. I know because I checked as soon as I got home from
school by calling her, and when I said, "Hi, it's Billy!" she said,
"Dude, take it easy!" so I knew it was her for sure. Grandma's always
telling me one of the main reasons people don't like me is because
I'm too eager, but maybe this time it's actually working out for me.
It's not like that time in eighth grade when I asked Alice Comstock
for her number, but when I called it, I got some answering service
that said, "You've been dissed!" and played fart noises, and when I
asked her about it the next day, she just started laughing, and her
friends started laughing, and they wouldn't stop laughing, so I just
walked away and learned from the experience that maybe I shouldn't
ask people for their phone numbers anymore, though obviously I
didn't learn my lesson.

After I called Lydia, I turned on the AA channel. There was
my favorite alcoholic, Lynn A., sitting in her usual spot and nodding sagely as a woman shared about relapsing on mouthwash after
seventeen years sober. "I made a friend today, Lynn," I told her, and
I swear she winked at me.

Something happened when Lydia pushed that napkin down on my heart. Something I can't explain. It's like she found some secret button that reset the world. Not just my world, but *the whole world*. Grandma always says I exaggerate stuff, and maybe she's right, but I know something happened, something bigger than me and bigger than Lydia. It felt like the whole earth took a big inhale, and everything was frozen for a minute while it held its breath, and then when it exhaled, it's like it messed up gravity and jumbled us all up with it. And even though I've never gotten anything better than a C in science, I still understand the basic idea that sometimes when you add one thing to a different kind of thing, it can create a totally new thing that looks nothing like the things that made it, and that new thing can start a chain reaction that does all kinds of surprising stuff all over the place, and I think maybe Lydia and me are like that, like our meeting has created some weird chemical reaction that's going to turn everything wonderful, except instead of chemicals it's magic or something, and when you think about it, magic is just science no one's figured out yet.

So I guess it feels a little anticlimactic now to be sitting here on this faded, stained couch, watching TV with Grandma like usual after one of the most unusual days of my life, but I'm choosing to focus on the positive and not waste my feelings on disappointment.

It's Monday, which means it's *Sexy Sober Survivor* night, which is Grandma's favorite show, which means she might throw the remote control at my head like the last time I made the mistake of talking during it. It's a show where fashion models go to rehab, except the rehab is on a deserted island and they have to break down and cry and/or tell sordid stories from their pasts and/or tell sordid stories from another contestant's past, to get the clue to lead them to food. And also, they're naked the whole time.

It's an interesting show for obvious reasons, but I find it kind of awkward to be interested in it for those reasons in the company of my grandmother, so when it's on, I try to think of something else. For instance, during the last episode, I tried not to look at the screen while the contestants splashed water on each other while bathing in a river; instead, I wondered whose job it is to put all those black bars on their interesting parts, and how they get the bars to move around so fast when the girls are running away from crocodiles and hornet swarms and bouncing around in the water, but then I inevitably started thinking about what's under those black bars, and then things got awkward again, and I had to excuse myself and go upstairs to my room and hope, as I always hope when going upstairs, that this won't be the time the house decides to finally collapse on top of me, burying me in a heap of rubble, and the whole time I'm waiting for the firefighters to dig me out, the most pressing thing on my mind will be how am I going to hide my boner when my arms are pinned under this thousand-pound beam?

I'm grateful we're not watching *Sexy Sober Survivor* right now, just the local evening news. Grandma has her feet on my lap because she's supposed to elevate them according to something she read on the Internet, which is basically her doctor since she can't afford a real one. I'm looking at the TV screen with what I'm hoping looks like an interested expression on my face, but mostly I'm just trying really hard not to look down because Grandma's ankles are so swollen, they're about as big around as a loaf of bread, and there are blue squiggly veins and pink splotches all over them and crusty white skin peeling off, and quite frankly they scare me.

I wonder how much of my life I spend trying not to look at stuff. Not Grandma's feet. Not *Sexy Sober Survivor*. Not in the eyes of the bullies at school. Not at the various scabby guys lying around town who are hopefully sleeping but might be dead. Maybe you could call this denial, but I call it choosing positivity.

The guy on TV is talking about how excited everyone is for the school year to start, but Grandma's just shaking her head back and forth the way she does when she yells, "Can you believe this liberal media crap?" because she thinks the fancy news people in Seattle are so out of touch about how "real people" live. I don't quite understand Grandma's idea that living in a town with no jobs makes us more "real" than other people, but I certainly understand that the people on TV live very different lives than me and Grandma and most of the people in Rome and Carthage and all of Fog Harbor County do, and the news they're talking about isn't usually about our lives. Maybe in Seattle people are actually excited about the school year starting like the news guy said, because they live in a world where people get excited about stuff, while we live in a world where everything seems to happen for the sole purpose of pissing Grandma off.

"Billy," Grandma says. "Rub my feet, will you?"

"Okay, Grandma," I say. I move my hands to her feet without looking. I feel my way around the warm moistness of her skin.

It could be so much worse.

I say this to myself several times a day. The phrase calms me.

It could be so much worse.

The therapy talk shows I like to watch after school are always saying the key to happiness is gratitude. Even people with the worst lives can be happy if they remember to be grateful for what they have. So I remind myself there are far worse ways to be an orphan. I could be in a foster home where I'd have to share a bedroom with ten other kids, with maniacs for parents who steal my foster-kid money for drugs and feed me dog food. Grandma could be a raging alcoholic, or a junkie like my mom (RIP). She could be fast enough to chase me around the house with a belt. I could be living on the streets. I could be sold into slavery. My house could collapse on top of me, and I could die with a boner caused by *Sexy Sober Survivor*, and firefighters would find me and my boner under the rubble too late, and even though it's tragic for a kid to die, they'd laugh about me to each other in secret for the rest of their lives, and that would be my legacy.

I take a deep breath. *It could be so much worse.*

The thing is, Grandma doesn't have to keep me. She could have kicked me out a long time ago, like she did my uncle Caleb, and *he's* her actual son. Sometimes I get scared that she's finally had enough and is sick of buying me food, but that's when I try to make myself extra useful. So far, this strategy has worked. As long as she needs me, I can stay.

Maybe not every newly minted high school senior has to massage his grandmother's swollen, discolored feet, but I choose to focus on the bright side. I only got shoved inside a locker twice last year, so things are definitely improving. The guidance counselor says I show an aptitude for customer service and rule-following, so if I don't become a heroin or meth addict or get anyone pregnant in the next few years, I can aspire to a promising future as a shift manager at a chain restaurant or big-box store at the Fog Harbor Mall. And they're always hiring at BigMart.

Grandma told me once that my optimism is a mental illness. But one of my favorite TV therapist's tagline is "Happiness is a choice," so I think the fact that I keep choosing it actually means I'm extra sane.

In addition to therapy talk shows, my other favorite thing to watch is the twenty-four-hour AA meeting channel. The meeting room has a bunch of posters on the wall with all these great slogans on them. I used to have a notebook where I'd write them over and over again whenever I felt sad, kind of like when I'd get in trouble in elementary school and as a punishment, the teacher would make me write a hundred times, "I will not hide in the bathroom at recess" or "I will not eat food out of the garbage can." I like "One Day at a Time," and "Progress, Not Perfection," and

"Keep It Simple, Stupid," but my all-time favorite is "Fake It Till You Make It," because it means all I have to do is pretend I'm happy and eventually it'll stick.

Lynn A. is this old lady who I swear is sitting in the same seat next to the coffee maker every time I turn on the channel, with her bluish-white fluffy hair and colorful sweaters, looking like Mrs. Santa, constantly knitting some kind of scarf with a serene look on her face, like even a nuclear bomb couldn't make her stop smiling. I've known her pretty much my whole life. Lynn A. has been sober for forty-three years, and now she just lives in this AA meeting on TV, and every now and then she'll tell the story about how she used to be a prostitute who lived in a van by the river and her liver was the size of a basketball and she was vomiting blood all the time, and she'll give a big speech about how she's found the keys to the kingdom of Heaven, and she knows a new freedom and a new happiness, and she doesn't regret the past nor wish to shut the door on it, and she comprehends the word "serenity" and she knows peace, and feelings of uselessness and self-pity have slipped away, and she's lost interest in selfish things and gained interest in her fellows, and her whole outlook on life has changed, and she's not afraid of anything anymore, and she always knows what the right thing to do is, and no matter how many times she says this I get excited every time, and I feel it in my whole body, and it feels like the truth, or at least what I want the truth to look like, and I want exactly what she has.

Ever since I was little, every time Grandma or someone at school would do something mean to me, I'd wait until Grandma went to bed and sneak into the living room to watch the AA channel and pretend Lynn A. was my real-life grandma and Grandma was just my nightmare grandma, and I swear she'd look right through the TV directly into my eyes and smile at me, and it would make me feel better every time, and for a second I could believe I was in that room with all those people sitting in a circle talking about their feelings and clapping for each other's bravery and handing each other tissues when they cried, and Lynn A. would be holding my hand and I'd get to stay there inside the TV for the rest of my life, just like her.

I honestly don't know who I'd be if it weren't for cable television.

LYDIA

IT'S HOODIE WEATHER TODAY, OVERCAST BUT NOT RAINING,
so I'm taking advantage of the dry roads and skateboarding the
three miles home from work. It's after eight, but the sun isn't anywhere close to setting, like nature hasn't gotten the memo yet that
school started and summer hours are supposed to end. The one
thing Carthage has going for it is that it's flat and easy to skate,
though most of the year it's usually too rainy. There's something
peaceful and almost beautiful about the long, empty road that
winds around the seashore, past the old docks and caved-in shacks,
the rocky beaches sharp with barnacles, with their monuments
of driftwood and old tires. But look closer and you see plastic
bags and garbage hanging from mud-spattered blackberry vines,
dumped mattresses and TVs on the side of the road in front of
the impenetrable wall of mossy, dripping, mosquito-infested rain
forest. My home—one big, wet garbage dump.

As far as I'm concerned, Carthage, Washington, is a ghost town,
and that makes the people who live in it ghosts too. The whole
place is just a memory of something that used to be. And maybe
that something used to be worth caring about, but not anymore.
The joke of a downtown is mostly boarded-up storefronts for drug

dealers to lean on. The only places to work are in the land of parking lots on the edge of town—fast-food restaurants, chain stores, the crumbling mall. Half the boats at the fishing docks have FOR SALE signs on them, and the other half are mostly-drowned houses for rats. The only thing the railroad's good for anymore is a way for drunks to find their way home from Larry's bar at night. The old sawmill is a home for raccoons and junkies.

What are you supposed to do in a town where there's nothing to do? Most everyone my age is so bored, they do whatever it takes to temporarily solve their boredom problem, just hoping they're not the one who gets pregnant or killed by an overdose or car crash this year, as if babies and death are things you catch, as inevitable as a cold.

But not me. Maybe something about growing up in a bar has ruined the whole being-reckless thing. Or maybe it's the fact that I don't have any friends to be reckless with. Or maybe I'm just smarter than everyone else. But probably not the last one.

I think I made a mistake giving that Billy kid my number. He called me as soon as school got out, but I strangely wasn't annoyed, which I should have been, and that annoyed me. Billy wants something from me, and I don't like people wanting things from me; that's one of the main reasons I stay away from them. But Billy's not letting me do that. I have a strange feeling that this, that *he*, is the beginning of something that's going to get way out of control. But I'm strangely not annoyed by that, either.

I tense when I hear the sound of a car approaching. The only problem with empty roads is when they stop being empty. "Looking good, baby," some douchebag yells out of a truck. I roll my eyes. Even sexist pigs in other places probably have more imagination than the majority of people here. I try to skate faster, but it's no use. I'm a skinny girl on a cheap skateboard and no match for this dude in a giant truck blasting aggressively bad music, as if his truck isn't offensive enough with its unnecessary size and ridiculous bumper stickers:

KEEP HONKING—I'M RELOADING

CAUTION! THIS VEHICLE MAKES FREQUENT STOPS AT YOUR MOM'S HOUSE

I'M ONLY SPEEDING CUZ I REALLY HAVE TO POOP

Keep it classy, Carthage.

The truck slows to a stop in front of me. I feel the familiar tightening of fear in my chest. Do boys even know this feeling? Do they have any idea what it's like to be a girl alone on an empty road?

I give the truck the finger as I pass it on my skateboard. It follows me, and the driver yells the things guys yell, and I could ignore him for the rest of my life if I had to, but I just don't have the patience today, so I turn around and say, "Hi, I have AIDS and gonorrhea and a very small tail fused to my spine. Want to fuck?"

He immediately stops doing the thing he was doing with his tongue between his fingers and scrunches his face up like *I'm* the most disgusting thing in the world. "Freak," he says, and drives off, and I am left again with the sound of waves lapping against the rocky shore, and the seagulls squawking about who knows what, and I have proof once again that loneliness is far better than the companionship of any of the losers I've met in this town during my very long and excruciating seventeen years of life. I almost wish the King would just go ahead and get World War III started like everyone's talking about and put the planet out of its misery. Humans were a mistake. Give this dying place back to the seagulls and raccoons.

When I get home from work, I stop in Larry's bar before going to our apartment in the back. I cringe as soon as I see him, remembering his promise/threat as I left home this morning that he was going to dye his hair before opening the bar. There are black stains all over his ears and around his hairline, but the worst part is that he doesn't even seem to notice. He has a big dopey smile on his face, like he's just grateful not to see any grays. As if pretending to not be old enough to be my grandfather makes up for the fact that he looks ridiculous.

"You look ridiculous, Larry," I tell him.

"And you look lovely as usual, Lydia," he tells me.

His positivity is infuriating. No matter how mean I am to him, he is still somehow capable of pretending this is exactly the life he always wanted. As if "refusing to make space for negative energy," or whatever the hell he calls his New Age denial tactics, actually makes the negative stuff go away. If it were only that easy.

I'm nothing like him, in so many ways. It's hard to say if this is a good or bad thing. All I know is if you put the two of us next to each other, you'd never guess we're related. I look exactly like my mom—brown skin, brown wide-set eyes, oval-shaped face with high cheekbones, and long straight black hair—while my dad is basically a stereotype of every potbellied old white guy who is not aging gracefully.

He's behind the bar, drying glasses. I'm the only one in here besides Old Pete in his usual booth, but Pete's more furniture than human at this point. I would rather be somewhere else, but I just got done with my shift at Taco Hell, the TV in our apartment is broken, and I don't have any friends, except for maybe potentially that Billy Goat kid, but the verdict's out on him, so my activity options are limited. Technically, it's against the law for me to be in here since I'm underage, but no one cares about laws like that in Carthage. Even the county sheriff comes in here to drink, and all he does is wink at me and tell me to work hard in school.

Maybe if I had agreed to help Larry like he asked, his hair wouldn't have turned out so bad. But what self-respecting girl wants to help her old-ass dad dye his hair? At least it's better than that time he got the dream catcher tattoo on his shoulder when he was going through his Native American phase and was convinced he was part Quillalish, even though he refused to take one of those DNA tests to prove it, and even though northwest tribes traditionally have nothing to do with dream catchers. White people love pretending they're Native American, and they don't care which kind.

Larry says living with a teenager makes him want to stay young, as if that's a good thing, as if it isn't completely inappropriate that he's obsessed with that horrible teen series Unicorns vs. Dragons that some second-rate author from somewhere else set here. It's almost like he's proud to be from the shit hole that is Carthage, Washington. I think he actually believes the great battle in Book Four took place in the woods behind his bar, and the fact that he's lived here his whole life means he has some role in the bestselling series, the movie franchise, the freaking theme park that used to be in Florida when Florida still existed, as if that is some excuse for the walls of his bar (where *grown men* go to drink) being plastered with posters from the book. Sometimes I think my sixty-five-year-old father is more like a teenager than I am. But if you gotta drink, you gotta drink, absurd posters or not, and the old drunks of Carthage need a place to go. If I were an alcoholic, I would totally drink alone.

I think Larry really, truly believes that unicorns live in the forests around here, that local tribes have been using unicorn saliva in traditional medicines for generations, and that dragons actually live on top of Mount Olympus in the middle of Olympic National Park and want to eat everyone. People believe what they want to believe, regardless of facts. For Larry, believing in unicorns and dragons probably feels better than seeing what's actually going on in his life, which is nothing.

Despite how many times I've pointed it out to him, the fact that the dragons favor the blood of white people over that of the Indians because it tastes "purer" doesn't strike Larry as a little racist. Or the fact that the vegetarian dragon hero keeps his unicorn love interest chained up in his mountain cave to "protect her" doesn't strike him as the least bit rape-y. People can overlook all kinds of problematic stuff when they want to believe in magic.

"Want a pop?" Larry says. "I cleaned the lines so it doesn't taste like moss anymore."

What is it about this backward little pocket of Washington that makes everyone call soda "pop"? People have TVs, for Pete's sake. They should know better.

The TV news is on low in the corner. Something about the King's new girlfriend being a reality star half his age. "Can you believe this guy?" Larry says. "He saw her on TV one night and told his people to bring her to him. And now she gets Secret Service protection on her way to sleepovers at the White House."

If there were more people in here, he probably wouldn't have said that. Fog Harbor County is definitely pro-King territory. The people who get fucked over the worst seem to love the King the best. Go figure.

"Kinda like you, Larry," I say.

"What?"

"The King ordered up a girlfriend, kind of like how you ordered up a wife from the Philippines."

He freezes for a moment. I hold my breath, waiting for any tiny sign that he's going to lose his cool. But he just smiles and sighs. "Lydia, your mother was a nurse at the hospital here on a work visa. We met at bingo. You know that."

"And then she ran away as soon as her citizenship went through." I don't say the part about how she died in a car crash just a mile from home the night she tried to leave us.

"Lydia," he says, "why do you say things like that?"

Why can't he just get mad? Why can't he just hate me as much as I hate him?

I don't say anything. I hate this conversation. I hate all conversations involving that woman. So why did I bring her up? It's almost like I want to torture myself. Like I want to torture everybody.

The answer to Larry's question is I don't know why I say things like that, why I have to be so mean to my dad, why I insist on demeaning the woman who was supposed to be my mother. Maybe it's because hating her, hating them both, is easier than the alternatives.

Larry looks at the TV for a moment, then at Old Pete nodding off in the corner. "What should we have for dinner?" he finally says.

"I brought home a bag from Taco Hell," I say. I pull the greasy sack from my backpack, a collection of now-cold mystery foodstuff that had been under the warmer too long and was about to get thrown away. I look inside, see a mess of greasy paper and cracked taco shells, close the bag, and throw it on the bar.

"Thanks, honey. You're so good to me," Larry says.

If this is good, what the hell is bad?

"We need to eat more vegetables," Larry says as he looks inside the bag. "I'm afraid you're going to get rickets."

"What exactly is rickets?"

"Beats me," he says. "I think we have a can of green beans in the cupboard. Want to heat that up?"

"Whatever, Larry."

It doesn't really matter that she died. I would be motherless either way. This way is actually better, because I don't have to spend the rest of my life wondering where my mother is or if she ever regrets leaving. She's dead. It's over. So I don't have to wonder about anything.

BILLY

EVERYONE'S PESSIMISTIC, BUT I THINK THE UNION OF Carthage and Rome High Schools may be the best thing to ever happen to Fog Harbor, or maybe I'm just speaking from my own personal experience, because so far it's pretty much the best thing that's ever happened to me, because all of a sudden I'm brand-new to someone, and I've never been brand-new to anyone. Except for maybe when I was born, but I don't remember that, and I'm pretty sure no one was happy to see me then, because according to Grandma, it was a "total shit show."

Maybe some people don't like things being brand-new, like how the Rome kids refuse to sit by the Carthage kids and everyone scoots their desks all the way to the side of the room so it's just me sitting in the middle all by myself like an island who wants to be friends with everyone but who nobody wants to be friends with. Maybe the reason some people don't like new things is because they're happy with the way things are, or even if they're not exactly happy, even if they're kind of miserable like Grandma, they think keeping things the way they are is easier and less scary than changing them. They're so used to being miserable, it's almost comforting. That's probably the way most of the people around here feel, and I've felt that way most of my life too, but things feel different now for some reason, and I'm pretty sure they're different for my new friend Lydia, too. Because *we're* different. We're the kind of people who want to be brand-new.

I know that's a lot to say about someone you just met, but it's the second day of school and I'm in Miscellaneous Science and for the first time I can remember someone sat by me *on purpose*, and when I asked Lydia to be my lab partner she said yes, and even though I know I'm not usually the best judge of these things, I'm almost positive she's not doing it to play a trick on me. We're the only two people in the entire school from different towns who are talking to each other, and that makes us pretty special if you ask me.

After those guys made fun of me in the locker room last year about not having any armpit hair, Grandma, in one of her rare instances of niceness, told me about how everyone comes of age at different times, how I'm just a late bloomer and that's good because it's better that I stay her sweet boy as long as possible instead of turning into a sex-crazed pervert too early like most guys do, including Uncle Caleb, who supposedly got a girl pregnant when he was fourteen and Grandma had to pay for the abortion because no one else would. I'm not sure about that last part, but I think it's true about the late-bloomer stuff because I finally got armpit hair over the summer, and I have a friend now who also happens to be the coolest person I've ever met, and I believe everything happens for a reason so there's just no way those two things can be a coincidence, and maybe now I'll finally be someone besides the kid who gets shoved in lockers and has a famous uncle, and maybe now I'll finally be able to shake off the label of "Smelly Kid" I got in third grade when our washing machine was broken for three months and Grandma couldn't get it together to go to the Laundromat.

Maybe all sorts of things will change now too, like maybe there will be some kind of scandal involving the student body president, and the student body will decide to impeach her, and when they ask themselves who has impeccable integrity and sound judgment, they will immediately think of me, because I will be the most ideal ruler, able to cross divisions and bring peace between the students of Carthage and Rome, and the students will bring that peace into their homes and change the hearts of their parents, and the parents will bring the peace to work and change the hearts of their coworkers, and it will be contagious and the whole county will be transformed and everyone will finally get along, and it will all be because I saved the day.

And then maybe Uncle Caleb will come home and he won't be so sad and angry, and we can hang out like we used to when I was a kid and he would pull me around town in that plastic wagon I was too big for, except now maybe we can go somewhere besides One-Armed Gordon's house, and we can do something besides me just sitting there while they get drunk, and maybe Caleb can tell me about the world outside Fog Harbor and how to get there and how to get good enough at something that people think I'm important.

"Billy!" Lydia yells. "Are you even listening to me?"

"Yes?" I say, but I wasn't. I was busy imagining a world way bigger than this one.

"You're supposed to put your safety goggles on."

And maybe Lydia and I will be elected Prom Queen and King, and Grandma will finally be proud of me for something and she'll stop being mean and actually let me pick what we watch on TV for once.

"Are we doing the experiment now?" I say. "Does this go in here?" And I pour a beaker full of clear liquid into a jar full of white powder just as I realize Lydia's saying, "Noooooo!" and the next thing I know, there's a loud boom and people are ducking for cover.

Lydia's face and goggles and hair are covered in thick white foam that, for all I know, could be dissolving her skin, and I go through a complicated series of emotions in a very short period of time—first, panic that I may have just killed my new best friend, then delight that I have a new best friend, then despair again that I may have just lost her, then surprise that she's not screaming in agony, then relief that her skin does not appear to be dissolving off her face, then guilt that the rest of the classroom is still running around screaming, then the bubbling of joy as Lydia removes her protective goggles to reveal the perfectly clean outline of skin around her eyes as she smiles a big slow Cheshire cat smile and says, "Rad."

LYDIA

THAT BILLY GOAT KID KEEPS FOLLOWING ME AROUND,
and there's nothing I can do about it. He's like a baby duck or something, like he imprinted on me because I'm the first person who's
ever been nice to him, and now he's mine forever, whether I like it
or not.

"Can you do a trick for me?" he says between heavy breaths as
he jogs behind me. Technically I'm not supposed to skate on school
grounds, but security has their hands full breaking up all the fights
between Carthage and Rome kids.

"I don't do tricks," I say.

"What's the point of having a skateboard if you don't do tricks?"

"It's a longboard. It's for transportation."

"Bicycles are better for transportation."

"Bicycles are expensive and they break and you can't carry them
around."

"The bus is good too."

"The bus smells and costs money."

"I have five dollars. Grandma paid me for stuffing her medical
billing mailers."

"I thought you said she was a travel agent."

"She does a lot of things. It's weird how she seems to work all the time but hardly makes any money."

"Tell me about it," I say. I get off my board and carry it. I'm afraid if Billy keeps running, he's going to have an asthma attack. "How long did you work for?"

"I don't know," he pants. "Like, four hours."

"You're working for a dollar twenty-five an hour. Dude, your grandma's running a sweatshop."

He blinks, considering this as he walks. Then he turns to me and smiles his toothpaste commercial smile. "But having five dollars is better than not having five dollars."

"I guess so."

"Do you have a driver's license?" he asks.

"Yes."

"Why don't you drive?"

"None of your business." I'm not going to tell him it's because my dad's van is the most embarrassing vehicle on the planet.

"If I gave you a short skateboard, could you do tricks?"

"What is your problem?"

"I just really want to see you do tricks."

"I'm not a circus animal."

"Do you want to go to Taco Hell?"

"I hate Taco Hell."

"Why?"

"I work there."

"Are you working tonight?"

"No."

"Do you want to come over to my house?"

"I guess I don't have anything better to do."

I can't remember the last time I went over to a friend's house. *Friend.* I guess Billy's my friend. Poor bastard.

We're just about to get off school grounds when a nearby mouth breather shouts, "Way to go, Billy Goat! You got yourself a girlfriend."

They all look the same—these large, soft boys. Doesn't matter if they're from Carthage or Rome. They're all named Graylon or Grayson or Braydon, and they are the reason for every stereotype about small towns. This one is accompanied by two of his female counterparts, these girls I can barely tell apart who are all named Kayla or Kaitlyn or Katelyn. Who the hell decided it was a good idea to wear sweatpants with high heels? I imagine knocking them over with my skateboard, and the thought almost makes me smile.

"Are you, like, Quillalish or something?" one of the girls says.

"She's not Native American," Billy says. "She's half Filipina."

"Fili-what?" the guy says.

I cringe. Why must Billy be so earnest? If he is unwilling to be embarrassed about the clueless things he says, then that means I have to do it for him, and that is not a responsibility I signed up for.

"She looks Carthagean to me," one of the girls says.

"Ewww," says the other. "So that's what that smell is."

"Yeah," says the first girl. "Smells like fish."

No one could write dialogue this bad. My life is a teen movie that tanked at the box office and ruined several people's careers.

It's time to put an end to this worthless conversation. "I smell loose morals, subaverage intelligence, and three dead-end lives," I say, grabbing Billy's arm and dragging him the rest of the way down the stairs before he has a chance to be nice to them.

"Bitch," one of the girls says, and I tug Billy a little too hard because I know he wants to look back with his big doe eyes and beg for forgiveness, because I can already tell he's the kind of person who gives assholes way more than they deserve.

"Why don't you go back to Mexico?" the other girl shouts after us. They're so ignorant, they can't even do racism right.

"Come on, dude," I say to Billy. "If you look at them, it screws up the drama of our exit." I put my arm around his skinny back and hold on tighter than probably necessary.

"Hey, Billy Goat," Graylon or Grayson or Braydon yells. "You heard from your uncle lately?"

If Billy were a dog, he'd be a golden retriever. One of those good family dogs. The ones who have been bred to never bite. The ones who stay loyal even when their humans are assholes. I'd probably be a Doberman. Skinny but muscular. Shifty-eyed. The kind that bites a lot.

BILLY

MY HOUSE IS ONE OF THE BIGGEST ON FIRST STREET. YOU could say it's also in the worst shape of any house on First Street, but I like to say it has the most character. There's a hole in the floor of the upstairs bathroom where you can see all the way to the kitchen below. Every day it seems like something new breaks and the house leans more to the south. When I was little, I used to race my cars by letting them go at the north end of the living room, and I wouldn't even have to push them to make them move. Grandma always says the house would probably be condemned if anyone official cared. But luckily no one in Rome cares about much of anything.

"Sorry my house is kind of a dump," I say as I lead Lydia past the doorless hallway closet piled with trash bags full of old clothes.

"It smells like something died in here," she says, leaning her skateboard against the wall.

"There's a possum family that lives in the crawl space under the house."

"There's a bunch of drunk old men who live in my house."

"Does it smell like dead things?"

"Dead souls."

"You're the first friend I've had over in a long time," I say. "Sorry my grandma's kind of a hoarder."

"She should go on that show."

"She's on the waiting list."

"Cool."

I have a funny feeling that Lydia's presence in my house has somehow changed it. I suddenly notice a bunch of things that weren't here before—the cardboard boxes stacked almost to the ceiling, the broken bookcase covering most of the window, the mountains of bags from Thrift Town's "Twofer Tuesdays" sales that Grandma never bothers to unpack. But they've always been here. It's just my seeing that's changed.

"At least she's a clean hoarder," Lydia says. "At least there're no cats or rotten food all over the place."

"I feel like now that you've been in my house, we can tell each other everything."

"Fine," Lydia says. "I'm not really in the witness protection program."

"My uncle's Caleb Sloat."

"I already figured that out."

"My mom died of a heroin overdose two weeks after I was born."

"My mom died in a car crash while she was trying to abandon me."

I swear the house shudders, like a tiny earthquake, and I feel wobbly for a second. It rattles sometimes when a lost semitruck goes down our road, but never quite so powerfully, and not with such impeccable timing.

"Did you feel that?" I say.

"Feel what?"

"Never mind. Do you want to sit on the couch?"

"Are cats going to come out of it?"

"Probably not."

"Okay."

Lydia sits down in Grandma's spot. No one's ever sat in Grandma's spot before, not even me. The house shudders again.

"Do you have any food?" she asks.

"Not really," I say. I ate the last two packs of ramen for dinner last night. "I think there's some mustard in the fridge? Grandma's supposed to go grocery shopping tonight."

"That's all right. I'm used to being hungry."

"Me too."

The light coming in from the one window that's not covered by something is making everything kind of golden, and even though the room is full of old cheap stuff, something about the light makes it look enchanted, like we're in a fairy tale and all this junk is actually antiques with magic keys hidden inside, and all the dust floating around catching light is actually some kind of fairy powder. It's like a little bit of magic blew in and made everything buzz and shine. Maybe everything's not as ugly as it always seemed.

"Do you like Rainy Day Knife Fight?" I ask.

Lydia is the orphan princess locked in a tower, and I am the brave knight who saves her.

"Their music makes my ears bleed."

Or maybe it's the other way around. Maybe she's the one who saves me.

"They're pretty popular, though," I say. It's strange—I usually try to avoid talking about my uncle and his band with people. But for some reason I want to talk about it with Lydia. I want to talk about him.

"Popular does not mean good," she says. "In fact, being popular is most often a sign that something is garbage. The majority of people in this world have no taste. Therefore, if they like something, it must be bad. That's just science."

"But what if they never got popular?" I say. "What if they never got discovered and they stayed indie or whatever you call it? Would you like them then?"

"I don't like anything that comes from here."

"What about Unicorns vs. Dragons?"

"Especially Unicorns vs. Dragons," Lydia says. "And the author of that crap is from, like, Delaware or something."

"Did you know he's getting out of rehab soon?" I say. "My uncle."

"Everybody knows that," she says.

"His music kind of sounds like here, you know? Like fog and rainstorms and rocks on train tracks and old trees cracking."

Lydia looks at me for a long time without saying anything, and something about it makes my stomach feel mushy, but not in a bad way. I said something weird like I usually do, but I think maybe she's close to the same kind of weird that I am, and maybe she actually thought it sounded smart.

"Yeah," Lydia finally says, and then she looks out the one window that is not covered by a broken bookcase or piled boxes, as if she's expecting someone or something to arrive at this exact moment. As if she knows something I don't.

"Do you like your uncle's music?" she says.

"I don't know," I say. "I think I just like hearing his voice."

I decide I am probably not the knight who saves Lydia. This is not that kind of story at all. She is not a princess, not someone who needs saving, but something closer to a wizard. This is one of those stories where the kid grows up thinking she is some kind of wrong and broken version of a normal girl, but the whole time she actually has superpowers, and that's why she feels so different.

"Yeah," I say about nothing in particular, and I look out the window too.

Just then, a huge gust of wind blows and the whole house creaks, every single wall and floor and beam and window and nail and screw. Everything shakes and shifts a few more inches to the south, and I feel myself move with it. My body is displaced. I am suddenly in a different part of space.

"I think we're going to fly away," Lydia says calmly.

"This is how it starts," I say, and I'm not completely sure what I mean. But Lydia knows, and she nods in agreement, and something is settled, and something is just beginning.

LYDIA

MY LEGS BURN. I LOVE THE WAY MY LEGS BURN.

Cheap speakers blast music from Larry's old stereo in the corner. It's amazing, all the cool weird CDs you can find at Thrift Town. No one in this town has any taste. They throw away everything good.

It's ridiculous that people actually pay thousands of dollars for dance classes and college when basically everything you need to know is on the Internet for free. Not that I'm not still pissed at Larry for not paying for dance classes, and not that I won't be pissed at him until the day I die, but at least there is an infinite number of YouTube videos of technique instruction and choreography, and there are plenty of websites about dance history and theory, and there are even teachers who answer my questions when I e-mail them. Maybe my makeshift studio in the garage behind the bar isn't quite ideal, and maybe I don't have a teacher on hand to correct my form, and maybe I don't have any partners to dance with, but I think I'm doing pretty damn well, all things considered, and the best thing is I don't have to deal with anyone knowing there's actually something in this world I give a shit about, that there's something I love so much I'd die if I lost it.

The thing is, you can't tell people your dreams. When someone knows what you love, they know how to hurt you.

Or worse, what if they start dreaming for you too? What if you become responsible for not only your own disappointment, but theirs, too? That's certainly not a responsibility I want.

Ever since Billy and I started hanging out, it's like everything has come alive in some strange new way, and all the green things are growing an extra few inches every time I blink, like if I close my eyes for too long I'll wake up to find myself covered in vines and moss and they'll be dragging me through the mud away from civilization to be consumed by the forest. It's like I can smell the appetite of this place. It's mud steam and fir needles. It's the ocean breeze, salt water, decomposing seaweed. It's the tang of creosote from the docks. As ridiculous as those Unicorns vs. Dragons books are, at least the author got the setting right. If I didn't know any better, I'd say it's starting to smell like dragons.

I'm used to being alone, but now all of a sudden I'm not, and I find myself almost not hating the world for whole minutes at a time when I'm with Billy, which is pretty much a miracle. I've only ever felt that peace in here, never with another human, at least not recently. But as nice as it is, I know it's only temporary. The minutes always pass. No one can ever really get inside another person. That peace is not real.

I'm not going to tell Billy about my dancing.

This pain is what's real. When my thighs burn so hot I can

barely walk afterward, when I push myself to the point of agony. The pain tells me I'm worth something. It tells me I've finally earned the right to catch my breath. My body is all that exists. It is the only thing I can depend on. Music or no music, there is a rhythm that cancels out all the other noise, all the nonsense that keeps screaming for attention, all the pain of the world outside.

I point and leap and spin, and sweat whips off me, showering the duct-taped boards under my bare, calloused feet. I see myself in the fractured shards of mirrors I glue-gunned to the wall. This is how I know myself—in this tattered leotard; in these ripped tights; in this broken, salvaged room. This is the only place I'm real.

This is the place I come when I need to remember who I am. This is where I come when I need to forget everything else.

But I had dreams about my mother last night. This is not normal. Not only have I trained my body all by myself, but I've trained my mind, too. For years, whenever a thought of my mom comes creeping in, I've just pushed it away, into the dark, like I have muscles in my brain that have gotten stronger and stronger, along with my legs. I thought my mom was gone. I thought I got rid of her. I thought the dark places gobbled her up and she was no more, but maybe she's been lurking there, waiting to come out, like a crazy, hungry ghost.

I don't want her back. Because with her comes the old Lydia, and I definitely don't want her—the girl who used to cry all the time, who used to follow Mom around and grab on to her leg until she had to kick me off. Mom was always tired, and I was the needy little girl, begging her to love me more. But she never could.

I cried when she died. I cried at the funeral. I cried when Larry told me we couldn't afford dance lessons anymore without Mom's income, and paying the bills was more important than my dreams. I cried and cried and cried until everyone was sick of me and I was sick of myself, and then I decided not to cry anymore. Because I realized, what was the point? It didn't fix anything. The more I cried, the less other kids wanted to play with me. I was the weird girl who cried, and then I wasn't, then I was just the weird girl, and everyone else stayed the same, and nobody cared how much strength it took for me to stop crying.

It wasn't one of those dreams full of metaphors and emotions. I didn't wake up in a pool of sweat, or terrified, or missing her, or any emotion, really. Mom was just there, as if she was always there. We were eating breakfast. She had her nurse's scrubs on, and it was a rare occurrence when she looked more beautiful than tired. It was nine-year-old Lydia sitting there next to her, but teenage now-me was watching from somewhere else, from a cheap piece of art on the wall maybe, one of Larry's framed posters of some famous painting in an attempt to look classy, but really it just looked sad. And my eyes were inside it, and my nose, too, because I could smell the way the house used to smell—like clean laundry. Mom was always doing laundry, even when she was so sad she couldn't do anything else. She used extra dryer sheets because she wanted everything extra soft.

And that's it—that's the entire dream. Just my dead mom and my dead little self, sitting there eating breakfast, as if it were any normal morning, as if Mom wasn't planning her escape, as if she wouldn't die in a few days trying to leave us.

I dance harder. I dance so the pain will push the dream away.

Then something catches the corner of my eye. A figure, moving, small and quick. I turn my head, and it is gone. Probably one of so many feral creatures that live here in the shadows.

And now the shadow is just a shadow. The wall is just a wall.

BILLY

"I'M BY NO MEANS AN EXPERT ON VEGETABLES," LYDIA says as we cross Main Street in downtown Rome, which is totally empty except for a few people milling around outside the methadone clinic. "But I'm pretty sure lettuce is not supposed to be white." She's been telling me about what goes into the tacos at Taco Hell. I think she's trying to scare me, but mostly she's just making me hungry.

I get depressed every time I go to Grandma's office, so I avoid it as much as possible, but I need a computer with Internet to do research for a report for my American Patriotism class, and we don't have one at home, and I can't use the computer lab at school like I usually do because the Coding Club meets there on Wednesdays, and even those guys pick on me. But I don't care about that today, because Lydia agreed to come with me, even after she said it's not healthy for people to spend so much time together. If it were up to me, Lydia and I would hang out every day after school and both days on the weekend, but she has a job and something she calls "boundaries" that I still don't quite understand, though it's been covered plenty of times on my therapy talk shows.

Grandma's Sloat Travel and Local Tours office is in downtown

Rome, with a pawnshop on one side and a failed pet grooming place on the other. The front window has a crack in it and needs cleaning. A dusty rack of old, faded brochures for exotic vacations lines one wall. On the other side of the room is a table with information about local excursions and attractions—hiking, river rafting, mini golf, whale watching, salmon fishing tours, the annual razor clam festival, and the Quillalish Indian Casino and Cultural Center. In the middle of the room, on the coffee table in front of the drooping floral-print couch and wicker armchairs, are her handmade, xeroxed pamphlets about her own signature boutique tour packages.

The irony is not lost on me that my grandmother runs a travel agency and I've never been outside western Washington State.

Lydia drops her backpack on the floor and flops onto one of the wicker chairs. It makes a brittle, squeaking sound as she leans backs and puts her feet up on the coffee table. "Where's your grandma?" she says.

"Probably at her friend Shirley's salon down the block," I say. "I think that's where she spends most of her time when she's at work because she usually comes home with a lot more gossip than money."

Lydia leafs through a brochure about the Logging History Museum. "So how's business?"

"Honestly, not great. Most of her clients are old people who don't know how to use the Internet to book their own flights and stuff, but they're all dying off. So Grandma's trying to get her local tour business off the ground. She named me her director of online marketing, but our Facebook page only has eleven followers and she never pays me."

I pull one of Grandma's handmade brochures from the display on the coffee table and hand it to Lydia, the one for her Caleb Sloat, Lead Singer of Rainy Day Knife Fight, Childhood Tour™, which includes a drive past the hospital where he was born, the elementary school he attended, the wall where he got arrested at fifteen for spray-painting INBRED INFRAREDNECKS, the water tower in the Rome Hills where he claims he slept for a while, and his old friend Gordon's house, where he lived for the last two years of high school after Grandma kicked him out. One of the tours even caught Gordon on the front porch in his boxer shorts smoking a cigarette. Many photos were taken. I posted one on the Facebook page, and it got four likes. Grandma finally drove away when Gordon whipped out his penis and started peeing in the tour's direction.

Lydia looks up at me in disbelief. "She has a tour about her own son?"

I nod.

"No offense, but isn't that kind of . . . sleazy?"

"They're estranged."

"I can see why."

"The tour ends at our house," I say. "My bedroom is the grand finale."

"They go in your room?" I can tell Lydia is less than impressed with the Caleb Sloat, Lead Singer of Rainy Day Knife Fight, Child-hood Tour™.

The look on her face is making me feel a weird mix of relieved and defensive, like I'm sort of grateful she's seeing all these things about me, but also scared of her opinions about them. "It was Caleb's room growing up, so it makes sense the tourists would want to see it, right?" I say, and my voice seems to have gone up an octave.

"But it's your room now," Lydia says. "Shouldn't you have some say in the matter? I mean, aren't you, like, pissed?"

"I don't really mind," I say. I don't tell her that Grandma stands at the bottom of the stairs while the tourists are up there completely unsupervised because she developed a debilitating fear of heights right around the time she kicked Caleb out, or that I've noticed something missing after each tour—a postcard of the Space Needle I taped to the wall, an almost-empty tube of lip balm, a pair of (dirty) boxer shorts. What would someone want with my dirty underwear? I don't even want to know.

I guess it bothers me, but I've never said anything. Grandma would probably smack my chin for telling her how to do her job. "You can start having opinions when you start paying rent" is one of her favorite sayings, except I can't pay rent because she won't let me get a job because that would mean I wouldn't be around to help her all the time.

Lydia pulls her books out of her backpack with a sigh. "I guess we should do some homework or something."

I want to tell her more, but I also don't want to tell her more, and I have no idea what this feeling is.

I try to work on my American Patriotism project for exactly twelve seconds before changing my Internet search from the assigned topic of "why political resistance is unpatriotic" to "Caleb Sloat interviews." It's like an addiction, the way I watch the videos of my uncle on YouTube. I've seen most of them so many times, I have them memorized. I know the whole timeline, how in the first few months of interviews, Caleb is freshly shaven, his enthusiasm showing through his signature snarky angst. But over time, he gets more pale and hunched over. His hair is greasy, his skin all blotchy and pocked. You can practically smell him through the screen. His eyes, when not covered with sunglasses, are bloodshot, unfocused. He stares out into space like a dead doll.

I'm watching one of the earlier interviews because I'm in no mood to get more depressed on purpose. This one is from a few months before Rainy Day Knife Fight's second album *You Can't Go Home Again* came out, before they made it big. The whole band is together, backstage after a show, and very drunk. Even with the sound off, I know every word by heart. The interviewer keeps trying to ask them questions, but they keep making jokes and hitting each other over the head with empty pizza boxes. Eventually Caleb sits down and lights a cigarette while the two other guys continue wrestling behind him.

The camera zooms in on his face. I don't think I'll ever get used to this close-up of him so relaxed and smiling. His dirty-blond hair is out of his fluorescent blue eyes. He's arching his eyebrow the way he does, which everyone says makes the girls go wild. "So what do you want to know?" he says, and even though I have it on silent, I swear I can hear his voice.

"How does it feel?" I know the woman behind the camera says. "The *Seattle Times* just named Rainy Day Knife Fight the band to watch out for next year. You're the darlings of college radio stations. There's a lot of buzz about you guys."

"Yeah?" Caleb says, taking a long drag of his cigarette. "Well, I can tell you it sure beats getting my ass kicked every day as a kid."

And then someone pours a beer on Caleb's head, and he jumps over the back of the couch to join in the wrestling, and the interview is over.

Even though the Caleb in this interview is happy, I'm still depressed. Because that Caleb doesn't exist anymore. It's like watching a ghost. I haven't seen that Caleb, or any Caleb, for a very long time.

I change my Internet search again. Quick, before the sadness has a chance to seep in too deep. Before the tears come. I type "cute kitten videos." I put a smile on my face. "Hey, Lydia, look at this."

But she was already looking.

Lydia takes the bus back to Carthage, and I get a ride home with Grandma. What I really want to do when I get home is turn on the AA channel and check in with Lynn A., but that's just not an option with Grandma here. Lynn A. is my secret. I don't want Grandma anywhere near her.

We're eating fried chicken while the news is saying something about the new miniature ponies the King bought for the White House so his grandkids from his third marriage can have something to do when they come over. His grandkids from his second marriage have already covered the walls of the East Sitting Hall with crayon. A government TV channel will have a twenty-four-hour live video feed of the ponies' barn.

"Oh, how sweet!" Grandma says, grease dripping down her chin. "The King has the best ideas."

"Didn't he take your health care?" I say.

The Styrofoam tub of mashed potatoes falls off her lap gravy-side-down on the rug. "Dammit, Billy, look what you did!"

I run to the kitchen for paper towels. When I get back, Grandma is staring at the TV with her hand over her mouth, completely still. She is watching a grainy video of Uncle Caleb onstage, taken with someone's phone at a show. The caption BREAKING NEWS scrolls across the bottom of the screen. Caleb's tiny, sweatpantsed figure is swinging a guitar around, chasing his bandmates, who are fleeing off the stage. The audio is a bunch of muffled voices, some nervous laughter. Then he throws the guitar into the audience, then the mic stands, then the drums, and the muffled voices turn to screams. Someone says, "Holy *[bleep]*." Someone else says, "I think someone's hurt." Someone else says, "Are you getting this? We have to put this on YouTube."

My uncle, Caleb Sloat, lead singer of Rainy Day Knife Fight and best thing to ever come out of Rome, Washington, is on the huge stage, completely alone, screaming into the microphone. All I can hear are the TV bleeps over his curses. Then Caleb throws the microphone into the audience, and the screen cuts back to the newscasters. They're barely even trying to look calm and neutral like they're supposed to. There's a twinkle in their eyes, like the look Grandma gets when she hears juicy gossip from one of her chain-smoking old lady friends. People love bad news about other people, especially famous ones.

I don't feel gravity. The house feels like it's floating, and I'm floating within it. Everything is on pause.

"Details are still coming in, but this is what we can tell you now," the news lady says, a dramatically lit head shot of Caleb in the little video box by her head. "It appears that Caleb Sloat, lead singer of Rainy Day Knife Fight, suffered some sort of mental breakdown during a live show in New York City this evening. It was the band's first show since Sloat's most recent rehab stay, where he was reportedly being treated for heroin addiction. Several videos were posted online moments after Sloat left the stage, showing the lead singer attempting to assault his bandmates just seconds into their hit song 'You Can't Go Home Again.' Eight people were rushed to the hospital for injuries suffered after Sloat threw musical equipment into the audience."

The video starts playing again, this time zoomed in closer on the grainy blob of my uncle. "At this point," says the newsman, "no one knows where Caleb Sloat is—not his bandmates, manager, or his on-again, off-again girlfriend, Shannon Smear, lead singer of the band Olympia's Consent. Sloat is arguably one of the most recognizable celebrities in the world, so there's no doubt he'll be located soon." The reporter looks into the camera gravely. "Hopefully alive."

I look at Grandma, and her hand is still over her mouth. "Grandma?" I say.

The phone in the hallway starts ringing. "Should I get that?" I say.

She doesn't say anything. Why isn't she telling me what to do? Am I supposed to answer the phone? Am I supposed to ignore it? Last time I answered it she got mad at me. But it keeps ringing. "Grandma?" I say again. Nothing. How am I supposed to know the right thing to do if she doesn't tell me?

I finally run to the hall and answer the phone because the biggest thing on my mind is maybe it's Caleb, and the possibility of hearing his voice is way more important than the possibility of getting in trouble.

"Hello, may I speak to Tammy Sloat, please?" the voice says. It's definitely not Caleb.

"May I ask who's calling?" I say.

"This is Ronda Rash from KING 5 News in Seattle."

"Grandma!" I yell into the living room. "Someone from Channel Five wants to talk to you!"

"Tell him to kill himself!" she scream-cries.

The phone starts ringing again as soon as I hang it up. So does Grandma's cell phone buried somewhere in the living room.

"Turn it off!" Grandma hollers. "Turn them both off!"

I run back into the living room. Grandma has picked up the fallen tub of mashed potatoes and is wiping off the rug-contacted layer with a napkin. She sets the tub back on her lap and digs in with her plastic spoon. The same grainy video of Caleb is still playing, now with the caption ROCK STAR HAS MELTDOWN ONSTAGE AND DISAPPEARS.

"Grandma?" I whisper. "Are you okay?"

She squishes the spoonful of mashed potatoes in her mouth. Is this when she starts crying? Is she finally going to break from the years of watching her only son, her only living child, destroy himself on TV? Is she thinking about all the times he's nodded off in the middle of interviews, all the reports of him destroying hotel rooms and being violent with fans, all the rumored overdoses and near-deaths, all the stories he's told about how horrible his childhood was, how horrible she was?

Her face is still. It could go either way.

Then the loose skin on her cheeks starts moving. "This," she croaks. I hold my breath. Then the rest of her face jiggles as her mouth transforms into a crooked smile. "Is *fantastic*!" A glob of mashed potatoes sprays out of her mouth and sticks to her lip. "This is going to be great for business!"

The house shakes. I have to hold on to the wall to keep from falling.

"Shouldn't we call him?" I say, even though I know she doesn't have his number. He changed it a few years ago and never told us the new one.

"Grab me another drumstick," she says as she digs back into the mashed potatoes.

"Aren't you worried about him?" I say, but she's not listening. "Do you feel that?" The house shakes harder. Some old books fall off the top shelf of the bookcase. The hanging light fixture sways overhead and unleashes a thick cloud of dust. "I think we're having an earthquake."

"We need to call them back," she says.

"Call who back?"

"Channel Five!" she yells. "Billy, you're my director of online marketing. You have to call them back!"

"I don't have their number!" I yell in response. I normally never yell at Grandma, but this is not normal. I'm feeling about a hundred different things all at once, and none of them are good. The house keeps shaking and I'm the only one who can feel it and my uncle is missing and I'm the only one who seems to care.

LYDIA

I HAVEN'T HAD MUCH EXPERIENCE WITH FRIENDS, BUT I'M pretty sure what I should do now is call Billy. All night long, whichever channel Larry turns to, there's Caleb Sloat's face staring out at the bar, with headlines like TORMENTED ROCKER ON THE LAM, and SUPERSTAR MISSING, and FANS FEAR THE WORST, and CALEB SLOAT'S 15 MINUTES MAY FINALLY BE UP.

"What a shame," Larry says, shaking his head sadly at the TV. "That kid had some talent."

"What'd you expect?" says one of the old guys at the bar. "With a family like his."

I pull out my crappy cheap phone and look at it. Maybe if I had a nicer phone, this wouldn't be so hard.

I have never called a friend on the phone, never mind a friend who might be emotional and needing me to know how to be a friend. What are you supposed to say to a friend who's emotional?

Hi, Billy, how are you feeling about your uncle disappearing?

Hi, Billy, are you excited for everyone to harass you at school tomorrow?

Hi, Billy, what do you think about everyone's theory that when your uncle is finally found, he will probably be dead?

What are you supposed to do with someone else's feelings when you barely know what to do with your own? Does having friends mean having to do this kind of thing all the time?

The TV is playing a clip of an interview from about a year ago, right before Caleb went to his second rehab. He's with Shannon Smear from that band whose music I actually kind of like, but nobody in Fog Harbor will ever admit that out of some weird allegiance to Rainy Day Knife Fight and the suspicion that Shannon is responsible for Caleb's downward spiral, but really it's just that everybody's sexist and Shannon dares to speak her mind and not worry about being "likable." I have seen this interview before. Caleb is lying on a couch with his head on Shannon's lap. She's wearing some kind of vintage fifties pinup girl swimsuit and a cowboy hat, her thin arms covered with tattoos, her face made up in its usual drunk drag queen style. He's in old tattered pajamas and white tube socks.

She's doing all the talking, while he just lies there with his eyes closed and a serene smile on his lips. Shannon talks fast and leaves little space for even a breath, let alone someone else's voice, like she lacks whatever mechanism filters and organizes thoughts between the brain and the mouth. She just talks and talks, first about how they met backstage at a show, about how they fell in love immediately and made out in the bathroom of the club, how the combination of piss and beer and toilet cleanser will now always be her favorite smell, how sex that night was amazing, how the next day he bought her a taxidermy vulture and that's how she knew he was the one, how sex that afternoon was amazing, how they want to make a bunch of babies and populate the world with beautiful, intelligent, sensitive children who will become an army and bomb all of Washington State west of Olympia so they can give it back to the trees.

That's when Caleb lifts his head and says, "But if we bomb it, what will happen to the trees?"

"We won't bomb the trees," she says sternly.

"There will be tree collateral."

"There is always collateral in a war, dummy," she says, then pulls his face up almost violently and starts kissing him, and then she straddles him right there on the couch and starts unbuttoning his pajama shirt, and then the interview is over.

"That woman is not right in the head," an old guy at the bar says, and everyone, including me, nods in agreement.

And then my phone rings, and I know who it is without looking. No one calls me besides Larry, which is the only reason I can even afford having a phone, because I hardly ever have to buy new minutes. I consider not answering it.

I look up at the TV and there's a close-up of Caleb Sloat, his dirty-blond hair in his eyes just like Billy's, the same jaw, the same thin face, the same sad blue eyes staring right at me.

"Hey," I say, walking away from the bar and settling into a booth for privacy. Only Old Pete is within earshot, but he doesn't have much to say about anything.

Billy doesn't speak for a while. I just sit there with the phone to my ear, listening to his silence. Is this what I'm supposed to do? Or am I supposed to start asking questions? Am I supposed to wait for him to speak? How the hell do people talk on the phone? Where do people learn these things?

I hear Billy take a deep breath. I swear I can feel his warm exhale on my cheek and smell something meaty and slightly sour on his breath. Gravy? I must be hallucinating. After all these years hanging out in a bar, some of the alcohol must have seeped in through my skin and caused permanent brain damage.

"He made really good mac and cheese," Billy finally says. "I think he put, like, a whole stick of butter in it."

"Yeah?"

"We'd draw and paint together for hours sometimes. He was a great artist. He'd draw all these weird magical creatures he invented himself."

"That's cool."

"He was a hide-and-seek master. I could never find him."

"Oh." *Oh?* Is that the best I can do?

"My house is perfect for hide-and-seek. Because of all the stuff, you know? It makes good hiding places."

"Uh-huh." I keep saying these useless non-things. I'm failing at this conversation. I should just hang up now and put us both out of our misery.

"Do you know there's a bedroom upstairs that's full of nothing but blankets and pillows? Whenever there's a sale on bed stuff at Thrift Town, Grandma always buys it all and makes me put it in that room. She's been doing it for years, even before Caleb left. That was always his favorite place to hide. He'd, like, burrow into a spot and I'd find him and we'd just hide out in there together talking about stuff. And he'd tell me all these weird made-up stories about all the creatures he drew. And we'd just float in this soft place together."

I imagine a little-boy version of Billy alongside an older, scowling, heroin-addict Billy look-alike, floating in a cloud. Safe. Impenetrable.

"He sounds like he was a really good uncle," I say, and I feel something thick in my throat.

"He was. For a while. Then he wasn't anymore."

Then silence again. I don't trust myself to say anything. I'm not helping Billy. I'm not making him feel better or fixing anything. I don't know how to do this. I'm not being a good friend.

"I'm really scared," Billy whispers.

"Okay."

"I really miss him."

"I know."

"He was an asshole sometimes, but I think he was the only person who ever loved me." Billy's voice breaks, and then he starts sobbing. I can feel the percussion of his breath in my ear, the great intakes before the exhalations, like he's inhaling parts of me, borrowing them for the seconds the breath is held inside, and then he exhales and gives them back again. I am okay with this. I can sit here and be inhaled, with the protection of the phone between us. I can be sturdy while he needs these parts of me. I am no less solid for being needed. For now, anyway. He is a few miles away, in a different town. He cannot take too much of me from there.

When his breaths calm and become little more than whispers, I finally speak. "I'm so sorry, Billy," and I'm pretty sure that's the nicest thing that's ever come out of my mouth, and that makes me a new weird kind of scared, like all this softness is making me a target.

I see something move in the shadows. I feel like I'm being watched.

He sniffles. "For someone who's never had any friends, you're pretty good at it."

"Really?"

"Yeah. Thanks for listening."

Is that all he wanted? For me to listen?

"Lydia?" he says.

"Yeah?"

"You're my best friend."

"Okay," I say, and immediately regret it. Am I supposed to say "you too"? Or "me too"? I don't know if I'm ready to say either of those things. I barely know him. What if the only reason we're friends is because no one else wants to be friends with us?

"I'm gonna go to bed now," he says.

"Okay," I say, and I feel the air sucked out of my chest. Maybe I don't want him to go to bed. Maybe I wish he were right here, sitting across from me in the booth, so I could tell him about how jumpy I've been feeling. About my dream. About my mom.

"See you tomorrow," he says.

"Okay," I say again.

I put my phone down on the slimy wood table. I hear Old Pete clear his mucusy throat in the booth behind me. "Time to wake up," he grumbles.

I feel a thin tear stream down my cheek and settle into the side of my mouth. A brief burst of anger rips through me as I taste the salt, and I don't know if I'm angry at Billy, or my mom, or myself, or the tear. Or everything.

BILLY

THERE'S NOTHING LIKE A GOOD NIGHT'S SLEEP TO remember what your priorities are.

I woke up this morning determined to stay positive. I learned from one of my favorite therapy talk shows that just forcing yourself to smile can actually trick your brain into thinking it's happy. So even though thoughts of Caleb keep flashing into my mind, even though I can't find any clothes in my dresser that aren't slightly damp, even though I woke up with seven spider bites in a straight line on my stomach, and even though the hole in the wall next to my bed got bigger overnight and I can hear mysterious things scurrying around in there and the lights in the bathroom started blinking on and off while I was brushing my teeth like in a horror movie, I'm smiling so hard my cheeks hurt as I recite today's gratitude list in my head:

A roof over my head (though it's got some holes and leaks and probably bats living in it and is connected to a house that is starting to act like it wants to kill me).

Food to eat (though it has little nutritional value and is probably giving me diabetes).

Living by the sea (though I don't know how to swim and the water is too cold anyway and it usually smells weird and the beach is often covered by all the fish and seals and whales that keep dying in the ocean).

~~*Family?*~~

A best friend!

I don't even have to force my smile for the last one.

I keep smiling all the way to school, despite the possum that lunges at my ankles as I walk out the front door, despite the rain, despite my crappy raincoat that's not even waterproof, despite the hole in my shoe that cardboard and duct tape couldn't fix, despite the fact that I'm too late for free breakfast and I have to wait until lunch to eat. I keep smiling even though everyone stares and laughs at me all day, even though Graylon Jennings trips me in the hall, even though people keep singing Rainy Day Knife Fight songs in my face, but with the lyrics changed:

Fishing in the mud
Look at all my blood
Don't clean me up
I'm all done dying

If I act like nothing is wrong, then nothing is wrong. I manifest my own reality. I am made out of love and light.

It could be so much worse.

I smile when I sit across from Lydia at lunch. "Hello!" I say. "How are you today?"

"How are *you*?" Lydia says, with a confused look on her face. She doesn't get it. She has not discovered the power of positive thinking.

"I'm great!" I say, biting into my corn dog.

"How are you *great*?" Lydia says.

"Aren't these corn dogs delicious?" I say. "I saw a really cool moth on my way to school today."

"You saw a moth?"

"It was really cool."

"Moths are not cool."

"Sure they are."

"What is wrong with you?"

"That's the thing," I say, taking another bite of my corn dog. "Nothing's wrong. It's all a matter of perspective. I have to let go of Caleb, you know? Because I'm powerless over what happens to him. And his path is his own. I can't walk his path for him. What happens to him doesn't really affect me all that much, if you think about it."

"You sound like you're in a cult," Lydia says. "You can't just decide to not have feelings."

"Sure I can." I smile even bigger. I just need to keep smiling. I just need to Fake It Till I Make It.

Lydia sighs. "Between you and my dad, I think I got stuck with the two most infuriatingly positive people in all of Fog Harbor."

"You must be lucky," I say, squirting a packet of mustard on my corn dog. "I saw a show once about this girl who lived entirely on mustard and Diet Coke."

"How'd that work out for her?"

"She died." I smile and take another bite.

LYDIA

IT'S BEEN A FEW DAYS SINCE BILLY'S UNCLE WENT missing, and he's still got that goofy smile plastered on his face like nothing's wrong. "Sorry I'm late," he says, walking toward my locker. "I had to go the long way to avoid Mrs. Ambrose because she keeps trying to tell me about college scholarships."

"How dare she."

I've been wondering lately if I should tell Billy about my dancing. It's feeling stranger and stranger to keep it a secret, especially since Billy tells me literally everything that goes through his head.

"Want to come over?" Billy says.

"Yeah, why not." I close my locker with a slam.

"Did you hear Channel Five said someone reported seeing my uncle in Mongolia?" Something in his face gets droopy, like maybe he's actually having a feeling besides his forced perkiness.

"I thought it was Italy," I say.

"No, that was on Wednesday."

He looks sad for approximately three seconds before he smiles again. Am I supposed to say something? Would a friend try to get him to talk about it, even though he said he doesn't want to be sad?

What's more important—letting someone do things their own way, or trying to make them tell the truth?

"Where's your skateboard?" Billy says.

"I don't want to talk about it." I don't want to tell him about how I accidentally broke it in half when I tried to do a rail slide yesterday. Everyone knows you can't do tricks on longboards.

The brand-new FOG HARBOR LUMBERJACKS sign in front of the school has been spray-painted over with UNICORNS KILL DRAGONS! which is actually not how the story goes at all; the dragons were the ones terrorizing the unicorns for most of the series. We don't have much use for a mascot anyway, since pretty much all the sports teams have been canceled because Rome and Carthage students refuse to be teammates.

As we walk away from school, Graylon or Grayson or Braydon says, "Heard from your uncle lately, Billy Goat? By the time they find whatever ditch he died in, he's gonna be pretty ripe."

"God, that whole family's crazy," Kayla or Kaitlyn or Katelyn cackles through her chewing gum. "Just a bunch of white trash junkies."

Like either of them can talk.

"Do you want to see my attic?" Billy says when we get to his house. It's only a ten-minute walk from school. His house is a ten-minute walk from everything in Rome.

"Sure," I say. His house seems even more broken than the last time I was here, like it's been beating itself up.

Before we go up to the attic, Billy shows me his room on the second floor. "It's not much," he says as we stand in the doorway. That's an understatement. There's almost nothing in it. A mattress on the floor with an unzipped sleeping bag as a blanket, a crooked lamp, an old dresser and bedside table, and a big hole in the wall. No decorations or anything personal. It's like the room of someone who thought they wouldn't be staying.

"How long has this been your room?" I ask.

"Ever since Caleb left, so, like, ten years."

I think about my own room, how I've spent literally my entire life decorating it. The walls are completely covered with a collage of posters and art I've found for cheap and pictures I've cut out of magazines. I've kept almost every stuffed animal I've ever owned. I have a whole table dedicated to random crap I've found on the ground.

I feel a mix of sad and angry that this is Billy's room. He deserves more. He at least deserves some goddamned pictures on the wall.

"Show me the attic," I say.

"Okay," Billy says.

We climb a narrow set of stairs hidden behind a door I didn't even notice. The air seems to change as we go up, become lighter somehow, and everything doesn't seem so broken.

"It's like a different house up here," I say when we reach the attic. There is exactly zero stuff in it. It is empty and clean.

"I can't even remember the last time I came up here," Billy says, looking around like it's as new to him as it is to me. "I forgot it existed." He walks slowly around the open space, all exposed rafters and brown wood, with ceilings that meet the floor in sharp corners all around. "Doesn't it feel a lot more stable up here than it does in the rest of the house?" He kicks a column that connects the floor to the ceiling. "It's totally dry, even with all the holes in the roof. It's like the leaks just skipped this floor or something. I don't even see any spiderwebs or mouse poop. Isn't that weird?"

"Yeah," I say. I'm looking out the one small window at the view of the clear-cut hills in the distance.

He joins me by the window. We're on our knees, side by side. We can see all the way to the hills in the east and the ocean to the west, where the fog is rolling in. I'm used to fog, but it's usually something I wake up to in the morning, already there. Or it filters in so softly and gradually in the evening that no one really notices. But somehow, watching from up here, it feels different. More intense or something. More on purpose.

"It seems thicker than usual, doesn't it?" Billy says.

"Yeah," I say. "That's not normal fog." It's like the fog in Book Two of Unicorns vs. Dragons, when the war's about to start.

I've never watched it from the outside, never seen the edges, never seen where the sky stops and the fog starts. I've only ever been in it.

"Is it just me," Billy says, "or do things seem weird around here lately?"

"Things have always been weird around here."

"But they're getting weirder."

I think about the shapes I've been seeing in the corner of my eye, the strange movements in the shadows. But if I say it out loud, will that make it more real? Is it worth the can of worms it'll open?

"Yeah," I finally say. "Things are getting weirder."

"The fog is coming in really fast," Billy says.

"Yeah," I say again.

"It's almost here."

Five. Four. Three. Two. One. And now we're gone. Now there is nothing but white.

I feel strange, like the ground has dropped away, like we are suddenly suspended, no longer attached to the rest of the house, to Rome, to Fog Harbor, to even the earth for that matter. It's just me and Billy in the attic like a ship, adrift in this sea of white, with no map, no compass, and no way to steer.

I wonder if Billy notices that I'm trembling. I'm used to having so much control over my body. I've been training it for years. I know every muscle and tendon and bone. But right now it's like something inside me has taken over, and there's nothing I can do to stop it.

I remember studying the nervous system in biology freshman year, how there's this phenomenon in prey animals where after they escape a predator, they'll shake uncontrollably to get rid of their adrenaline, to flush out the trauma of their fear. Maybe this is like that. Maybe this fog is more than weather.

The corners are full of shadows. There is something moving. Something human-shaped. The thing that's been following me. I can almost see it.

"I have to go," I say. Can he hear the fear in my voice?

"Not yet," Billy says. What is that look on his face? Is he scared too?

"I have to go," I say again, standing up too fast. I feel light-headed. When was the last time I ate?

I open the attic door and hurry down the rickety, steep staircase to the second floor, all the while hearing wood creak and crack beneath me.

As I reach the first floor, the front door swings open, revealing a large, panting woman carrying several plastic Thrift Town bags. She drops them in the entryway and wipes her wet forehead with the back of her hand.

"Grandma!" Billy shouts. "This is my friend, Lydia."

Billy's grandma narrows her eyes. "So she *is* real."

"Of course she's real," says Billy.

"I thought you made her up."

I look at Billy, at the temporary hurt on his face before he makes the choice to smile again.

"I have to go," I say. "I'm sorry."

I need to run. I need to get away. It's not safe here.

Billy's grandma is still between me and the exit, and she doesn't appear to be moving anytime soon. I say, "Excuse me," and I squeeze by without looking her in the eye, open the door, and take the biggest breath possible as soon as my face hits the cool air outside, but then I immediately start gagging. It smells all wrong. It smells like death and decay and bad things coming.

"What a rude girl," I hear Billy's grandma say as the door closes behind me, then "Billy, what's for dinner?" and my heart cracks imagining Billy standing there with that woman, in that house, without me. I will call him later. I will.

The world outside has been transformed. Visibility is only a couple feet, and beyond that, a thick wall of white. Streetlights glow like fuzzy, floating orbs. A car drives by, and the red taillights create a smoky trail through the fog, as if the water particles have caught the light and are holding on to it on purpose. I can hear the world, but I can't quite see it.

Something darts in front of me, something large and fast and silver. I hear what sounds like hooves on pavement.

I close my eyes and tell myself to wake up.

I open my eyes, and everything is the same.

This is real. I'm awake.

I start running, even though I can't see. As long as I keep the sidewalk under my feet, I'll be okay. I'll follow it to where Rome ends, where it meets the country road that will take me home. I'll run blind. I'll outrun whatever it is that's chasing me. I'll run as far away from that haunted house as I can.

As soon as I get home, I'm heading straight to my studio. I won't even bother changing into tights. I'll dance naked. I'll play something loud and frenetic, and I will shake my body like the deer who barely escapes. I will dance until I have nothing left, until I sweat out the fog and whatever it brought with it.

BILLY

MY EFFORTS TO STAY SMILING ARE STARTING TO FALTER.
There just aren't enough positive thoughts or gratitude or TV or distractions to keep the sad thoughts away. Everywhere I turn, there's a screen with my uncle's face on it, or Grandma talking on the phone to some news station or potential tour client, or bullies at school laughing about how Caleb's dead, or random people on the street conveying their "thoughts and prayers" with a manic glint in their eyes. Two detectives came by the house last night to ask questions about Caleb, and Grandma slammed the door in their faces.

I think I caught her crying this morning. She was watching the news, and it was saying something about how the success rate of rehabs is super low, and even lower for heroin addicts, so basically Caleb is a lost cause. I said, "Grandma, are you okay?" and then she screamed at me to leave her alone and threw a spoon at my head.

Everything feels upside down. My house is getting more aggressive. I barely slept at all last night because I swear I could hear voices coming out of the hole in the wall of my bedroom. I did the thing I've always done when life gets especially bad, like when I was little and I'd be trying to go to sleep with Caleb and Grandma screaming at each other all night long. I lay in bed and rubbed my feet together and went through my favorite fantasy of the best day ever: I wake up and Lynn A. is in the kitchen making me pancakes; then she drives me to school and hands me a lunch bag; then when I open the bag at lunch, there's a note inside written on a napkin, which changes depending on my mood but is usually something like "I love you, kiddo!" with a heart and a smiley face; and then she picks me up from school and there's homemade muffins when I get home, still warm from the oven; and I don't even want to watch TV, and maybe I even do my homework; and then after a perfect homemade dinner, Lynn A. sits on the edge of my bed, singing some old-timey song, rubbing my back until I fall asleep. Usually that does the trick and I'm out cold, but I had to go through it a ton of times last night, and I kept changing the food, I kept changing what she wrote on the note, I even changed the board game we played before bedtime. I thought all I needed was to get the perfect combination of details, and that would be the magic cure for my sleeplessness, but all it seemed to do was make the house madder.

I almost got lost on the way to school because the fog was so thick. I begged Lydia to hang out with me after school, but she had to work today. She kept saying she was sorry. She said it so much, I started feeling bad about how sorry she was, and then I started saying sorry, then I couldn't even remember what we were so sorry for or what we were talking about in the first place.

She has no idea I need supervision. I can't control myself. I keep coming back to the worst thing for me even though all it ever does is make me feel worse.

I'm in the computer lab, at my favorite desk in the corner where no one can see what I have on my screen. Headphones are on and YouTube is cued up with an infinite supply of Caleb Sloat interviews.

"Yeah, my dad was abusive," Caleb says in one interview. "His dying was the best thing that ever happened to me. But then Ma just started where he left off."

Then he commences to talk about how growing up in Rome was like being in a family with ten thousand abusive parents.

"You have to understand one thing about growing up surrounded by white trash." I flinch when he says "white trash." People say it all the time, but it hurts the most coming from him. "If they suspect you're smarter than them, they will kick your ass. They have nothing else to work with. That is their one skill—kicking people's asses. It's pathetic, really. But as a kid, I didn't know that. I just knew I was getting my ass kicked. I knew I hated them. I knew I wanted revenge."

"So have you succeeded?" the interviewer says. "Is your success your revenge?"

Caleb takes a long, thoughtful drag from his cigarette. "Yeah, I guess so." He smiles. "And not just revenge on the dumb rednecks in Fog Harbor. But also all those fucking elitist hipster bands who were so rude to us on our first couple tours. All because we were wearing sweatpants and T-shirts instead of fucking ties and loafers and fedoras and shit. All those turds with master's degrees in, like, philosophy and art history who looked at us like we were an alien species. And the worst part is, people call their music 'rock.' But there's nothing rock about it. There's no soul. There's no grit. It's like a poetry thesis with a fucking ukulele and a cello."

"How does it feel?" the interviewer says. "All your success."

"How does anything feel, man?" Caleb says, taking another drag of his cigarette. "We're all fucking numb in the end, aren't we?"

In the next couple interviews, Caleb basically says the same things over and over again. He talks about everybody being assholes in Rome and Fog Harbor, and while I mostly agree, I suspect the real problem is that everyone's just kind of sad, and being sad turns people into assholes sometimes. What choice do they really have when it's cloudy 95 percent of the time and no one has any money?

Caleb talks about being poor and different, how he had no choice but to be angry and full of rage. The Fog Harbor he describes is similar to the one I know, but I'm not sure it's true that Caleb had no choice in how he turned out. People pick on me, too, but I'm not angry and full of rage. Or maybe it's just a matter of time. I wonder if maybe I'm a late bloomer to anger the way I was to puberty. Maybe it's my destiny to end up just like Caleb.

But mostly what I wonder is, if Caleb thinks everyone he left behind is white trash, what does that make me?

YouTube starts playing the next video. I hate this one. It's one of Caleb's most recent interviews, and very short. He's grouchy and combative from the beginning, sweaty and squirming like his skin hurts. I made the mistake of reading some of the comments once, and the consensus is that Caleb was going through heroin withdrawals.

The interviewer asks him about the rumor that he hasn't written any new music in two years. Caleb gets angry immediately and starts ranting about how everyone's a critic, how it's their job to tear creative people down because deep inside they're jealous because they can't create anything themselves. "You people don't understand the creative process," he says. "You're robots. You're cogs in the capitalist machine. All you care about is a fucking product. Do! Do! Do! Stay busy at all times! Show us something shiny! There's more to art than that, man. You don't fucking get it."

"So explain it to me," the interviewer says. "What exactly have you been up to? Can you describe your creative process? When can we expect something new from Rainy Day Knife Fight?"

"None of your business," Caleb says, lighting a cigarette. "Next question."

"Okay," the interviewer says. He clears his throat. There is the sound of papers rustling.

Caleb takes a drag of his cigarette and fidgets in his seat. "Can you get me a beer, for fuck's sake?" he yells to someone offscreen.

"So," the interviewer finally says, "there's something I've always wanted to ask you about. You've always been very open about your childhood, sharing some pretty dark stuff about what happened to you."

"Yeah," Caleb says, grinning. "Like that time I screwed that old lady for twenty bucks and a case of beer? True story."

The interviewer clears his throat again. "You had an older sister who died young, when you were around ten years old, correct?" he says. "Sarah. You hardly ever mention her. Can you tell me a little about her?"

Just then, an arm reaches in from offscreen and hands Caleb a beer. His hand wraps around it slowly. He stares at the interviewer sitting behind the camera, so much hate in his eyes I can feel heat on the skin of my own face.

And then, in slow motion, Caleb tears the mic off his shirt, jumps out of his seat, and smashes his beer bottle on the camera, and the interview is over.

Caleb got sued for that one, for the cost of the camera and the suffering caused by the punches he landed on the interviewer's face before a security guard pulled him off. They settled out of court.

I close the YouTube window. I can hear the janitor shuffling outside the computer lab. Any second now he'll be in here shutting off the lights, telling me to go home.

I wipe the tears off my face with my sleeve. My shirt smells like mildew. I left it in the washer too long. Now my face probably smells like mildew too.

Caleb's never said much about my mom, but at least he's mentioned her a few times. At least he's acknowledged her existence. At least he's said her name.

But in all the hundreds of interviews I've watched, Caleb's never once mentioned me.

LYDIA

"I CAN'T FIGURE OUT HOW TO BREAK IT TO MRS. AMBROSE that I don't want to eat lunch with her anymore," Billy tells me at lunch. He doesn't look good. Not that he's ever looked all that well-put-together, but now he's got bags under his eyes like he hasn't been sleeping and his hair is more tangled than usual. I'm poking around at my sloppy joe with a plastic knife because ever since the air started smelling like rotting dead things, I'm having a hard time with mystery meat products. No one else seems to be having this problem as they're blindly shoving lunch into their faces with their plastic utensils. The school doesn't let students have metal silverware anymore after a Carthagean girl stabbed a guy from Rome last week with her fork.

"You haven't eaten lunch with her all year," I say.

"I know, but I think she keeps waiting in there every day for me."

"That's weird, Billy."

"I don't know. I find it kind of flattering."

"Don't you think she'd be happy you found someone your own age to eat lunch with?" I say, sawing my bun into tiny pieces.

"I guess. But I still don't want to tell her."

"Maybe what you need is closure," I say. Where did that come from? I almost sound like I know what I'm talking about.

"Have you been watching therapy talk shows too? They're good, right? It's like getting free therapy."

"Bite me," I say, but it's the nice version of "bite me" I save just for Billy.

"It's weird to be avoiding someone," Billy says. "Since I'm the one people usually try to avoid."

"You're moving up in the world."

"Hey, Billy Goat," says one of the Graylons. "Have they found your uncle yet?" He is the seventh person to say some version of this to Billy during lunch alone. I know this Graylon from Carthage, and I know for a fact that he was born with a sixth toe on his left foot and he had to wear diapers to bed until he was ten years old, but somehow he's still qualified to be Billy's bully? "Is anyone in your family *not* crazy?" he says.

"Is anyone in your family good at anything besides drinking beer and hitting their wives?" I say.

"Fuck you, Pocahontas."

"Really? That's the best you can do? First of all, for the millionth fucking time, I'm Filipina. *Fil-i-pi-na*. Second of all, Pocahontas was from, like, three thousand miles from here. If you're going to diss me using a racist historical reference, you should at the very least do your research and make sure it's accurate."

Graylon backs away with a screwed-up look on his face and mutters a half-hearted "freaks."

"Fucking people," I say, going back to sculpting the squishy pile of bun and runny meat into a mound on my plate. "Garbage, all of them." Billy's looking at me funny. "What?"

"He looks at you like you're weird different from the way he looks at me like I'm weird," Billy says.

"What are you talking about?"

"It's like I'm just pathetic weird, but you're some kind of powerful and scary weird. I wish I had more of your weird."

"You can have it," I say. "I have plenty to go around." I honestly don't know how Billy has survived this long.

I go back to my sloppy joe sculpture. I am building a second layer. It looks like a miniature meaty wedding cake. "You could just say thank you and goodbye," I say.

"To Graylon? Why?"

"To Mrs. Ambrose. Maybe that's what closure is."

"You make it sound so easy."

"Maybe it is."

"Are you trying to trick me?"

I look up and see Natalie Morris walk across the lunchroom. Tall and thin, with smooth dark brown skin that has apparently never been blemished by a pimple or even a mosquito bite. I knew the moment I saw her on the first day of school that she's a ballerina. You can tell by the way she holds her chin up at a much higher angle than everyone else does, like even her chin thinks it's better than the rest of us. Natalie is one of the only Black kids at Fog Harbor High, though she's adopted and her parents are very white and part of the tiny upper class that still remains in Fog Harbor.

Billy turns around. "What are you looking at?"

"Natalie Morris is such a snob," I say.

"No, she's not," Billy says. "She's just shy."

Natalie sits at a table with two thin girls with long, flowing hair, impeccable posture, and bagged lunches that probably contain nothing but celery and air. As far as I can tell, they don't really talk to anyone besides each other. Like they're too special to even want to be popular.

"Ugh," I say. "Ballerinas."

"What's wrong with ballerinas?"

"I hate them."

"Why?"

"I have my reasons," I say, smashing my meat cake.

"You sound like everyone else."

I feel like Billy just punched me in the guts. That's pretty much the worst thing anyone could ever say to me.

I'm sitting at the bar after work, and once again Larry and I are sharing "food" that was too gross to sell to people at Taco Hell for ninety-nine cents. I felt like puking doing food prep, so my manager Alfonso moved me to the register where I had to deal with customers, which in a way is almost worse. I swear the fog is making me sick. Can someone be allergic to fog?

"Do you have homework?" Larry asks.

"No," I lie, picking at the white spongy chunks in my "chicken" burrito, which is only slightly better than the gray gelatinous "beef."

I'm trying to keep my eyes glued to the TV because every time I look away, I lock eyes with Drunk Ted, who has been staring at me since I was thirteen. Every time I see him, he feels the need to tell me I'm pretty enough to be a supermodel, which he apparently thinks is a compliment, but it's really just gross because it proves that he's looking at me the way drunk lonely men look at girls that are way too young for them.

This is not a healthy environment for a teenager.

"So listen to this," Larry says to no one in particular. "I told you about the research I did on the big fight in Book Four of Unicorns vs. Dragons, *The Fog Arriveth*, right? To figure out where all the main events happened? And how I did some triangulation and discovered that the battle occurred in the forest right behind here, just across the river?"

No one shows any indication that they're listening to Larry, but he continues anyway. "What I'm thinking is, we just have to cut down a few trees to clear the space, and then we could make life-size replicas of the dragons and unicorns, and you know how when unicorns bleed, it burns a hole in the ground straight through to the middle of the earth? We could dig really deep holes and put some red lights in the bottom so they'll shine out and it'll look like the glow of magma. It could be, like, a tourist attraction!"

I'm not quite sure who the "we" Larry's referring to is, but I know I have to put a stop to this immediately. "Isn't that forest technically part of the reservation?" I say.

"Yeah, but I'm thinking they'll let me do it if I give them part of the proceeds."

"You do know the Quillalish tribe officially boycotted the entire Unicorns vs. Dragons franchise, right?"

Larry looks sad, but only for a moment. "We could do it in the parking lot, then," he says. "It's not ideal, but I think it could work. We'll have to get some investors, of course."

"Yeah," I say. "Maybe Old Pete could lend you a few dollars. Oh wait, isn't his tab up to, like, a thousand bucks?"

Larry just smiles and refills my soda.

The reality show about professional hit men has just ended, and the local news comes on. As usual, the whereabouts of Caleb Sloat is top news, even though the King accidentally bombed the wrong village somewhere this morning and killed a few thousand innocent people. But instead of covering that, the news is replaying an interview from three days ago with Caleb Sloat's ex-girlfriend, Shannon Smear. She looks a little better than usual, like maybe the people at the news station did her makeup instead of letting her go on looking like she usually does, which is like she let a toddler draw all over her face. She also seems closer to sober than usual. Her words sound like words, though the way she puts them together is almost as unintelligible as the King's.

"It's just so sad," she says, shaking her head. "I mean, he's a genius, you know? And, like, a guy like that is fragile. That's why he needs me, because I'm the strong one. He's always needed me. We love each other so much, it's, like, not even human. I was trying to help him, you know? He's like my baby. My beautiful, sensitive baby. And that's why he's in trouble now, because he didn't let me take care of him, because he's got so much pride, and he doesn't know how to let people love him. That's all I ever wanted, but he's so lost. He doesn't know. He's, like, this puppy, right? But, like, a *bad* puppy. He's my bad little puppy."

"I think she did it," Drunk Ted says. "She killed him."

"Yup," says another guy at the end of the bar.

"And you know what?" Shannon Smear continues. "He really loved my band, Olympia's Consent. He loved our new album, *Survive This Storm*, which is coming out tomorrow and will be available everywhere music is sold. He said it was our best yet." Then she starts fake-crying.

"You guys know his mom?" Drunk Ted says. "Tammy Sloat, over in Rome?"

The other guy spits in response to the word "Rome."

"She's a piece of work, that one," Drunk Ted says. "Two junkie kids, something must be wrong with the mama." "That's my best friend's grandma you're talking about," I say, even though I wasn't too impressed the one brief time I met her, and the woman sounds like a tyrant no matter how much Billy tries to candy-coat his stories. But I still feel the need to defend her, because Tammy Sloat is Billy's. And anything belonging to Billy is mine to defend.

I imagine throwing my half-eaten burrito down the bar and watching it land perfectly in Drunk Ted's glass, splashing chicken and cheese and beer into his droopy pervert face. But Drunk Ted is probably a major reason why Larry's bar is still even in business and why I have a roof over my head.

"Oh, that scrawny kid?" Drunk Ted says. "Isn't he retarded?"

"No, he's not retarded," I say. "And by the way, it's not okay to call people retarded." Screw the burrito; I'm this close to grabbing a pint glass and throwing it at his head.

"Naw, he must be retarded. Heroin baby and all. And I heard his mom was still turning tricks long after she was showing."

"Okay, that's enough," Larry finally says. But it's too late. I can feel the sting of something in my eyes, tiny daggers that should be tearing apart Drunk Ted's rotted liver instead of poking around my eyeballs. Everything's been getting so weird—the fog, the dreams about my mom, Caleb disappearing, hallucinations of small figures in the shadows and hooved creatures in the fog. And now I feel like crying? Because of something a drunk old man said that doesn't even have anything to do with me? What is happening? What is wrong with me?

"Well, he's a gay, I know that," says Drunk Ted. "Why else would he be *just friends* with a girl as pretty as Lydia here?"

And then I do throw the glass. My arm moves all by itself,

without asking me what I think about it. The glass barely misses Drunk Ted's face as it smashes into the wall behind him.

"Lydia!" Larry shouts.

"What the hell?" Drunk Ted yells. "Larry, get a handle on your bitch daughter."

The other guy at the bar just rolls his eyes and looks back at the TV. Old Pete burps in his booth by the door but doesn't wake up. Why can't all men be as easy to get along with as Old Pete?

I storm out of the bar and into the apartment. I know Larry won't leave the bar to come talk to me. I'll be asleep before he closes for the night, and by the morning he'll lose his nerve. That's how we deal with things—by walking away, by hiding until things blow over. Out of sight, out of mind.

But the apartment isn't much better. The stinging in my eyes has turned into real tears, like a broken faucet I can't turn off, like this isn't even my body anymore; it's the body of some little girl who cries and can't help it. This isn't me. I don't know what to do with myself. I'm too tired to dance. And it's not the kind of feeling I can dance away, not a feeling my muscles can burn through. It's a feeling that's settled on me heavy and is not going anywhere.

I get ready for bed and lie down in the dark. I look at the blackness of the ceiling and push away a memory of fresh-smelling sheets, of hands in the dark tucking me in. I push away the memory of being a kid who likes getting wrapped up tight. In the darkness, I can imagine a smile on my mother's face instead of the scowl she usually wore. In the darkness, it is easier to believe she loved me.

Stupid, I tell myself. *You're so stupid.*

I think about Natalie Morris. Did Natalie come home from three hours of elite dance classes to a home-cooked meal made by her loving mother? Does her bed smell like roses? Has she ever had to train her mind the way she's trained her body—to be strong, to push through pain, to make every move look easy? Or is dancing the hardest thing she's ever had to do?

I can't tell Billy the real reason I hate Natalie. I can't tell him it's because I'm jealous. Because then I'd have to tell him why I'm jealous, because he'd keep asking and asking until there was nowhere deeper to go, because he has this annoying habit of always knowing when there's somewhere deeper to go. And then he'd know my dance secret, and then he'd know too much.

The thing is, there's only so much good stuff to go around for people in Fog Harbor, and Natalie got all of it. It's bad enough she gets to take classes and follow her dream and I don't, but why'd she have to get so lucky in the parent lottery, too? Why not me? Why'd I get stuck with my pathetic dad who can't afford dance lessons and doesn't defend me against creepy alcoholic old men? And for that matter, why'd Billy get stuck with his asshole grandma? People act like living with blood relatives is automatically better, but sometimes maybe it's better to start over from scratch and get a whole new family that actually wants you.

Maybe in some alternate universe, I could have been Natalie.

Maybe I could have been the one who got adopted by rich parents and was given everything I ever wanted, my future full of possibilities. Maybe I could have been the ballerina snob everybody hates, instead of just being hated.

I hear something moving under my bed. I shut my eyes tight and hold my body completely still the way I used to when I was a kid. The monsters won't get you if they think you're sleeping. It's when you wake up that things start to become a problem.

BILLY

GRANDMA THINKS THERE'S NOTHING IN REAL LIFE AS
good as what's on TV, but I think she's just not looking right. Like
at this very moment, she's inside watching some courthouse TV
show when she could be sitting on the front stoop with me watching a real-life drama across the street. Some guy let his dog poop
in Cult Family's front yard, and Cult Dad went ballistic. The guy
was just like, "Whatever, old dude," and kept walking. But then
Cult Dad ran into the house and came out with one of those big
scary guns people only use in wars and mass shootings and started
chasing the guy down the street, and then another neighbor started
shouting, "Dammit, Dwight. Calm down!" but then Cult Dad
pointed the gun at her, and she screamed, and then more people
came out of their houses, and a car stopped and the driver said he's
calling 911, and then Cult Dad pointed his gun at that guy, and
now he's standing in the middle of the street, spinning around and
pointing his giant gun whenever he hears a sound, and the whole
neighborhood is watching, and some people's lips are all tight and
judgy like Grandma's get, and some people are laughing, and it is
way more entertaining than any TV show I've seen recently.

But then Cult Girl peeks through the tiny sliver of curtain I can see through the five giant trees blocking the house's front windows, and she's got the saddest look on her face I've ever seen, and when she meets my eye I try to use all the psychic powers I possibly have to tell her I'm sorry she got stuck with this guy as her dad, and I'm sorry I thought it was entertaining, and then I wave and she actually waves back, for the first time ever, not quite a wave but more like a sad little flop of the wrist, like she's too exhausted to do a real wave and that's the best she can do under these circumstances, and I use all my psychic powers to tell her that it was enough and to not feel bad and no matter what hang in there, but then a hand grabs her shoulder and the curtains fall where her face used to be, and then she is gone.

Fog is rolling down the street like a slow-motion tsunami of mashed potatoes, and that smell like an old man's breath is heavy in the air like the stench of someone dying from the inside. It's quite a scene, this guy with a gun on top of his car about to get squished by a giant fluff ball, and he has no idea what's coming behind him. I remember Grandma saying something about the military and the Middle East and PTSD, but I don't know if it was about him or one of the other men with guns on the block who work at the prison and sometimes drink too much and start yelling, or maybe it was about all of them. All the dads work at the prison, and all the moms work at BigMart. Except for Cult Girl's mom, because she's not allowed to work, because they go to some weird church in a trailer by the freeway that says women are supposed to stay in the home and kids should be kept pure and not have any contact with sinners, aka everybody else. I don't know what the church says about terrorizing your neighborhood with a giant gun.

The thing is, every neighborhood in Fog Harbor has a guy like this who occasionally loses it and goes outside with a shotgun and shoots at the sky, only those guys are usually drunk or high on meth, and as far as I know the only thing Cult Dad's been smoking is his trailer-church God and PTSD. Most everybody in Fog Harbor has some kind of gun, and mainly they're just for hunting or shooting cans or for guys to show off how tough they are when they don't have any actual muscles. It's just the way things are. Grandma says the people in Seattle hate us for it.

A cop car rolls up like it's in no hurry, with no lights or sirens. It parks, and the two cops get out and say hi to Cult Dad all friendly, like they're running into each other at the grocery store. "Hey, Dwight," one of them says. "What's going on?" The fog inches down the street toward them. The neighbors' houses disappear, as if swallowed. No one seems alarmed.

"The dogs," Cult Dad says, gun still surveying the neighborhood. "They're after me, Shawn."

"Damn dogs," Officer Shawn says.

"Infidels," Cult Dad says. "Bottom-feeders."

"Yep," says Officer Shawn. "Hey, Dwight, what do you think about putting your gun down? You're scaring your neighbors a little."

"Property rights, Shawn," says Cult Dad. "It's in the Bible."

"Get in here, Billy!" Grandma hollers. She's peeking out through a crack in the front door.

"Come out here, Grandma," I say. "It's just getting good." But then I remember the look on Cult Girl's face, and I remember this is her actual life, not a TV show.

"You have no business snooping on the neighbors," Grandma says.

"But you snoop on the neighbors all the time."

"Come in right now or I'll smack your chin."

I sigh and get up. I do what Grandma says. I always do. The possum who lives in the crawl space under the house pokes out her pointy face and hisses at me as I walk inside.

Maybe my life isn't that different from Cult Girl's. Except I get to leave the house. I get to talk to other people, whether they like it or not. When I think about it, I could hypothetically do whatever I want. But I don't. Because even when Grandma's not with me, it's like she is. And even though I could do what I want, I have no idea what I'd even want to do. Caleb did what he wanted and look where it got him.

Maybe Cult Girl is the lucky one. She doesn't have to go to school and get picked on all the time. She doesn't have to make any tough choices because all of her decisions are made for her. Her world is small and figured out and right now that sounds pretty nice to me. Except for the whole being-in-an-oppressive-cult thing, of course.

"Come over here," Grandma says as she shuffles into the living room. "The King's making an important speech."

"Grandma, have you noticed how weird the fog is lately?" I say as I follow her.

"There's always fog," she says, plopping down on the couch in her usual spot, sending a cloud of dust flying. "This county is called Fog Harbor, for Pete's sake."

"But it's way thicker and it smells weird."

"Stop thinking so much, Billy," she says. "It's not your strong suit."

The King's on TV standing at a podium in what looks like a fake pressroom set up at a tropical resort. Ocean and sandy beach are visible in the corner of the screen, like the camera guy wasn't trying very hard when he framed the shot. A slight breeze blows the fluff on top of the King's head.

"Look, let me tell you something about nuclear—I'm practically a scientist. My brain, it's that good, PhD material, smart genes, it runs in the family. It's in the guts, it's all about instincts, and I got plenty of instincts. I'm like a fox, they're real smart and they have that fluffy orange hair, but not when they're dirty. Have you seen a dirty fox? Not a pretty picture. See, you don't need a fancy degree to know stuff like this. I know nuclear is powerful. That's my whole point. I don't think you're listening. And look at me, I'm one of the smartest people in the world. My point is, they're going to kill us. They're going to kill us if we don't kill them first."

The King looks very pleased with himself, and Grandma nods her head earnestly and says, "Now that's a leader."

I'm about as nonpolitical as you can get, but on what planet does that sound like somebody who knows what he's doing?

I wonder what would happen if I just ran away. One night, while Grandma's sleeping, I could sneak out. Lydia would be waiting behind the bush by the trash cans, with a backpack full of her Taco Hell money, and maybe I could save up by selling plasma, whatever that is, the way Uncle Caleb says he did in interviews, and we could swoop Cult Girl off her front stoop, and then we'd hide in a gas station bathroom and cut our hair and dye it different colors like fugitives do in movies, and maybe I would wear a fake mustache and a suit as my disguise, and Lydia and Cult Girl could wear whatever they want, and then Grandma would wake up in the morning and she'd yell, "Billy, where are you?!" up the stairs, but I wouldn't be anywhere. For the first time in her life, Grandma wouldn't know where I was and I wouldn't come running when she called.

I wonder how long it would take for her to realize I'm really gone. Maybe a few minutes, and then maybe she'd be so worried that she'd actually overcome her fear of heights and find the strength to walk up the stairs to the second floor, where she hasn't set foot in ten years, and the house would groan under the extra weight, and then it'd shift a little more to the south, and the wood would start splitting, and the foundation would start cracking, and when she got to the top of the stairs and found me gone, maybe then, finally, she'd realize how much she loved me. And as the house falls apart around her, she'll be consumed with regret for all those seventeen years of bossing me around and smacking my chin, seventeen years full of love she never figured out how to feel, and she'll be so overwhelmed, she'll fall to the ground, convulsing with tears of heartache from how much she misses me, and she'll realize she didn't treat me right, she'll realize how much she needs me, how helpful and selfless I've been, how she can't live without me, and dramatic music will play, with violins and other fancy instruments, and the house will finally collapse, but it will be *her* trapped by a beam, not me, and underneath all that rubble of her broken home Grandma will finally realize I'm good; she will realize I'm not like Caleb, and I'm not the one who killed my mom.

But Grandma will be too late. I will be long gone, speeding into infinity with Lydia starring as my sidekick and Cult Girl starring as the girl I save, and I will be the hero, finally.

"This just in," the news guy says. "There has been a new development in the missing persons investigation for Caleb Sloat, lead singer of the hit band Rainy Day Knife Fight, who disappeared after an apparent breakdown onstage over two weeks ago. Investigators have just discovered that several hundred thousand dollars were withdrawn from Caleb Sloat's bank account days after his disappearance. We have no more information at this time, but we will keep you posted with any new developments."

I look at Grandma and she has murder in her eyes. I can practically hear her thinking, "That money should be mine."

The smell of a dead giant's burp fills the house, and I know it's the fog and not from Grandma this time. I peek out the window and everything has been swallowed by white. The world looks like a fresh piece of paper.

I know escapes have to be really well planned. That's the only way they work. One mistake and you're more trapped than you ever were to begin with.

LYDIA

I NORMALLY WOULDN'T BE SO AGREEABLE, BUT I'M HAVING a hard time saying no to Billy since all this Caleb stuff started happening. I'm not sure I like this version of myself. It agrees to do things like go hiking in the rain, even though I slept like crap last night because I had another dream about my mom, and I'm feeling so irritable and pissed off that even the trees are annoying me, and we've barely even started this hike.

We're wandering around an old logging road in the forest by the train tracks. Moss hangs off gnarly old Douglas firs like long green beards, like something out of *Lord of the Rings*. I can almost see faces in the bark, mouths built out of shelves of giant fungi, eyes dug out by woodpeckers. The trees are going to start talking any minute. The slugs and spiders and swarms of mosquitoes are all part of their sinister plan. I look up, and the canopy is so thick I can't see any sky. Just a ceiling of different shades of dark green. I can hear rain falling hard somewhere up there, but all that hits us are thick, sporadic drips.

"Why are we doing this again?" I say. We've stopped so Billy can look at the map he took from his grandma's office. I have the sudden strange feeling that we're being watched, that the deeper we go into the forest, the more alive it gets. I keep hearing something crunching around in the undergrowth, but when I look, nothing's there.

"I've spent my life looking at brochures about all the cool stuff to do around here," Billy says. "I figured maybe I should try some of it. Plus, hiking's free and I don't have any money."

"Do you want to go kayaking next?"

"Sure."

"I was kidding."

Billy looks up from the map and says, very seriously, "I need a hobby."

"Okay?"

"Do you know what I do when I'm not at school or hanging out with you?"

"What?" I say, but I'm not sure I want to know. Boys do gross things when nobody's around.

"I watch TV with my Grandma," he says. "Or I watch old interviews of my uncle. It's not healthy."

"So you think hiking's going to be your new hobby?"

Billy looks into the dense wall of forest. "Let's go this way," he says.

"There's no trail."

"It'll be an adventure."

"Fine," I say. I'm probably due for an adventure. Anything is better than Taco Hell and Larry's bar.

We walk for a while in silence, slowly due to all the tree stumps and ferns and rotted logs and rocks in our way. "Isn't this fun?" Billy says, inspecting a red mushroom. "We're hanging out, getting in touch with nature. At least we're not at the mall."

"At least we're not at the mall," I repeat. The small consolation of my sad, empty life.

"Hey, look at this!" Billy says, pointing at a tangle of long shimmering white hairs snagged on a tree branch. "They're *glowing*." His eyes look like they're going to pop out of his head. "Oh my god," he says. "Do you think they're from a uni—"

"No," I say. "It's just those glitter hair tinsel extension things girls get."

"Feel it," Billy says, caressing the strands. "It feels like real hair."

"I'm not going to feel it," I say. "And you shouldn't either. You don't know where that hair's been. It could have lice or something."

"I don't think unicorns get lice."

"For fuck's sake, Billy, there's no such thing as unicorns!" I am so close to leaving him stranded out here by himself. "I know, why don't you get a job? You're always broke, you don't do any extracurriculars, and no offense, but you don't really have any friends besides me, so you have tons of free time."

"I have to help Grandma."

"Help her do what?"

"Everything. I don't know. I have to be available when she needs me. If it weren't for me, the trash would never get taken out. Can you imagine what that house would be like if the trash didn't get taken out?"

"I'm sure you could take the trash out between school and a part-time job."

"But her health is bad. She needs my help with all kinds of stuff."

I stop walking. I'm sick of everyone's excuses for choosing to be miserable and pretending they're not. "You want to know what I think?" I say.

"Not really."

"I think you're terrified of not being needed. I think you secretly want to believe your grandma is dependent on you because that makes you important. Because if she didn't need you, who would you be? It's like you wouldn't even matter anymore."

I don't know why I felt the need to say that, but I know as soon as it comes out of my mouth that it's true. I watch as Billy's face goes through a series of emotions—surprise, confusion, suspicion, alarm, and then something I've never seen before—anger.

"Screw you," he says, his face all red. "You're not being a very nice friend." He stomps away deeper into the forest.

"Maybe a real friend's job is not to be nice all the time," I say, following him. "Maybe a friend's job is to tell the truth."

"Did you read that on a tea bag?" Billy says, with an edge to his voice I've never heard before.

"Whoa," I say. "Stop. Talk to me."

He spins around. "The last interview of Caleb I watched, he was all hunched over, like he was too weak to even hold himself up. He was wearing sunglasses, and his sweatshirt was all stained, like he hadn't bathed or changed his clothes in days, and he could barely stay awake. He's twenty-seven years old, but he's, like, a feeble old man. He looked like he was dying."

"I'm sorry."

"No one ever helped *him*."

"Oh, Billy."

"I think he's dead."

I reach out—to do what, I'm not sure. I'm too far away to hug him, so it's unclear what exactly I'm expecting my arms to do. I don't have much practice at this stuff.

Did Caleb ever hug Billy? Does his grandma? Does anyone?

Larry's not a big hugger, but he tries sometimes and mostly I just push him away. My mom was a hugger on her good days, but on her bad days she wouldn't let me touch her. I'd chase her, crying, and she'd lock herself behind her bedroom door while I pounded on it with my tiny fists. It's like the little affection I got from her just made me hungrier for more.

Something twists in my chest. It's my mother's ghost-hand refusing to let me go.

"I'm sorry," I say to Billy's back, but he won't look at me. He just keeps walking deeper into the forest. "Really, I mean it. I could have said all that stuff much nicer. I didn't know you were so upset. I was just trying to help. You should understand that, of all people."

He spins around to face me. "I help people by doing stuff for them. That's different."

"Maybe that's not really helping them," I say.

We look at each other for a long time. Isn't he supposed to say something? Are we fighting? Is this our first fight?

After what seems like forever, Billy sighs and looks away. "I just want to change into dry clothes and make a box of mac and cheese and watch TV."

"Should we go back?" I say, but then all of a sudden, a huge gust of wind almost knocks me over, and my heart jumps into my throat. Even though I'm standing, I feel like I just landed on the ground after falling, like gravity just seriously kicked my ass. Everything feels heavy, like the air itself is weighing me down, and my ears pop under the pressure. "Wait a minute," I say, looking around the forest, which is way darker than it should be in the early afternoon. "Do you hear that?"

"Hear what?"

"I don't hear any birds." Everything alive stopped breathing and moving. The only sound is the dripping of the rain filtering down through the trees. "Let's get out of here," I say. I try to make my voice sound strong, but I don't think it worked. I start to walk, but I stumble, my boots sucking up mud. The ground is trying to hold me hostage. The forest can smell my fear.

"You're going the wrong way," Billy says.

"No, I'm not. The road is this way." I point in the direction of a wall of green. I could swear there used to be an opening in that direction. I could swear I saw sky.

"No, it's this way." Billy points in the direction of another identical wall of green.

We stand there looking at each other. "Shit," I say.

"I'm scared," says Billy.

He needs me to be the brave one. I have to be the brave one.

"It's okay," I say, pulling my phone out of my pocket. Of course it has no bars. I try to smile. "It'll be fine. We just have to retrace our steps, and—" But then Billy spins around faster than I've ever seen him move, then spins back and looks at me with terror in his eyes.

"Did you see that?" Billy says. He sounds like he's being strangled. "Lydia, did you see that?"

"No," I whimper.

Did he see the thing that's been following me? Did he see the thing that ran by me in the fog at his house?

"Something really big," he says. "Something dark. Way over there. It was moving fast."

"Was it a bear?"

"No, way bigger than that."

"Wouldn't we have heard it?"

He takes a deep breath, and so do I. "You're right," he says. I feel a little better.

But then the drips of the forest get louder and faster, and pine needles start flying around us like tiny sharp torpedoes. We both look up at the same time and see the forest canopy swaying and thrashing. Trunks creak in protest. Gusts of wind beat us from all directions like they're trying to knock us down. My ears pop again.

A sound like a deep, sad moan rips through the forest, and I swear I can feel it in my bones.

"What the fuck?" I say.

"There wasn't a storm on the forecast," Billy says. "I checked three times."

"What kind of storm makes a sound like that?"

Then I see something moving fast, in the distance, through layers and layers of leaves, white and maybe even kind of sparkly, like a car catching sunlight, but that's impossible because we're nowhere near a road that people actually drive on and there hasn't been sunlight around here in weeks. It has to be the thing I heard outside Billy's house the night the fog came. The thing with hooves.

The trees shake even harder as pine needles and wet leaves and twigs and soft bits of decaying wood fly sideways and upward. The wind is moaning even louder, like the whole forest is crying, and that stink like rotting death is everywhere.

And then the fog comes, out of nowhere. One moment, we are surrounded by thrashing green, the next moment swirling white. I didn't even see it coming.

"Ow!" I scream as something cuts my cheek. I can feel my long hair flying around my head like some wild Medusa.

"What happened?" Billy yells, and I can barely hear his voice over the moaning. Even though he's just steps away, I can't see him.

I pull my hand away from my face, and there's blood everywhere. "I think a rock hit me."

Then the forest is full of the loudest, most bloodcurdling noise I've ever heard.

"The air raid siren," Billy shouts. "It's coming from the coast guard station." He finds my hand in the fog. "This way!" He pulls me in the direction of the sound.

We run as fast as we can, but the forest floor pulls at our boots, like it doesn't want to let us leave. All of our movements are in slow motion as the wind keeps beating at us, trying to push us deeper into the forest. I run into a spiderweb that wraps all around my face and neck, then fall into a mud puddle that goes up past my knees. Billy has to pull me out, but my boots don't come with me. "Those were expensive!" I scream, but I know we're not stopping to fish them out. We slow-motion run toward the sound of the siren, the forest whipping around us, invisible in the fog, branches like arms coming out of nowhere, grabbing at our clothes, spiderwebs all over the place, our faces and bodies getting pelted with sticks and stones and everything else without roots, like someone has made the forest their weapon, and we got caught in their war zone, and now we're just trying to make it out alive.

Then, as soon as it appeared, the fog clears. A sickly, pale gray-green light shines through the thinning branches, and the wind calms, and the forest seems to let go of its grip. We fall to the ground where the forest canopy finally opens above the train tracks. I lie on my back and look up at a sky I do not recognize, with a color and texture I cannot name. My clothes are heavy with mud, my hair tangled with sticks and leaves. Everything stills and settles, but somehow I know everything has changed and there is no going back.

The siren rings in my ears. I can hear Billy crying softly next to me. I roll toward him and put my arm around his heaving chest until I can feel his heart stop trying to jump out of it.

"Strange weather today, huh?" the bus driver says as I limp onto the bus. I put Billy on the bus going the opposite direction.

"Don't talk to me about the weather," I croak back. I've lost my voice from having to scream over the sound of the storm. I am shoeless, caked with mud almost up to my waist, and I'm pretty sure I have a cut on the bottom of my right foot, and I'm pretty sure it's bleeding, but it's impossible to tell because whatever blood that's there is mixed up with the mud. There's not a single place on my body that is dry.

I leave a wet trail behind me as I walk to a seat in the middle of the bus. It's completely empty except for Old Pete asleep in the back in a mildewed camo poncho. A brown puddle forms beneath my seat, and I think about the pointless fight Billy and I were having when the storm started, and for some reason I start laughing uncontrollably, and I totally don't care because it's just me and Old Pete and this bus driver who has most likely seen his fair share of people having meltdowns on his bus.

Pete somehow knows to wake up right when we get to the stop outside the bar, and we walk in together without speaking. As he sits down at his usual booth and I walk away, he mumbles, "They're here," then falls back asleep. I'm too tired to ask him what he's talking about.

I expect my dad to see me and freak out, but his eyes are glued to the TV, along with the three other guys sitting at the bar in various states of wetness, one who looks almost as muddy as me. A banner on the bottom says BREAKING NEWS, and that reporter Ronda Rash, with her perfect blond hair that must be a wig and her signature pastel suit with the tasteful hint of cleavage, is standing on the edge of a giant hole in the ground as big across as the high school lunchroom and about two stories deep. Disheveled people are gathered around the pit, looking down into it, as police work to put up a flimsy barrier around the border.

Ronda Rash is saying something about an F2-level tornado touching down right at the border of Carthage and Rome, the first tornado ever documented in Fog Harbor County.

"A goddamned tornado," says the muddiest guy at the bar. A glob of mud drops off his nose into his beer, but he takes a sip anyway.

The screen cuts to the meteorologist back in the studio, and he is standing in front of some graphics about a tornado, literally scratching his head. "Tornadoes just aren't possible with our topography and weather system," he mumbles like a guy having a conversation with the voices in his head. An offscreen voice whispers, "You're live, Lewis," then he snaps out of it and goes back to meteorologist voice to explain how tornadoes are made.

I notice a cup of hot tea in front of me. "Thanks," I say to Larry, surprising myself. This day is full of surprises.

Larry hands me a beer and says, "Will you take that to Pete?"

I squish my way over to Old Pete's booth and set the beer in front of him. "Hey," I say. "You're not even wet."

"I've lived here a long time," he says, eyes still closed. "Nothing surprises me anymore." He reaches out his trembling hand to lift the beer to his face, which is cracked and dry like tree bark, and tips it into the opening behind his long, thick gray beard. I think those are the most words I've ever heard him speak.

I squish back to the bar, and the TV is showing the pit again, except now people are divided onto two sides of it, yelling across at each other. "It's ours!" shout Carthageans one side. "It's ours!" scream people on the Rome side.

"At this point," says Ronda Rash, "it is unclear if the tornado pit falls more in Carthage or Rome city limits. Residents of both towns appear to feel very strongly that the pit belongs to them. A survey team is en route as we speak."

I take a sip of tea and realize it's from one of the stale tea bags Larry keeps at the bar in case anyone ever orders a hot toddy, which they don't. I touch my hair and feel it matted with mud and sticks and leaves and spiderwebs and tree sap and who knows what else. There's no way I'm ever going to get these tangles out.

I realize I'm trembling, but I'm pretty sure it's not because I'm cold.

BILLY

I'M IN THE BATHTUB, TRYING NOT TO THINK ABOUT WHAT
just happened in the forest with Lydia. I've stopped shaking, so that's an
improvement. This is an opportunity to be grateful that I can fully relax
in the tub because Grandma isn't here to yell at me from the kitchen
through the hole in the floor. After this, I'll turn on the AA channel and
Lynn A. will be there and everything will be okay.

Relax, I tell myself.

It's not working.

I don't want to think about how long it's been since I cleaned
the tub or what's growing on the sides of it, so I squeeze in a bunch
of dish soap to make bubbles so thick I can't see through them,
which will hopefully do double duty of cleaning me and cleaning
the tub. I know dish soap is not ideal for a bubble bath, but it's the
only soap we have in the house right now.

Rich people don't have to think about soap. They have different
soaps for every kind of cleaning—for washing dishes in the sink, for
washing dishes in the dishwasher, for washing windows, for washing counters, for washing floors; soap for laundry, soap for hands,
soap for bodies, soap for hair, even separate soap for faces. Last week
I had to decide between deodorant and a jar of peanut butter while

doing our grocery shopping at BigMart. For the sake of everyone at school, I chose deodorant. But now I want a peanut butter sandwich more than I've ever wanted one in my life.

I hear what sounds like footsteps, but it's probably just a new noise the house came up with for a new something that's breaking deep inside it. Something splashes into the bathwater. I look up and a section of plaster about as big as my hand is missing from the ceiling. I fish it out of the tub and throw it into the corner of the bathroom, but it left little chunks of white chalky stuff in the bathtub that will probably get stuck all over me.

As broken as the house is, at least I'm not outside. At least I'm not in that forest, with whatever else was running around. It may not be completely safe in here, but it's way worse out there.

I try not to look at how dirty brown the bathwater is as it drains. I towel myself off and feel pretty clean, all things considered, then dress in my room quickly. No doubt new things will disappear after Grandma's upcoming Caleb Sloat, Lead Singer of Rainy Day Knife Fight, Childhood Tour™, which have been increasing steadily since Caleb went missing. I think maybe I should hide my most important things in the attic, but then I realize there's nothing important enough to go through the effort of hiding, and that's kind of a sad feeling when you think about it, to not have anything you particularly want to protect.

Or I could flip that to something positive: I'm not materialistic. That's a good quality for a person to have.

For some reason, the usual comfort of watching TV suddenly doesn't seem so appealing. I want to go somewhere that's dry and quiet and empty, where even if Grandma comes home and starts screaming at the top of her lungs I won't be able to hear her. So I grab the sleeping bag off my bed, throw it over my shoulders like a cape, and climb the rickety steps to the attic so I can stare out the window and watch the fog until I fall asleep.

When I open the door to the attic, the first thing I notice is a wet trail from the door to the deep black shadows under the eaves, even though I didn't notice any trail coming up the stairs. Fear freezes my body before my brain has a chance to make any kind of intelligent decision. And that's where I am—frozen in place, head empty, blanket over my shoulders—when a hunched figure emerges out of the shadows, swathed in rags, greasy blond hair covering his eyes, a mirror image of myself.

"Dude, you smell like fucking dish soap," says my uncle Caleb's voice.

LYDIA

LAST NIGHT I DREAMED I WAS NINE YEARS OLD, JUST before Mom left. I'm at dance class, in my little pink tights and leotard and skirt, the nicest clothes I've ever owned. Mom put my hair in a bun, taught me about the secret world of hairnets and bobby pins.

Dance was the only thing I did that my mother ever showed interest in. She'd drive me to class and put her phone away and actually watch the whole thing. I would look back at her often, in the mirror, hoping she wouldn't notice me gauging the softness of her face—her frown wasn't so frowny, her eyes weren't so empty, and that meant I was doing a good job.

In the dream, nine-year-old Lydia is dancing, and I can see her little body, but somehow I know it's the older now-me inside it, because her face is too serious, her muscles are too tense, her point is way more arched than her foot should allow, her leaps way higher than humanly possible, her pirouettes faster. But she doesn't look like some prodigy, she's not beautiful—it's grotesque. I'm inside her like some kind of torture device, tearing her apart. And the whole time her body is doing these impossible things, her head's whipping around, looking for Mom, and I think I'm going to break her, I'm going to break her neck, I'm too much, I'm always too much, but Mom's nowhere, even though we can feel her eyes, the little girl and me, Mom's watching us from somewhere, in the wall maybe, the ceiling, behind the mirror.

The mirror. We walk toward the mirror. We're still in character, still ballerinas. We're always performing. It's always a show.

We watch our faces get larger, mine and little Lydia's, in split screen, then superimposed, then combined in some weird layering effect, but our eyes are the same, almond-shaped mirrors reflecting the mirrored wall, creating a feedback loop, turning our image infinite, and the mirror turns to liquid, and we pass through, and there is nothing on the other side. Just white. Just emptiness. There is no ground, no up and no down, no one but the girl and me, suspended in space, unable to move.

When I opened my dresser drawer this morning, the framed photo of my mom that usually hangs on the living room wall was sitting on top of my T-shirts. Have I started sleepwalking and moving things around while I'm unconscious? Sleep-*redecorating*?

I am looking in the bathroom mirror now, in the apartment behind Larry's bar where I've lived my whole life. Mom hated living here. When she was in a particularly bad mood, she called it a dungeon. And Larry was her captor, as if his love was a curse. Just like in Unicorns vs. Dragons, when the dragon king kept the unicorn princess locked up in his tower, and the wind would carry the sound of her cry all the way to the ocean.

There is nothing magic about this mirror. It's just me looking back at myself with a gash on my cheek and my tornado hair. The mirror is solid and cheap and scratched. It hasn't been washed in a long time. Flecks of toothpaste and floss projectiles dot the surface like dirty constellations.

Even after shampooing three times and using a whole bottle of conditioner to get the tangles out, my hair is still a rat's nest. It will never be clean again. The forest won.

So I raise a pair of scissors and start cutting.

BILLY

ON THE WAY TO SCHOOL THIS MORNING, I SAW ABOUT A hundred cats sitting on top of someone's roof. A couple blocks later, three deer were walking down the middle of the street like it was no big deal while a whole line of backed-up cars honked at them. Lydia wasn't at breakfast so she missed the impromptu prayer circle about how the tornado was a sign from God that the rapture is coming and only the righteous will ascend to Heaven in the coming apocalypse and the rest of us will be burned to a crisp in hell. She would have loved that.

A whole trailer park in Carthage was demolished, which Carthageans are saying is proof that the tornado pit belongs to them, and Romans are saying is proof that God hates Carthageans, because apparently even weather takes sides in the Carthage versus Rome feud. I know the tornado was a big deal and all, but even though it almost killed Lydia and me in the forest, I've totally moved on because now I have way bigger news hiding in my attic.

Technically, Uncle Caleb specifically said to "not tell a living soul" that he's hiding in the attic, but the way I see it, Caleb doesn't know Lydia or understand the depth of my trust for her, so when he made that pronouncement he didn't have the full information, so Lydia doesn't really apply to his "not tell a living soul" rule, because he didn't even know her soul existed. He was talking about everyone else's souls, not Lydia's.

By the time lunch comes, I can barely breathe, I'm so excited. There's also the fact that I didn't sleep last night, which may have something to do with how weird I feel.

"Lydia!" I shout as soon as I see her, and she jumps and almost drops her lunch tray, and I'm about to start telling her everything, but I get distracted by the fact that she doesn't have any hair.

"You don't have any hair," I say.

"That's not entirely true," she says. "I have some hair. It's a pixie cut. You like?"

I can't decide. She doesn't look like Lydia.

"What are you all jazzed up about?" she says. "You look like you're going to fly away."

I lean into her and she recoils. "What the fuck, Billy? Are you trying to kiss me?"

"Get a room, freaks!" someone passing by shouts. Someone else makes vomiting noises.

"I was just trying to tell you a secret!" I cry. This isn't going well so far.

I follow Lydia to our table in the middle that no one sits at because it's in the no-man's-land between the Carthage and Rome sides of the lunchroom.

"So tell me," she says, sitting down.

I lean in.

"Watch it," she says.

"Can you hear me?" I whisper.

"Yes," Lydia whispers back sarcastically.

I wait a few seconds for ultimate effect.

"Come on!" she says, throwing a tater tot at my forehead.

"CalebSloatishidinginmyattic" comes tumbling out of my mouth too fast. It is not the delivery I was hoping for.

Lydia doesn't say anything. She tilts her head to the side, kind of like a bird.

She doesn't say anything. And she still doesn't say anything. I'm starting to feel dizzy from not breathing.

"Say something!" I finally blurt out.

"I don't know what to say," Lydia says very softly and slowly, which is the opposite of how she usually talks, which proves definitively that this is a Really Big Deal.

I tell her everything I know, which isn't much. Caleb didn't exactly want to chat. I had all sorts of questions, but every time I started asking one, Caleb told me to "shut the fuck up" and go get him some food and dry clothes. So basically what happened was Caleb just ordered me around for about twenty minutes as I went up and down the stairs getting him stuff. I start telling Lydia all the things I had to go up and down the stairs to get—blankets, frozen pizza, Pop-Tarts, water bottle, bucket, toilet paper—and finally she cuts me off and says, "I don't get it. How did no one see him the last two weeks? How did he even get there?"

"I asked him the same exact question," I say. "I said, 'How'd you get here without anyone seeing you?' and he said, 'I can't tell you,' and I said, 'Why not?' and he said, 'You'd never believe me,' and I said, 'I'm pretty gullible,' and he said, 'Drop it,' and I said, 'Did it have anything to do with the tornado?' but then he just told me to shut the fuck up again and go get him another pillow."

"Billy Goat," Lydia says with a grin, "this is a damn good secret."

The compliment gives me sparkles in my chest. I lean in closer, and Lydia actually leans in too this time. "There's more," I say.

"What?" she says.

"He gave me his bank card and told me his code. He told me to get a bunch of cash out and buy him a computer."

"Won't the police be able to trace the card or something?"

"That's exactly what I asked him! He said not to worry because it's a secret bank account that's not under his real name, because his old drug dealer also sold fake IDs and dead people's social security cards. Isn't that great?"

Lydia arches her eyebrow and I realize that sounded really bad.

"Are you going to do it?" she says.

"I need your help."

"Why?"

"I don't know how to buy a computer."

"You just go to BigMart and buy one."

"Will they sell it to me? Won't they be suspicious I have so much money?"

"Dude, they just want to sell computers. They don't give a crap where the money comes from."

"Lydia," I say, "I just really want you to come with me. I need your help. I don't have anyone else."

Lydia's face does something weird.

"You get to meet my uncle," I say.

"I have to admit, I'm curious," she says.

"Curiosity is the root of all innovation!" I shout, because I'm so excited.

"That's on a sign in our chemistry class," Lydia says.

"I've always liked that sign."

"Curiosity also killed the cat," she says, and I shudder.

LYDIA

"DUDE, WHY ARE YOU SWEATING?" I ASK BILLY. HE WOULD make a terrible criminal.

We're in BigMart looking at computers. Neither of us knows anything about computers. Billy doesn't even have one at his house, and Larry's laptop is, like, twenty years old and so slow that I hardly ever bother using it.

"It's scary having this much money in my pocket," Billy says. "It's like everyone knows and they're all looking at me."

"They're looking at you because you look like a tweaker. Just breathe or something."

I'm acting calm because Billy's not. One of us has to be the calm one, and Billy's made it pretty clear he's the drama queen in this relationship. But the truth is, I don't really feel calm at all. I keep thinking about my recent dreams, and my mom, and the tornado, and all the weird stuff that happened in the forest, and the photo that showed up in my T-shirt drawer, and the creepy figure I keep seeing but not quite seeing, and how one of the most famous people in the world suddenly appeared in Billy's attic out of nowhere, and now we're buying him a computer, and if you actually stop and put everything together and start thinking about how absurd it all is, it could really make a person freak out, and I'm not in the mood to do that right now.

"He said he wanted one that was good for watching videos," Billy says, poking at some buttons randomly.

If you start thinking about stuff and how it all might be connected, then you start thinking about things like fate and destiny and the bigger picture and what's the meaning of all this and what's your part in it and where do people go when they die, and none of these are things I ever intend to think about.

"I need to sit down," I say, and I plop down on a chair in front of a tester computer.

I haven't been dancing enough lately. I've been hanging out too much with Billy. That's the problem. Dancing is always the best way to keep me from thinking.

"He said if he's going to be up there awhile, he needs something to do," Billy says.

"How long is he planning to stay up there?" I say.

"He didn't exactly let me ask questions," Billy says. "I told him we don't have Internet but he said it's easy to hack into a neighbor's Wi-Fi."

"Your uncle's a hacker?"

"I don't know. He's supposed to be a genius or something. Everyone knows that."

"Lot of good it did him," I say. "Being smart is just asking for trouble." Where did that come from? Now I'm starting to sound like my mother. She was always so good at seeing the worst in things.

"I think we need help," Billy says.

"That's the understatement of the year." I feel like my skin's going to snap off. I'm wound so tight, I'm going to explode. "We need to get out of here," I say.

"Should we ask this guy?"

"Hey," I say to the clerk who has passed us about a million times and never asked if we need anything. "Which one of these computers is good for streaming videos?"

"Uh, all of them?" Nobody who works here knows anything about anything. They just wander around like blind zombies while hordes of teenagers shoplift right in front of them.

"Just point at one," I say. "We have six hundred dollars."

He points at one that's five hundred forty-nine dollars.

"Okay. We'll take it," I say.

"I'm just warning you," Billy says as we climb the steep stairs to the attic, "he's kind of cranky."

Billy opens the door and says hi, but Caleb doesn't even look in our direction. He's sitting by the window in a broken-looking lawn chair, wearing Billy's dorky clothes. A dull puddle of cold gray light makes a circle on the floor in front of him, but only his ratty-socked foot is illuminated; the rest of him is hidden in the shadows. Torn potato chip bags and candy wrappers litter the floor around him, and the faint smell of pee is coming from somewhere.

I am not impressed. He looks like someone who should be

sleeping on a bench at the bus station, not like one of the most famous people in the world.

Finally Caleb turns from the window and sees us. "Dude, what the fuck!" he shouts, and he throws the moldy paperback that was sitting in his lap at Billy's head, and Billy ducks just in time for it to hit the wall behind us.

"Don't freak out!" Billy says.

"Is this part of the fucking tour now?" says Caleb. "I bet you told Ma, too. Is she on her way here with the news crew? Is she going to charge fucking admission?"

"Don't be mad—"

"You're just as bad as her," Caleb says. "You're as bad as all of them. I thought I could trust you. I can't fucking trust anyone. You're all a bunch of fucking liars."

"Is he crying?" I say.

"I'm not fucking crying, you fucking bitch!" and Caleb tries to throw a candy bar wrapper, but it just gets stuck in the air and we all pause for a moment to watch it float down to the floor. For a second, I forget to be angry.

But as soon as the wrapper lands, I say, "What did you call me?" and stomp over to where Caleb's sitting. He smells like B.O. and garbage.

"Lydia, stop," Billy says weakly, but I don't think he means it. I think he likes watching me get mad at people. I think he likes hearing me say all the things he never can.

"I'm not doing any favors for some washed-up junkie in an attic calling me a bitch," I say.

"What'd you call me?" Caleb says.

"Please stop," Billy says, a little stronger.

"Why'd you bring me up here?" I say.

"Yeah, why'd you bring her up here?" Caleb says.

"I need her help," Billy says.

"You need me to help you do what?" I say.

"Help me help him."

"Yeah?" I say. "And who's going to help me?"

"Me?"

"You're going to help me help you help him?"

"Jesus fucking Christ," Caleb says.

I've known Caleb Sloat for two minutes, and already I hate him. It'd be one thing if I loved his music, if I thought he was some artistic genius who could get away with being eccentric and not caring how he treats people, but he's just an asshole and a mediocre guitar player who got famous for feeling sorry for himself and sold out as soon as he got the opportunity.

I stay as far away from Caleb as I can while Billy helps him unpack the BigMart bag, and then we basically just sit around watching him set up the computer. I can't believe I wasted a day off work for this. I could be making money or at home dancing right now.

"Jackpot," Caleb says. "Some dumb-ass neighbor's Wi-Fi password is 'password.' People in this town are such fucking idiots."

I look at Billy, but he's just staring at his uncle like he's some kind of god. Whatever this is that's happening, I am certain it's not going to be good for Billy.

"You need to get me some different clothes," Caleb says. "I feel like a retard."

"Don't say retard!" I say. What the hell is wrong with people?

"Was I talking to you? Billy, you need to get me some weed."

"Didn't you just go to rehab?" I say.

"Let me tell you something about rehab," Caleb says. He's the kind of guy who's used to people listening to him. I hate people like that. "After detox, rehab is pretty much just expensive summer camp for adults."

"What'd you do there?" Billy says. "Did you talk about your feelings a lot like on *Sexy Sober Survivor*?"

"No."

"Why not?"

"I don't have feelings," he says with a smug look on his face. He thinks he's so clever. I hate people like that, too.

"Are you a sociopath?" I say. "Sociopaths think the world revolves around them, and they don't have a conscience or the ability to feel empathy."

He glares at me, and I feel a small thrill of accomplishment.

"Dude," he says to Billy. "Just get me some fucking weed. I've been through hell. It's not like I'm asking you to get me fucking heroin."

"Do you have to say 'fuck' so much?" Billy says.

"Yes," Caleb says.

"I don't think I can get you weed," Billy says.

"Why not?"

"First of all, I don't know anyone who sells weed."

"You're a teenager in Fog Harbor. Everyone sells weed."

"Second of all, I don't want to contribute to your relapse."

"Dude, let me tell you something. In the great scheme of things I've done, weed is barely a drug."

"It's a gateway drug."

"Okay, yeah, maybe. Don't do drugs. But for *me*, it's a little different. It's going to be my gateway to sobriety, okay? Like, I just need it to ease my transition. *¿Comprende?*"

"Wait," I say. "Are you gonna go through withdrawals and shit? Are you going to be up here puking and shitting yourself and expecting Billy to clean it up?"

"Don't worry, princess. I already did that part."

"Are you running from the law?" Billy says.

"Worse," Caleb says, looking out the window like some forlorn dude-version of Emily Dickinson. "I'm running from the whole goddamned world."

I roll my eyes quite possibly the hardest I've ever rolled them in my entire eye-rolling life. This guy is so full of shit.

BILLY

EVEN THOUGH GRANDMA'S SEPARATED FROM CALEB BY
two floors and has bad hearing and never notices anything I do
and probably even forgot the attic exists, I'm still terrified of getting caught. It's like she's drilled a part of herself into my brain and
knows every time I even think something bad, and then she punishes me immediately with guilt. I watched TV with her for a while
before she went to bed last night, and my heart was pounding so
hard I was sure she could hear it, and every time the house creaked
I'd jump a foot off of the couch like I was getting electrocuted.

"Dammit, Billy!" she yelled. "Why the hell are you sweating so
much? You smell like a pig."

"Sorry," I said, and then I went upstairs and sat alone in my
room looking at the wall because I couldn't sleep. As soon as I
heard her stomp into her bedroom, I went back downstairs and
watched AA TV for a long time. I told Lynn A. about Caleb hiding in my attic, and she just knitted her scarf and listened the
whole time without saying anything, which I appreciated. I have a
feeling she probably doesn't think it's a very good idea, but luckily
she's not the judgmental type. Grandma's guilt-voice yelling in my
head got a little quieter, and I fell asleep on the couch listening to

the soothing sound of people talking about their rock bottoms.

I begged Lydia to come over again today because I've been assigned the task of carrying over a decade's worth of hoarded thrift store blankets and pillows from the second-floor bedroom up to Caleb's attic. On the walk home through the stinky mist, we saw a raccoon jump into a stroller and grab a bottle right out of a baby's hand while the mom wasn't looking. I swear this fog has everyone acting a little extra bonkers.

"This is bullshit," Lydia says, carrying her seventh load up the narrow staircase. "Tell me again why I agreed to help you with this."

"Because you're my best friend." I keep calling her this, but she still hasn't confirmed one way or the other. I figure if I keep saying it, eventually it'll stick.

"Whatever," she says.

We're both drenched in sweat while Caleb just sits on his broken lawn chair by the window staring at his computer. I understand he has just been through an enormous ordeal to get here and probably isn't in prime physical form, but maybe it'd be nice if he helped a little.

"Aren't you going to fucking help?" Lydia yells at him. Further proof that we're best friends: she can read my mind.

"Nope," he says. "I'm quite comfortable, thanks."

She drops the comforter she was carrying and storms downstairs. I follow her. Why can't they just get along? Don't they know how much easier life is if you don't pick fights?

"Why are you letting him treat you like this?" Lydia asks.

"He needs my help," I say.

"But that doesn't mean you should let yourself get used."

"I'm not," I say, but I know that's not completely true. So what if he's using me a little? Lydia doesn't get it. She doesn't understand how things work in our family.

"What do you even owe him? Why do you want to help someone who's so mean to you?"

"He's my family."

Lydia shakes her head and sighs.

I want Lydia to understand that Caleb isn't all bad. He's not just that asshole she's seen on TV. He's not even just that asshole in the attic right now. There's something good in him, and I know it, and Lydia needs to know it too. Because Caleb and me, we come from the same place. We're made out of the same stuff. If there's nothing good in Caleb, what does that say about me?

"Did I ever tell you about that time we found the bird?" I say.

Lydia sighs. "No. But—"

"I think I was five or six or something. It's one of my earliest memories. We had just left Gordon's house where I played video games while they got stoned."

"Yeah, you're not really helping your case right now, Billy."

"We had this old plastic wagon that Caleb would pull me in whenever we went anywhere. Gordon's house. BigMart. The park."

"He took you to the park?"

"Yeah, all the time. He pushed me on the swings and everything." I decide to leave out the part about how most of the time, Caleb would just sit on the bench and tell me to play by myself, or that one time he said he'd be right back but he left me there so long it got dark out and a cop had to drive me home.

"This one time, we found a bird half alive on the road. Caleb was really upset. He wrapped it up in his hoodie and took it home and tried to nurse it back to health. He was really serious about it. He was so gentle with that bird."

"Did it live?"

"No," I say. "It died and we buried it."

"Was he sad?"

I think about this. I remember standing over the little grave in the backyard in the rain. I remember us bowing our heads and taking a moment of silence. Then Caleb looked up with a blank face and said, "Fuck it. It's just a fucking bird." Then he walked into the house and turned on some loud music in his room and left me out in the rain with the dead bird, and we never talked about it again.

"I think so," I finally say.

Lydia sighs.

"Just a few more loads," I beg. "Caleb said he'd buy us pizza. Real delivery kind, not frozen."

"I can buy my own pizza," Lydia says.

"I can't," I say.

"Fine," Lydia says. "Just a few more loads. But I want to make it clear that I'm doing it to help you, not your asshole uncle. Okay?"

"Okay."

When we drop off another load in the attic, Caleb looks up from his computer and says to Lydia, "I like this butch Mexican thing you have going on."

"First of all, I'm not Mexican," she tells him. "Second of all, I'm not even butch. I have short hair and I'm wearing jeans and a hoodie. That's, like, normal clothes. But I guess you think all women should dress like your girlfriend and drip sex diseases everywhere they go."

"She's not my girlfriend anymore," Caleb says.

"I don't care," Lydia says. "And by the way, that's not what she's telling people."

Caleb covers his face with his hands and emits a strange, loud, guttural combination whine/moan and starts rocking back and forth.

Lydia looks at me. "What's wrong with him?"

"He told me very specifically not to mention anything about what's happening outside," I say. "Especially things that involve him."

"Billy," Lydia says. "He needs professional help. Like, seriously. We are not qualified to deal with this." I know she's probably right, but Caleb asked me to help him. He asked *me*.

"Hey!" Caleb says. "Stop talking about me when I'm right here."

"Sorry," I say.

"Don't apologize to him," Lydia says.

"Sorry," I say again.

"Hey, kids," Caleb says. "Where's my weed?"

Lydia gives him one of the meanest death stares I've ever seen, which is saying a lot, but it doesn't even faze him.

"What's the fucking holdup?" Caleb says. "Come on, Billy. You have the money."

"Listen," Lydia says. "I don't give a shit if you're rich and famous and his uncle. You do not get to talk to him like that."

"I can talk to him however I want."

"Fuck you."

"Fuck *you*."

They stare at each other for a long time. My heart is pounding in my throat. They need to stop fighting. I need them to stop fighting. How do I make them stop?

"Guys?" I choke. "Please don't fight."

Then Caleb starts laughing. "Hey, Billy," he says. "You tap that yet?" He smirks and motions toward Lydia with his chin.

I look at Lydia and she is frozen. She is supposed to have a witty comeback. Where is her witty comeback? I have never seen her speechless like this. I am supposed to defend her. I am supposed to stick up for my friend. But I'm frozen too.

"Don't talk about her like that," I manage to say weakly.

"It's a legitimate question, man. She's hot. She's a bitch, but she's hot."

I look at Lydia, and now her anger is directed at me, and I open my mouth but I have no voice, only a pathetic whimper, like someone deflated me, like I'm some kind of malfunctioning whoopee cushion, and somewhere inside I know there are words to defend her, but they are too lost and I am too late and she is down the stairs before I ever have the chance to find them, and by the time I get it together to follow her she is out the door, and the house shakes so hard it throws me down the staircase, and the side of my face slams against the bottom step, and I know I totally deserve it.

LYDIA

I WOKE UP THIS MORNING TO FIND MOM'S PICTURE IN THE kitchen cabinet next to a box of cereal. As I took a shower, I kept seeing something moving behind the curtain, but every time I pushed it open nothing was there. I know it's all in my mind. It's like how after watching a horror movie you get extra jumpy and everything feels scary for a while. The only difference is this feeling is getting stronger, not fading away.

It's not even Halloween yet and already it's freezing, even though it hardly ever freezes in Fog Harbor. The fog spent all night sticking to things, and when I stepped outside to wait for the school bus this morning, the whole world was sparkling and frozen, icicles hanging off of everything like glistening swords. It'd be beautiful if it weren't so cold. My Advertising History teacher said this is proof that global warming is a hoax, which is just further validation that going to school is making me dumber.

I didn't return Billy's calls last night. He left a total of seventeen messages, all apologizing for not sticking up for me when his uncle was spewing his nonsense. I probably should have called him back, but I didn't want to talk about it. Because talking about it would mean it mattered. It would mean I got hurt. And who the hell wants to talk about that?

I don't think I'm mad at Billy. How can I expect someone who can't even stick up for himself to stick up for me? But maybe it'd be nice if someone would. Maybe I'm tired of always having to do it myself. It's exhausting feeling like I have to defend myself all the time. From people at school, the guys at Larry's bar, asshole customers at work, random dudes on the street—everyone, everywhere, butting into my life uninvited, or wanting something I don't want to give.

Really, I'm way sadder for Billy than I am for myself. He still wants attention from his uncle so badly, he'll put up with anything to get it. He doesn't understand that you don't have to let people in your life who hurt you. You can just shut them out, easy peasy, even family if you have to. You just push them away and they're gone.

"Whatever," I say at breakfast after Billy's fifth version of *I'm sorry*. "I'm over it."

"Really?" Billy says.

"What's up with your face?" I say. He's got a cut on his cheek and big reddish-purple bruise.

"I fell down the stairs."

For a moment, I forget what I was so mad about to begin with, and my chest is full of a brand-new rage that cancels out every other feeling. Nobody just falls down the stairs. That's exactly what people say to hide who really hurt them.

"Did he do that to you?" I say. I think I am growling. I could kill Caleb Sloat.

"What?" Billy says, and he seems genuinely surprised. "No! He would never hurt me."

But does he know that for sure?

"Was it your grandma?"

I could kill that whole goddamned family. I really could.

"No! I swear to God, I fell down the stairs." I search his face for a lie, but I don't see one. "I'd tell you if someone hurt me," he says, and I know he's telling the truth.

I take a deep breath and the rage dissolves a little, and now mostly I just feel something heavy sloshing around in its place.

"It doesn't really hurt," Billy says, trying to sound cheerful, and for some reason that strikes me as the saddest thing of all.

"I made a decision," I say, trying to sound calm. "I'm never coming over there again. Not ever. We're still friends and everything. But I never want to see your uncle again."

"That's fair," he says.

"I think so."

It's so easy. Poof, just like that, Caleb Sloat is out of my life.

Things are tense for about a minute as we poke at the sugar-covered ball of processed white flour that passes for a breakfast pastry, but then a fight breaks out a couple tables over. Everyone watches as one guy pummels another, shouting something about icicles, and then blood starts flying and a drop lands in my syrupy fruit cocktail.

Nobody seems surprised by this violence, just entertained. It's become so normal, we barely even see it.

BILLY

LYDIA WENT STRAIGHT TO WORK AFTER SCHOOL AND I feel a little sad that she didn't wait around to say goodbye, but I don't blame her for punishing me. That's how relationships work, right? Like how when I do something that really pisses Grandma off, she hides all the food in her room for a few days until she decides I've earned it back. The worst is when this happens on a weekend or over the summer so I don't even get school meals. Luckily, I've mostly learned how not to piss her off by now, but there were a few years in elementary school when I was really hungry.

Rumors are flying about the fight in the cafeteria, and I have no one to compare notes with. Apparently an icicle fell on the foot of a Carthage student's dad and sliced a hole straight though, boot and everything, and he's convinced that the dad of this other guy from Rome is responsible. I'm not sure how a person could plant an icicle on someone's house and time it perfectly right to fall at a certain time, like some kind of remote-controlled icicle. This is something Lydia would have an opinion about, but she is not here, and I am more confused than ever, because it's hard to know what to think without her opinions.

When I get home, I'm so cold I can barely feel my hands and

my face is completely numb. Cult Dad is marching up and down the street with his big gun like he forgot his shift is over as a prison guard, and I'm not really sure who he's trying to protect or who he's trying to protect them from, but I definitely don't feel safer. I wave at Cult Girl, whose face is poking through the curtains, and she raises her eyebrows in a *Can you believe this shit?* kind of look, and I feel like we've made some real progress in our relationship. Then she points at a black car sitting in front of her house with a guy in sunglasses in the front seat who is staring right at me, and I run inside the house and the door slams shut behind me all on its own and just barely misses smashing my hand.

I take some deep breaths and watch five minutes of AA TV to calm down. "There's an unmarked car outside my house," I tell Lynn A. She puts down her knitting and takes a sip of her coffee and nods. "I don't know if I can do this." She smiles warmly, and it makes me feel a lot better. Sometimes just telling her my fears out loud makes me feel less scared.

My favorite therapy talk show comes on in four minutes, but I have to check on Caleb. I'm getting out of all my regular routines, including sleep, but this is certainly a lot more exciting, though also a lot more stressful. Grandma finally fired me as her director of online marketing and hired some free intern from Fog Harbor Community College, and she's hardly ever home these days until late at night, which I am definitely not complaining about. The only problem with Grandma being so busy is that there have been four Rainy Day Knife Fight tours in the last week alone, and I'm almost out of underwear since everyone has decided to take a pair as a souvenir. I'm on constant alert because I never know when the tours are happening, so I have to keep my eye on the window in case Grandma's van drives up so I can hide the door up to the attic in time behind a very tall, very heavy dresser. It's basically a death trap for Caleb up there if the house ever catches on fire, but I guess that's a small price to pay for privacy.

I've never had to keep a secret before, and I don't think it's my strong suit. How do people handle the stress? Grandma can smell when I'm lying to her, and for a split second, I think maybe it'd be easier to just confess and get it over with. Caleb's her son, and this is her house, so doesn't the combination of those two things kind of give her the right to know he's here? And maybe his being trapped would be the perfect opportunity to force them to make up, because they'd have no choice but to talk to each other. Kind of like on *Sexy Sober Survivor*—this is their desert island, and there's no way off (unless they break their contract with the television station, which I guess isn't applicable in this situation). Where else could Caleb go? He's certainly not going to walk out the door in front of all the neighbors, especially not now with that black car sitting out there. It'd be impossible for him to run away. He's basically our prisoner.

The truth is, the most likely scenario if I told Grandma that Caleb's in the attic is she'd probably call all the news stations and Seattle PD and sell him to the highest bidder. Not to mention the fact that Caleb would kill me. So I guess I'm just going to keep him a secret until he's ready to not be a secret anymore, at least until I die of a stress ulcer.

I climb upstairs and Caleb's sitting in his spot by the window. He's building some kind of nest with all the blankets Lydia and I brought up that has gotten so high, now only his head and the crooked lamp with the ripped lampshade I donated from my own bedroom poke out. The window doesn't open, so the smell is becoming unpleasant. He says he's still cold, even though Lydia and I already hauled up at least fifty blankets yesterday, even though he's wearing a beanie and three sweaters and a coat and two scarves and long underwear and two pairs of sweatpants.

I have so many questions, but Caleb never wants to answer any of them. Questions, like news, are outlawed.

"What's for dinner tonight?" Caleb says without taking his eyes off his laptop. The stubble on his face is on its way to turning into a real beard. He's created a kind of hatch on the side of his blanket fort that he can open so I can give him stuff. He's been binge-watching a documentary series about some smart and depressing topic I don't understand. I can practically hear Grandma say, *What, he thinks leaving Fog Harbor makes him some kind of goddamned intellectual?*

"I don't know," I say. "I could go to Taco Hell and pick something up?" Lydia already told me not to bother her at work because she got in trouble the last time I stopped by, but this would give me a legitimate reason to be there.

"You know we can afford better food, right? You could go to a real restaurant and get takeout, maybe even food that has nutritional value. Would it kill you to bring me a salad once in a while?"

I am having a hard time wrapping my head around the fact that my uncle watches documentaries and eats salad. What other weird habits has he picked up since he's been gone?

"Hey, I'm curious," Caleb says, shutting the laptop that is sitting on what used to be my bedside table. "How much are you skimming off the top?"

"What do you mean?"

"Don't play dumb. How much extra are you taking for yourself when you get cash to buy me stuff?"

"Nothing," I say. "I don't take anything."

Caleb looks at me for a long time, and I wonder if he can hear my heart beating out of my chest. He suddenly looks so much like Grandma, with that same grimace she gets when she tells me, "I can't believe I got stuck with you."

But instead what happens is Caleb starts laughing.

"Wow," he says. "You're serious."

"Of course I'm serious."

"Dude, I don't give a shit. I have so much money, I wouldn't even notice."

"I don't steal."

"Yeah, well, you're the only one. In, like, the whole world." He shakes his head, like he's disappointed in me for not stealing from him. "Man, she's got you good."

"Who?"

"Ma. She's damn good at making a kid feel like he's worth nothing, huh?"

I know we're not really talking about money, but I'm not entirely sure what we're talking about. The only thing I'm sure about is that it hurts.

There's no way I'm going to let Caleb see me cry. He already thinks I'm the biggest wuss who's ever lived, and I think he's probably right.

"I just wanted to help," I say. "I didn't expect you to pay me."

"How much do you think your time is worth?"

"I don't know." I'm holding my breath. I'm biting my lip. I will not cry in front of Caleb.

"Seriously. How much do you think you're worth?"

I am holding everything so tight, I think my blood has stopped moving. I squint my eyes so no tears will come out, but I feel them, seeping into my eyelashes, and my throat hurts, and everything hurts.

I turn around so Caleb can't see my face, but I can't do anything about my shaking shoulders. I can't do anything about the puffs of air coming out of my nose.

"Three hundred," Caleb says to my back, and I could be imagining it, but his voice sounds softer.

"What?" I sniffle.

"That's how much you're going to pay yourself. Three hundred dollars a week."

I whip around. "That's more than Grandma makes some weeks."

"Yeah, well, you're worth more than her. Way more. Doesn't take much."

"That's too much," I say. "I'm barely even doing anything."

"Dude, you are the world's worst negotiator." Caleb laughs, and I never thought an insult could make me feel so good. "It's the least I can do for making you clean up my shit. Hey, the bucket needs emptying, by the way. It's getting ripe in here."

"What would I even do with that much money?"

"I don't know. Buy some drugs. Have some fun. Eat a fucking salad. Take that feisty girlfriend of yours on a date or something. Do what people with money do. Speaking of drugs, did you get my weed yet?"

"I told you, I don't know where to get it."

"Just ask Gordon."

"One-Armed Gordon?"

"Yes, of course One-Armed Gordon. Jesus, Billy. Do I have to do everything for you? And put some ice on your face, for fuck's sake. You don't want CPS sniffing around, do you?"

LYDIA

I WAS HOPING I'D NEVER HAVE TO BRING BILLY TO THE
tragedy that is Larry's bar, but it was pretty much inevitable. Now
that I've refused to go to his place anymore, that doesn't leave us many
options. Today seemed like as good a day as any because it's Halloween
and Billy definitely needs a pick-me-up after getting bullied all day
for being the only person who showed up to school in a costume
besides a few nerdy freshmen dressed as unicorns and dragons, and
some girls dressed as sexy nurses and sexy devils and even one sexy
baby, which I found particularly creepy. Billy arrived in a weird old-
timey outfit and a fake mustache, carrying a broken lantern. When I
asked him who he was supposed to be, he was appalled that I didn't
recognize Hilliard Cod, the founding father of Rome. I mean, you
can't just let a guy walk home alone dressed like that.

Plus, there's the fact that we've been pretty much inseparable for
two months now, and he still hasn't met Larry. I'm totally fine with
this, but Billy is attached to certain ideas about arbitrary friendship
milestones that he learned from sitcoms. He's been begging to come
to my house for weeks, and I finally gave in because after a while it's
no fun to watch anyone grovel, and honestly hanging out at Larry's
bar is probably a healthier environment for him than that attic with

his uncle, which is a sad statement when you think about it. Our standards for healthy environments are pretty low.

"I've never been in a bar before," Billy whispers excitedly as we enter. We rode the county bus here and even that seemed to excite him.

"I'm sorry this has to be your first bar experience," I say. On the other hand, it may turn him off of bars completely, which would probably be a good thing considering his family's tendency toward going overboard with the mood-altering substances.

Larry's got the place covered with Unicorns vs. Dragons–themed Halloween decorations. There's a cardboard zombie unicorn guarding a cauldron full of candy on a table by the entrance. What looks like a miniature dragon skeleton hangs from the ceiling, along with tufts of white fluff that I'm guessing are supposed to be fog and/or dragon smoke.

"That's Old Pete," I say, pointing to the still figure in the corner booth. His beard is taking on a greenish hue. "Those are the other booths no one ever sits in. There's the jukebox that no one ever uses. There are the old guys at the bar watching TV." Billy looks disappointed. "I told you," I say.

"I thought there would be more . . . glamour," he says.

"But this is Carthage, Billy. You have to drive, like, a hundred miles before you find any glamour."

"I see someone's a big Unicorns vs. Dragons fan."

"I don't want to talk about it."

We take a couple of stools at the empty end of the bar just as

Larry steps out from the back, wearing the same cheap dragon costume from BigMart he's worn for the last three Halloweens, which is basically a giant black onesie with a hood and a lumpy little tail. His wings are looking a bit droopy. "Well, hello there! You must be Bill!" he says, and I cringe at his enthusiasm. "Quite a shiner you got there."

"Hello, sir," says Billy, with a weird old-timey accent to match his costume. His lantern is long gone after a couple of guys played catch with it after third period and it smashed in the hallway. "Nice to meet you. I'd like a dirty martini."

Larry and I both look at Billy like he's lost his mind. He gets a big goofy grin on his face. "I just always wanted to say that. I don't even know what a dirty martini is."

Larry laughs. I knew he'd love Billy. He has a soft spot for people who say weird stuff and smile for no reason. "How about a pop?"

"Can I have a cherry in it?"

"Absolutely."

"How about two cherries?"

"Now you're pushing it," Larry says with a smile.

Larry busies himself with something while the three guys at the other end of the bar stare at us. "You're that Sloat boy," one of them says, with a slur in his voice.

"You heard from your uncle?" says another one.

"Um, no?" Billy says, popping a maraschino cherry into his mouth. I'm pretty sure it's from the same bowl that's been sitting behind the bar since I was twelve. "Mmm, this is delicious. I used to get a jar of these for Christmas every year. It was my favorite gift."

"Pretty nice reward they're offering," one of the guys says.

"But you don't get them anymore?" I say to Billy. One thing I've learned is you've got to ignore drunk men or they'll just keep talking to you.

"We don't really do Christmas at my house," he says, looking at the TV. "We used to go to my great-aunt's house in Shelton for dinner, but Grandma says we're not doing that anymore because all Aunt Cynthia does is rub in her face how much better her life is than Grandma's."

"Is it?"

"I don't know. They both seem pretty miserable, if you ask me. But Aunt Cynthia's husband isn't dead and her kids play soccer and her house is a lot nicer than ours, and they live in one of those neighborhoods where everyone decorates their houses for Christmas with, like, a million lights and ten-foot-tall inflatable Santas."

"Sounds tacky," I say, stirring my drink.

"I think it's pretty," Billy says, and I immediately feel bad. "Do you think your dad would give me another cherry?"

I reach over the counter and put the whole bowl in front of Billy. "Here," I say. "Knock yourself out."

"Wouldn't it be nice to have a family you actually looked forward to seeing?" Billy says as he pops another cherry into his mouth, closes his eyes, and smiles. "I think these are my favorite food."

"We don't really do Christmas either," I say. "Larry has to keep the bar open for these losers."

"So, Bill," Larry says, the plush dragon head on top of his onesie bouncing as he walks toward us. "Can I get straight with you?"

"Um, okay?"

"What are your intentions with my daughter?"

"Jesus, Larry!" I say.

"Uh, I think we were going to have a campfire?" Billy says. "We got marshmallows."

"Larry," I say, using my best adult-scolding voice. "He's not my boyfriend."

"But are you planning to woo her?" Larry says. Billy looks like he's going to throw up from nerves. He shakes his head and takes a sip of his soda.

Larry squints his eyes and looks like he's thinking hard about something. "Don't hurt yourself, Larry," I say.

Then he smiles an actually pretty nice smile. He leans in close to Billy and whispers, "I get it, kid. I'm a progressive guy. No need to hide in the closet here."

"That's it. We're leaving," I say, hopping off the stool. What is wrong with people that they assume a guy is gay just because he's capable of being friends with a girl? Billy sits there smiling, like he hasn't quite figured out what Larry's implying because he's too busy enjoying the fact that an adult is speaking to him kindly.

"Honestly," Larry says, "I couldn't be happier. Now I don't have to worry about my daughter getting pregnant."

"Come on, Billy." I tug on his arm. "We're going."

"Wait, I want to see this real quick," Billy says.

"Turn it up, Larry," says one of the guys at the bar. "Sasquatch in the news again."

The TV news lady is saying something about a bunch of recent sightings in the Olympic Peninsula, but this time it's black instead of the usual brown and some say as big as a bus.

"That's a big Sasquatch," says one of the guys.

"It sounds like what I saw in the forest the day of the tornado," Billy whispers.

"Let's go start the fire," I say. "We have a whole bag of marsh-mallows to eat."

But his eyes are glued to the TV like everyone else's. "Local experts think it may be a mutated species of grizzly bear that migrated down from Canada after the Kamloops nuclear reactor meltdown two years ago," the news lady says, and everyone at the bar nods in tandem. "In other news, Caleb Sloat has reportedly been sighted at a mosque in Istanbul. The King has agreed to delay plans to bomb the region until the lead singer of Rainy Day Knife Fight can be safely brought home."

"That's quite a swim," says Larry. "All the way across the Strait of Juan de Fuca."

"He's a good swimmer, that Sasquatch," says one of the guys, nodding sagely.

"Jesus Christ," I say. "I can't take any more of this."

"Tell me something, Bill," Larry says. "Have you read Unicorns vs. Dragons?"

"Larry, stop!" I say, maybe a little louder than necessary. Old Pete burps over in his booth.

"Okay, fine," Larry says. "But how about Samhain? Do you know about Samhain?" He pronounces it *saah-win*, which, according to him, is how real witches pronounce it.

"What's that?" Billy says.

"No," I say, standing up. "Don't encourage him, Billy." Larry's Wiccan phase was even worse than his ongoing Unicorns vs. Dragons obsession.

"Samhain is the ancient pagan holiday marking a time when the boundary between this world and the spirit world thins and can be more easily crossed. It's where Halloween gets its origins."

"Um, okay?" Billy says.

"It is an excellent night for a fire. If you'd like, I can tell you some incantations you can use to summon the spirits. If there are any souls of the dead you'd like to communicate with, it's a great time to do that."

Billy looks at me with a raw, terrifying hope in his eyes, and my heart sinks to my stomach. This is how people get brainwashed and believe in lies. Because they're desperate for the impossible to be possible.

"We're good, Larry," I say. "We don't need any magic. We just want to roast some goddamned marshmallows." As I pull Billy off his barstool, I can feel him trying to hold on.

The freezing cold has let up, and it's actually a nice night, for a change. For the first time in weeks there are no clouds in the sky. The moon is full and extra bright. A warm fire crackles in front of us, the river rushes behind the trees, and we're eating crispy, melty balls of sugar, but even that isn't cheering Billy up from his sudden bout of moping, thanks to Larry and his talking-to-dead-people nonsense.

I add a couple of logs to the fire. It hisses and pops as we sit on old chairs on either side of it, left over from Larry's sad attempt a few years ago to create an outdoor patio, but even on nice days his customers just want to sit inside and watch TV. Billy and I face each other, the orange, dancing light projecting onto our faces and the wall of trees around us, making patterns that almost look like things.

"It's nice out here," I say.

"Yeah," Billy says, but I can tell he doesn't mean it.

"Did you want to stay inside?"

"Not really," he says. "I don't know. I feel sad in both places."

"Yeah."

"I'm thinking about my mom."

"Oh."

"I should be happy," Billy says.

I don't mean to, but a laugh escapes my mouth. "Why?" I say. What do any of us have to be happy about?

"My uncle came back. That's all I've wanted ever since he left. But it's nothing like I hoped it would be."

"What did you hope it would be?"

"I guess I wanted things to be like they were when I was little. I wanted to go back in time. I know that's impossible."

Billy looks up at me, the fire dancing in his eyes, and he looks like someone possessed, like it is more than just a reflection, but something coming from inside. "I just want a family," he says, and then his tears start flowing, and I swear the fire jumps and gets hotter, and I feel it in my chest, heavy and dense and burning, like a miniature sun the shape of my heart.

The temperature suddenly drops. In just seconds, clouds come out of nowhere and cover up the moon, and then snow starts falling, big, thick flakes of it, and the whole world turns silent and slow-motion and white, and it feels like we are the only people in it. Half of me knows this is some weird shit, but the other half isn't surprised at all.

"Me too," I say softly.

I just want a family.

And then it's like the rest of the world gets sucked away. I can't see Billy, can't hear the river. I'm alone, totally alone. It's just me and the fire and the ache inside me. I'm gripping the arms of my chair because it's the only thing that is solid. I can no longer feel my feet on the ground. Everything is twisting in the shadows. The fire is throwing itself around. It's like the tornado again, except everything's hot and dry. I'm in an oven. I'm being burned alive.

I've been drugged. That's it. One of those old bastards at the bar put something in my soda. That's the only explanation for the way the fire is dancing. It's the only explanation for the fire burning a hole in my chest.

Why is it windy all of a sudden?

Where is Billy?

Why am I crying?

Why is it black? Suddenly and completely black. The fire and wind and heat, gone. Billy and the bar and my apartment, the forest and the river, gone. Like I blinked and everything got sucked away, and now I'm stuck in an empty vacuum, a nowhere place. It's just me and the fire.

But there's someone else. I can see a little now, just enough to make out the outlines of another figure, like someone turned up a dimmer switch on a light somewhere, except it's impossible to tell where the light's coming from. It's almost like the figure is making the light itself, like some kind of phosphorescence, like one of those creepy deep-sea creatures who make blinking lights to attract their prey.

But the figure is not a predator. Somehow I know this. I know it is the thing that's been following me, hiding under my bed, darting into shadows, just out of reach. It is small, a child. It is sitting alone, surrounded by black. My heart rips open in my chest. The pain cannot be contained. The figure looks up. She. I can tell it is a girl. The girl looks at me, into the mirrors of my eyes. She is made of shadows. I cannot see her face, but I know exactly who she is.

I open my mouth, but I cannot speak. My throat is full of dust.

Somehow I know it is not my own heart aching, not my grown heart, strong from years of training. It is a smaller heart, a little girl's heart, taking residence in my chest—a stowaway, an exile, squeezed tight with longing.

Relax, I say without words.

But she can't. The girl can't. How can she relax when she has so much to do? How can she relax when she knows there is no one who will help her?

I see a scene like a movie with the sound turned off, a motherless girl with long black hair who can't stop crying. An empty space, no one to hear her. The girl's mouth opens and her eyes squeeze tight. She screams into nothingness. There is no echo, no walls, nothing to reflect her. No one to listen. She learns she does not exist. So the girl stops crying.

As she fades away, I hear a whisper. I know it is the little girl speaking, but it is in my own voice: *I am so tired.*

Tired of what? I ask her. But she is gone.

I touch my wet face. The wind has stopped. Everything is cold and quiet.

The fire comes back into focus. I feel pressure on my shoulder. Someone is squeezing me, shaking me.

"What happened?" I hear Billy cry, but his voice sounds far away. Everything is buzzing, like I'm waking up from fainting. "Did you have a seizure? Did you cross into the spirit world?"

"Jesus Christ, Billy," I say. His face slowly comes into focus. I remember where I am. I look around for the girl, but the only things I see are trees dusted with snow, and Billy's face, full of fear, and his eyes, full of flames.

"It looks like we're on a different planet," I say. Everything is white. I blink my eyes and stand up, a little wobbly.

"Are you okay?"

"I'm fine." But I think I may be lying.

"You were, like, possessed for a minute. I kept saying your name, but you didn't respond. You were just staring at the fire and crying and—"

"I'm *fine*, okay?"

But I'm shivering and lost and I feel like something inside me broke open.

Then I look at Billy, and the love and concern on his face feels like a punch in my stomach, but it's a warm punch that almost feels good, and a weird sound comes out of my throat, a combination of choking and crying, and I want to hug him so bad but I don't know how.

And then the cold of the night slices through me, and something becomes clear: I trust him. He is the first person in my life I have ever really trusted. And there are no rules for this, no script, no blueprint for what we are. We are making this up as we go along. But one thing I do know is that keeping a secret from him feels like lying.

I am tired of living in the shadows. I want him to see me.

"Billy, I want to show you something," I say. For once, he does not ask any questions. I start walking, and he follows.

I lead him to the back door of the building, though the dark narrow hallway lined with boxes and crates, and into my apartment behind the bar. It's nothing fancy and way smaller than Billy's house, but at least we can see the floor and there aren't bags of stuff piled all over the place, and everything isn't the color of dust. It strikes me now how, even though it's kind of weird to live behind a bar, there's something almost cheerful about how everything is brightly colored, how Mom actually made an effort to put art on the walls, but also something sad in how Larry has never bothered redecorating in the eight years since she's been gone, like this place is still some kind of shrine to her.

My eyes focus on the family photo hanging on the wall, the one we took at the Seattle zoo when I was seven. We look so happy, but it's a lie. And there's the photo of Mom I put back in place after I found it in the medicine cabinet this morning. She stares at me with her dark eyes, an empty smile painted on her face, full of mysteries I will never have the chance to solve. She took that chance away from me. She was buried with all her secrets.

I feel a twinge of something I can't name, which quickly turns into something I can: I hate her. I hate what she stole from me. I hate what she's done to us.

I meet Billy's eyes for a second, and his love helps dissolve the hate just enough for me to keep going. I turn around, walk the few steps it takes to get to the other side of the kitchen, and open the door to my studio.

BILLY

WE ENTER A SPACE THAT USED TO BE A TWO-CAR GARAGE,
but the garage doors have been boarded up. The floor is covered
by a puzzle of particleboard and duct tape, and a long wooden bar
runs along one side of the room. One of the walls is covered with
old thrift store mirrors, cracked and mismatched, catching the light
of the single dull light bulb hanging in the middle of the ceiling.
It's like somebody took a picture of a dance studio, crumpled it up,
stepped on it a few times and dragged it through the mud, then
flattened it out again.

Lydia looks tenser than I've ever seen her, standing in the middle
of the floor, looking at her feet.

"What is this place?" I say.

"I'm a dancer," she says. "This is where I dance. I don't tell people.
I've never told anyone."

"You made this all yourself?"

She nods. "It's kind of a work in progress." She pauses and looks
up. "Dude, I feel naked."

"You're completely covered with clothes. I can't see anything."
That makes her smile a little.

"So I dance," she says, shifting on her feet. "It's a thing I do."

"Do you take lessons?"

"I used to. When I was a kid. Before my mom died. But I've mostly taught myself since then."

"Wow."

"You want to hear a secret?"

"Yes," I say, sitting in the one rickety chair in the corner and trying to stay calm. There's nothing I want more in this moment than to hear a secret from Lydia.

"I have this sort of dream about getting on that reality show *Show Me Your Moves*."

"I love that show!" I say. "But Grandma never wants to watch it with me because she says it makes her feel fat."

"Most of the people who get in the top twenty have been hard-core training since they were, like, three and can do flips and all kinds of acrobatic shit. But the show always leaves a couple spots for break-dancers and random self-taught people because viewers love the underdog stories, right? I mean, look at how your uncle got so famous. And I thought maybe I could do that, you know? And if I get that far, even if I get kicked off early, those people always get offers from top dance schools for full scholarships. It's like free publicity for the schools. And then I could get some real training finally. And then, I don't know, maybe travel the world as a professional dancer."

In our long two months of friendship, I am pretty sure that's the most Lydia's ever told me about what lives inside her head without any sarcasm to mask it. I think it's also the longest she's ever talked at one time, because witty comebacks are usually pretty short, and this is the furthest thing from a witty comeback she's ever said to me.

"I think that's an awesome dream," I say, and as the words come out of my mouth, I realize I don't have anything close to a dream. I have all kinds of weird fantasies, but nothing actually based in reality. Nothing I've been working for. Nothing I care about so much I'd build a whole room for it.

"Show me," I say.

"Show you what? This is it. This is my pathetic Frankenstein dance studio."

"No, show me your moves!" Lydia doesn't laugh. "You know? Like the show?" Still nothing. "*Show Me Your Moves?*"

"I don't dance for people," she says. I can tell she's trying to not look at herself in the mirrors, but she's also trying to not look at me, so there aren't a lot of places for her eyes to go.

"You were just talking about dancing in front of millions of people on TV and around the world," I say. "You need to at least dance in front of one person."

"You're harder."

"Dancing for one of me is harder than dancing for a million strangers?"

"Yeah," she says, like it should be obvious. "A lot harder."

"I don't get it."

"You don't have to."

"I showed you my uncle in the attic."

"I never asked you to do that."

"What are you so scared of?"

Finally, she looks at me. "Are you calling me chicken?"

Bingo.

"Yes," I say. "I am calling you chicken. You act so tough, but really you're terrified of letting anyone see the real you."

"I am going to break your TV so you can't watch any more goddamned therapy talk shows."

We stare each other down for a long time.

"I'm not leaving until you dance for me," I say. I'm a total wimp about almost everything, but for some reason I can do this.

We stare each other down some more.

"Fine!" Lydia finally says, pulling off her coat. She throws her hoodie at me. And her shoes. And socks. She starts pulling off her jeans.

"Oh, hey," I say, and I can feel my face getting red.

"Calm down, you prude," she says. "I have leggings underneath." She throws her jeans at me too.

"Okay, I'm ready," she says. She's barefoot in the middle of the room, in leggings and a T-shirt. "I'm not warmed up, so don't expect me to do anything crazy." I try to imagine her in some kind of sequined tutu with her face all made up, but I can't. Maybe she's not that kind of dancer.

"See that CD player next to you?" she says. "Find the CD on the floor called *Satie* and play track number three."

"Ooh, a CD player," I say. "How retro."

"Shut up."

I follow her directions and the music starts—sparse piano that sounds like rain and fog and loneliness, like the classical, even-more-depressed version of Rainy Day Knife Fight. With the first note, Lydia is transformed. Suddenly, she's neither the cynical girl with a snappy retort for everything, nor the lost girl I caught a glimpse of by the fire, but someone fluid and graceful and not fighting anything. And even though she's moving all over the place, it's like deep down, some part of her is really still, and that still place travels with her wherever she goes, as she lifts her arms and points her feet, as she closes her eyes and arches her back and spins and leaps across the floor, and for some reason I think of a blue heron, how they're always so still and dignified and focused, so long and beautiful and always alone, and how I always feel a weird combination of lucky and sad when I see one.

Lydia stretches and slinks across the room, like someone waking up who's not quite sure she wants to wake up. She starts close to the ground but gradually gets taller, longer, until she's whirling around the room. She's a slow-motion tornado. She's performing some kind of spell, a conjuring. I feel my insides swirl. She leaps and I half expect her to never land.

The song is short, probably only around three minutes. But I don't think I could have handled anything longer. I feel like the air's been knocked out of me. I don't know anything about dance, but I am one hundred percent sure Lydia is brilliant.

"Billy, why are you crying?" she says, sweaty and a little out of breath. "Was I that bad?"

I can't speak. All I can do is shake my head.

I know exactly what I'm going to spend my new money on.

LYDIA

I'VE BEEN TRYING TO FORGET WHAT HAPPENED TWO
nights ago. But every time I close my eyes I see the fire, and every
time I open them I see the little girl. She's not hiding anymore, not
sneaking behind me and rushing out of sight when I try to get a look.
She sat beside me on the bus to school this morning, for Pete's sake.

But she doesn't speak. She doesn't make any noise at all. All she
does is kind of hang around, appearing randomly throughout the
day and disappearing just as randomly. She's like the world's most
boring ghost. Now that I can see her clearly, I'm not really scared of
her anymore. What I am is pissed. I don't have time for this shit. I
don't want some little kid following me around. I yell at her when
no one's looking. I tell her to leave. But she just ignores me, and that
just makes me madder.

Fog Harbor has always been weird, but the weirdness has
started speeding up since the tornado. Flocks of Canada geese are
flying north instead of south. A bald eagle snatched up some lady's
Chihuahua yesterday in the BigMart parking lot, and then she
found the dog's collar hanging on her mailbox when she got home,
like the eagle knew where she lived.

There's some new app that's got everyone walking around

school with their faces glued to their phones because they score points based on how long they let their retinas get scanned. People are running into walls and knocking over trash cans and yelling at each other for talking or doing anything else people do in real life that might distract them from staring at their phones. Who knows what kind of brain-scrambling powers those fancy phones have, or what kind of subliminal messaging might be happening? If I were so inclined, I might say this is the beginning of the zombie hordes and the end of civilization. But that sounds a little too much like one of Larry's conspiracy theories.

The lunchroom is eerily quiet. Billy and I are the only ones actually talking to each other, plus the handful of doomsday-prepper kids in the corner who have been grumbling in hushed tones and comparing their rations with extra vigor ever since the tornado. Even the other poor kids without fancy phones aren't talking, as if their silence is some kind of sad, secondhand participation in the richer kids' absurd game. The quiet is oddly freeing, like we're on a vacation from the usual nonsense.

But I'm having a hard time looking Billy in the eyes since I danced for him. I showed him too much and now I want to take it back. I want my secret back. This is probably something close to how people feel after they sleep with someone and regret it. Embarrassed. Exposed. Like some kind of vulnerability hangover. He kept bringing it up all day yesterday, kept telling me how great I am and begging me to dance for him again, and it made my skin crawl. I think I hurt his feelings a little when I told him to leave me alone, but he bounced back. He always bounces back.

Billy's been excited about something all day, but he won't tell me what. "I can't talk in here," he whispers. "It's too quiet." His black eye is starting to fade to a yellowish brown, and now the skin just looks kind of dirty.

"Dude, nobody's listening to us. They're too busy getting brainwashed." One of the prepper kids nods at me like we're in this together. I have to admit, it feels a little comforting. They're not bad people to have on your side in an emergency.

"A kid in my Blog Studies class got so mad when he had to put his phone away that he started punching Mr. Belding in the nose and had to get taken away in handcuffs," Billy says.

"That's what you were so excited to tell me?"

"This other kid was talking about how he went hunting with his dad over the weekend and saw an albino stag as big as an elephant with a weird antler, like, *one long antler*, and don't you think that kind of sounds like a uni—"

"Don't say it!" I reach my hand out to cover Billy's mouth, but a little too forcefully, so it ends up more like a slap.

"Ouch!" Billy says, rubbing his chin.

"Sorry," I say.

"I can't stand this anymore," Billy says. "I have to tell you." He leans in. "Are you ready?"

"Sure." Sometimes he is so melodramatic.

"Okay, so I was reading the *Fog Harbor News*."

"That thing still exists?"

"Mostly it's just advertisements and classifieds. Stop asking questions!"

"Sorry. Go."

"You know that dance school Fog Harbor Dance Academy?"

Of course I know that school. It's the best dance school in all of coastal Washington, and it's where I took lessons until I was nine. "Yes, Billy. I know the school."

"They had a big half-page ad in there about how they're holding auditions to give a new student a full scholarship for a year. All the classes they want."

I feel a weird kind of weightlessness in my ribs, like a tiny person leaping inside of me. "Do you still have the newspaper?" I say calmly, with as little emotion as possible, like I don't care, like this news barely interests me at all.

"Um, no," Billy says. "I threw it away."

"Why'd you do that?!" I accidentally yell.

"Shut up, Lydia Chlamydia," hisses a girl on the Carthage side of the lunchroom, without ever taking her eyes off her phone. I went to a sleepover at her house in second grade, when I was still marginally normal.

"Don't worry," Billy says. "I have the phone number. And I already called them to find out about it, and they said you should call to set up the audition."

I'm trying really hard not to smile, to not let that leaping thing inside my chest get too full of itself. I'm trying to rein everything in so it won't get out of control, because hope can do that; it can get dangerous if you let it.

"Do you have your phone with you?" Billy says.

"Yes." I can feel my heart pounding in my ears. And there she is, my little stalker, dancing happily behind Billy, skipping and spinning between lunch tables in a pink leotard. I give her a nasty look, but it doesn't faze her at all.

"Let's call now," Billy says. "Make sure you ask for Mary. She's the one you need to talk to. Don't talk to anyone else. She's expecting your call. *Mary.*" Billy's being really intense about this whole Mary business, but Billy is often intense about odd things. He passes me a piece of paper with the phone number written on it in his chicken-scratch handwriting.

I dial the number. I try to breathe. A million tiny feet are tap-dancing on my heart. The little girl spins on top of a lunch table. I feel like I did in my dance studio with Billy on Halloween night, a weird combination of terrified and free.

"Fog Harbor Dance Academy," the perky woman who answers the phone says. "This is Belinda. How may I help you?"

"Um, hi. May I speak to Mary, please?"

"Let me see if she's available," the woman says. "May I tell her who's calling?"

"My name's Lydia Lemon? She's supposed to be expecting my

call?" The tap dancing gets faster as I wait for Mary to pick up. If I have to wait much longer, I'm pretty sure I'm going to start hyperventilating.

I look at Billy and he has this hopeful look on his face, like he's counting on this working out as much as I am, and then the tap dancers in my chest all collapse. Their feet are broken. My heart is cracked. I never should have danced for him. He should not know this about me. He should not care this much.

"This is Mary," says a raspy voice that sounds vaguely familiar. Is this the tight-bunned woman who taught my ballet class as a child?

"Oh, um, hi." I turn around to face the Carthage side of the zombie lunchroom. I cannot look at Billy. I can barely deal with my own feelings, let alone his. But the little ghost girl is wherever I try to look. She won't let me ignore her. "My name's Lydia Lemon? My friend Billy said he talked to you about my coming in to audition to take some classes at your studio?"

"He sure did," Mary says with what I detect to be a stifled laugh. Billy must have made an impression. "Sweet kid. So when do you want to come in? Tomorrow? Teen classes start at four, so if you can get here by three thirty, you'd have time to show me your stuff."

I'm supposed to work tomorrow, but fuck it. I can call in sick. I've never called in sick before in my life.

"Yes, that's perfect," I say. "I'll see you then."

I turn around and Billy still has the smile on his face. "So?" he says.

"I'm going in tomorrow."

"Can I come with you?"

"No." Absolutely not. "I think I need to do this myself."

He's trying not to show it, but I can tell he's disappointed. It's one thing to perform for him in my garage, another thing entirely to feel the pressure of his expectation as I do the most important dance I've ever done in my life.

"Oh," he says, trying so hard to look happy. "Okay."

It shouldn't be this quiet in here. There should be noise to drown out the war of hope and terror in my brain.

"Are you excited?" Billy asks.

I nod yes, but what I really want to do is throw up.

"Awesome!" he says. "Now I just have one teeny-tiny favor to ask you. What are you doing after school?"

BILLY

"I CAN'T BELIEVE I LET YOU TALK ME INTO DOING THIS,"
Lydia says. "If I get arrested, I'm going to kill you. The only reason
I'm here is to supervise so you don't do anything more dangerous
and foolish than what you're already doing."

"Thank you," I say. Lydia just rolls her eyes.

I know it's asking a lot of a friend to come with you to buy drugs,
especially when the drugs are for someone she hates who is technically not supposed to be doing drugs, and I do feel a little bad about
it. But I know Lydia will totally forgive me when she starts taking
dance classes. Except she won't actually know I have anything to do
with it at first, and that's going to kill me, but it'll be worth it because
she's going to be so happy she'll forget to be mad at me, and then
when she's at the peak of her happiness, I'll make the big reveal and
tell her it's me who's responsible for the greatest joy she's ever known,
and she'll be so grateful she'll never be mad at me ever again.

I'm trying not to wonder what Lynn A. would think about my
being at a drug dealer's house. I'm trying not to picture the gently
disappointed look on her face, like, *I love you, but I know you can
do better.*

"Yo, did you see me on TV last night?" One-Armed Gordon

says as he emerges from his kitchen with a large can of some kind of energy drink. "I did a dope-ass interview on Channel Seven."

To say Gordon's house is filthy would be an understatement. My house is full of crap, but at least it's clean crap that mostly stays in bags. But I get the impression that Gordon just throws things at the wall when he's done with them. Soda bottles and moldy pizza boxes cover the floor. There's a pile of chicken wing bones in the corner, like roadkill after crows have their way with it. The house smells of greasy hair and old socks. Lydia and I are sitting on the lumpy couch, and she looks like she's trying to make herself as small as possible, as if that will help her not touch anything dirty.

"Oh, where are my manners?" Gordon says. He's wearing a pair of wrinkled khaki shorts with stains all over the crotch and a T-shirt advertising a local pawnshop. Only one of the sleeves has an arm coming out of it. "Do you guys want one of these?" He holds up the energy drink. We both shake our heads. "Best scam ever. You call up a company and tell them their product made you sick and you're thinking of suing them, and then they send you a lifetime supply! I have, like, thirty cases of this shit in the back."

"Billy," Lydia says. "If this isn't over in two minutes, I'm leaving without you."

"It's good to see you, Billy," Gordon says. "Where you been? I haven't seen you since you were a snot-nosed little kid following your uncle around."

"I was supposed to follow him around," I say. "He was baby-sitting."

"You know Caleb used to live here with me and my pop?" Gordon says, sitting down on a chair across from us like he expects us to stay awhile.

"I know," I say. Gordon's house is a stop on the Caleb Sloat, Lead Singer of Rainy Day Knife Fight, Childhood Tour™ after all.

"Did he ever tell you I was in the band?"

"What band?"

"Rainy Day Knife Fight, dumb-ass. I was one of the founding members."

"Right," Lydia says.

"But I don't think the touring musician lifestyle would have really worked for me, you know?" Gordon lifts some kind of con-traption with water in it from the table, grips it between his legs while the hand of his good arm holds a lighter to it, inhales, and exhales a giant cloud of sweet but slightly rancid-smelling smoke. "I like it right here in Rome. I'm a hometown boy."

Lydia squeezes my knee hard. "Ouch!" I say.

"I was bummed when I lost my arm in the accident at first, 'cause I couldn't drum anymore. But then the disability checks started coming in, and I was like, sweet, best thing that ever hap-pened to me."

Are all drug dealers like this? Do they just talk and talk forever, counting on their customers to be too scared to leave?

"Billy," Lydia says. "Just give him the money."

"Disability's great and all," Gordon continues as I pull my wallet out of my pocket, "but not quite enough to afford the nice things in life, you know? Which is why I need to supplement my income."

I look at my wallet and am suddenly embarrassed. It's the same blue Velcro wallet with a cartoon dolphin on it that I've had since I was ten years old.

"I'll tell you, things weren't looking good there for a while after they legalized weed and everything went legit, but then luckily the King fixed that and people like me are back in business."

Lydia stands up. "We have to go," she says. I hand the money to Gordon.

"Oh," Gordon says, obviously disappointed. He hands me a plastic baggie of dry greenish-brown clumps, and as soon as it's in my hand, Lydia pulls me out of the house. Gordon calls, "Do want to take one of these energy drinks to go?" but the door closes before I have a chance to respond.

Lydia says she has to go home to practice for her big audition, and she won't let me come with her, even though I promised not to talk. I saw a therapy talk show one time about introverts, and I'm pretty sure that's what Lydia is, so I'm trying not to take it personally.

My heart races the whole way home because I have a bag of drugs in my pocket and I'm pretty sure everyone for miles around can smell it, and any minute now an undercover drug-sniffing dog is going to jump out of the bushes and attack me. I'm also pretty sure I'm being followed because I keep looking behind me and I swear I see the same black car that was sitting outside my house the other day, but it's far enough away that I can't see any details. I've watched enough detective shows to know that's part of their strategy.

When I get home, the possum under the front porch lunges at my ankles, and I'm pretty sure she knows something.

How is it possible that in just a few weeks I went from having no secrets to having so many I can't sleep and I feel like I'm going to have a heart attack all the time? All I used to do was hang out with my grandma and watch TV, and now I'm basically a criminal mastermind.

LYDIA

I REALLY, TRULY THINK I'M GOING TO THROW UP. THAT extra corn dog I ate at lunch was a bad idea. If I'm actually going to start training seriously, I need to start eating healthier. Eggs and fresh fruit every morning. Smoothies. Grilled chicken breasts and avocados and whole grains that aren't gluten. First I need to figure out what gluten is.

But I'm getting ahead of myself. I haven't even done the audition yet. I could blow chunks on the dance floor and ruin everything, and all these thoughts about training and smoothies could be a total waste of time.

I get off the bus and for once it's not raining. The dance studio looks just like I remember it from when I was a kid, except the strip mall it's in has definitely seen better days. There used to be a pizza place next door where Mom would take me after class sometimes, just the two of us. "It's not good for a girl to eat dinner on a barstool every night," Mom would say, but back then I still thought being a little different was like an adventure.

I walk into the studio and luckily it's early enough before the afternoon classes that there isn't anyone here except the receptionist. "You must be Lydia," she says way too cheerfully. "Mary will be ready in just a sec. Do you want to go get changed?" She motions toward the changing rooms, which I remember well. "Then go straight into the big studio and warm up, okay? Do you know where it is?"

"Uh-huh," I say, but my voice sounds like a nine-year-old's. The big studio is where the big girls dance.

The changing room is dark and windowless, all splintering wood benches and shelves and cubbies. I remember how you couldn't ever sit on the benches or else your tights would get snagged. The floor is a stained industrial carpet. The smell is moist and earthy—old wood and girl sweat. A long mirror is on one wall, with a shelf of old shoeboxes full of used bobby pins, combs, rubber bands, and tangled hairnets and bun covers. A couple of crates are stacked nearby for the little girls to stand on. I remember standing on those boxes, barely five years old, looking at my face and my mother's in the mirror as she did my hair. I could barely stand how beautiful she was, and how proud I was to look so much like her, how when she pulled my hair back into a tight ponytail, I suddenly had cheekbones like hers, and I caught a glimpse through my baby fat of myself as a woman, and I knew what I wanted to do for the rest of my life.

I look in the mirror now, and the sickness in my stomach has been replaced with a heavy weight. And there's that infuriating little girl staring right back at me with her big, sad eyes, like she wants something from me, like I'm even capable of giving it.

I wish my mother were here. I wish she could see me do this.

Fuck. I am not going to cry. This is the worst possible time to cry.

"Get out of here," I tell the girl. "Leave me alone."

I watch her shrink into herself, become less solid. "I don't want you here," I say, and she dissolves even more. "I don't want you."

She turns around and retreats into the mirror. I won this round.

I want to feel a weight lifted off me. I want to feel triumphant. But the words I spoke left a bitter taste in my throat, and my heart feels heavier than ever, and even though she's a hallucination, she's still just a little girl, and I feel ashamed, like I want to apologize. And what sane person wants to apologize to a ghost?

I pinch myself in the soft part under my arm. Hard. I haven't had to do that in a long time. My elementary school guidance counselor taught me that trick after Mom died and I wouldn't stop crying in class and parents started complaining because I was making their kids uncomfortable. In retrospect, a school counselor teaching kids borderline self-harm techniques is maybe not super professional.

But it works. For a couple seconds, I'm distracted enough from my feelings to get my shit together. I take a deep breath and shake out my arms. I dress quickly in my ratty tights and leotard and put a couple clips in my short hair. I block all thoughts of my mother out of my mind. I ignore the little girl now sulking in the corner.

I walk through another door straight into the studio. I never got to take classes in here as a kid, but I'd sometimes watch the older girls dance, imagining myself as one of them. There's a piano in the corner and a stereo on a shelf, a couple speakers mounted near the ceiling. Besides the mirror along one wall and the barres on the others, that's it for decoration. I love how sparse dance studios are, how honest, how unpretentious despite all the big egos they often contain. I trust these rooms way more than I trust the people in them.

I find a place at the barre and try not to look myself in the eye or at the figure darting around in the mirror as I do some quick warm-ups. Just my arm, my leg, my foot. I tell myself I am only my body parts.

After a few minutes, Mary walks in. I remember her from when I was a kid. I remember wondering if she ever took out her perfectly round gray bun, and if her hair was as long and witchy as I imagined it to be. I have no idea how old Mary is—fifty? Sixty? Older?—but her body is still all muscle and tendon and poise. I'm pretty sure this woman lives in a ballet skirt.

"Lydia," Mary says. "Hello." She shakes my hand firmly. Her lips are in the shape of a tight smile I have a feeling she doesn't really mean. This lady means business. I am nothing to her.

"Hi," I say. "It's so nice to meet you. Thank you so much for this opportunity. I used to take classes here as a kid, and—"

"Are you warmed up?"

"Yes," I lie. I only had time to do one side.

"Do you have music?"

"Oh yeah," I say, "I left it in the dressing room. Can I go get it?"

"No time," Mary says. "The next classes start arriving in five minutes. Can you do without?"

"Um, sure," I say. Saying no to Mary is not an option.

She glides to the corner of the room and leans against the piano. "Whenever you're ready."

"Okay," I say, moving to the center of the room. I taste corn dog in the back of my throat. I pretend not to see the girl staring at me from the mirror.

I decide to play it safe and not do any of my own choreography. I'm doing some of the sequences I picked up from a *Show Me Your Moves* solo that won an Emmy last year.

I get in position, close my eyes, and hear the music in my head. I open my eyes and start to dance, and Mary and the girl disappear.

It only takes three minutes, but I'm out of breath when I'm done, and I feel a tweak in my right hip. I have a sinking feeling that Mary could tell I was trying too hard, that she was turned off by my eagerness, that she's disgusted by how obvious it is that I want this more than anything I've ever wanted in my life.

"We need to work on your endurance," Mary says dispassionately.

"Okay," I pant. Hope twirls in my chest at the sound of "we."

"We'll start you in intermediate ballet to work on your technique. Advanced is the highest level we offer for the contemporary/lyrical/jazz combo, so we'll put you in that. I'm going out on a limb here, but I think you might be ready for preprofessional modern. If not, we'll move you down to advanced. That'll be three afternoons a week, plus a three-hour block on Saturday mornings. Are you ready to commit to that?"

"Intermediate ballet?" I say. "Is that with, like, middle schoolers?"

"Would you rather not dance here at all?"

"No, ma'am," I practically shout. "Intermediate is great."

"And I don't know what you might have heard, but this is a No Eating Disorders Tolerance school, okay?"

"Okay."

"Belinda can give you a printout of some sample meal plans and recipes."

"Okay."

"Good. We'll see how you do. If you seem to pick everything up in the first few weeks, we may decide to move you to advanced ballet. But don't count on it. You've been dancing feral for, what, eight years?"

"When's the next class?" I say. "Can I start today?"

Mary's thin lips twist. "I don't think so, dear. It's the preprofessional pointe workshop."

My body actually recoils at the word "pointe." Fucking fancy-shoe ballerinas. No thank you.

"You can get your schedule from Belinda. And the dress code for each class so you'll know what to buy."

"Dress code?"

Mary looks me up and down. If she were forty years younger, she could fit right in at Fog Harbor High. "You didn't think you could come to classes in *that*?" she says with a smirk.

I'm too happy to want to tell Mary to go fuck herself.

The little girl is bouncing up and down in the mirror with a big smile on her face, showing all the excitement I'm trying not to, and somehow this pains me more than her sadness. Even after I was so mean to her, even after I pushed her away, she's still here, still happy for me, still loyal.

The dressing room is packed now, pink nylon and pink skin everywhere. It's all spider legs and arms and shoulder blades and jutting hip bones, girls chattering like hens at the mirror as they do their hair. A couple of girls are bent over a bench pounding new pointe shoes with a hammer. Another girl looks beastly as she gnaws on a chunk of beef jerky. Everyone thinks ballerinas are so pretty and graceful, but really, they're animals.

I grab my stuff and try to get out as quickly as I can, but as I turn around, I run straight into Natalie Morris, Miss Prima Ballerina herself.

"Watch it," Natalie says.

"You watch it," I say.

A bunch of girls stop what they're doing, like they just noticed I'm here, and there seems to be a consensus around the room that I do not belong among them.

I lift my chin even higher than those long-necked princesses and walk out of the dressing room, the little girl trailing behind me. I am going to prove them all so wrong.

The only problem with going to dance school is having to deal with other dancers.

BILLY

THIS IS WHAT'S ON THE SHOPPING LIST CALEB GAVE ME
late last night:

BigMart:
Glue gun w/ lots of extra glue
Staple gun w/ lots of extra staples
Large sewing needles
Thread, many colors
Fishing line
Button variety packs, many colors
Extra-strength laxatives

Thrift Town:
Every single doll and stuffed animal they have
More blankets and pillows

I spend the whole afternoon shopping, but my thoughts keep returning to Lydia. As I select a pack of fluorescent-colored buttons, I think she must be getting off the bus at exactly this moment. As I stand in the BigMart checkout line, I think she must be getting ready to dance.

I could tell she was excited all day today but she was trying to hide it. I don't know why she acts so cool all the time, like she doesn't care about stuff. Who's she trying to impress? Certainly not me. I'm so easily impressed, it's kind of embarrassing. And anyway, who decided not caring about stuff was impressive?

Lydia has no idea I lied to her about the audition. She's going to get there and dance for that Mary lady, and Mary's going to see she's as good as I told her she was, and they're going to sign her up for all the classes she wants, and Lydia will have no idea it's me paying for the whole thing. Mary promised she'd keep my secret, and I guess I don't really know if I can trust her, but what choice do I have?

I thought about just telling Lydia I wanted to pay for her classes, but that idea didn't last long. I know she'd never let me. She's weird like that. I'm guessing it has something to do with pride, which is not something I know a whole lot about. Why would you say no to something you really want just because someone's trying to give it to you?

I know the whole situation is a little dishonest, and probably technically a lie, but I think sometimes being sneaky is okay if it's for a good cause. Sometimes people don't need to know when they're being helped, because sometimes people won't let you help them.

The checkout lady at Thrift Town doesn't bat an eye when I show up with my cart full of the store's entire doll selection. She's used to me doing Grandma's weird shopping. She even lets me borrow a shopping cart to haul everything home, which I know for a fact is against the rules because she calls the cops whenever homeless guys try to "borrow" carts. As I head out the door, I think Lydia must be done with her audition by now. I wish I had a cell phone so I could call her.

I thought if I hurried, I could make it home before the fog came, but I was wrong. I exit Thrift Town and walk straight into thick white soup with zero visibility. It's half a mile of this as I make my slow way home, running off the curb several times. Cars pass by, but I only see their fuzzy, disembodied trails of light. Pedestrians pop up out of nowhere. One second, all I see is white, and the next, there's a face right in front of mine, yelling at me to "Watch it!" It's like trying to play a video game with the screen turned off. At one point, I have a head-on collision with the cart of a homeless man coming from the opposite direction. I never even saw him coming.

And then I'm alone again, just me and the white, and I hear the sound of hooves and feel a swift cold wind that makes my lungs sting. The sky darkens and something big and black passes over-head, and then a sound like thunder, but from way closer than the clouds. Then everything is still and quiet, and I can feel my teeth chattering, and the smell of rot is overwhelming. It's impossible to tell how much is real, how much is my imagination, and how much is the effect of my sleep problems slowly disintegrating the already fragile state of my mental health.

When I get home and carry everything upstairs, Caleb says, "Just leave it by the door." He doesn't even bother opening the hatch of his blanket fort to look at me.

"What are you going to do with all this stuff?" I ask from the doorway.

"Just leave it," Caleb says again.

"Is it for an art project?"

"Leave it," Caleb says for the third time.

I stand there for a moment, wondering if I should tell him about the black car I keep seeing, even though he told me not to tell him anything about the world outside. But wouldn't he want to know if he's in danger? Which one would make him madder at me—telling him or not telling him?

How can I keep talking so I get to stay up here longer?

"Are you constipated? Is that why you needed the—"

"Jesus, Billy. Just get out of here and leave me the fuck alone!"

So I leave Caleb alone and go back downstairs. The whole house shakes with each step I take, and the lights blink on and off. A weird sound comes from the walls, like a bunch of people are in there throwing themselves into things. It sounds violent.

I use the house phone to call Lydia to see how the audition went, but she doesn't answer. What if the whole thing backfires and she's humiliated and hates me? Or what if she's thrilled beyond belief because she did great and got in? Either way, why doesn't she want to share it with me?

I sit on the couch and search for something to watch. I turn to the AA channel to say hi to Lynn A., and then I keep clicking; I'm not really in the mood for a meeting right now. I know they're just going to talk about how important honesty is, and that's not really helpful when I'm trying to keep a bunch of secrets.

All those years sitting here with Grandma, all I ever wanted was a chance to hold the remote and decide what we watched, but now that I have that power, I spend the next two hours just clicking through the channels. Nothing I land on feels right. Without Grandma here making all the TV decisions, I don't even know what I want.

I spent so much of the past several years wishing I could see Caleb. For a few of those last weeks, I made my wish even smaller—all I wanted was for Caleb to be alive, even if it meant I never got to see him again. No one ever taught me how to pray, but I did it anyway. I got on my knees and everything. I asked God or whoever to protect my uncle and keep him safe. And my wish actually came true, and I got more than I even dreamed of—Caleb is now living under the same roof as me for the first time in ten years. I should be happy. I should be grateful. I have more to be grateful for than I've ever had in my life.

The lights flicker as I take a deep breath in. I hold my breath and remind myself to be grateful. *It could be so much worse.* The house groans as I breathe out, twisting and settling in a big cloud of dust that makes me cough.

Honestly, I feel more alone and confused than ever. The problem with wishes is once they come true, you have to figure out something else to wish for.

LYDIA

"WATCH YOUR TURNOUT, LYDIA," MARY SAYS. I AM POSI-
tioned between two twelve-year-olds at the barre. The little girl is
in the mirror, running around like she's purposely trying to distract
me, and I'm trying to concentrate on my dancing at the same time
I'm fighting the impulse to start screaming at her, and this is really
the last place in the world I need to have an outburst. Sometimes
I'm pretty good at ignoring her, like she's nothing more than an
annoying mosquito bite, but sometimes, like right now, when I'm
already a ball of nerves, it hits me how incredibly twisted it is that
ignoring a ghost seems to have become a normal part of my life, and
I don't know how long I'm going to be able to keep this up before I
just can't hold it together anymore.

I can dance circles around all these kids, but they're not the
ones under the microscope. Of course, Miss Prima Ballerina herself
is here assisting Mary. Natalie Morris walks up and down the rows
correcting each student, wearing some extra-long leg warmers that
go up to her thigh gap and a flimsy pink ballet sweater that probably cost a hundred dollars and provides exactly zero warmth. I had
to spend nearly all the money I've saved up to buy the pink leotard, tights, skirt, and new slippers required for ballet, and the black

tights and leotard for modern, and black shoes for jazz—that's over two hundred dollars right there, gone in an instant. Not to mention this whole meal plan I'm supposed to be on. Organic fruits and vegetables and free-range meat? Yeah, right. I don't think they even sell that at BigMart. This scholarship is turning out to be pretty damn expensive, not to mention the fact that I'm losing two work shifts a week to make all the classes. I don't even know how I'm going to afford tampons this month.

Larry's so clueless, he doesn't even notice anything's different. He never saw any of the money I made when I was working more shifts, and I'm gone now pretty much the same amount as I was before. But even if things changed drastically, he probably wouldn't notice then, either.

Natalie is getting closer. I square my shoulders and tuck my pelvis as I do a goddamned perfect grand plié in second position. "Don't touch me," I snap as Natalie hovers next to me.

Natalie looks hurt. "I was just going to say your arms look nice."

"Whatever."

I'm pretty sure I killed it on the barre warm-up. The choreography for the floor is easy, though I'm a little slow with some of the words. I have to watch the other girls to see what they're doing, but it's not too hard to catch on. So what if I can't perfectly translate the moves from French? It's doing the moves that counts.

I make up for that weakness with my dancing. I know my arabesques must be higher than everyone else's. I add embellishments wherever I can—a battu in the jetés, an extra turn in the pirouettes. Because when people expect you to fail, for whatever reason—because you're an outsider, because of your lack of training, because your hair's weird and your skin's brown, because you're here on a scholarship and they know you can't afford any of the pink shit you're wearing—you have to be ten times better than the best kid in the class.

"Turnout, Lydia," Mary says again.

"Fuck," I mutter in the middle of a tour jeté. The prepubescent girl next to me gasps and stumbles on her landing, nearly knocking over a whole line of tiny blond creatures. I am a monster towering above them. The little girl laughs at me from the mirror. What is she even doing here? Why does she pick the most annoying times to show up?

I catch my breath and wait by the wall as the old lady playing piano in the corner starts the song again for the next group. As I pant, I remind myself I really need to work on my endurance. Maybe I should start jogging.

"Relax," Natalie whispers, gliding up noiselessly beside me. "This isn't a contest. You're doing great."

I think she's trying to be nice, but it feels like a judgment. She is telling me to calm down. She is telling me I shouldn't be feeling what I'm feeling. Natalie doesn't understand. This *is* a contest. Maybe she doesn't have to work so hard because she's the teacher's pet and her rich parents pay for everything and she's been a part of this world since she could walk. But I have to earn this. I have to prove I deserve to be here.

I get ready to dance again, but Mary says time's up, so everyone gets in lines and the old lady plays something ridiculously flowery while we do our bows, and then all the dancers run to the changing room and I'm left in the middle of the studio, alone, the little girl grinning across from me in the mirror. Natalie smiles at me as I leave, and it's not a bitchy ballet-princess smile at all. For a moment, I'm disarmed by surprise and a warm feeling spreading through my guts, and for some strange reason I don't completely understand, I smile back.

"Point taken, Miss Lemon," Mary says without looking up from the cell phone she's poking at. "You can move to advanced next week. And I recommend you study up on ballet terms in the meantime. Flash cards can be helpful."

BILLY

"WHAT ARE YOU DOING AFTER SCHOOL?" I ASK LYDIA AT lunch.

"It's Tuesday," she says. "You know I have dance class."

"Oh yeah," I say. I guess I knew that. Even though it's been a few weeks since Lydia started taking dance classes, I still ask every day.

She looks at me funny. "I'm sorry I've been so busy," she says.

"It's okay." I try to smile. I'm happy for her. I am.

"Are you sleeping okay?" she says. "No offense, but you kind of look like shit."

"I think there are raccoons or something in my walls. They kept me up all night."

"You should call an exterminator."

"Yeah." Or maybe an exorcist.

"What'd you do after school yesterday?"

"First, I stopped by Mrs. Ambrose's class, but she just started talking about some new life coach she met online who's teaching her about how her body's made out of light so she needs to do everything at a higher vibration, and how for only five hundred dollars she got her own unique personalized mantra."

Lydia laughs, her mouth full of french fries. "You should introduce her to Larry." She takes a bite of her second hamburger. "And then what'd you do?"

"Oh, you know. Hung out with Caleb."

She grimaces. She does not approve of our relationship.

"He was in a surprisingly good mood, actually," I say, which is partly true, meaning he wasn't being mean to me, though he was sort of in the middle of a panic attack because he accidentally signed into his e-mail account and was reminded that outside the attic there's still a whole world of people who want something from him. But then he smoked some pot and felt a little better and he let me sit next to him while he watched a movie that was all in French and I couldn't read the subtitles fast enough.

"Are you sad about all the Unicorns vs. Dragons signs?" I say. This morning's big news is that someone vandalized all of Carthage's prized Unicorns vs. Dragons–themed street signs, but only the ones featuring dragons.

Lydia laughs. "I could not give any less of a shit," she says. "But Larry was practically catatonic."

"How's dance class?" I ask. Is this small talk? This feels like it might be bordering on small talk. Or is this just how normal people talk? Is a normal conversation just calmly asking questions back and forth?

"Good," she says. "Really good." She smiles, her face so relaxed and happy, and for a second I feel the air knocked out of me. I wish I were a part of that smile.

Just then, everyone on one side of the morning prayer circle table stands up from their seats in unison and shouts, "Who's in the house?" Then everyone on the other side of the table stands up and says, "J.C.'s in the house!" Then they all cheer and clap for themselves at the successful completion of their cafeteria Christian flash mob, then Grayson Landsverk shouts, "Fuck you!" Then they sit down and pray over their burgers and fries, and all I can think is who in their right mind would thank God for any of this? And then I think, that's the exact opposite of gratitude and not how I should be thinking if I want to be happy, and then I wonder if I even want to be happy.

Lydia just keeps eating with a smile on her face, not even bothering to say something snarky. I should feel happy that she's happy. But mostly I just feel alone.

I'm pretty sure I saw the black car sitting outside of school as I was leaving, but it drove away before I could get a good look. I've been seeing it several times a week. I told Lydia about it, but she says I'm being paranoid. She won't let me come to dance class with her, even though I promised not to embarrass her. She says there are rules about no visitors, but I'm not sure I believe her.

I spend the whole walk home trying not to hyperventilate. Every sound makes me jump. Maybe I'm being paranoid like Lydia said, but it's entirely justified. I pass a tree with about a thousand crows in it, and they just sit there silently watching me walk by, their heads turning slowly as their beady eyes follow me. I heard somewhere a bunch of crows is called a "murder," so I'm definitely not taking it as a good sign.

I check under the porch when I get home to make sure the possum isn't waiting there to ambush me. When I turn around, I see Cult Girl across the street, hiding something in the bushes on the side of her house. She looks up and meets my eyes with a look of pure terror, like a deer about to get run over by a bus, or maybe a possum preparing to attack, but then I use all my psychic powers to tell her she can trust me and not to be scared, and then her face relaxes and she puts a finger in front of her mouth, like *shhh*, and now I have yet another secret to keep.

The house greets me by breaking a shelf in the doorless hallway closet as soon as I enter, throwing about six dusty Thrift Town bags on top of my head that explode on impact like mildew bombs and knock me to the ground. I lie on the floor for a minute on my back with the wind knocked out of me, covered by old clothes that have been sitting in those bags for who knows how long, strangely calm as I watch a new crack in the ceiling grow before my eyes. What's the point of even getting up if the house is just going to knock me back down again? I wonder if this is what Lynn A. means when she talks about acceptance.

Eventually, I manage to shove most of the clothes back into the pile in the closet. I turn on the TV, ready to relax after my crap day, but all of a sudden there's my uncle's face staring right at me, and I start hyperventilating all over again. BREAKING NEWS flashes on the bottom of the screen, and the house shakes so hard a lamp falls over.

"The ongoing investigation into the disappearance of Caleb Sloat, lead singer of Rainy Day Knife Fight, just got an exciting new lead after several frustrating weeks of false starts and dead ends. Details at this time are limited, but a source has revealed that someone claiming to be an acquaintance of the rock star has offered information in exchange for the recently increased reward that may lead to proof that Sloat is alive and operating under a false identity, which investigators hope has the potential of being traceable. This is welcome news for an investigation that had been quickly losing steam as repeated inquiries to Sloat's friends and family have yielded little helpful information, and the consensus among most people that were close to him is that he's dead."

I can't listen anymore. I turn to the AA channel. I really need a meeting.

"Lynn A.!" I say as soon as I see her. "I don't know if I can do this anymore." The scarf she's knitting today is yellow. Such a cheerful color for such a sucky day. She smiles and nods, encouraging me to keep talking. "Do you think I should just tell Grandma that Caleb's here and get it over with? Should I tell Lydia about the dance classes? Should I tell Caleb about the black car and the news? Do you think a person can die from keeping too many secrets?"

Lynn A. frowns and looks at me like, *You're really thinking about giving up now, Billy? You're better than that.* Sometimes she's into tough love.

"You're right," I tell her. I sigh, and the house sighs with me. I can't give up just because something's hard. If everyone in the meeting did that, they'd all be drunk or dead or in jail. "I don't know what I'd do without you," I tell her, and she winks at me.

I turn off the TV. I don't feel 100 percent better, but at least I know what to do now. Lynn A. told me not to give up. So I won't. It's nice having someone to help me make these difficult decisions.

All things considered, I feel pretty good on my way up to the attic to visit Caleb, and I manage to stay upright the whole time even though I step through another rotted stair and almost lose my shoe. The giant blanket fort is nearly as tall as the ceiling now, expanded on the inside to make space for the twin air mattress I bought him at BigMart and a couple of milk crates stacked on top of each other to house his growing library of Thrift Town paperbacks, which would certainly be weird enough, except the walls are now topped with a couple dozen ratty, dismembered Frankenstein dolls he's constructed out of the stuff he keeps making me buy him, all of them wearing the heads and body parts of the others, their mismatched pieces held on by glue and staple-gun sutures and messy multicolored thread stitches. Some of their eyes have been dug out. Some have several pairs of eyes. Some wear a mosaic armor of buttons. Mouths are stapled shut. They face into the circle like followers of some cult leader they think is God. It looks like the set of a horror movie, or like a serial killer lives here.

From the top of the stairs, I can see the faint, unnatural glow of the computer screen somewhere inside the structure, illuminating the dolls' faces from below with a creepy blue light. Of course I know they are just dolls, just objects, but I still feel something in their presence, as if they are real people staring down at Caleb so intently, like an adoring audience, like replacements for all the fans he left behind. Is Caleb lonely? Is this an attempt to make friends? I wonder if there's a difference between friends and fans, a difference between being loved and being worshipped. I wonder if Caleb knows.

"I hear you creeping around out there," Caleb says, his voice muffled from deep inside his blankets. "Did you take down that bag of garbage I left by the stairs?"

"Yes," I say.

I move a column of stacked blankets and smell Caleb's B.O. before I even enter his space. His beard is getting so bushy, he's starting to look like one of those sensitive guys in those bands he hates. Either that or a lumberjack, which he also hates. As usual, he is watching a show on his laptop, with his most cherished things on the table next to it—his bag of weed, a lighter, some rolling papers I managed to buy at a convenience store all by myself without throwing up from nerves, a water bottle, a half-eaten bag of baby carrots, and an old soup can he's using as an ashtray. "I'm almost out of weed," he says. "Go see Gordon soon."

"Okay."

"You can hang out with me on one condition," he says. "Don't talk about the news or anything happening in the world."

My stomach lurches. Can he read my mind? "You've told me that, like, a million times."

"You need a reminder. I don't want to hear what people are saying about me. I don't want to hear about the fucking King and who he's fucked over today. I don't want to hear about war or people dying or what asshole celebrities are up to."

But what about black cars following me? What about old drug dealers selling information to the police? What about Breaking News about the whole world trying to find you? Does that count? Where is Lynn A. when I need her? And what do the King and war even have to do with Caleb's life? Life is hard enough without worrying about politics and all those people I don't know doing things far away, like they're playing some giant board game and I'm not even a piece of it.

"Okay," I say.

"I don't want that shit in here at all, okay?"

"Okay." It suddenly strikes me how weird it is that this house is the safest place Caleb could think to go, but for me it is literally a death trap.

Caleb looks out the window for a minute. Light glistens off the grease on his hair and skin. I make a mental note to pick up some face wipes, which are things I've seen on commercials that are like an extra-fancy kind of soap built into a napkin for people who are too lazy to wash their faces.

He starts rolling a joint as I sit down on the other broken lawn chair he lets me keep up here for when I visit. We both look at the laptop screen. It's some show about penguins. A sea lion is tearing one apart.

"Goddamn, nature is fucking brutal," Caleb says, sucking on his joint. Now a bird is pecking at a newly born penguin chick as the parents stand by wailing their penguin wails. Caleb mutes it.

"Are you ever going to talk to Grandma again?" I say for some reason.

Caleb looks at me like I have poop smeared all over my face. "Really, dude? I'm having a nice, relaxing afternoon, and you bring up the woman who slapped me around my whole childhood, who kicked me out when I was sixteen, who's tried to blackmail me on multiple occasions into giving her money, who's been trying to sell me out my whole life? That bitch?"

"Don't call her a bitch," I say weakly.

Caleb sucks in another big puff of smoke. "Name one nice thing she's said to you, one nice thing she's done in the last week. The last month. The last year."

"She picks up dinner on the way home sometimes."

"That's her fucking job," Caleb says, exhaling smoke in my face. I make a mental note to add breath mints to his shopping list. "She's supposed to feed you."

"She's taken care of me my whole life," I say.

Caleb doesn't say anything for a while. He just looks out the window and takes a couple more puffs off his joint. "Yeah, well," he finally says, "it's the least she could do."

"I don't get it," I say. "If you hate it here so much, why'd you come back?"

"It's the only place no one would look for me." Caleb looks at the remaining nub of his joint sadly. "This is bullshit," he says. "I need something stronger."

Then he looks at me. His eyes are droopy. He doesn't look angry, which is a nice change, but he looks empty and gone, and maybe that's worse.

"You know you're never going to get out of this town, right?" he says. "No one ever gets out."

"But you got out."

He laughs cruelly. "Have you noticed where we are right now?" He pauses. "It doesn't matter. I could be across the world, and I'd still be here. We're infected, man."

I don't know how I feel about this. I've always had some vague desire to leave Rome, but nothing specific, nothing resembling a plan. If what Caleb says is true, then even my fantasies are probably a waste of time.

The images on the screen reflect backward in Caleb's eyes.

Am I going to be stuck here for the rest of my life?

How long can someone live in an attic before they can't anymore?

"Are you getting better?" I say softly.

Caleb just looks at me, his face unreadable.

"What do you *want* exactly?" I say, even softer.

Caleb clenches his jaw, and I am scared for a moment. How well do I really know my uncle? Is he capable of violence? Is all this isolation and pot smoking and lack of fresh air going to turn his depression into rage? Will he break like he did onstage before he disappeared? Will he take it out on me?

But all Caleb does is sigh. He says, "I just want some peace, man. That's all I've ever wanted."

"Then what?" I say. "What happens after that?"

Caleb sucks down the last of the joint and doesn't even flinch as the burning paper reaches his fingers. He throws the brown wet wad into the soup can.

"Seriously, dude, what is up with you and that girl?" Caleb says.

"Who, Lydia? Nothing," I say. "We're friends."

"Are you in love with her?"

What exactly does being "in love" with someone mean? Do you have to want to have sex with someone to be in love with them? Though Lydia's certainly beautiful, and though I would probably jump at any opportunity to do anything the least bit sex-related with an even non-beautiful girl who miraculously wanted to with me, strangely I don't think I want to with Lydia. I don't really know what having a sister is like, but maybe that's the closest thing to describe how I feel about Lydia.

"I love her," I say. "But I'm not *in love* with her."

"Sometimes you sound like a bad movie."

"Maybe I'm a little bit in love with her," I say. "But maybe you're supposed to be a little bit in love with everyone you love."

Caleb rolls his eyes. "You're thinking too deep for me, kid."

"Did Grandma ever hug you growing up?" I say, surprised at the question as it comes out of my mouth. Maybe I'm getting high from secondhand smoke.

"What do you think? The only time either of them touched me was to kick my ass."

People talk about sex all the time, but there are so many other kinds of touching. I've seen it on TV—those families who are always hugging, those parents who put their arms around their kids' shoulders, who pat their kids on the back, the kids who rest their heads on their parents' shoulders when they feel sad or discouraged. They make it look so easy. "I don't even remember sitting on Grandma's lap when I was little," I say. Those TV kids are the ones who grow up with life skills like how to pay bills and cook and talk through conflicts and fix toilets. They grow up knowing how to touch people. "I don't want to have sex with Lydia. But I think maybe other kinds of touches would be nice. Maybe there's some subset of being in love with someone that doesn't involve having sex with them but just involves hugging. Maybe we can figure out how hugging works by practicing on each other."

I realize that as I've been thinking all these things, Caleb's been staring at me, and then I realize I was thinking out loud, that I did that thing I always do of not having a filter, that Caleb heard all my weird thoughts, that at any moment he's going to burst out laughing and make fun of me and call me a stupid piece of shit like everybody else does.

"Dude," Caleb says, his voice thick with something new and unexpected, a kindness that makes me gasp. "We gotta get you out of this town before it kills you."

For a brief moment, for a tiny millisecond, I feel a softness settle over me, and the house feels sturdy, and Caleb is home, and I am with him, and I think, *This is what I wanted.*

But then it's gone. I touched it, so briefly, but now all that's left is the aching want cutting through me.

Caleb looks out the window. "Fuck!" he says, and just like that everything sharpens and speeds up. "Fuck fuck fuck! Get out of here!"

I lean over him to look out the window, and there's Grandma pulling up in her van. The back door slides open, and a tour group starts spilling out.

"Billy, get the fuck out of here!" Caleb pushes me, and I fall face-first into the wall of the blanket fort. I try to get up, but the more I move, the more tangled in blankets I get, like they're some kind of plush quicksand. Caleb finally pulls me out and drags me toward the staircase, and I fall all the way down just as I hear the front door opening.

"And here is where Caleb grew up, right in this house!" I hear

Grandma say. "He was such a sweet kid, so creative." The sound of the fake shutters of camera phones.

I push the dresser to hide the door, but it gets stuck on a dislodged floorboard. I push harder, but it won't budge. "If you'd like to go up those stairs, you can see Caleb's old bedroom on the right," Grandma says downstairs.

They are going to catch us. They are going to take Caleb away from me and I'm going to be all alone and Grandma's going to kick my ass and I'm so stupid and why did I ever think I was smart enough to handle any of this?

Someone says, "Ooooh!" and I hear the first footstep on the staircase just as I finally push the dresser in place.

A girl in pink sparkly sweatpants and a Rainy Day Knife Fight T-shirt with Caleb's giant face printed on the front emerges from the staircase and yelps when she sees me. "Hi," I say, leaning against the dresser all casual, like I was hanging out here all day, like I'm totally relaxed and not about to have my tenth heart attack of the afternoon.

"Are you his ghost?" she says with big eyes and trembling lips.

"I don't think so," I say, but I have no idea what's true anymore.

Then she points her phone, the flash blinds me, and all I see is white.

LYDIA

PREPROFESSIONAL MODERN CLASS MAKES THE TORTURE of ballet worth it. This is where I don't have to think, where the teacher's instructions skip my brain and go straight to my body. The little girl seems happiest here too. She just sits quietly in the corner of the mirror watching with starstruck eyes, the way I used to look at the big-girl dancers when I was little. For this brief hour and a half, I don't even hate her.

The modern teacher, Luz Hernandez, has danced with some of the top avant-garde dance companies in the country. She is also a very different kind of teacher from Mary. She swears in class. Her hair is blue. Her skin is brown. She once told a girl to "get out of your head and dance with your fucking ovaries." She is definitely my kind of people.

But Mary is here today too, perched in the corner on a stool, watching the class with her laser eyes and permanently frowning thin mouth, making my safe place suddenly toxic.

"What is she doing here?" I whisper to Natalie Morris as we move through our floor warm-up. "This isn't even her class."

"She oversees all the preprofessional classes when it comes time to pick soloists for the big annual show."

"Jesus."

"Don't worry."

"All right, women!" Luz yells. I like how she calls us "women," instead of "girls" like the other teachers. "Let's move on. We're adding another sequence to the choreography today. First, let's run through what we've already got. How's that sound, Miss Lemon?"

"Um, uh, good?" I manage to say. Dancing in Luz's class is fine, but for some reason I turn completely incoherent anytime I actually have to talk to her.

"Um, uh, great," Luz says with a wink, and I can feel every millimeter of my skin from my collarbone to the top of my head turn red. Just as I feel the blush start to fade, I catch Natalie's smiling eyes as she gets in position, and the blush flares right up again.

It's times like this I most wish I were in my studio, dancing alone.

I take a deep breath and close my eyes. I feel my feet on the solid floor and the air holding me. I feel my warm muscles, my elastic tendons, my strong bones. The music starts, I open my eyes, and I dance.

Luz's choreography is strange, reptilian, full of odd angles. It is at once jerky and luscious and fluid. It makes a dancer's body do everything it is capable of, and then forces it to do more. The other dancers struggle to make the right shapes. They're too worried about being pretty. Their brains tell their bodies the mathematics of it all. You can see it in their eyes—they're thinking. But I dance somewhere beyond thought. These are the movements of an underground world I already know. This is how my body breathes.

When we are done, I stand in the middle of the floor, panting. I feel weightless, floating, triumphant. Most of the other girls' faces are twisted in frustration, confusion, even anger. They are not used to things being this hard.

I look at Mary in the corner, her chin in the air, obviously disappointed. She glances at me, and for one brief moment her face changes, and I have no idea how to read it.

"Maybe go a little slower with the next round of choreography, Ms. Hernandez," Mary says, "to make sure everyone gets it."

"Yep," says Luz, then turns toward the class. Did she just roll her eyes?

I study Luz's movements as she shows the new choreography. I study the tiny details, the tilt of her head, the flex of her wrists. I mirror what I see.

"Miss Lemon," Luz says. "Will you come to the middle of the floor and demonstrate, please?"

I try not to smile or look at the other dancers' faces. Just pretend this is no big deal, that I'm used to being called out for doing something well.

I dance the new series. "See that micro bend in her elbow?" Luz asks the class. "See that arch in her back?" The class nods solemnly. "There aren't words for that. This isn't ballet, folks. I can't recite a bunch of technical terms to program you like freaking robots.

There's no vocabulary for *feeling*. You have to experience it. You're not looking hard enough."

I look at my feet. It's all I can do to keep from floating off the ground.

"Again," Luz says, and the class dances again.

By the end of class, the floor is soaked with sweat. Two girls are in tears, and a few more look on the verge of them. I follow the slow, sad progression to the locker room, and this time I'm standing taller than everyone, even Natalie Morris.

"Miss Lemon," calls Mary from her perch in the corner. "May I have a word with you, please?"

A handful of students are still in the studio, watching me walk toward Mary, getting ready for something juicy. They are not going anywhere.

Neither is the little girl. She's perked up in her corner of the mirror with a new glint in her eye.

"I know you feel in your element in this class," Mary begins, "and I'm glad you're enjoying yourself."

I can tell a big "but" is coming. I look around for Luz, but she is gone.

"But," Mary continues, "when you dance in an ensemble, your job is to blend in with the other dancers. You must not stand out too much during performance. The goal is not to show yourself; it's to take on a larger identity with the group. You may bristle at this, but right now your job is to fit in. You've been dancing alone for so long, you don't know how to dance with other people. Save your personality for your solos, okay?"

I say nothing, but I have plenty I want to say. Part of me is thinking this is the worst metaphor in the history of all metaphors—*You've been dancing alone for so long, you don't know how to dance with other people*? What bullshit. Another part of me wants to say, "I'm getting a solo?" And another part of me just wants to punch Mary in her perfect pointy chin.

"Miss Lemon, you're here to learn how to be a dancer, right? I'm teaching you how to be a dancer. If you really want to do this, you're going to have to be part of an ensemble. No one's career is just solos. You have to earn that."

"Is that all?" I say. I can't look at Mary. I'm in that volatile place between anger and hurt. Eye contact with anyone might make me burst into tears or start punching.

"You know I'm on your side, right?" Mary says.

"Yes," I say, but sometimes, like right now, I'm not so sure.

"Go get cleaned up," Mary says. I turn around and head to the dressing room. I pretend not to notice the other students making eyes at each other and snickering. I know what they're thinking. *Serves her right, thinking she's so special. She shouldn't even be here.* I refuse to look at the sad-eyed little girl only I can see, watching me from the corner.

I pull my clothes over my drenched tights and leotard, even though it's freezing and I have to stand outside for half an hour to catch the bus home. But the fear of hypothermia is nothing compared to my desperate need to get out of the locker room, which is eerily quiet even though it's full of my stuck-up classmates. I can feel their eyes burning holes into my skin. They hate me for not being good enough, and they hate me for being too good. I can't win.

I hurry out of the building and immediately feel the sweat on my face start to freeze.

"Hey," someone says.

I turn around, and Natalie is sitting in a car that's nice but not too flashy, not brand-new but not too old. Safe, dependable. It looks warm inside.

"Hey," I say between chattering teeth.

"Are you okay?" Natalie says. "Mary was kind of a bitch."

"I'm fine."

"It's okay if you're not."

I look into Natalie's eyes then, so surprised by how this simple statement from this beautiful girl takes my breath away. Either that, or my lungs are freezing.

"Will you get in the car, please?" Natalie says. "You look really cold."

My survival instincts outweigh my other instincts to avoid being in close proximity to people who want to talk to me.

The car is warm, as I expected. A ballet shoe key chain dangles off the rearview mirror. It smells like vanilla, but not cheap artificial air freshener vanilla, actual vanilla, like someone's been baking cookies in here.

"I love the way you dance," Natalie says.

"Thank you," I say, looking at my lap.

"Mary does too, you know? She's just trying to get you ready."

"By making me quit?"

"You're not quitting, are you?" She seems genuinely concerned. "You can't quit, Lydia."

"No," I say, looking out the window at the other students filing out of the building, getting into their own parked cars or their parents' warm minivans. "I don't know. Just maybe I'm not cut out for this. Maybe I'm only capable of dancing by myself."

"I doubt that," says Natalie.

"I'm like one of those kids who are raised by wolves their whole lives and can never be a part of civilized society."

"I don't think that's a real thing," Natalie says. I look at her. She smiles. She has a beautiful smile.

"It's a good story, though," I say, maybe also smiling a little too.

"Let me give you a ride home," Natalie says, and she starts pulling out of the parking lot before waiting for an answer. "Where do you live?"

"Carthage," I say. "The north part just outside of town, before the rez."

"Cool," Natalie says. Is she really this nice? If she's really this nice, why doesn't anyone know about it?

"Thanks for the ride," I say. "I probably would have frozen to death without you. Then who would Mary have to pick on?"

"You know she never got to solo, right?" Natalie says. "Not professionally. She went to Juilliard and all that, danced for a few years before her injuries made it impossible. Tulsa Ballet, I think. And then she came back here to start this school. But she was only ever an anonymous girl in the company. Which is awesome, don't get me wrong. So few dancers even get that far."

I'm not quite sure what Natalie is trying to tell me. That Mary hates soloists? That Mary hates me? That Mary's *jealous*?

"Anyway," Natalie says, "I love the way you dance."

"You already said that."

She smiles. "Do you really hate ballet as much as you act like you do?"

I don't answer right away. I don't want to tell this ballet dancer that I hate what she loves.

"I don't hate it," I finally say. "I guess I don't really understand it."

"Okay," Natalie says. "That's fair."

We drive the rest of the way to Larry's bar in silence, but it is not uncomfortable. Something soft and singer-songwritery is playing low on the stereo, but I can't make myself ask who it is. I don't want to waste my breath on small talk about music. Not with her.

I am strangely not embarrassed as we pull up in front of the bar. "My dad owns this place," I say. "We live in back."

"It's nice you're so close to the river," Natalie says.

"Yeah," I say, but all these years living here, I never once even considered that.

"I'll see you at school," Natalie says.

"Thanks for the ride."

"Anytime."

I get out of the car, and the little girl and I watch Natalie turn around and drive away, and even though it's started to snow, I still feel warm all the way through.

BILLY

IT'S CHRISTMAS AND THE BUSES AREN'T RUNNING AND
Grandma refuses to drive me anywhere and Larry loaned his van to someone for the night. "Why don't you just walk there?" Grandma said, but it's miles away and it's about twenty degrees outside, and I'm pretty sure I'd die by the time I got there. So here I am, stuck in my homicidal house, and there Lydia is, sitting in a bar with a bunch of drunk old men. It isn't right.

Ever since the new lead about Caleb's false identity was announced, everyone in Fog Harbor thinks they're detectives. Grandma says people stop by her office every day to ask her questions and she has to chase them out with a broom, and our home phone stays unplugged all the time now until one of us has to use it, and as soon as we plug it in, it starts ringing. In addition to the black car making more appearances, there is a constant stream of vehicles that slowly drive by our house at all hours of the day and night. There's one in particular that's covered in Rainy Day Knife Fight bumper stickers and has set up a semipermanent camp across the street, and a girl with bulging eyes just sits there in the driver's seat staring at our house and crying until Grandma calls the cops and they tell her to leave, but then she just comes back the next day. Luckily, Caleb's window faces a direction no one can see from the street, but really it's just a matter of time until someone flies a drone or something up there and our whole cover is blown. I'm surprised no one's thought about that already. Maybe stalkers aren't the most intelligent people on the planet.

Grandma and I already did our customary five-minute Christmas gift exchange. As she inspected the lumpy mug I made her in art class, I told her way too enthusiastically, "You can put pencils in it!" She was not impressed. "Customers will love it," I said. "People trust people with homemade art by children on their desks." That seemed to get her attention. She nodded in approval. Then she handed me a plastic BigMart bag and said, "Hurry up. I don't want to miss the start of my show." It contained new socks, underwear, strawberry-scented bath gel, a five-dollar bill, and a box of snack cakes. It's actually the perfect gift because the tourists have taken almost all of my socks and underwear, and I'm sick of smelling like dish soap. I felt kind of bad about the five dollars since I actually have my own money now, but I think Grandma would have been suspicious if I tried to give it back. She made me give her two snack cakes, but I didn't mind, because it's Christmas.

Lydia and I ran out of things to talk about on the phone, and I don't want to sit in my room by myself while an endless stream of spiders keeps coming out of the hole in my wall. It's not worth trying to go to sleep because I know the house will do something to wake me up the second my eyes close. So I sit on the couch with Grandma while she eyes the box of Christmas snack cakes in my lap every couple of minutes during the made-for-TV Christmas romantic comedy. "Are you going to eat those or what?" she asks at least three times.

"I'm saving them," I say. For what, I don't know. For a moment that feels cake-worthy.

She gives me the look I get so often, the one that tells me I'm an alien, that I do not really belong to her.

"You're too skinny," she says.

"I know," I say.

She eventually falls asleep on the couch, snoring loudly. I cover her with a blanket, whisper, "Merry Christmas, Grandma. I love you," and take my box of snack cakes up the two flights of stairs to the attic. My foot goes straight through another rotted stair, but I keep my balance. My one tiny accomplishment of the day. The house shakes like it's laughing at me.

I pull my foot out of the hole and open the door without knocking. The nest is there as usual, the Frankenstein dolls standing guard on top, looking down at Caleb almost affectionately, and the movable column he uses as a door is already wide open, revealing him inside, sitting in his chair looking at his computer screen. His body is more relaxed than usual, his face softer, and something about seeing him when he thinks he's alone, without that extra barrier of blanket wall to open first, makes me feel embarrassed. It's not like he's naked or anything, but it almost feels like it, like he hasn't had a chance to decide how he wants to be seen, and there he is just raw and exposed with nothing to protect him.

But maybe that's a good thing. Maybe he left his fort open for a reason. Maybe this is a sign he's getting better.

And then a sudden feeling of dread squeezes my heart. What happens then? What happens when Caleb gets better and leaves? Will he go back to his old life? Will he forget me all over again?

Is there a part of me that hopes he never gets better? Then he'll have to stay here. Then I get to keep him.

"You again?" Caleb says, finally noticing me.

"I brought dessert," I say. But I do not deserve these cakes. I am not a cake-worthy person.

Caleb perks up. "Mmmm, sugar," he says as I hand him one. "God, how I love high-fructose corn syrup and hydrogenated oils." He tears the cellophane wrapper, and we eat the whole box in silence as we watch the Christmas movie on the computer screen, the one about the bullied kid in the olden days who wants a BB gun and the dad who's always yelling and the mom who never sticks up for herself. I don't know why everyone thinks it's so funny. It's one of the saddest movies I've ever seen.

"This guy," Caleb says. "What a fucking bastard. But my dad makes him look like a saint."

"What was he like?" I say.

"Why do you want to know?"

"I don't know. Because I never met him, and he's my grandpa, and I should get to know something about him, and Grandma never says anything."

"Yeah, that's what she does, right? Says nothing about anything that matters. But says way too much about shit that doesn't."

"He was a logger, right?"

"Ha!" Caleb laughs. "The bastard worked at the shingle factory. He was just a foreman on an assembly line carrying a clipboard."

"Oh."

The movie dad is trying to fix his lamp that's shaped like a leg after the mom "accidentally" broke it because she hated it so much. No one in the family has the guts to tell the truth, so everyone goes around being sneaky.

"Your grandpa was a fucking drunk and smashed up the house on a regular basis," Caleb says. "Smashed *us* up on a regular basis. And Ma didn't do anything, just watched her TV and yelled and slapped us around too. Especially when he'd leave. Did you know about that? He'd just disappear for a week and never tell us where he went, and as far as I know Ma didn't even ask him. She just accepted it like she didn't have a fucking choice what he did, and then she took her misery out on us. Sarah was convinced he had another family somewhere that he was supporting, and that's why we were so poor all of a sudden, but who knows. Who fucking cares? I don't."

Sarah. It's alarming to hear her name out loud. Like my grandfather, it's as if she never existed, as if Grandma erased her from the family. As if I lost all rights to my own mother.

"Tell me about her," I say, so quiet I can barely hear my own voice.

"I don't want to talk about her," Caleb says quickly, eyes on the computer screen.

"But she's mine," I say. I reach out my hand and slam the laptop shut.

Time freezes. I look at my hand, wonder for a moment if it has a mind of its own, because I don't do things like slam other people's laptops shut.

"She's mine and I want to know about her," I say. "I deserve to know about her. Grandma doesn't tell me anything except that she was a disappointment and a junkie. But she was someone before that."

I know I'm crying, but I don't care. Grandma's not here to make fun of me and call me a sissy. Caleb might, but so what. What can he really do? What power does he have? He's a prisoner in an attic.

"She was mine, too," Caleb says. He looks at me, all of his usual sarcasm and irony drained from his face. "You should have known her." He hands me a paper towel from the roll he keeps by his table.

I wipe my eyes with the scratchy paper. "Was she nice?"

"Yeah," Caleb says. "For a while, anyway. Do you know what Ma used to say to me all the time, after Sarah died? That she was the good one. She was the one who was supposed to make it. I wasn't even supposed to be born. And I was *ten*. Imagine saying that shit to a ten-year-old. I wasn't even an asshole yet."

I have no idea what to say. I have never had anyone to talk to about all this unspeakable stuff. It's like I grew up in two dimensions, and now, in this attic, in this pile of musty comforters and pillows, the third dimension has just been discovered, with all kinds of weird new gravity, and I feel wobbly. Upside down. Inside out.

"I was seven years younger than her, you know? She was out of the house by the time I was nine, and the year leading up to that was rough. She changed a lot. She and Ma were always yelling at each other. But that wasn't really her. It was the drugs talking." He laughs bitterly. "After seeing what happened to Sarah, I should have steered clear, right? Talk about a cautionary tale. But it's almost like watching her go through it made it seem even more inevitable. I knew we were made out of the same stuff."

This is not the part I want to hear about. My whole life, this is the only part I've known. But what about before that? Why can't anyone in this family ever talk about anything good?

"What did she like to do?" My voice is almost a whisper. I don't feel like I'm even allowed to ask these kinds of questions, allowed to know anything that would make her three-dimensional.

"She loved singing," Caleb says. "The only thing we ever did together as a family was watch those silly singing competition shows. Even Dad liked them."

"Did she have a good voice?"

"It was decent. Nothing spectacular. But the amazing thing was she seemed so *happy* when she sang. Like all of a sudden, she wasn't a Sloat anymore. She was a happy person who ended up with us by mistake." Caleb looks at me with a sort of melancholy smile. "Kind of like you."

I feel my throat close up and a new batch of tears form in my eyes. I suddenly don't want to know any more. I don't want my mother to be a real person. It hurts too much. The realer she becomes, the more it means I lost.

"You know she's who taught me how to play guitar?" Caleb says. "The basic stuff, anyway. I'd strum these simple little three-chord songs while she sang and danced, and then she started making me sing backup." He laughs. "Who knows? If it wasn't for her, maybe I'd never have even picked up the guitar. I probably would have ended up working at BigMart or the prison like everyone else, or selling drugs like Gordon."

"Maybe you'd be happier if you did that," I say.

"Yeah, you're probably right. But there's no hope of that anymore, is there? You can't go back to being like everyone else after you realize you're not."

"I've always known I'm not like everyone else," I say. "Ever since I was a baby. That's all anyone's ever told me."

"Yeah, you're different. That's why I like you."

My chest is suddenly full of bubbles.

"Everyone tries so hard to be homogeneous, you know?" Caleb says. "To not stand out. To not be different. They hate us because we're different. But I hate them because they're the same."

"I don't hate anyone," I say.

"Well, maybe you should." Caleb chuckles. "How did we grow up in the same house? How are you not totally furious and full of shame?"

"Maybe I am but I'm in denial."

"No, you're made out of something else," Caleb says, shaking his head. "I wish I was more like you."

"But I'm nothing special. I'm nobody."

"I spent the last ten years trying to be somebody," Caleb says. "That shit's the loneliest gig there is."

We're quiet for a long time. Caleb keeps looking out the window even though it's pitch-black and all he can see is his own distorted reflection. I want to tell him he should cover up the window, but that would mean I'd have to tell him why, which would mean telling him about how the investigation is closing in and we're running out of time and pretty soon the world's going to catch up to us, and that's not something either of us wants to talk about. I'm also pretty sure all this talking about our feelings means Caleb's getting better, which I think means he's going to leave soon. So no matter what I do, I'm going to be alone again any day now.

"You know what's sad?" Caleb finally says. "Growing up in this shitty house with our shitty parents—it should have brought Sarah and me closer together. It should have made us a unit. Me and Sarah against the world. That's what should have happened. We should have known that's what would have made it bearable, that we had each other even if we didn't have them, that we were stronger together."

He pauses, swallows. He looks at the place in front of him where the computer screen should be, but it's still closed. There's nothing to distract him.

"But we didn't do that," Caleb says. "We turned against each other. Like in those nature documentaries where there's, like, an epic drought or something and there aren't enough resources to go around, and the animals just start fucking killing each other or jumping off cliffs, or they just wander off into the wilderness to die. That was like me and Sarah. Totally on our own, competing for resources. And there was never enough."

"And she wandered off into the wilderness to die," I say.

Caleb looks away and doesn't say anything for a long time. Is that what he's doing here? Is this the wilderness?

"You ever seen those documentaries about the Serengeti during the wet season?" Caleb finally says.

"You know we don't watch documentaries in this house."

"Good point." He almost smiles. "Well, the Serengeti is basically, like, this giant meadow in Africa where at a certain time of year, there's, like, all these rivers and lakes and a shit ton of food for all the animals, more than anyone can eat, and there's a bunch of lions hanging out next to a bunch of zebras and gazelles, and they're all buddies just taking a nap together, and there's no such thing as predator or prey because everyone's bellies are so full, they can't even move, and they're so goddamned happy, they forget they're enemies."

"That sounds nice," I say.

"Yeah," Caleb says. "But people aren't like animals. No matter how much they have, they always want more."

I look down at the empty box and cellophane wrappers at our feet. The cakes are gone. And I'm still hungry.

LYDIA

I HAVEN'T SEEN A WHOLE LOT OF THE WORLD, BUT I'M pretty sure Larry's bar is high on the list of most depressing places to be on Christmas. I'm sitting in my usual spot, the little girl sitting silently on the stool next to me, with the usual suspects at the other end of the bar, and Old Pete in his booth. It's disturbing how much time I spend with these guys but know close to nothing about them. Do they have families they could be with today? Are they choosing this place over somewhere else? Or is this their only choice?

I keep trying to tell myself this is any old day, that Christmas is just a marketing conspiracy in the guise of a religious tradition I don't even believe in, so it's not worthy of acknowledging, let alone celebrating. But I still wish Billy were here. He takes things like holidays seriously. He wants them to be special. He shouldn't be with those people in his house, even if they are technically family.

That movie that always plays all Christmas day is on the TV. It's the kind of comedy that, if only a few things were changed, would easily become a tragedy. Those are my favorite kinds of comedies, the ones just a razor-thin line from something else entirely, the ones that make you laugh about things that would normally make you cry. This one could easily be a tearjerker about a terrorized kid in an abusive family, with a bully of a father and a beaten-down mother. But instead you're supposed to laugh at all the yelling and shaming; it's supposed to be funny instead of cruel.

Larry's bad dye job is growing out, showing his gray roots. Right now, I can't really think of anything more terrible about him than his hair. That, and his dream catcher tattoo. And his Unicorns vs. Dragons obsession. He's embarrassing and clueless, but those things are superficial. Compared to the dad in this movie, Larry's an angel. I can't remember a time he's even raised his voice to me. So why have I always hated him so much?

Something contracts in the pit of my stomach. I feel off. It's like somebody grabbed my brain and shook it up real hard, and now all the memories and feelings that had been safely contained in there are floating around, bumping into things, making a mess. I can't stop thinking. The thoughts keep coming and coming, like a stampede, carrying garbage bags stuffed with feelings, and the bags keep breaking, and the feelings get thrown all over the place, and the cleanup crew I've always relied on to quickly mop up all these kinds of messes appears to be on strike.

I remember Larry when his hair was still actually the color he keeps trying to dye it. I had forgotten this version of Larry, but now here he is, bumping around in my brain with all the other stuff that got dislodged. There he is with a bouquet of flowers, dressed up for a night out at the fanciest restaurant in Fog Harbor, but Mom's in her nightgown claiming she's too tired. There he is asking Mom what's wrong, asking how he can help, and she just closes the bedroom door in his face. There he is at the mini golf course during one of his short-lived attempts at family night, trying to stay smiling despite Mom's refusing to play. And there is little me, holding my tiny pink rented golf club, wanting so desperately to play, but instead hiding my excitement and joining Mom sitting sullen on the bench.

He was always trying to make things better. It was Mom who refused to try. And for some reason, I thought I had to choose a side, and for some reason, I always chose hers.

What kind of mother forces her kid to make a choice like that?

There Larry is, after Mom's death, trying to hug me, asking me if I want to talk about it. And there is little me, pushing him away. Just like Mom always pushed him away. I told him to leave me alone enough times, and he finally did.

How can he stay so positive when his life sucks so bad, when all the people he cares about turn out to be such assholes? Same with Billy. It's like some people are just born to see the bright side of things. No matter how bad things get, that's their special survival technique; it's how they stay motivated to keep going. But then there are people like me, people like Billy's grandma and my mom and Caleb. We're programmed to always see the negative, so we can prepare ourselves for the worst. But I'm starting to think maybe sometimes that's not always the best approach. Maybe sometimes survival techniques can turn into prisons.

I have the sudden urge to hug Larry. He's on the other side of the bar, pushing a cup of coffee in front of a guy who's already half passed out, even though it's just the afternoon. I think Larry actually loves these losers. He loves this terrible town. Maybe someday he'll find something that can love him back.

Larry and Billy have so much in common. Foolish optimists, both of them. So what does that make me? A tortured artist like Caleb? Someone who will feel alone no matter what I do, no matter how many people adore me?

The Christmas movie cuts to a commercial for the King's family's company's brand of hot dogs: Royal Wieners. The leader of the United States appears on a jet boat holding a hot dog in one hand, his other arm around a bikini-clad woman who is much closer to my age than his.

This world is too bizarre to even attempt to figure out.

My strange desire to hug Larry has thankfully passed. But now another thought has rushed in to take its place. I think about my last ballet class, how Natalie takes the advanced class for extra practice even though she's in preprofessional, how she was in the place next to me, how noticeable it was that she didn't reek of perfume like the other girls. How aware I was of her body the whole time, even when I was facing away from her, how I could sense her behind me. How the more I look at Natalie, I don't see a stuck-up ballerina, but someone maybe lonely like me, someone who has also made her face a mask, but who opens when she dances, who lights up, who takes off her mask when she's doing the thing she loves.

I take a sip of my flat soda and think about how Natalie whispered so close I could feel the warmth of her breath on my naked earlobe, "You seem to actually be enjoying yourself."

"Ballet is a necessary evil," I said.

"Whatever," Natalie said, but there was a smile in her voice.

We turned in tandem, and when our arms accidentally brushed against each other, I felt a small shiver. Could Natalie see the goose bumps on my skin? Did she notice how my first arabesque on the next side was half a beat too late? Did she notice how desperately I was trying not to look at her for the rest of class?

What is Natalie doing right now? Maybe sitting around the fireplace drinking hot cocoa with her family, a Christmas tree twinkling behind them, tastefully decorated with matching, color-coordinated ornaments and a few handmade ones Natalie has brought home from school over the years.

Did she get everything she wanted for Christmas? Has she already forgotten what she got?

I shake my head. I try to dislodge her. I try to dislodge everyone.

Then the little girl swipes her arm across the bar, knocks over my drink, and spills soda all over my lap. "You fucking idiot!" I scream without thinking, fire and fury exploding from my belly like some kind of dragon. But the girl is gone.

Larry comes over with a towel and starts wiping up the mess. "It was just an accident," he says, so much dopey kindness in his eyes I want to punch him. I want to punch everyone. I want to strangle that horrible little ghost, but every time I try, my hands go right through her.

I slide off my stool. It's time to go to my studio. It's time to lock the door and dance everything away.

Dancing is a relief, but it can't be everything. I am starting to realize this. I can close my eyes and will myself to stop thinking for three, maybe five minutes at a time. I can dance my way out of my head and into my body, where things briefly make sense, but which I always have to leave eventually. Relief never lasts forever. The world is always there, waiting for me with its relentless weirdness. I must always eventually come back. I must stand still. And it is in that stillness that the other parts of me return, the parts of me that intersect with and bump against the rest of the world. The parts that remember and feel.

There is so much to remember and feel now. It has always been there, but there's some new portal back to that forgotten place, and it is too wide to plug or patch. Things have escaped that can never be shoved back in again.

For some reason, I feel compelled to walk over to Old Pete's booth, where he is hunched over the grimy table with his eyes closed, his gnarled, cracked hands around his beer. His beard is definitely green. It has what appear to be tiny strands of moss and lichen growing in it. "Merry Christmas," I say. He opens his eyes, looks straight ahead, does not seem to even register my presence.

I see movement in the corner of my eye and turn just in time to catch the little girl darting behind the jukebox.

"Oh, this is about to get good," Old Pete says to nobody in particular.

BILLY

HERE WE ARE AT BIGMART WITH ALL OF ROME'S AND Carthage's most thrift-conscious citizens looking for post-Christmas deals. Grandma would be right here with them if she weren't busy giving a tour of our house. Luckily, Caleb is letting me store my Christmas underwear in the attic so the tourists don't steal it.

Hordes of blue-haired women cram the seasonal aisles, throwing 90-percent-off greeting cards and Christmas ornaments into their shopping carts. Lydia and I go straight for the Advent calendars. An ancient woman with a ratty platinum blond wig and purple lip liner has the same idea and glares at us as we pull stacks of calendars off the shelves.

"There's enough for everyone," I tell her.

"No, there's not," she spits, then grabs a pile of calendars, cradles them in her arms, and scuttles away.

"How was your Christmas?" I ask Lydia. She's been pretty quiet ever since she picked me up.

"Quit it with the small talk, Billy Goat," she says.

"Why won't you just tell me how your Christmas was?"

"It sucked, just like yours. Nothing to report."

"Mine didn't totally suck," I say. "I think Caleb and I bonded or something. He told me about my mom a little bit."

She looks at me kind of sad but doesn't say anything.

"Isn't it weird how both our moms are, like, total mysteries?" I say.

"Maybe that's why we get along so well." She sighs and looks at the messy rows of Advent calendars. "Why would anyone think this is a good idea?" she says as she inspects a dented calendar covered with illustrations of bloody zombies in Santa hats. She's pretty good at changing the subject when she doesn't want to talk about something.

"Look at this one," I say, holding up one with kittens in sexy lingerie.

"What is wrong with people?"

"Do you think we have enough?" I say. We each have two full shopping baskets.

"It's never enough, Billy."

I don't think she's talking about Advent calendars.

Larry's van is impossible to miss in the BigMart parking lot. It's got a giant airbrushed dragon head on the side, and the doors are so high off the ground it has an extra little step that folds out on the bottom so you can get in. One person passing by looks at it in horror. Another person smirks. A little kid says, "That is so cool!"

"I know, right?" I say to the kid. Lydia rolls her eyes at both of us.

When we get in the car, I grab my backpack out from behind

my seat. "I know we promised not to get each other Christmas pres-ents," I say, "but I kind of cheated."

"Yeah, me too," Lydia says.

"Really?" I fight the urge to throw my arms around her. I know she's not a hugger. But she's also not a surprise-gift-buyer, so you never know.

"You go first," she says, not meeting my eye. If I didn't know any better, I'd say she was nervous.

"Okay." I pull the gift out of my backpack and hand it to her—a misshapen, newspaper-wrapped package held together by masking tape.

She opens it slowly, carefully, like she's trying not to rip the newspaper, and pulls out the first of two things inside.

"I remember you saying how expensive tights are and how yours were getting ratty," I say. "Did I get the right size?"

"They're perfect, Billy. Thank you." She pulls out the second gift and looks at it for a long time.

"It's Filipino folk dance music," I say.

"I can read the CD cover," she says, still staring at it.

"Because you're Filipina and a dancer and you can listen to it and get in touch with your roots or something." Is she mad at me? Did I offend her?

But then she looks up and smiles with that weird sad-happy look she gets in her eyes sometimes. "I love it," she says. "It's a really thoughtful gift."

But then why does she look like she's going to start crying?

"Okay, my turn," Lydia says. She reaches behind the driver's seat and pulls out something large and flat and wrapped in actual wrapping paper with a bow. I think I actually gasp. I almost don't want to open it because it's so pretty.

"You wrapped that yourself?" I say.

Lydia just shrugs. "I found the wrapping stuff in a closet. It's, like, ten years old."

"It's the nicest thing I've ever gotten."

"You haven't even opened it yet."

She has no idea how low the bar is.

"It's not much," she says. "I just saw it at a thrift store and thought you'd like it."

I try not to rip the wrapping paper as I open it, but I'm too excited. I hold the gift out in front of me—a framed painting of an abstract blue swirl with a glowing yellow ball at the center, like a galaxy or a tornado with a mysterious life inside, and I think, if there could be picture that perfectly illustrates what it feels like inside my brain these days, this is it. This painting could be my self-portrait.

"I thought your room could use some decoration," Lydia says. "What do you think?"

"I think it's perfect," I say. I want to say so much more, but I have no idea what. I think giving someone art is just about the most intimate gift a person can give, except for maybe sex toys or something.

"Okay, great," Lydia says with an almost-sharpness in her voice.

She buckles her seat belt and turns on the car. I guess that means the gift exchange is over.

I don't ask where we're going as Lydia drives us across town, across the flat blocks of Criminal Fields, across the Rome bridge, and up into the hills where all the big, fancy houses are.

"I bet Natalie lives up here somewhere," Lydia says, and I startle awake. I doze off a lot these days since my house keeps finding new sounds to keep me up at night.

We get out of the neighborhoods and enter what used to be an old-growth Douglas fir forest, but it's all been clear-cut now. As far as the eye can see, it's rolling foothills covered with moss and fern and flimsy saplings. And in the middle of it all is the famous Rome water tower that people around the world have heard of because Caleb supposedly slept there when he was homeless and then put it in a song. It doesn't look like anything that deserves to be famous. The giant red ROME painted on it is barely decipherable after so many years of weather, the formerly white tank is discolored with some kind of greenish-black mold, and the hundred-foot-tall metal frame is rusted. A ladder hangs off of it, the bottom at least ten feet off the ground, like you already have to know how to fly just to start climbing.

"*Water tower home*," I start singing with my squeaky voice that's nothing like Caleb's. "*Look at what I've sown. No cover from the rain. Liquefy my brain.*"

Then Lydia joins in: "*A view of dirty memories from my hovel in the sky. Everywhere's a cemetery. I'm dead but I can fly.*"

"I didn't know you knew the words," I say.

"Everyone knows the words."

Lydia parks the van right where the ladder meets the sky.

The wind whips around us as we climb. Our bags full of discount Advent calendars act like sails, catching the wind, trying to pull us off the ladder. Maybe other people would decide to abort this mission. But those people are not us.

My lungs and every muscle in my body burn by the time we reach the top of the water tower. "There's no way your uncle lived up here," Lydia says as I pull myself onto the narrow walkway surrounded by a flimsy rail. "He totally would have fallen off."

"You should see where he lives now," I say, panting. "He doesn't take up much space." I really need to get in better shape.

Everything within reaching distance is covered with graffiti— Rainy Day Knife Fight song lyrics, several I LOVE YOU, CALEBs, some weird poetry by anonymous fans, and one RIP CALEB SLOAT with the date of his disappearance. My stomach seizes at the sight of this, even though I just saw him last night.

We find a spot out of the wind, with a view of all of Fog Harbor below us. It's been cloudy all day, but that's nothing compared to what's coming. The real weather is hugging the ocean maybe a mile out—a wall of thick, white, inevitable fog advancing toward land.

"What does he do up there all day?" Lydia says as she hands me one of the Advent calendars from her bag. We start popping open the days and fishing the little pieces of chocolate out from inside. I start at the biggest one and pick the rest randomly from there. Lydia starts at the beginning and systematically works up to the best piece of candy at the end.

"He just smokes pot and watches shows on his computer," I say. "He had me change all his passwords and security questions so he can't read his e-mail, and he did something to block any news and social media sites from coming up. He's, like, totally cut off from the outside world."

"He can't do that forever, can he?" Lydia says, inspecting a piece of candy from her zombie Christmas calendar that looks like a severed elf head.

"I don't know." I look at one of my candies. It's either a drum kit or a machine gun.

"*You* can't do that forever."

"I guess not."

"Do you think they're going to find him soon?"

"I don't know."

"They just have to figure out the Social Security number that guy sold him, and then they can trace his bank account to here."

Why is she saying this? Is she *trying* to make me have a panic attack?

The fog is advancing fast. It's nearly to the shore.

"Hey, Lydia," I say.

"Hey, Billy."

"Will you come with me to Gordon's again?"

Lydia sighs her biggest sigh of the day. "Ugh," she says.

"Pleeeease?" I plead.

"It's so wrong in so many ways."

"I don't want to go by myself," I say. "I always end up staying for, like, two hours because I'm too scared to leave."

"I wouldn't want to go if I were you either. Why can't you just say no to Caleb?"

"He's family."

"And it's good to enable him?"

"At least he's not doing heroin."

"Jesus, Billy. You sound like an abused wife. 'At least he doesn't punch me in the face.'"

"He doesn't punch me in the face."

Lydia sighs again. She doesn't get it. Saying no is so easy for her. Besides dancing, it's probably her greatest talent.

"So will you come with me?" I say.

"Maybe," she says. "If I have time." But I know that's pretty much a no. Lydia never has time anymore.

We eat our candy in silence for a while, throwing the empty cardboard over the edge and watching it drift slowly to the ground, catching wind occasionally and changing course. The only sounds are the wind, the popping open of the little windows of the calendars, and a lone hawk somewhere in the distance crying about something.

"Do you think I should eat this?" I say, showing Lydia a disfigured chocolate from my fourth, maybe fifth, calendar.

"It's green," Lydia says. "The last time I checked, chocolate isn't supposed to be green."

"It's not green. It's just a different shade of brown."

"It might be poisonous."

"I paid good money for this."

"Billy, that calendar cost twenty-five cents. That piece of chocolate cost a penny. I will give you a penny to not eat it if it means you won't die of food poisoning."

"Look at you, throwing money around." I thought that was pretty funny, but Lydia doesn't laugh.

I look at the greenish-brown blob in my hand. I throw it over the side and watch it fall until it's so small I can't see it anymore. There's no satisfying sound to tell me when it hits the ground, and I feel cheated. I throw the whole calendar overboard and feel cheated again by how slowly it glides. I want to throw something heavy and hard, something that will really make an impact.

We are silent as the fog swallows the shore, as it advances inland, gobbling up trees and roads and houses and every other solid thing in its path. It has become so normal, this disappearing.

LYDIA

THE FOG IS SILENT AND FAST IN ITS TAKEOVER. IN JUST a few minutes, Rome and Carthage are gone. Everyone who ever thought anything about Billy and me are gone. Now it's just the two of us left, at the top of the world, with no one to define us. The longer we are silent, the more time the bullshit has to fall away. The fog has reached the water tower now, has swallowed up the metal structures that hold it in the sky, but it stops just below the tank. We are floating above the sea of white—unmoored, untouched.

Somehow this changes things. Suddenly, with the rest of the world gone, there are things I can say out loud.

"Everything feels out of control," I say. Billy doesn't say anything for a while. I wonder if he even heard me over the sound of the wind. "I think it started when we met."

"I think it's like chemistry," he says after a long silence. "You've got two volatile elements that are used to doing their own thing, and then you put them together and *bang*!" He claps his hands together and I jump, the sharp sound so shocking and out of place up here in the clouds. "The explosion sets off a bunch of other explosions."

"That makes no sense, Billy," I say. "That's like some pseudo-science anti-vaxxer shit."

"Haven't you been paying attention in chemistry class?"

"No. And neither have you."

"There's a fine line between madness and genius," he says.

"Did you get that from one of your talk shows?"

"No. Caleb said it."

"Whatever," I say, but my heart's not in it. I don't feel like being sarcastic or funny. I just feel confused and pissed off about everything.

We sit there for a while saying nothing. I can't see any of Carthage or Rome or my life below. What if it were this easy to break free from it? What if I could just be right here, right now, without what's down there to define me?

"I think my house is trying to kill me," Billy finally says.

I look at his face. He's totally serious. "Is that why you haven't been sleeping?"

"It keeps me up all night. I'm afraid it's going to kill me in my sleep. It's breaking faster and faster, but only around me, like it's reacting to stuff I do, like it has an *opinion*. I barely avoided a huge piece of plaster falling on my head the other day. It leaves nails all over the floor for me to step on. I feel like it's watching me, like it can see whatever I'm doing, whatever room I'm in." He seems genuinely scared.

"Maybe it's not trying to kill you," I say. "Maybe it just wants you to leave."

Normally, I probably wouldn't entertain Billy's ludicrous ideas.

But these are not normal times. I'm starting to accept that most of the logic of the universe is basically not applicable in Fog Harbor anymore. I'm being stalked by a ghost kid, so it is perfectly plausible that Billy's house is trying to kill him.

With the fog all around us, it feels like we are hiding inside a stack of down pillows, like we are insulated. Safe. I can see why Caleb liked it up here so much he wrote a song about it. It's like up here, we don't have to be who we are down there.

"Why would it want me to leave?" Billy says. "It never did before."

"Maybe it didn't think you were ready."

He's quiet for a minute as he thinks about that.

"I think I'm going crazy," he finally says.

"That makes two of us."

"But you're the sanest person I know."

I don't tell him about the nine-year-old girl in a pink tutu sitting next to me, her bare feet dangling over the edge as she silently works on her own Advent calendar, opening the doors one by one. I don't even know how I'd begin to talk about her. And once you talk about something, it usually means you have to start dealing with it, and I certainly don't know how to do that.

Billy sighs. I sigh. The little girl sighs. Maybe way below us, down there on First Street, enveloped by fog that smells like something dying, Billy's house sighs too.

"I hate my mom," I whisper. "I wish she could come back so I could tell her how much I hate her." My heart is as soft as the fog. I feel it in my throat, expanding.

Billy doesn't say anything. He just reaches for my hand, and I let him. I don't even cringe. I must have left my defenses down there somewhere, in the place now buried. And we sit here, holding hands, feet dangling a hundred feet in the air, looking at the erased context of our lives below, sitting in the fabled place where Caleb Sloat may have slept when he had no home, and I feel like shit, but I also feel safer than I've felt in a long time, also freer, and the combination of these feelings makes no sense. It's like a tornado inside me with the sound on mute, and the only thing anchoring us in this cold place in the sky is the few inches where our skin touches, a tiny opening for trading each other's warmth.

BILLY

IT'S THE FIRST DAY BACK AT SCHOOL AFTER BREAK, AND all anyone can talk about is a New Year's Eve party in Rome that ended in a bloody riot after Carthage students crashed it. Rome police had to call in county deputies so they'd have enough handcuffs and cars to transport kids to the station. More than a few students are absent today due to injuries, and several more have some form of black eye or split lip. Braydon Hansen has his right arm in a cast.

But everything changes in fifth period, when the principal announces over the loudspeakers that school's getting out early because the mayor just declared today a new holiday, tentatively titled "Liberty Day," after news reports that the King pronounced the Olympic National Park no longer protected and now open to logging. Students and teachers start cheering in class, Carthageans and Romans holding each other and crying tears of joy, forgetting their hate because the good news and promise of abundance suddenly makes their rivalry unnecessary. It's an emotional roller coaster, to say the least.

Lydia and I haven't talked about what we talked about on the water tower. Somehow up there, anything seemed possible, but down here it's the same old crap. I couldn't find her after school got out, so I'm on my own again. It's just like when she showed me her dancing; anytime she lets her guard down, she goes into hiding immediately afterward.

I get why everyone's excited about the forest thing, but I don't think I'll benefit too much since Grandma definitely isn't getting a job cutting down trees, and if I tried I'd probably die the first day on the job, and to be honest I kind of think the forest should stay a forest, but I will never in a million years admit that to anyone around here because they'd probably murder me and tie my dead body to a tree and write on it with my blood, ARE YOU HAPPY NOW, TREE HUGGER? as a warning to anyone else who might think trees should have more rights than red-blooded Americans.

Everyone's celebrating as I leave school grounds. In the streets, people are setting off fireworks and firing guns into the sky, the colorful flames and sparks glowing eerie in the misty fog all around. It's a little scary to be walking around in the middle of a bunch of explosions when visibility is only a block or two and people can't really see where they're shooting, but it's kind of pretty and I guess I'm glad everyone's happy, and for once they're too busy to harass me about Caleb.

I hug my coat tight to my body, but it does nothing. I haven't been able to get warm all day. Those crows I saw the other day are waiting for me in a tree down the block. I try not to make eye contact as I walk by, but then I hear a bunch of wings flapping, and they all land on another tree ahead of me. As I walk by a second time, they all start cackling, and it's so loud and shrill it makes my ears hurt, and it feels just like when the popular girls at school huddle together and don't even bother whispering as they make fun of me. And now I feel embarrassed in front of a bunch of birds.

It takes Gordon a long time to answer the door. I have to ring the doorbell three times. Finally the door opens, revealing a shirtless and crusty-eyed Gordon in boxer shorts. "Oh hey, little man," he says. "I just woke up. Come on in." The stump of his missing arm moves back and forth as he leads me into the house, which is in the same general state it usually is. "Do you want to play video games or something?" Gordon says as he pulls on some wrinkled pants from the floor.

"No thank you," I say. "I'm just here for, you know."

"Sit down," Gordon says. "Stay awhile. Let me get you something to drink."

"Um, no. I have to go," I say, but Gordon's already in the kitchen. I wonder when the last time he went on a date was.

He brings back a beer for himself and one for me, which I set on the table without opening. Gordon sits on the couch next to me, turns on the TV, puts it on mute, and we watch live news footage of people dancing around the Rome/Carthage tornado pit. "Pretty wild, huh?" Gordon says.

"Yeah, I guess."

"You got some serious bags under your eyes. You want an eye mask or something? I got a nice gel one in the fridge that's great for inflammation."

"No thank you."

"Let me know if you change your mind." Gordon takes a big swig of his beer. "It's lavender-scented."

"Can I ask you something?" I say.

"Yeah, sure."

"Did my uncle ever actually live up on the water tower?"

Gordon spits out his beer, spraying all over the coffee table. "Oh man," he laughs. "I was not expecting that. I thought you were going to ask me to get you some Molly."

"So? Did he?"

Gordon gulps down half his beer. "We used to go up there a lot. He loved it for some reason I never could understand. But the true story is we got drunk up there one night and passed out. So I guess he could say he slept there once, on accident. But he sure as hell didn't live there. All that time he claims he was homeless, he lived right here with me and my dad."

"Oh," I say. I can't tell if I'm disappointed or relieved.

"You know he cried when I called to tell him my dad died? He was on tour in Germany or something. He wanted to cancel that night's show, but I talked him out of it. I was like, think of the fans, man. What would Pop want you to do?"

"Oh," I say again.

"Let me tell you something about your uncle's stories," Gordon says, leaning back and putting his bare feet on the coffee table. "Maybe he's a musical genius or whatever like everyone says, but the whole 'I'm this poor misunderstood artist from this super-oppressive place' thing? That's bullshit. All those stories he tells on TV about growing up here, they're only about half true. He might actually believe them, because he's constructed this whole persona, you know? And it's based on this whole Caleb Sloat, poor abused kid from Rome mythology, poor victim, boo hoo hoo. And he, like, *needs* that, you know? But the truth is, if you took away his fame and money, he's still just like the rest of us. And that shit's not interesting."

For a moment, I forget how much I want to get out of here because I'm in shock that Gordon's saying some pretty deep stuff.

"The thing is," Gordon continues, "back in the day, *he* was the one following *me* around all the time. He wasn't some cool artist. He was just some kid who wanted to get high and noodled around on his sister's old guitar. He used to steal from your grandma all the time too. Did you know that? He pushed her down the stairs once. That's how she broke her hip. I hear she hasn't been upstairs since. She didn't kick him out—he just left. That's what he does."

I really don't want to cry in Gordon's house. I can't think of a worse place to start crying than Gordon's house.

"Hey, but I'm not bitter," Gordon says. He drinks the rest of his beer. "I got a good life. And what's he doing? Hiding out in Korea from a billion fans, but with no real friends in the world? Who's the loser now?"

"Um, I have to go," I say. "Can I just get the stuff?"

"Yeah yeah, okay." Gordon scratches his crotch, then opens a

258   AMY REED

wooden box on the coffee table full of mysterious plastic baggies.

"Are you sure you don't want to play video games?" Gordon says. "I just got *Kill the Bitches 5*."

"No thank you," I say, pulling money out of my dolphin wallet.

"Are you hungry? I could heat up some taquitos."

"Um, no." I hold the money out to Gordon. I hold my other hand out to receive the bag of weed. I lean in closer, to make sure Gordon notices my hands. But he just keeps talking.

"Oh, I know!" Gordon says. "I got some nitrous cartridges around here somewhere. You ever done nitrous?"

I grab the baggie from Gordon's hand, drop my money on the couch, and stand up. "Sorry, but I really have to go."

"Oh, okay," Gordon says, looking about as sad as I could imagine a one-armed shirtless drug dealer could look.

"Thanks and everything," I say, backing toward the door.

"Yeah, no problem," Gordon says. "Come by anytime. Even if you just want to hang out, you know?"

"Okay," I say. Are all drug dealers this lonely?

When my hand reaches the doorknob of the front door, I feel immediate relief. But before I go, I have one last question.

"Hey, Gordon," I say. "How'd you lose your arm?"

"Oh, that?" he says. "I fell off the water tower."

I had two official Caleb-related tasks to do after school—buy weed and buy more doll-making supplies—but I just couldn't help myself.

In the glass case at Thrift Town where they keep all the nicest stuff was an acoustic guitar that, even though I know nearly nothing about guitars, looked to be in excellent shape and a steal at twenty dollars. So what if it had a couple of pink heart stickers on it and WWJD? written in Sharpie? As soon as I saw it, I knew Caleb must have it.

I know Caleb said he wanted to leave his whole rock star life behind, and maybe this guitar doesn't seem like a great gift at first glance. But before he was a rock star, Caleb was just a musician. He was someone who loved music, like Lydia loves dancing. It made him happier than anything else in his life, except for maybe drugs, but those stopped working. I think that person is still inside him, and maybe part of him getting better is about him finding who he was before his life got all out of control. Maybe he doesn't see it that way right now, but sometimes what people say they want is different from what they actually need.

This is some advanced helping.

When I get home, there's a new camper van parked outside the house. A man and a woman in matching sweatpants are roasting hot dogs on a little portable grill, like they're tailgating and my house is some kind of show. They stare at me as I walk by, their heads turning slowly, just like the crows.

"Hey, Billy," the man says with a friendly and surprisingly sane-sounding voice. "Heard anything from your uncle?"

"No," I say. "How do you know my name?"

"The Internet knows all," he says, and I keep walking.

As I approach the front door, I hear a rustling coming from behind the house. Could be the possum and her family, but it sounds bigger. Maybe it's one of those nuclear reactor bears from Canada. Maybe it's that thing with hooves that sneaks around in the fog that Lydia refuses to call a unicorn. My normal response to scary noises is to ignore them and pretend they're not happening, but I'm feeling kind of confident with this guitar in my shopping cart, so I park the cart and walk through the knee-high weeds around the side of the house. I peek my head around the corner, and there, rooting around in the stacks of old paint cans and broken coolers and a rusty lawn mower, is Cult Girl.

"Um, hello?" I say. She jumps, then kind of recoils like a scared cat. "What are you doing?"

She doesn't say anything, just stares at me with her big eyes, all tense and nervous like she's getting ready to bolt. She's got her hair up in a tight bun like she always does, and she's wearing a drab sweater and ankle-length skirt, but I get the impression that she's undercover, that it's all a disguise, and she's got a cape and super-powers under there somewhere.

"It's okay," I say, slowly walking toward her. "I'm nice. Too nice, really. It's kind of a problem. Are you looking for something?"

And then she hikes up her skirt and runs away, and she's gone before I have a chance to try to convince her to stay.

Somewhere in the distance, I hear crows squawking.

I stand there for a minute after she's gone. Why do I feel so sad? Why does it feel like the air got sucked out of the sky?

I look through the pile of garbage she was digging around in, and I find a bundle wrapped in plastic bags. I open it, and inside is a cellophane-covered library book—*The Handmaid's Tale*. I think that's one of the books that's banned at my school. If I'm not even allowed to read it, I'm pretty sure Cult Girl would get grounded for a million years if her parents caught her with it, though I'm not sure how you'd ground someone who already can't do anything. Her whole life is basically like being grounded all the time, so this book must be pretty good if she wants to risk whatever punishment she'd get if she were caught.

I wrap the book up tight and put it back where she hid it. I guess I have room for yet another small secret.

The possum doesn't attack my ankles as I enter the house, so that's one small consolation for this very weird day. As I climb the stairs to the attic with Caleb's new guitar, I almost don't notice the house shaking, it's become so normal. I think about Lydia and her dance classes, how she hasn't once suspected anything besides the story I told her about the scholarship. Even I know the story had holes, and I certainly know Lydia is more skeptical than the average person, especially when it comes to good news, so I'm kind of surprised my gift/lie has gone over so easily. But maybe when someone really wants something, they're more willing to put on blinders, to see what they want to see and ignore what they don't.

Maybe desperate people are easier to fool. Even Lydia, who pretends not to want anything. Maybe especially Lydia, because she secretly wants so much.

I knock on the attic door and hear Caleb's muffled "Come in." I open the door and haul the plastic Thrift Town bags behind me, like some skinny, half-rate Santa. "I got your stuff," I say as I drop the bags at the entrance of Caleb's structure, now permanently open, more like a horseshoe instead of the previous closed circle. "And a surprise!"

Caleb's watching something on his laptop that's making him laugh. Last time I came up, he was actually outside his nest, doing push-ups. He gave himself a sponge bath yesterday and even washed his hair. He's been requesting that I bring him salads and brown rice bowls from Rome's one healthy restaurant that's always empty and will probably go out of business any day now.

"Caleb," I say. "Did you hear me? I got you a surprise."

"Did you finally go to Gordon's?" he says without looking away from the screen. "I'm living on stems right now."

"Yeah, but I got something even better."

Caleb looks at me, his face relaxed and almost pleasant. "Did you bring me a woman?" He laughs at his own joke.

"Happy late Christmas!" I pull the guitar from where I was hiding it behind a wall of blanket.

Caleb's face could be a movie screen. It tells a whole story in the next few seconds. From calm, to surprise, to confusion, to something that looks like yearning, then heartbreak, then anger, then fury, then rage, then something so hot it is unnameable.

"Get that fucking thing out of my face," Caleb growls. Low, slow, primal. He's an animal, cornered.

I don't get it. Caleb's reaction does not compute. I am the king of knowing what people secretly want. My greatest talent is helping people. It's the only thing I'm good at.

"What were you thinking?" Caleb says. "How can you be so stupid? What is wrong with you?"

It is Caleb's voice, but those are Grandma's words. Sloat words. Family words.

"I just thought—"

"No," Caleb says. "You weren't thinking. I came here to get away from this shit. I don't want a fucking guitar. I don't want to see a fucking guitar for the rest of my life."

"But it made you happy once," I say. I can feel my bottom lip trembling, pathetic. "I remember from when I was little. When you played music, you weren't like us anymore."

Caleb says nothing. He will not look me in the eye. He just stares at the twenty-dollar thrift store guitar like it's a grenade about to go off.

"Music's what got you out of here," I say, extending my arm, offering Caleb the guitar one more time. "Don't you want to get out of here?"

There is a moment of silence, of stillness, when both of us stop breathing. I swear the monster dolls lean forward to get a better view. The top of the blanket fort is lined with an audience peering out of mismatched plastic and glass eyes.

Caleb reaches out his hand, takes the guitar from me, and chucks it into the corner of the attic, where it lands with a hollow thud and the dissonant ring of untuned strings.

"Why do you give people shit they don't even want?" Caleb says. "All I asked you to do is bring me food and weed and to dump my shit. I'm paying you good money to do those very simple things. That's the only shit I want from you. I don't want your fucking friendship or bullshit psychobabble. I don't want you coming around here to hang out."

I open my mouth to say something, but all I do is choke.

"You know what I really want?" Caleb spits. "I want you to leave me the fuck alone."

And then I go on autopilot, like his words flipped a switch inside me. I am numb as I walk out of the attic and down the stairs. I focus on my breathing like the therapy talk shows have told me to do my whole life.

I breathe in.

I failed.

I breathe out.

I'm useless.

I breathe in.

I'm pathetic.

I breathe out.

Caleb hates me.

I breathe in.

I hate me.

I breathe out. I push the bookcase at the bottom of the stairs back in place. I hear the front door open and close, Grandma's heavy breaths as she walks into the house. All I want is to watch a therapy talk show or the AA channel. I want to hear about somebody else's problems so I don't have to think about mine. But that is not an option now.

So I go into my almost-empty room. I lie in my bed and stare at Lydia's painting on the wall, at the endless spiral inward.

Black holes suck in all the light around them. They consume everything that comes near.

I don't know how to help Caleb. I don't know how to help anyone. There is one thing I thought I could do, and I can't do it.

I turn onto my side and face the hole in my wall. I watch as a stream of ants poke their heads over the edge of the opening and take turns throwing lifeless bodies off the side, all their brothers and sisters and fathers and mothers and various distant relatives who have died somewhere inside the walls of my house, as if they have decided my room is some kind of ant cemetery.

I don't bother cleaning it up.

LYDIA

I WAKE UP TO THE LITTLE GIRL'S GHOST FACE JUST INCHES away from mine. The first thing I see is her eyes staring into me, and for a moment I think I am dead. I think, this is what hell is—staring into yourself for eternity.

When I scream, I half-expect to hear nothing, like in dreams, like in my worst nightmares, where I scream and scream and nothing comes out. But my voice is loud and clear, and it scares the girl into the corner. I jump out of bed and chase her out of my room and into the living room, knocking the lamp off my bedside table in the process, running into the coffee table with my shin, ramming into the side of the bookcase with my hip so hard, one of Larry's prized Unicorns vs. Dragons snow globes smashes on the floor.

"I hate you!" I scream, as if that would make her stop, as if hurting her feelings could somehow cure mine. But she just keeps running.

"I don't want you here!" I scream as I chase her. "Nobody wants you. You're pathetic."

But it isn't me speaking, it isn't my voice, and it isn't her I am talking to, and every word I say feels like a punch in my own heart, and by the time we are both exhausted and stop running, I am the one who is crying.

And then she just stands there, looking at me, calm and emotionless, never breaking eye contact as she reaches over and takes the picture of my mother off the wall, the one she's been moving and hiding and taunting me with. Time stops as our eyes turn to the photo in her tiny hands, at the woman trapped and motionless inside the frame. Then the girl looks up at me, a new glint of something cruel in her eyes, something sociopathic, like she takes pleasure in hurting me, and as I scream, "No!" she hurls the picture at my head with the aim and force of someone much more powerful than a nine-year-old girl.

I duck just in time for it to smash against the door to Larry's bedroom.

After all the screaming and running, it is this that finally wakes Larry up. He opens his door and pokes his head out, sees the picture on the floor haloed by broken glass, and then looks up at me full of hurt and betrayal, like I'm the one who killed her.

"I was dusting," I manage to say. "It fell."

He just stares at that broken glass like it's eight years ago all over again, like that morning we woke up to an empty apartment and a knock on the door and the rain-drenched cops standing there with their bad-news faces, and we both knew Mom was gone before they ever said anything.

"Clean it up," he says, with no breath behind his words. And he retreats back into his room, and I retreat back into mine.

And the girl is gone, whatever version of her that was just here, not the annoying one who follows me to dance class and school, not the one who spins in circles or plays harmless tricks, no longer the boring ghost she started out as. I had almost gotten used to her over the past couple of months, but now it's like she decided she's not okay with me just tolerating her presence. Now she *wants* something. Every time I look in a mirror, there she is, staring back at me with her needy, unblinking eyes. She keeps knocking things over, spilling my drinks. I try to ignore her, but it only seems to make her stronger and more solid. Like pushing her away feeds her.

The girl who showed up this morning is dangerous. She is capable of hurting someone. She is capable of hurting me.

I feel shaky all day, almost dizzy. I keep seeing the girl's eyes in front of mine, blocking my vision, blinding me from everything else. I keep seeing my mom's eyes, empty and glossy inside that frame. I keep seeing the glass smashed on the floor, and Larry's heartbroken silent stare, keep hearing the sound of my own scream echoing inside my head, and I look around for the girl, like she could give me some kind of answer, like she holds the missing clue, but her absence now is almost worse than her stalking. I need her to tell me what to do. I need her to tell me how to end this.

I'm so unhinged I even think about telling Billy. But the bags under his eyes are darker than ever and he's making less and less sense, and he has enough to deal with without worrying about me. There is only room for one of us to be haunted.

And I know the trap of letting him in. Once I tell him something, he wants more. He's never satisfied. The problem with Billy is he wants to talk about everything all the time. Like, you mention one thing one time in a moment of weakness, and he thinks that means you want to start talking about every little thing that goes through your head, and the more secrets you share, the better your score is as a friend. It's like that app that's got everyone's eyeballs glued to their phones; the longer they stare, the more points they get. It's like Billy's keeping a tally of my friend points according to some impossible relationship grading system he learned on those therapy shows, and I am constantly failing.

Or is this actually how friendship is supposed to work? You just share all your personal shit back and forth until you don't have any secrets left, and then you win?

At lunch I say nothing. I just sit there listening to Billy rattle on about how he thinks his relationship with his uncle is improving, and how it's nice to have someone you love as a prisoner, and I don't even have the energy to explain to him how fucked up that is.

So needless to say, I definitely am not my best self when Natalie finds me at my locker after the surprise early dismissal for "Liberty Day" and asks if I want to come to her house to practice before class. I can't think of a good excuse in time, so now here I am, sitting in the passenger seat of Natalie Morris's car as she drives through the neighborhoods of Rome Hills, and I have no idea how to define what I'm feeling.

Being with her makes me feel better, and for some reason that makes me feel guilty, like I'm stealing something I have no right to.

The farther away we drive from the flats of Rome and Carthage, the less anxious I feel. When we break out of the fog and into clear sky, for a moment, I can almost believe it's that easy, that I can just drive away from my problems.

Despite living just a few miles away my whole life, I've only been up here a handful of times. But when I was little, sometimes Mom would get in one of her moods to "see how the other people lived," and we'd drive slowly through the winding streets, the houses getting grander the higher we went in elevation, until we reached the top where the Rome Mansion—now part local history museum, part event space for ritzy weddings—overlooks the whole town out to the ocean. I remember being confused by how, from up here, Fog Harbor looked like a completely different world than the one where I lived, how all you could see was the beautiful stuff like the sparkling ocean and forest and river and sky, but none of the details of boarded-up houses and crumbling businesses, which were really all you noticed when you were down in the flats.

Mom would examine the fancy houses and their immaculately kept gardens with squinting eyes, showing a strange thrill of satisfaction whenever she'd discover a blemish in the perfect facades. By the time I came around, the logging and fishing industries had already been kaput for half a generation. Fewer and fewer people could afford to live up here, and many who stayed had a hard time keeping up appearances. Now, several years later, driving through the same roads with Natalie, the decay is even more apparent. Whole blocks full of FOR SALE signs. Abandoned mansions with boarded-up windows, unruly rhododendrons, and overgrown lawns. The streets are eerily quiet.

"It's like a ghost town up here," I say.

"Where have all the rich people gone?" Natalie sings to the tune of that old folk song, "Where Have All the Flowers Gone?"

For a moment, the car is silent as I stare at Natalie, as my brain tries to compute that this girl I always thought was stuck-up just made a joke and that joke was in fact very funny.

Natalie meets my eye and we bust out laughing.

Just when I thought I couldn't be more surprised by this girl, I am.

"My house is up here," Natalie says. "We have, like, two neighbors."

Because there is a total of zero male dancers at Fog Harbor Dance Academy, and because Natalie and I are the school's strongest dancers, Mary decided that, in addition to featured solos in the group routines, we would also costar in a modern pas de deux together, choreographed by Luz. The old me, after getting over the high of being chosen for this honor, would have been pissed to have to share the stage with a *ballerina* faking her way through *my* style of dance. But the new me was excited to dance with such a good dancer.

Since when is there a "new" me?

Natalie pulls in front of a two-car garage attached to a beautiful old house with two lion statues guarding the front door. It's not the biggest house on the block, but it's the best kept. All the hedges and trees are perfectly trimmed. All the withered plants of winter have been cleared and covered with fresh mulch.

"Here we are," says Natalie as she turns off the engine.

"Are your parents home?"

"No. My dad's at work, and my mom's at church volunteering at the blood drive."

"That's nice of her."

Natalie rolls her eyes. "Yeah, my mom is the queen of nice."

She seems nervous as she leads me quickly through the house. "This is the living room," she says without looking at the huge space to the left of the entryway, with lush carpets and furniture that doesn't look like anyone's ever sat on it. Inoffensive paintings of landscapes and floral still life line the wall. Silver candlesticks hold candles that have never been burned. But when we enter the kitchen, there, standing at the counter island in the middle of the vast space of white cabinets and shiny marble and chrome, is a petite woman with a perfect blond bob, matching baby blue cardigan set, and pearl earrings.

"What are you doing here?" Natalie says, with a sharp edge to her voice that surprises me.

"Hi, honey," says the woman I assume is Natalie's mother. "Who's your friend?" Her voice and smile are perfectly friendly, but friendly like someone told her to be, maybe not like she actually means it.

"This is Lydia," Natalie says, sullen-faced and monotone, so much like a caricature of a teenager I have to fight the impulse to laugh. "She's a dance friend. We're going to practice before class. Aren't you supposed to be at church?"

"I heard about school getting out early, so I came home to see if you wanted a snack," she says, then smiles at me. "Hello, Lydia. It's so nice to meet a friend of Natalie's. She doesn't bring many friends home."

"Jesus, Mom!"

"Honey, you know how your father and I feel about you using the Lord's name in vain."

"I can get my own snack."

"It's nice to meet you too, Mrs. Morris," I say. You have to be as polite as possible with these people. You can't give them any reason to think you're trash.

"Are you hungry?" Mrs. Morris says. "Can I make you a snack?"

"No," Natalie snaps, already moving toward a door on the other side of the kitchen.

"No thank you," I lie, and my stomach rumbles as soon as the words leave my mouth. I don't want Natalie, and certainly not her mom, to see me eat. It's never been something I cared about before, but I'm suddenly overly conscious of the fact that I've grown up eating most of my meals from a microwave or take-out container in a run-down bar, while Natalie and her family have eaten most of their meals here.

You can't let these people know how hungry you are.

"This way," Natalie says, opening a door off the kitchen.

"It was nice to meet you, Mrs. Morris," I say as I follow Natalie.

"You too, Lydia," she says, her straight white teeth sparkling. She looks like she's in a commercial for something expensive and unnecessary. "Come back anytime."

"Yes, ma'am," I say. I fight the urge to cringe. Being this polite hurts.

I follow Natalie down a narrow stairwell. Houses in the flats don't have basements. If they did, they'd immediately fill up with water.

Natalie turns on the light, revealing a dance studio that's even nicer than the one at Fog Harbor Dance Academy. "Whoa," I say.

"It's ridiculous," Natalie says, looking genuinely embarrassed. "I mean, I'm grateful and everything. But my mom had this built when I was *six*."

"What if you'd turned out to want to be, like, a drummer instead of ballerina?" I say, kicking off my boots and placing them carefully on a custom shoe rack by the door. I hang up my coat on a shiny gold hook.

"Yeah, no," Natalie says, pulling her sweater over her head. "That wasn't an option."

I feel awkward as I take off my many layers of clothing. Somehow being here alone with Natalie is a completely different experience than being in the locker room full of girls. I'm suddenly self-conscious. My skin feels hot.

Natalie scrolls through her phone. "Any music requests while we warm up?"

"I don't know," I say. I fold my arms over my breasts, then drop them to my sides, then put one hand awkwardly on my hip. "What kind of music do you like?" God, I sound like a loser.

"How about this?" A song starts playing on the custom stereo system. It's definitely rock, but a pretty and melodic twist on rock, with a guitar and cello and simple drums.

"This is cool," I say.

"It's not really what you'd expect a ballerina to listen to, is it?" Natalie says with a smile.

"Yeah, aren't you supposed to listen to classical music all the time?"

"You know there's such thing as avant-garde ballet, right?"

"That's an oxymoron if I've ever heard one," I tease.

"Oh my God!" Natalie says. "You're such a snob." She's smiling. I wonder if she knows what people say about her.

We spend the next two songs stretching in silence. I try to focus on my body, but my head keeps getting in the way. I have so many questions, but I don't have the guts to ask any of them.

Then all of a sudden Natalie starts laughing. She's sitting on the floor, stretched forward over her widespread legs, and her back is heaving with laughter.

"What?" I say.

Natalie sits up and folds her long legs against her chest. "We're like the Fog Harbor High diversity club down here. This can be our first official meeting."

I start laughing too. In addition to a handful of Native kids and a few Latinos and Asians who mostly keep to themselves, Natalie and I represent a good chunk of the racial diversity at our school.

"I don't know," I say. "Can we have a club with only two members? Maybe we should invite my friend Billy. He can be the token white guy."

"He's gay, right?" Natalie asks. "So he should totally be in our club."

"Actually, he's not," I answer, relieved to see no hint of judgment in Natalie's face. "But he gets that a lot."

"Oh," Natalie says, with a look that almost seems like disappointment. "Is he your boyfriend?"

"No!" I say, a little too forcefully. And just like that, the moment of ease during our laughter is gone, replaced by a new, intense awkwardness. "We're just friends," I say, looking away. "He's like my brother."

"That's cool," Natalie says, looking away too, bending into her stretch. But we accidentally catch each other's eyes in the mirror, and somehow it is more comfortable to hold contact there than face-to-face.

Miraculously, the little girl's not here, not staring back at me from the mirror, not dancing around trying to distract me. I don't feel that tug at my heart, that seizing in my chest that's not quite pain but the memory of pain. I don't hear the voice in my head, that begging whisper: "Look at me." Somehow, being here with Natalie has silenced the child, at least temporarily.

"Should we practice?" I finally say. I need to dance. I need to stop thinking.

"Okay," says Natalie. She cues up the music on her phone.

The choreography's smart. It plays on each of our strengths and lets us bring our own styles to our characters. Luz knew it was a hopeless endeavor to try to get us to match. There are so many reasons I like Luz, but one of the main ones is how all her choreography tells a story, even the simplest practice routines. In this story, two alien girls from different planets meet for the first time. The dance is a scene of them sizing each other up, Natalie's movements fluid and upright, mine jerky and close to the ground. We start out at odds, but by the end we are dancing in tandem. It's a little out there, I'll admit. But somehow pretending to be an alien dancing modern feels a lot more natural than being a human dancing ballet.

The routine is only four and a half minutes long, but we are soaking with sweat after the first run.

"I don't think you're supposed to look at me that early," I say.

"What do you mean?"

"You're supposed to avoid eye contact at the beginning. Pretend to ignore me. It isn't until we touch hands the first time that you look me in the eye."

"Oh, I get it," Natalie says. "That makes sense." She glides over to a watercooler and gets us each a paper cup of water, even though there are perfectly fine glasses upstairs.

"No offense," I say, sipping from the cup, "but I totally didn't expect you to be any good at modern."

Natalie laughs. "No offense taken. That was a kind of a compliment, right?"

"I guess," I say. "That's about as close as I get."

"Well, thank you."

"I thought you were just a ballerina."

"Just a ballerina?" she says, raising an eyebrow.

"You know what I mean."

Natalie's quiet for a moment, and my chest constricts. Why did I say that? Why do these things always come out of my mouth that hurt people I don't want to hurt?

Finally, Natalie locks eyes with me. "Thank you," she says.

"For what?"

"For seeing that. For thinking I'm more than a ballerina."

"You're an incredible dancer," I say.

Natalie's smile seems almost sad. "It's more than that."

"Yeah," I say. "I know." Maybe I don't know all of it, but I'm starting to. I know that Natalie is way more than a ballerina. I know that not a whole lot of people see that.

We should run through the routine again, but neither of us moves. I take another sip of my paper cup of water because I don't know what else to do.

"Can I ask you something?" Natalie finally says, turning to throw her cup into a small trash can.

"Of course."

She keeps her back to me for a few moments. I see her shoulders tense. I don't want to be responsible for that tension.

"Why do you hate ballet so much?" she finally says, turning toward me. "Be honest. You never really answered the first time I asked."

"I don't hate ballet."

"Don't bullshit me." She takes half a step forward, and without thinking I take half a step back. She is still several feet away, but she feels too close. Suddenly, I want to run away. I want to hide. I want to undo this whole conversation.

I look up briefly. The little girl is here now, staring at me in the mirror, but not the evil version from the chaos of this morning. Her eyes are sad and full of yearning, but for what, I don't know. For a brief moment, I'm filled with rage. How dare she come here? How dare she saddle me with the burden of her feelings? What the hell am I supposed to do with her sadness?

But Natalie's eyes bore into me too, and their kindness cools my anger just enough for me to keep talking.

"It's not so much that I hate ballet," I say, looking down at my feet. "It's just, I know it's not for people like me. Modern is. It reflects the real world, how real people live, all of our emotion and messiness. It can be raw in a way ballet can never be. As soon as you put on pointe shoes, you've made dance elitist. You put on classical music from hundreds of years ago, you dance these old stories about fairy tales and princesses—they're not real. Those aren't my stories. That's not my life." I look up, and her eyes are there waiting for mine.

"It's not my life either," Natalie says. "It's not supposed to be. It's just supposed to be beautiful. It's magic. And magic isn't elitist. We all deserve some magic."

"Some people can't afford magic," I say.

Natalie doesn't argue. She doesn't get defensive. She just lets my words fill the room. She gives them space with her silence. "Let's dance," she finally says, after the words settle onto the floor, sharing space with the expensive polished wood and our raw, naked feet.

The little girl wanders off, and we get ready to dance again.

BILLY

EVERYONE AT SCHOOL IS TALKING ABOUT THE UPCOMING
Unicorns vs. Dragons festival, even though usually most people
over the age of thirteen and under thirty pretend to hate it, but I
guess people forget to be cool when confronted with the possibility
of getting on TV and dressing up like magical creatures for a weekend. Carthage replaced their vandalized street signs, but now they
all exclusively feature vicious-looking dragons, and Rome commis-
sioned their own even bigger signs, and of course theirs are all of
sparkly and disturbingly Aryan unicorns.

It's been a few days since the whole guitar fiasco, and Caleb
and I have barely talked. Lydia's been more distant than usual too. I
keep asking her what's wrong, but she keeps saying "nothing," and
maybe she's telling the truth, but I just can't tell anymore, because
all my usual psychic senses seem to be malfunctioning. And then
this weird thing happened at lunch where all of a sudden she said,
"Didn't Natalie Morris used to have this lunch?"

"I guess her schedule changed after winter break," I said.

"Huh," she said, then kind of smiled, but it wasn't a smile
meant for me, it was for some inside place only Lydia can see, and
why won't she let me in there?

Of course she has practice after school, so I'm on my own again, which shouldn't bother me because being alone is my only talent besides helping people, but apparently I'm forgetting how to do both of those things, so now I have exactly zero talents.

Everyone's lives seem to be getting better all of a sudden, and mine's just getting more confusing. I try to remind myself to be grateful. I repeat my mantra: *It could be so much worse.* But then one of the Braydons yells, "They catch your fuckup uncle yet, Billy Goat?" and one of the Katelyns says, "God, why doesn't he just die already?" and when I get outside I take a deep breath but it tastes like farts, and the fog's so thick I can just barely see what's across the street, and there are those crows again in a tree and now they've got a few seagulls with them as extra muscle, and there's that black car that's been following me, and now its doors are opening and a man and a woman in suits are getting out and they're staring at me and the woman is on her phone and I bet she's calling a SWAT team and any second now a helicopter is going to swoop in and someone's going to swing down on a rope and grab me and we're going to disappear into the fog and they're going to blindfold me and torture me until I tell them every bad thing I've ever done.

It could be so much worse. There is no end to how much worse it can get.

The lady detective puts away her phone. I'm frozen solid on the sidewalk outside school. The guy waves with a fake friendly smile on his face. That's how they get you. I've watched enough shows to know how they pretend to be your friend, then they throw you in a van and waterboard you.

"Billy Sloat?" he calls from the sidewalk across the street. "I'm Detective Runyon. I'm one of the detectives on the case to find your uncle. Can I ask you a couple questions?"

I shake my head. I'm not moving. If I stay on this sidewalk, I think I'm safe. There must be some rule about weird people in suits not being allowed on school grounds.

"You're not in trouble, buddy," the woman says. They both start walking across the street toward me. An audience is growing, the whole student body of Fog Harbor High, hoping for a show. "We want to find him as much as you do."

Where is Lydia when I need her? She'd know what to do. She'd know how to be strong for this.

"I bet Caleb's dead," someone says. "I bet they're here to break the news."

They're here to arrest me. They're going to take me away in handcuffs. They're going to put me in a jail cell and never let me out.

"Why don't we go somewhere a little more private?" the lady detective says. "Come on. We'll give you a ride home."

That's what they say when they want to handcuff you to a metal table in a tiny room with a one-way mirror. I know I am no match for the interrogation. All they have to do is give me one mean look, and I know I'll start talking.

They are just an arm's length away. I smell cologne and stale coffee. They could reach out and grab me right now if they wanted to. No one would care.

"Billy," the woman says, "we understand how stressed and scared you must be." You have no idea, lady.

"Come on, Billy Goat," someone says.

"What a loser," someone else says, and then all of a sudden I'm running, and then I'm half a block away, the sounds of taunting and laughing and crows squawking fading away behind me, and I expect sirens to start any minute, the car to screech up beside me, strong hands pulling me by the shoulders into a dark backseat, but no one comes, like I'm not even worth the trouble. But I keep running, even though my lungs are burning, even though I think I twisted my ankle, even though I have never run this far in my life, even though I keep looking behind me and no one is chasing me, not even the crows.

The possum under the porch jumps at me as I enter the house. The house is shaking so bad I barely make it up the stairs. Chunks of plaster fall from the walls and ceiling as I stumble into my room, as I crawl into bed and throw my sleeping bag over my head and tell myself it's only a dream, the way I used to when I was little after Grandma or Caleb did something that made me cry and then made fun of me for crying. I pretend that any minute I'll wake up in my real life, where Lynn A. is my grandma and she's rubbing my back and singing some lullaby a little out of tune, and I have a whole collection of ugly scarves she knitted me buried in my closet, and I have a mom and dad downstairs somewhere, and they borrow the faces of people from shows, whatever family I'm in love with at the time, the shows that always have an episode where the kid has a hard day at school, but instead of keeping it inside he comes home to tell someone about it, and then his mom or dad or grandma makes him something homemade and warm to eat, and they eat it slowly while he talks, the grown-up just listening and looking at him with their loving eyes, and then he gets to lie in bed getting his back rubbed like this, and that is the life I pretend is mine.

No one ever makes shows about poor, sleep-deprived kids being stalked by crows and detectives, about kids whose houses are trying to kill them, about kids who have to keep so many secrets their heads are about to burst, about kids who keep losing everyone they love. No one ever makes shows about kids like me.

The house shakes hard, over and over again, but it's almost rhythmic, like rocking, and I close my eyes tight and pretend the house is Lynn A. rocking me to sleep, and I imagine my breath going in and out like waves, and I hide myself under the sleeping bag and curl into the smallest ball I can until I disappear.

I think I actually sleep for, like, two hours because when I wake up it's dark, and I can hear the TV downstairs, which means Grandma's home. I think about telling her about the detectives but decide against it because I'm sure she'd find some way to turn their existence into my fault, and I just can't add that to all the guilt I'm dealing with right now. And the more she freaks out, the more I have to freak out by default, because her feelings always inevitably become my feelings, and quite frankly I'm running out of room for feelings.

So I go downstairs to watch TV with her like old times. Maybe that will make things feel normal again. I sit in my spot on the couch and she doesn't even acknowledge my existence, and I feel better already.

The TV news is about to show one of the King's signature fireside press conferences, which was recorded a couple hours earlier. Grandma's on the edge of her seat. She says part of the fun is the surprise of finding out where he's vacationing.

"Grandma, have you noticed the house is kind of falling apart?" I say. The entire first floor is covered in white dust and chunks of plaster.

"The house has always been falling apart," she says. "Shut your trap."

I'm not a saint or anything, but really? The house has Grandma and Caleb to choose from, and *I'm* the one it's decided to pick on?

The King is sitting on a plush leather couch in front of a large stone fireplace, in what appears to be a ski cabin, white snow slopes visible in the window behind him. A mug of something steaming sits on the table next to him. He is wearing a fuzzy, sky blue bathrobe as the small press corps seated at his feet attempt to ask him about the tanking economy and the refugees from Florida and the giant bomb he's threatening to drop on some island in East Asia.

"That's boring," the King says, taking a sip of his drink. "I thought I told you guys to stop asking me boring questions. Better be careful or I'll kick you out like I did those other guys."

"It's true," Grandma says, nodding her head. "Those are boring questions."

"He looks warm," I say. "I wish I were warm." The house is always freezing these days. I can see my breath. It's like the walls have stopped working. Grandma doesn't seem to be having this problem.

"Oh, I know!" the King says. "I have exciting news. I'm excited. So excited. You should be excited too. I mean, really. This is huge. Let me tell you, I have the smartest scientists in the world. They make things happen. This new technology is the best thing you've ever seen. It's going to revolutionize logging. I love wood!"

"Ooh!" Grandma says, clapping excitedly. "I love wood too!"

"Firstly, you know how I opened up all those forests over there in Washington to logging? In that big park or whatever? Well, Royal Industries is going to have exclusive rights to them. Having just one company in there will streamline production instead of having a bunch of little local companies doing stuff. Plus, it's federal land, so that means I own it. Because I'm the King."

I watch one side of Grandma's face spasm as her mouth turns downward and her chin flexes. Is she having a stroke?

"And we won't have to bother with local labor because—wait for it—we have *robots* to do all the work! Isn't that exciting? Robots! Human labor can be so messy."

The handful of reporters the King still allows to talk to him all raise their hands in tandem and start asking questions, but the King stands up and says, "Well, gotta go now. I have a date—I mean, a meeting. Special envoy from Slovenia. They make 'em nice over there. Real quality."

There's a war happening on Grandma's face, and, as unpleasant as it is, I can't look away. The TV reflects in her wet eyes as her worldview crumbles. Her beloved King just betrayed her and all of Fog Harbor County. He's betrayed her plenty of times already, but I don't know how she's going to rationalize this one to herself, because this time it's personal.

The screen cuts to Ronda Rash on location at the tornado pit. "I'm standing here live at the Rome/Carthage tornado pit, which just a few days ago was surrounded by people from the rival towns celebrating the opening of the formerly protected local forests to logging after more than two decades of economic free fall due to deforestation that led to the closing of almost all local logging-related businesses."

Behind her, a shirtless man throws a burning tire into the pit.

"But now," she continues, "the same people have returned to protest the King's recent announcement of a decision that will presumably exclude local businesses and workers from benefiting from the expanded logging territory."

No one got it together enough to make any signs yet, so mostly people are wandering around aimlessly, shouting at each other. One man pushes another, who falls into another man behind him, and then all hell breaks loose, the crowd a flurry of pushing, punching, shouting, glass breaking, and random things on fire. Ronda Rash looks behind herself, a faint glimmer of fear cracking her confident reporter facade, then back at the camera. "Things are volatile here in Fog Harbor, to say the least."

A woman smashes a beer bottle on a man's head, then the bloody-faced man throws her into the pit, and the crowd erupts in feral cries. "Back to you, Jill," Ronda Rash says. The screen cuts back to the newsroom, but the sound is still on Ronda as she says, "Get me back to Seattle, Brian. The rednecks are rioting."

Grandma presses the mute button. Her face twitches.

"Grandma, are you okay?" I say.

Her face twitches again.

"It's going to be all right," I say. "Nothing's really changed from before." But I know that's not true. People who aren't used to hope got a taste of it and went on a bender, and now they're going through withdrawal.

"Do you need anything?" I ask. "I picked up a box of day-old donuts on sale."

Grandma nods slowly. I retrieve the box from the kitchen, open it, and set it on the couch next to her. Without even looking, she reaches over and picks one up. With the other hand, she changes the channel to the first thing that is not news.

"I'm going to my room, okay?" I say.

She doesn't respond. She has half a donut in her mouth and is being soothed by a detective show. I trust she's in good hands. TV and donuts are the best babysitters.

I climb the stairs to my room, stand outside the door, but don't go in. I hung the painting Lydia gave me on the wall across from my bed and have been staring at it every night as I try to fall asleep, and I think it's the only thing keeping me sane besides Lynn A. The blue spiral swirls and swirls, giving me something to focus on that's not inside my head, while the yellow center throbs, sucking in the infinite supply of blue, sucking in everything and burning it up and making it new on the other side, and I can almost feel the gravity, like it wants to suck me in too, and I want it to take me, to pull me out of this place and into that one and turn me into something new, but this world is too strong, it holds on too tight, and the gravity of the painting is no match for the gravity out here.

No matter how much looking at the painting relaxes me, there is still everything outside it, and that stuff usually wins. The hole in the wall next to my bed keeps growing, and the room is extra freezing, and I keep hearing the wind howling inside the walls like it's screaming at me, and the creatures scurrying around in there seem to be getting bigger.

So I just stand here now staring at the door, thinking about how my buying-Caleb-a-surprise-guitar plan backfired because now he hates me, and how my buying-Lydia-dance-classes plan backfired because now she's busy all the time and I'm more lonely than ever, and how depressing it is that I keep finding new ways to be depressed, and how if I were smart I might think there was some kind of metaphor involved in staring at a closed door not wanting to open it because you're pretty sure there's nothing good on the other side.

So I walk down the hall, move the dresser hiding the door to the stairs, and start the ascent to the attic. I've never done this before—gone up there when Grandma's home and awake—but something is making me feel reckless, some tiny desire to see what would happen if everything fell apart.

When I get to the top of the stairs, I stop. I can hear, just barely, the sound of music coming from inside. An acoustic guitar softly strumming a melody I've never heard before.

I open the door quietly and sit out of sight, in the shadows. I watch my uncle play guitar, and it's nothing like all the videos I've seen, nothing like the angry snarling rock star with greasy hair in his eyes. It's a side of Caleb I only vaguely remember from when I was a kid, one I'd occasionally get glimpses of when no one else was looking. The Caleb I see now is someone without his usual wall of rage, someone exposed, someone vulnerable. He is not performing. His only audience is his dolls, all turned toward him, leaning forward, their button eyes glistening. I swear I see one of them blink.

He starts singing, his voice soft, some weird, dark story about a mad scientist experimenting on dead bodies, dissecting them, lining up their organs on a chrome table in a basement lab, creating order out of their blood and chaos. Even though the words are so morbid, the melody is beautiful. The combination of those opposites is haunting, and somehow perfect.

Caleb closes his eyes as he sings the last verse:

The dead bodies,

so willing to do what they're told.

You know them so well.

Your skin's as cold as theirs.

And they sing to you.

They are perfect lovers.

They say thank you

As you tear them apart.

They sing, "Please don't put me back in the freezer.

I'm not nearly through.

There's still pieces of me that resemble something alive.

And I'm not gone yet.

I'm not gone yet.

And you're not gone yet too."

The dolls perk up, as if cued, as if Caleb's voice has given them life, as if he has conjured them to serve him. They start to dance, their bodies swaying back and forth in time to the music, like puppets being controlled with invisible strings. Then they join in with a startlingly cheerful chorus of "do-do-do"s with the pure, innocent voices of a prepubescent children's choir. They bob their heads in rhythm, as if this is any old pop song, as if it can be reduced to the hook of a chorus. Somewhere inside, I know this is shocking, that there's no good reason Caleb's creations should be dancing and singing, but there's no good reason for a lot of things that have been happening lately, and I think maybe I'm getting used to it, and quite frankly the dolls' singing is not the singing that surprises me the most.

The timid glow of an outdoor streetlight seeps through the single window and washes over Caleb like the softest of spotlights. I can't tell if it's the mad scientist or the dead bodies Caleb identifies with. Or maybe he is both.

When the song is over, Caleb looks up, right at me, like he already knew I was here. The dolls turn in my direction and cock their heads curiously.

"I came to get your bucket," I say. Caleb nods.

The dolls watch me as I walk across the room and into the shadowed corner. I remind myself that all these visits to the attic are just business transactions now. I am getting paid for this. I am Caleb's employee. He's paying me to keep his secret, and that's the only reason I'm doing it. I don't care one way or another if he leaves or gets taken away.

I made the mistake of thinking this relationship was something more. I forgot what the therapy talk shows taught me about unrealistic expectations, about those foolish hopes that will only ever lead to disappointment.

Better to not expect anything. That's my new motto.

I've perfected the art of picking the bucket up by the handle and carrying it down to the bathroom with my head turned, so I never have to look at the contents, and the smells that reach my nose are kept to a minimum. After I dump it, I come back upstairs and place it back in its spot. As I walk toward the stairs, I hear Caleb's voice: "Thank you."

For what? Emptying the bucket? For the guitar? For the food and weed and running his errands? It's certainly not an apology, but it's something. Some tiny drop to fill the hole of hurt inside me. I feel a lightening of my heart, a momentary bliss, a relief of pain, but then, as quickly as it came, the nice feeling is gone, and I am left empty again.

Thank you. Sorry. Such simple, nothing words. They come out of most people's mouths like air. But for me, never from anyone who's mattered. I can't remember Grandma ever apologizing or telling me thank you for anything.

What kind of life is one built on chasing thank-yous? They don't fill the hole inside my chest. It seems ridiculous, but I think I've always sort of believed that I could collect people's needs and store them inside me like some kind of permanent collection, like a museum, and I could fill the hole bit by bit, good deed by good deed, until I filled myself all the way up. I thought I could do that with Lydia. I thought I could do that with Caleb, and Grandma, too. But no one ever needs me as much as I need them.

"You're welcome," I say, and head back downstairs.

The hole inside me does not have solid walls. It's more like a mesh bag. And people are mostly water; they seep right through. They need and want and take and take, and at the end of the day, no matter what I do, I'm alone with myself, emptied out all over again.

LYDIA

POOR KIDS IN CARTHAGE AND ROME DON'T HAVE A LOT of options for places to hang out during the coldest winter on record. The movie theater, bowling alley, and coffee shops all cost money, and there's no way in hell Billy and I are going to wander around BigMart or the mall with the rest of the zombies. Anywhere outside is out of the question because right now it's approximately seven degrees Fahrenheit with the windchill factor. Gusts of ice crystals are forming over the ocean, then blowing inward at almost tornado speeds like tiny sparkling knives, slicing winter coats and exposed skin, drawing pinpricks of blood. The only indoor options that don't cost any money are people's houses, and Billy's house is off-limits for obvious reasons, so that leaves no other option but Larry's bar.

I'm sitting next to Billy at what has become more or less the official kids' section of the bar. He's nursing his Shirley Temple while I munch on a microwaved egg roll. The usual handful of guys is here. Even though it's well into January, there's still a small plastic Christmas tree in the corner, decorated with Unicorns vs. Dragons–themed ornaments. A sad single strand of multicolored Christmas lights droops over the bar.

Larry and I haven't talked about Mom's picture, of course. I cleaned up the broken glass, bought a new frame at BigMart that was identical to the old one, and hung the picture over the same slightly darker, unfaded rectangle on the wall where the paint had been covered for years. It's like nothing ever happened.

"How's practice going with what's her name?" Billy says flatly. His skin has taken on a slightly gray, zombielike tinge.

"Good," I say. "She's cool." I can't help smiling. Both at the thought of my last few practices with Natalie, and at Billy's fake forgetting what her name is.

"I never heard you call anyone cool," he grumbles into his pink soda. "I thought you said she was a stuck-up ballerina."

"Yeah, well, maybe I was wrong."

"I never heard you say that, either."

I look at the TV, but I'm not really interested in the news report about the King's new logging robots getting smashed in the forest. I can feel Billy staring at me, wanting answers, wanting me to let him into this part of my life that he's not a part of. Maybe I'm being mysterious on purpose. Maybe I don't want to let him in. Maybe, at least for now, I want to keep Natalie just for myself.

I look at Billy and now he's slumped over, his face in his hands. "Dude, are you *crying*?" I say.

"No," he says, lifting his head and wiping his eyes on his sleeve.

"Seriously, though. Are you okay?"

"I'm just feeling a little emotional lately," Billy says. "How long do you think it takes for someone to get permanent brain damage from lack of sleep?"

Something inside me constricts, makes me want to pull away, as if whatever Billy's going through is contagious and I don't want to catch it.

I feel a sharp pain in my calf. I look down and see the little girl crouched below me with a devilish look on her face, her fingers in pinching formation. She's been doing this lately, taunting me when other people are around, like she wants me to lose my shit in public. "Stop it!" I say without thinking.

"What?" Billy says, looking more hurt than ever.

"Nothing," I say. "My muscles were cramping."

"You talk to your muscles?"

"It's a dancer thing."

Billy sighs dramatically and buries his face back in his hands.

I fidget in my seat, look at him for a moment, then away. I open my mouth, then close it. Finally I say, "Do you want to talk about it?"

"There's nothing to talk about."

I look at Billy for a while. What happened to the guy who was always happy, who stayed positive no matter what? I'm kind of missing that guy right now, as delusional as he was sometimes. There must be a balance, something between blind optimism and hopeless despair.

Before I have a chance to say anything, Larry yells from the other end of the bar, "Hey, Billy. I've been meaning to talk to you. I'm thinking about contacting your granny about partnering on some tours. I have a vision for a combination Rainy Day Knife Fight and Unicorns vs. Dragons Carthage and Rome tour. People will love it! I think we could get it off the ground in time for the Unicorns vs. Dragons festival. You know about the festival, don't you?"

"Who doesn't?" Billy says.

"Oh God," I moan. Now is so not the time, Larry.

"This is the first annual," Larry says proudly. "I helped the Carthage Merchants' Association plan it. I was on the *committee*. Did I tell you about the attraction I'm going to build? I need to dig some holes in the back, but the ground's too frozen."

"We could help you," Billy offers. "Right, Lydia?"

"I'm going to kill you."

The TV is showing grainy pictures caught by a security camera at one of the King's logging sites. Blurred giant figures—some black, some white—dash around in the dark of night. It almost looks like they're herding the robots together.

"Don't be too disappointed if she's not interested, Larry," Billy says. "My grandma's not really a team player."

There's a huge burst of fire on the screen, then it turns to black with the caption VIDEO CAMERAS DESTROYED. The screen cuts to the newscasters' professionally blank faces. "The culprits behind the destruction of the equipment are still on the loose, and investigators so far have no leads. Sources say Royal Industries' losses are already in the tens of millions and that the King intends to reevaluate the company's plans in the region. This could be good news for local businesses and workers who were hoping to capitalize on the opening of the forests to logging."

"Those weren't no people on that video," says a guy at the bar.

"It's that Sasquatch again, I'm telling you," says another guy. "He's pissed. And now he's got friends helping him."

The unicorns and dragons in the posters hung around the bar seem to be laughing.

"Billy, I'm getting kind of worried about you," I say.

"I'm fine," he says, sucking on an ice cube. "I just need some sleep, that's all."

All of a sudden Old Pete emits a wet snort from his booth. The moss in his beard has thickened and spread all over his face and head. Only a small oval containing his eyes, nose, and mouth is still skin. "The most humane way to cook crabs," Old Pete mumbles, "is to chill them first. You gotta lower their body temperatures slowly so they get numb and drowsy. Then they won't feel it when you spike them in the head."

I shiver. I think that's the most I've ever heard him speak, and I've known him most of my life. It's nonsense of course, but it feels important.

"Just drink your beer, old man," says one of the guys at the bar.

Larry slides two new bright pink Shirley Temples in front of Billy and me. "With double cherries," he says with a wink.

"How festive," I say, rubbing the rim of the glass clean with my fingers.

Billy looks at the TV, his eyes blank, momentarily distracted from his feelings by what's on the screen. He needs something and I don't know what it is, or how to give it, or if it is even mine to give. What are you supposed to do when someone says they're fine but you know they're not? I'm so used to him being transparent, telling me every little thing that goes through his head. He's not the one who's supposed to brood and hold things in. That's my job.

There's a part of me that wants to say, "Fuck it," that doesn't want to deal with his feelings, that only wants mine to matter. It's the part of me that's shaped like my mother.

Why is this shit so hard? Does anyone know what they're doing, or is everybody faking it?

The little girl is sitting on the counter now, between me and the TV screen, forcing me to look at her. "Really?" I say. One of the old guys at the bar looks at me like I'm nuts, but I don't care. Why can't she just talk? Why can't she just tell me what she wants? Why does she have to be so goddamned passive-aggressive?

I could say something right now, could ask Billy to tell me more. But I don't. I just let him sit there and watch TV. Because maybe this, whatever this is that Billy's going through, is something he needs to do alone. Maybe my job as his friend is to let him.

The girl smiles at me mockingly, digs her finger inside her nose, and then sticks it in my drink.

I look over at Billy, and he's fallen asleep sitting up.

After I get back from dropping Billy off at home, I hurry into my studio. But something feels off. Something is missing.

I try not to think of Billy as I do a quick warm-up. I try to ignore the little girl darting around the room like a kid who ate too much sugar. But the more I try to ignore her, the angrier I get.

"You're useless," I tell her. "All you do is get in the way." I want the cruel words to make me feel better. I want to hurl my pain onto her. But as she cowers in the corner, I just hate both of us even more.

I take a deep breath. Too much thinking. I cue the music and move to the middle of my spliced-together dance floor to practice the ballet choreography Mary's been building over the last few classes. I focus on my turnout and force myself into the unnatural shapes ballet requires, these torture devices disguised as beauty.

I imagine myself as a hollow-boned bird, light as air, a girl who is empty, waiting to be filled with whatever role I am supposed to play. I try to imagine myself as a ballerina, as someone pretty and perfect and pure. I try to feel the magic Natalie says she feels.

But I am not like Natalie. I am a dancer who hunches her shoulders. I am a dancer with no goddamned turnout. I am a dancer who rolls on the ground, barefoot, sweat-drenched and covered with bruises. I am not pretty or perfect or pure.

I stop dancing. I stand completely still as I listen to the rest of the classical piece playing on my cheap speakers, the soaring violins and flute and piano. I have no idea what this music is supposed to make me feel. Does this music even have a story? It's a soundtrack to lives that are nothing like mine.

I pull off my ballet slippers and change the music to something loud and fast. I throw my body around the room, and the little girl follows me. Fuck my turnout. Fuck the French lexicon. Fuck Billy and fuck Larry and fuck my mom and fuck that little girl who won't leave me the fuck alone.

I try to find the anger, the rage I use like fuel. But something heavier has taken its place and it's weighing me down, throwing me off, messing with my balance. Rage, I can deal with. Anger, I can use. But not this, whatever it is. Not this feeling like a tiny hand squeezing the blood out of my heart.

I use my reflection in the mirror to spot a series of turns. I laser my focus on the image of my own eyes. I turn once. I turn twice. But the third time I whip around, my eyes are no longer there. I am staring into nothing, not even a reflection of the wall behind me, not even black. Just nothing. Just the absence of myself.

I have no breath. The wind has been knocked out of me from the inside. I am sobbing, gasping for air. I reach for my throat, but nothing's there.

The whole room is empty. It's the Halloween fire all over again. The world has disappeared and I'm in a vacuum and the only thing I can see is the little girl cowering in front of me, long black hair cascading over her shoulders, skinny brown arms wrapped around pink-covered legs, the tights never designed to match skin like ours.

Alone. Totally alone. A whole world between us and everyone else.

I look away. This is too much. I don't want to see this, don't want to see *her*. I don't want to care. Why can't I just dance this away? Why can't this be enough anymore?

"I hate you!" I scream. "Leave me alone!"

These are not my words. This is not my voice.

Everywhere I turn, the girl is still there, daring me to look at her. "What the fuck do you want?" I scream at the mirror.

The girl looks up, face streaked with tears. She makes no sound when she speaks, but the word painted on her lips is undeniable: *help*.

My muscles give out. I am not strong enough to fight this. I surrender. I let go.

My sobs shake the rickety room. They make the earth move. They make the one place in the world where I feel safe fall apart.

Is this the big earthquake we've been warned about for years? Will it tear the Olympic Peninsula off the rest of the state and send us drifting out into the ocean? Or have I caught what Billy has? Is my home going to drive me to madness? Is this the end of what little I have left that makes sense?

As the room shakes, the mirror fragments I glue-gunned and bracketed on the walls start shattering around me. The duct tape holding the particleboard floor together splits, and the boards buckle and shift like tectonic plates. I back into the corner, arms covering my head from the glass raining down, while everything I worked so hard to build is destroyed.

I am the shattered glass on the floor. I am the puzzle with too many pieces missing.

Then I feel the warm imprint of a smaller back leaning against mine, the birdlike spine fitting into the grooves of my own. We are two pieces fused together, two pieces that fit nowhere else, holding each other up while the world crumbles around us.

And there we sit until the room stops shaking, waiting for the stillness after the storm when everything is broken and done, when there is only one set of choices: give up or build something new.

BILLY

IT'S CLOSE TO MIDNIGHT AND GRANDMA STILL ISN'T
home. I've been calling her phone all night, but she won't pick up.
She doesn't exactly have an active nightlife, so this is totally out of
character. She's never stayed out this late.

I'm trying not to panic, but I'm not really in the optimal condition for staying calm. I can't remember the last time I had a decent
night's sleep. All these thoughts keep banging around in my brain,
spiraling down faster and faster and faster, and now Grandma's
missing, and when I turned on the AA channel, Lynn A. wasn't in
her usual seat by the coffee maker. She wasn't anywhere. I stared at
her empty seat for a long time, waiting for her to come back from
the bathroom or something, but the screen just cut to a new shot
of a poster with a message in bold cursive writing, YOU'RE ONLY AS
SICK AS YOUR SECRETS, which is pretty much the understatement of
the year.

These things happen sometimes. People have lives. Maybe
Grandma went out with her chain-smoking old lady friends and
didn't bother to call home, which would totally make sense since we
leave the phone off the hook most of the time these days to avoid
all the people asking questions about Caleb, and Grandma probably

wouldn't call even if the phone was on. Maybe Lynn A. had family business somewhere. Maybe she's in an airplane right now, flying to some city where she has a grown-up kid with a brand-new baby waiting to meet their grandma.

I look at the painting on the wall of my bedroom. It has changed from the beautiful hypnotic swirl to something darker, more black than blue now, faster and more violent than before, like an out-of-control tornado that wants to destroy everything in its path. The throbbing center is no longer warm and inviting. It's too hot. The pull is stronger. It wants to suck me in and burn me up.

Things aren't going well. Not only am I sleep deprived, not only are Grandma and Lynn A. missing, and not only is tomorrow Monday, meaning the usual problem of having to go to school, there is also now the additional problem of my only winter coat, which wasn't that warm to begin with, having a huge hole in it after being slashed open by a splintered board that shot out of the wall right as I walked by, barely missing my body. By the time I get to school tomorrow morning, I'll be an icicle. If the house doesn't kill me first.

I know I could buy myself a new coat. Ever since Caleb started paying me to run his errands, buying things is a strange new freedom I haven't quite accepted. Nearly all of my money, besides the large chunk I set aside to secretly pay for Lydia's dance classes, is still wadded up in a shoebox under my bed. The last time I counted, I had over sixteen hundred dollars, and my hands itched the whole time I was handling the cash and I swear I had heart palpitations, like I'm allergic to it or something.

Lying in bed now, I feel uncomfortable just thinking about it. I've heard of money burning a hole in people's pockets, but is it possible to burn holes in people's beds? Could it spontaneously combust under there and set the bed on fire right under me? Am I sleeping on top of a fire hazard? Despite the fact that I'm freezing, being burned alive is not an appealing proposition.

For some reason, I cannot bring myself to spend the money. *My* money. There's never been such a thing as "my money."

I've run to the store daily, sometimes multiple times a day, for whatever Caleb's requested. I've cleaned bucket after bucket of piss and shit. I've endured Caleb's insults and bad moods. I've kept an entire person a secret and bought illegal drugs, for Pete's sake. But somehow none of that is enough to convince me I deserve a ten-dollar secondhand coat so I don't freeze to death walking to school in the middle of the coldest January ever recorded in Fog Harbor.

But worse than possibly freezing to death is the fact that I'm pretty sure Lydia is sick of me. It was bound to happen, I guess. She found someone better to replace me. Natalie and Lydia certainly have more in common than we do. What do I even have to offer? Right now the only thing about me that's useful to Lydia is my money, and she doesn't even know it exists.

Maybe now is the right time to tell her it's me paying for her dance classes. Maybe that would bring her back to me. Maybe that would convince her I'm worth keeping.

Whatever's in the wall keeps moaning, and it won't shut up. The wind won't shut up. My mind won't shut up. The tornado keeps spinning, and nothing can stop it.

I'm getting so tired of keeping secrets. When you think about it, is there really a difference between a secret and a lie?

But if I told her, it could backfire so incredibly bad. I didn't really think that part through. The problem with trying to save people is, what if they don't want to be saved? If she finds out, she might hate me forever. And that's way worse than losing someone because they just get tired of you.

Maybe I never should have paid for those classes. Then Lydia would still be miserable and bored and mine.

I am a horrible person.

I have to focus on the positive. Why is it getting so hard to focus on the positive?

I'm so tired.

Where is Grandma? Where is Lynn A.?

I keep forgetting what I've learned from the therapy talk shows. The solution to my feelings right now is that I need to adjust my expectations. I must try not to be so attached. I knew my friendship with Lydia was too good to be true, but I got too comfortable, I got used to it, as if it would always be there. I've been so stupid. I, of all people, should know that no one sticks around forever.

I have to let Lydia go. That's the only way I'm going to survive losing her.

I don't know how my brain fits all these thoughts in it without exploding.

I want to sleep. I can't sleep.

The room shakes and the glowing center of the painting flares and I feel my skin burning for a split second as I fight the pull of gravity that wants to slam me against the wall, and then I'm more freezing than I was to begin with.

I know Caleb's still awake. Maybe talking to someone will help me stop thinking, even if it's someone who doesn't want me around. Maybe I should tell him about Grandma going missing. Maybe I should tell him about the detectives.

Or maybe I should tell him I love his new music. Maybe what Caleb needs is encouragement. Maybe I can help him.

Suddenly, I don't feel so cold.

I creep up the stairs in my pajamas, preparing what I'm going to say. *I've been listening to you playing music.* No. *I've heard the music you've been playing.* No. *I overheard you playing music, and I think it's brilliant.*

Then another little voice pipes up out of nowhere: *please love me.*

I shake my head, trying to dislodge the voice. But the echo is still bouncing around my skull, louder than all the other noises. I feel embarrassed already, and I haven't even done anything yet.

I knock lightly on Caleb's door and hear nothing. Maybe he's asleep for a change. I open the door slowly, but it stops at some kind of obstruction. I have to put all my weight behind my push to get the door open enough to let me in.

The first thing I notice in the attic is the heavy pile of blankets in front of the door. The room is dark, lit only by the glow of the streetlight coming through the window. There are blankets everywhere, in haphazard lumps all over the floor, as if a storm came through and ripped Caleb's nest apart. The guitar and creepy dolls are all safely huddled in one corner, but everything else—the broken lawn chairs, the cheap wooden bedside table, the lamp, Caleb's growing library, even Caleb's computer—are thrown around the room, like the attic became that stage where Caleb had his meltdown, where he lost his shit and became a tornado with the whole world watching.

"Caleb?" I say softly.

"Mmrrghmm," says a voice from a dark corner. Caleb's pale bare feet stick out of the shadows. He is lying belly-down on the floor, his eyes closed. I see an almost-empty bag of weed next to him, which I know was full just this morning because I had to go to Gordon's house in the middle of fog so thick I got lost, even though it's five blocks away in a neighborhood I've lived in my whole life, and when I got there Gordon was eating a frozen pizza that was still frozen, which he proudly called a "breakfast Popsicle."

Can someone die of a marijuana overdose?

"Caleb," I say, gently prodding his shoulder.

"Mmrrghmm," Caleb says again, rolling onto his side.

"What happened?"

His eyes open into narrow slits. He coughs. "Let me sleep," he says, his voice rough.

"You broke your computer."

Caleb's eyes open a little more. He stares at me. "Why'd you pick such an easy fucking password?"

"What?"

Caleb manages to prop himself up on his elbow. "*Sarah?* Really?"

After Caleb accidentally checked his e-mail a few weeks ago, he made me block a bunch of websites and search terms and change the system admin password to something he "could never guess." He gave me the responsibility of protecting him from the world. And I failed.

"Fucking stupid," Caleb spits as he lies back down, his eyes closed again.

Fucking stupid.

It's Grandma's voice. I am so sick of Grandma's voice. I am sick of everybody telling me who I am and who I'm not. I'm sleep deprived and I'm pissed off and I've lost my patience with everyone.

And I'm not fucking stupid.

I stare at my uncle's face in the dark, so stoned he can't even open his eyes. The dolls watch us, Caleb's loyal audience. I hear a familiar voice inside me, the one that wants to say *I'm sorry* over and over again until I can be sure Caleb stops hating me, at least temporarily, the part of me so eager to take all the blame, to give and give until it hurts, and then keep giving some more, because that's all I know how to do. Even then, after I've given everything, it's never enough. But the voice still says *I'm sorry*, as if doing and saying the same things the same way will somehow get different results. *I'm sorry.* As if apologizing for my existence is some twisted way to earn it.

But there's a new, different voice beneath the *I'm sorry*, one I don't remember ever hearing, one that knows I have absolutely nothing to be sorry about.

"I'm not responsible for your Internet searches," I say. The dolls perk up. I can hear them shuffling behind me.

"You were supposed to do one thing, and you fucked it up," Caleb says. "You can't even choose a password right."

"I can't protect you from yourself," I say. The dolls titter amongst themselves.

"You have to get me some dope," Caleb says. "Gordon won't have it, but he'll know who does."

"Are you kidding me?"

"Then I just need some tinfoil."

"No," I say. "Get up."

"Huh?"

"I said get up. You can't lie there on the floor forever. It's time for you to get your shit together."

But I know Caleb isn't getting up anytime soon. He can barely even open his eyes.

"So you know the plan, right?" Caleb says. "Ask Gordon where to get some dope."

"Did you even hear me? I said no. I'm not going to help you kill yourself. If you want heroin, you can leave this attic and get it yourself. I'm done."

Caleb says nothing. He just looks at me through the thin slits of his eyes, like he has no idea how this stranger found his hiding spot.

"I'm done with all of it," I say, a fire rising, burning away a layer of sludge inside me I didn't even know was there. "No more weed. No more emptying your bucket. None of it. You can come downstairs and do it yourself. I'm not your servant. I quit."

Is this what the house has wanted all along? Was the point of all my sleep deprivation to make me so unstable that I'd finally lose my temper? Is this why it's been torturing me, like how the military tortures prisoners until they tell the truth? Is this the truth?

"But I need you," Caleb says weakly.

Something squeezes inside me. For a moment, I want to take it all back. I look at Caleb's bare feet. How is he not freezing? He needs a blanket. There are so many blankets.

But there is something solid inside me, and that place says, "I can't save you."

A gust of wind shakes the house, nearly knocking me over. Something creaks and groans from deep inside, then the sound of breaking, splitting open. The attic is no longer immune to the rest of the house's madness. Something in the foundation has shattered.

And then Caleb starts crying. He pulls his thin body into a ball and lies in the shadows, wracked with silent sobs. I cannot see the details of his face, but I see the faint light from outside reflected in wet streaks down his cheeks. I see his teeth shining, and for some reason it makes me think of a documentary we watched together about an ancient city destroyed by a volcano, of mummified human remains caught in volcanic ash, everything scorched and preserved black, except the teeth still glistening white, like no one told them they were supposed to be dead too.

I lean down and put my hand on Caleb's trembling shoulder. I can say no and still love him.

But then he reaches his arm out and pushes me so hard I fall down.

Animals hide when they are wounded. They snarl at anyone who comes near.

I stand back up. I rub the sore spot on my butt, where I know I will have a bruise. My head is strangely clear as I walk downstairs, pull my wallet out of my backpack, and take out Caleb's ATM card. Caleb is raging on the floor when I return, now wailing so loud I worry for a moment that Grandma might hear him. But then I remember she's not here. And even if she were, I don't care. Let Grandma hear him. Let all those people camped outside hear him. It is not my job to worry about Caleb anymore.

I throw Caleb's card, and it lands next to him on the floor. He opens his eyes for a brief moment, looks at me with a split-second of focus, confused, like he doesn't know how he got here, like he doesn't even know who I am.

"I don't want your money anymore," I tell him.

Then I lift a blanket off the floor and cover Caleb's feet. I walk away. I go downstairs, to my room with the growing hole in the wall and the unseen creatures who live inside and never shut up and the painting with the black hole that I almost want to jump into. I lie on my bed and have never felt so heavy in my life, and my eyelids close, and I couldn't open them even if I wanted to.

I wake up around five in the morning, after almost four hours of sleep, the longest stretch I've gotten in weeks, to the sound of the front door slamming shut and the whole house shaking. "Grandma?" I shout as I hop out of bed. I run into the living room just in time to see her plop down on the couch, a cloud of dust exploding around her.

"Where were you?" I say.

"I'm in no mood to talk right now," she says with a raspy voice, hoisting her legs onto the couch, turning on the TV, and pulling a blanket up to her chin.

"Are you okay?"

"Do I look okay?" she snaps.

"Um, yes?" I say. "I mean, no? I don't know."

"Dammit, Billy," she sighs. "I was in the slammer all night."

Did she really just say "slammer"?

"You were in *jail*?"

"Damn police will think twice next time they try to come into my place of work," she grumbles, clicking through the channels.

"What did you do?"

"Since when is asking someone to leave 'assaulting an officer'?"

"Grandma, what did you do?"

"And since when is a broom a 'deadly weapon'?"

"What?"

"Everything's fine," she says. "They let me go when they realized I knew nothing about Caleb. Everyone wants to be the one who catches him. Well, they're barking up the wrong tree."

"Don't you want them to find him?"

She stops clicking through the channels. She looks at me, and I think I see a glimmer of something un-Grandma-like in her eyes, something maybe sad, something maybe a night without sleep in jail uncovered.

"Caleb's gone, Billy," she says, her voice cracking a little, maybe from a night spent yelling at cops, but maybe also from emotion, maybe because she misses her son and is ready to make amends like Lynn A. is always talking about.

"But what if he isn't?" I say. "What if he's here somewhere?"

This could all be over with just a few simple words. This is when I tell her that her son is sleeping two floors above her head. She's finally ready and I'm finally ready and maybe she can help him too, and maybe I won't have to hold this all by myself.

But in a split second, what opened in Grandma's face closes down once again, and her eyes turn mean. "If he's anywhere around here, you can bet your ass I'll find a way to make a dollar off him."

She turns the TV to the twenty-four-hour commercial channel and says, "Scram, Billy. I need to rest." And then her eyes close, and she starts snoring, and just like that she's fast asleep.

I stand there for a few moments just staring at her. How can she just decide not to care? How can she sleep so easily? How do Grandma and I even share the same blood? How can we live in this same house but I'm the only one it's hurting?

I go to my room and get dressed for school. Everything's completely upside down, but I can't think of anything else to do but go through the motions of my normal life. I'll get to school way too early, but the good news is I won't miss free breakfast.

LYDIA

IT'S SO COLD THIS MORNING THAT I'M FORCED TO GET over my embarrassment about Larry's van and drive to school because I'm pretty sure I'd freeze to death during the couple of minutes it'd take to wait for the bus. If I'm lucky, the van will get covered in ice so nobody can see what's painted on the side.

Things at school are tenser than ever. The King announced early this morning that the forests around Fog Harbor would once again be off-limits to logging after all his equipment was destroyed because, in his own words, "If I can't have it, no one can." Three fights break out by lunchtime. One kid has to go to the hospital for a broken nose after getting punched by a kid he accused of being an environmental terrorist for having a peace sign bumper sticker on his car. Apparently, everyone becomes a suspect for causing your misery when there's exactly jack shit you can do about it.

"What's wrong?" I ask Billy in Miscellaneous Science. It seems like that's been the bulk of our conversations lately. He's lying on his desk with his face turned away from me, watching the freezing rain fall outside the window and coat the ground with ice. "You barely talked at lunch," I say.

"I'm just tired," he says.

"At some point you don't get to use that excuse anymore, you know."

"Anything you'd like to share with the class?" Mr. Mosley says from the front of the room, interrupting his lecture about ionic bonds.

"Sorry," Billy says.

He told me a little about what happened last night, about how his grandma spent the evening in jail, how Caleb asked for heroin, how he cried like a baby when Billy said no. When I said, "I'm proud of you for standing up to him," I meant it as a compliment, but Billy did not seem to take it that way.

"If it was such a good idea," Billy said, "why does it feel like such crap?"

"I don't know. Maybe because sometimes doing the right thing is hard."

"Now who sounds like a therapy talk show?" he replied, with a new bitter edge to his voice.

"You seem angry," I said.

"I don't get angry."

"Maybe you should."

"Don't tell me what to feel."

The rest of lunch was pretty much silent after that. If we had fancy phones to stare at, that's probably what we would have been doing. My little girl companion sat with us at the lunch table, but she was kicking my leg the whole time. I just sat there, getting angrier and angrier, at her for kicking me, and at the fact that I couldn't do a thing about it. When she slammed her foot straight into my ankle, it sent a lightning bolt of pain up my leg, and I erupted before I could stop myself. "Fucking stop it!" I yelled, and Billy looked at me like I broke his heart. "My leg again," I said. "Cramps." And he just sighed and looked down at his lunch tray, and Kayla or Kaitlyn or Katelyn muttered, "Crazy bitch," as she walked by and bumped me in the back with her hip, and it took all my strength not to turn around and tackle her. If I don't get a handle on this soon, it's good-bye, dance career, hello, mental institution.

As Mr. Mosley drones on about electrons, I look at the back of Billy's head and feel guilty. He's the friend who needs me most, so it's him I should be thinking about, but my thoughts keep drifting to Natalie. Does her car have four-wheel drive? Will she be safe driving the steep hills to her house with all the ice on the road?

How do people manage having more than one friend?

The intercom crackles. Everyone looks toward the ancient speaker in the ceiling. Even Mr. Mosley seems relieved to get a break from his boring lecture. But then three alarms ring in quick succession. I know this means something important, but I can't remember what. Whatever it is, it's bad. Billy sits up. We lock eyes.

"Please remain calm, students," the principal says over the intercom. "We need to vacate the school immediately. Teachers, please lead your students to the off-campus safety meeting location in an orderly fashion."

This is not a drill. Nervous echoes of "What's happening?" fill the room. Even Mr. Mosley looks spooked. "Come on, everyone. You heard Principal Bensen. Leave your things and form a line immediately."

Only Billy and I think to put our coats on. The other students leave their belongings—coats, hats, books, backpacks—everything except their phones. Nobody leaves those. They're already texting their friends, already posting on their social media accounts, swapping theories about what the emergency is. Some people are even talking to each other in person with their actual voices.

Consensus seems to be there was a bomb threat. Even the teachers are pretty certain. It was inevitable, really. This is how wars escalate. First some angry words and tripping people in the halls. Then fistfights and broken noses and throwing people into tornado pits. Then mass annihilation.

Outside, ice crystals shoot from the sky almost violently, as if they have volition, as if they want to hurt people. I pull Billy with me in the opposite direction. Luckily the path to the senior parking lot is covered most of the way, but Billy's hair still gets turned into blond icicles, mine into little black spikes. The door of the van is frozen shut, but after a few good kicks I'm able to get it open. Billy and I huddle inside, the heat on full blast. The little girl comes out of nowhere and jumps into my lap, her bony butt drilling into my thigh. I flinch and Billy looks at me funny, but what's new?

After a few minutes, the ice on the front window melts away, and we have a perfect view of the parade of students and teachers making their way through the ice storm. They're covering their faces as best as they can, but the ice freezes their fingers in place, a hard, translucent shell in front of eyes, noses, and mouths, leaving just a small melted hole at the nostrils for air to go in and out. The only things that don't freeze are the body parts in motion, the legs moving the lines of students forward, across the street to an abandoned empty lot. But once still, the ice is able to accumulate in earnest. Within a few minutes, the entire student body and teachers of Fog Harbor High School have been turned into frozen sculptures, solid and completely immobile, many with their phones in front of their faces, the screens glowing eerily through the coating of ice.

"Zombies," I say from the warmth of Larry's van. "Nobody knows all they have to do is move to get free."

A whole fleet of police cars arrives, sirens blaring, bumping into each other as they attempt to park on the ice. Flashing red lights reflect off the sparkling students like a surreal heartbeat.

"Do you think they're in pain?" Billy says.

"Nah," I say. "They're numb. They can't feel a thing."

We drive past the lines of our classmates—shiny, still, and glistening white. How easy it would be to just tip them over.

"I've never skipped class before," Billy says.

"Don't worry," I say. "I'm pretty sure school is canceled for the rest of the day."

It's not easy to drive on sheets of ice with an invisible nine-year-old on my lap, but I manage not to hit anything, even with her tugging at the steering wheel trying to drive us off the road. Luckily, the streets are entirely empty. No one in their right mind is driving right now.

I don't realize I'm driving to Billy's house until I pull up in front. Covered with ice, it almost looks pretty, like an intricate ice sculpture. There are all kinds of vans and campers parked on the block that weren't here before.

For some reason, I'm waiting for Billy to make the first move to get out. But he just sits there, looking into the white glassy nothing in front of him, like he's as frozen as all the classmates we left behind in the cold.

"Should we go in?" I say.

"I guess." He doesn't move.

"Are you going to check on Caleb?" I say.

Billy stares ahead, silent, into the sheet of ice accumulating on the window. "No," he finally says. "He can come down if he wants to. For all I know, he's already frozen in a ditch somewhere."

"Jesus, Billy."

He sighs. "Do you think Gordon has some sleeping pills?"

"Stop it," I say. "Just fucking stop. We're going inside, okay? We're going to sit on the couch and eat junk food and watch TV like normal people."

He sighs again. "Okay."

It takes several kicks to break the ice and open the car door. We have to take tiny steps to Billy's front door to avoid slipping. I cover my face with my gloved hands, but Billy just lets his skin get pelted with the ice flying at him like shards of shattered glass. By the time we get inside, he has little beads of blood all over his face. My coat narrowly escapes being slashed by a board sticking out of the wall of the entryway.

Even inside, we can still see our breath. We keep our coats on as we sit on the couch and Billy starts surfing channels. I pick up the half-eaten bag of cheese puffs on the coffee table and offer it to him. The little girl is in the corner, playing with a dust bunny.

Billy shoves a handful of cheese puffs into his mouth and lands on a flashing BREAKING NEWS logo superimposed over a photo of Caleb. He gasps. The screen cuts to reporters in the newsroom: "We interrupt your scheduled programming with breaking news about Caleb Sloat, the legendary and troubled lead singer of Rainy Day Knife Fight, who has been missing for nearly four months and presumed dead by many." The screen cuts to the now infamous video of Caleb's onstage meltdown. "We have just received information from a reliable source that Sloat has been traced to a fraudulent bank account at Sound Bank and Trust, where regular withdrawals have been made from an ATM in Sloat's hometown of Rome, Washington, in the months since his disappearance. We will be working closely with investigators and law enforcement to get to the bottom of things, and of course our viewers will be the first to know any new details."

"Well," says the other reporter, "Fog Harbor is certainly having their time in the limelight lately, aren't they, Steve?"

"Looks like Caleb Sloat may be home again after all."

The newscasters chuckle.

Billy chokes.

His eyes are bulging out of his head. Did a cheese puff get stuck in his throat?

"Billy?" I say, but he doesn't respond, just stares at the TV screen wheezing like he can't get a breath in. I start hitting him on the back. Isn't that what you're supposed to do to a choking person? He keeps gasping for air, so I keep hitting, but it's not working.

I've seen the Heimlich maneuver on TV. It can't be that hard, right? I pull Billy toward me and try to wrap my arms around him, but he keeps swatting them and trying to pull away. "I'm trying to help you!" I say, attempting to catch him in a bear hug from behind.

"Stop!" he shouts.

"You can talk?"

"Why are you attacking me?"

"I thought you were choking."

"I just swallowed wrong," he says, pulling his body as far away from me as he can get on the couch. "Jesus, Lydia."

"Oh," I say. "Sorry."

We sit in awkward silence for three seconds, then simultaneously tilt our heads toward the ceiling.

"What should we do?" I say.

"I don't know."

"He can't stay here."

"I already told him that."

"This is the first place they'll look."

"I don't care."

"We need to hide him."

Billy looks at me in disbelief. "Since when do you care so much about Caleb?"

I'm not really sure how to answer that. I don't think I care about Caleb. I kind of hate the guy. But I wouldn't wish what's coming for him on anyone.

"Let them find him," Billy says. "It doesn't matter."

"But if they find him, they'll destroy him."

"There's nothing left to destroy."

"Oh, come on," I say. "I don't know what's going on with you right now, but it's getting really old."

"You don't get it."

"What don't I get?"

Billy looks sickly in the pale light coming through the windows. It seems to accentuate the dark bags under his eyes. He looks so much like Caleb. "Don't you see?" he says. "I can't help people. Neither can you. We can't make them better. So what's the point of trying? What's the point of caring at all?"

"You sound like an angsty teenager."

"Maybe I am an angsty teenager."

"No," I say. "You're not. That's why I liked you in the first place."

"Well, sorry to disappoint you."

"You sound like me."

"Whatever," he says, looking at the TV. "You're new to this whole caring-about-people thing. You haven't spent your whole life loving people who don't love you back, who just use you up until you have nothing left."

Billy starts flipping channels. I grab the remote out of his hand and throw it across the room even though what I really want to do is throw it at his head.

"Hey!" Billy says. "Grandma will kill me if the remote is broken. She will literally kill me."

"Fuck you, Billy," I say. I want to be angry, but it's something else. I feel the sting of tears in my eyes. "Don't tell me I don't know how to care about people." Billy looks at me like maybe he's sorry, but it's not enough. There is so much I need to say, and I need somebody to hear it.

"I loved my mom," I say. "I loved her so much. She was a fucking asshole most of the time, but I loved her anyway. I couldn't help it. She was my *mom*." I am ugly with tears, with snot. My whole head hurts with the pressure of all the pain that's trying to burst through. Everything hurts.

"I'm sorry," Billy says, looking down at his lap.

"And then she fucking died, and I decided loving people sucked and I wasn't going to do it anymore. And you know what? That was a mistake. I've been completely miserable and alone since then. Until I met you."

Billy looks up at me sheepishly for a moment, then looks away.

"Hating people fucking sucks," I say. "It doesn't punish them. It only punishes you."

He is quiet for a long time. There is so much pain in his face. He looks like he's aged five years in the last few weeks. "Loving them isn't any better," he finally says. "Am I just supposed to let Caleb walk all over me? I should let Grandma boss me around? I should keep being their slave, waiting for them to treat me right someday?"

"That's not what I said. You can love people without letting them use you."

"It's not that easy." Something in his face is shifting. His jaw is getting tight. His eyes are turning mean.

"Love isn't about living people's lives for them," I say. "And it's not about trying to get something in return."

"So what's it about, then? If you're such an expert all of a sudden?"

"I don't know. I really don't. All I know is I hated everyone until I met you. Because you were different. Because you weren't an asshole like everyone else." I look him in the eye. "And now you're being an asshole."

"Maybe I've wasted too much of my life trying not to be an asshole," he says.

"So, what? Now you're going to try to be an asshole?"

"I don't know. Maybe," he mumbles. "Hurt people hurt people."

"What?"

"Just something I heard on a show."

Those damn therapy shows. What a crock of shit. As if a person can get cured of all their dysfunctions in an hour. As if there's some one-size-fits-all solution.

"If you want to waste your time feeling sorry for yourself, go ahead," I say, wiping my face with my sleeve and standing up. "But I'm going to help your uncle."

I stomp up the stairs without waiting to see if Billy's going to join me. The little girl stomps up after me. The truth is, I'm not really sure why I suddenly feel so compelled to help Caleb. I don't even know the guy. What little interaction I've had with him was not good. I certainly don't like the way he's treated Billy. I don't even like his music. But I also know, despite whatever's going on with Billy right now, that he loves Caleb more than he loves anyone in the world. And whatever my impressions of the guy were, however flawed he may be, I believed Billy when he told me Caleb was good. I believe in Billy's love for him. And I believe in defending that love against the coming inevitable hordes of crazed mediocre humans looking for someone to tear apart.

I storm into the attic without knocking. It looks like someone let a horse loose in the Thrift Town bedding section. Caleb's in the corner pissing in a bucket, his skinny white ass peeking over the top of his gray sweatpants. The little girl next to me giggles silently.

"Time to go, Caleb," I say.

"What the fuck!" he shouts, spinning around, pulling up his pants. "What are you doing in here?"

"No time to talk. You can bring whatever you can fit in a milk crate. We have to go now."

"I'm not going anywhere with you."

"Fine," I say. "If you want to stay here and wait for all the reporters and private investigators and random psycho fans who are on their way, that is totally okay with me."

A look of pure terror washes across Caleb's face. "What are you talking about?"

"Someone at the bank sold you out, dude. It's all over the news. Everyone in the world knows you're in Rome."

Caleb reaches out his hand for the nearest wall.

I kick the milk crate in his direction. "I'm giving you, like, two minutes to fill this."

Just then, Billy enters the attic carrying two empty BigMart bags. "Here," he says flatly, letting the bags fall on the floor.

Caleb walks over and picks up the bags. "Thanks, man," he says softly. Billy doesn't meet his eye.

"Pack now," I say. "Feelings later."

I watch as Caleb packs as much of the pile of creepy dolls as he can fit in the grocery bags, and as many of the books as he can fit in the milk crate. Billy stands by the doorway staring at his shoes. The little girl looks out the window, like she's standing guard.

"I'm ready," Caleb says.

"I'm not sure I understand your packing strategy," I say. "But okay. Let's go."

Caleb carries the milk crate and I carry the bags. As we walk to the door, Caleb says, "Billy, will you grab the guitar?"

Billy doesn't move.

"Please?" Caleb adds.

"Come on!" I say, moving quickly down the stairs.

We stop in the hallway outside the front door. Caleb looks around at the house covered with the white film of plaster, at the new cracks in the walls and all the boards sticking out. "What happened?" he says.

"Focus, people," I say. These Sloat boys and their attention problems. "We can't just walk out the door. There are people out there."

"What people?" Caleb says.

"All the superfans parked up and down the street. They've been out there a long time, right, Billy?"

Billy just shrugs.

"What?" Caleb says, terror in his eyes.

"You didn't tell him?" I say.

"Why didn't you tell me?" Caleb says.

"You told me not to."

"We don't have time for this right now," I say. What is wrong with these people? It's like they have no survival instincts. "Billy, does your grandma have a large box somewhere? One big enough to fit Caleb?"

"You're going to put me in a box?" Caleb says.

"Would you rather be thrown to the fans and detectives?" I say.

He doesn't say anything to that.

"Grandma's got a big rubber tub full of a million scented candles," Billy says.

"Go get it."

Caleb and I stand in the hallway awkwardly, not making eye contact, listening to Billy rummaging around upstairs, then a big crash and what sounds like a bucket of rocks rolling around the wood floor overhead. He emerges pushing a giant rubber tub as big as a small bathtub down the stairs.

"Get in," I say. We all look in the tub, flecked with who knows how many years' worth of scented candle wax. Caleb climbs in almost gingerly and huddles into a ball. It's amazing how small people can get when they have to.

Billy secures the lid while I run outside to kick the new layer of ice off the van and open the side door. Larry's just going to have to deal with his beloved airbrush getting chipped. The girl is already inside, pushing buttons she should not be pushing.

"Lift with your legs," I tell Billy as we each take a side of the box.

"Please don't drop me," says Caleb's muffled voice from inside.

We manage to get him to the van despite slipping a couple times on the ice and Billy complaining that his arms are going to break off. I can feel the eyes of the fans huddled in their campers and vans, watching us, wondering if whether what they're seeing is worth getting excited about. But nobody moves, even when Billy runs back into the house and emerges carrying Caleb's meager possessions and the guitar strapped on his back. He could be any teenager moving out to live on his own.

Two news vans pull up in front of the house just as we drive away.

The drive to my place is very slow, very slippery, and very awkward. It's mostly silent, except for Caleb occasionally saying, "Billy, I'm sorry," then a few minutes later, "Dude, I said I'm sorry," while Billy sits stoically in the front seat. Billy took the lid off the box when we were safely a few blocks away, but only after I told him to. Caleb's still sitting in the box, his legs folded to his chest, like he doesn't think he deserves to get comfortable.

The little girl keeps tugging on the steering wheel and pushing down on my feet with hers. "Are you trying to crash us?" I grumble without thinking.

"Sorry," Billy and Caleb say in tandem.

"How is it a good idea to hide a drug addict in a bar?" Billy says as we push a blanket-covered Caleb through the back entrance to my apartment.

"Do you have any better ideas?" I say.

"Let's put him up at the water tower. He loves sleeping there."

"I told you I'm sorry," Caleb's muffled voice says from beneath the blanket.

I unlock the door to my dance studio and flip on the light. The walls are still bare, the floor still torn up and covered with broken glass. I haven't had the nerve to come back in here since everything fell apart.

"What the hell happened in here?" Caleb says.

"Apparently glue doesn't hold mirrors on walls very well," I say.

"You expect me to live in here?" Caleb says.

I turn around and face him. "Are you serious? I just saved you from two news vans, and who knows what else that made it to that house by now. Excuse me if this isn't up to your rock-star standards, but this is how people have been living back here since you've been gone touring the world."

Caleb opens his mouth, but I cut him off before he gets a chance to speak. "Larry never comes in here, but leave the door locked just in case. I'll keep the key. You can still get out if you want to. Seriously, feel free."

Caleb opens his mouth again, but I keep talking. "No way in hell I'm cleaning up your piss and shit. You can use the bathroom like a civilized human being. But not between the hours of two a.m. and noon because Larry might be home. And don't make any noise then either. Unless you want to meet my dad. I'm sure he'd be happy to meet you."

Caleb looks at Billy, but he's still giving him the cold shoulder.

"You can stay here until the end of next Saturday," I continue. "You have less than two weeks. That's it. You need to figure out what you're going to do, because you're out of here whether you figure it out or not. And let me make something clear. I'm not like Billy. I'm not going to baby you. You're a grown-ass man. You should be able to take care of yourself. And if you can't, then it's your job to get professionals to help you, not put that responsibility on a fucking kid. I don't care if you're rich and famous. I think this whole situation is bullshit. I don't like you. I don't like your overrated band's music. I think you're an asshole. I think you took advantage of Billy, who is way too nice for his own good and loves you way more than you deserve."

"Okay," Caleb says, his voice raw, his eyes shining. "You're right." I look at Caleb briefly and our eyes catch, and for a moment I see a glimpse of Billy, some spark in him of something good, something worth saving.

A rush of sadness nearly knocks me over.

But there are things that have to be done. I am all business. I set down the bags full of dolls on the floor inside the studio. I take the crate of books from Caleb and peer inside. "You brought a bunch of creepy-ass dolls and books about Buddhism? You're a weird dude."

I shove a broom that was leaning next to the door at him. "Here. Clean up all that broken glass. Try not to cut yourself. And if you try to commit suicide in my fucking house, I will fucking kill you."

I close the door and lock it. Billy and I stand in my kitchen, not talking, not looking at each other. Something is wrong, but I don't know what, and I don't know whose fault it is. I don't know whose job it is to say *I'm sorry*.

Maybe we're not built for this. Maybe we're so damaged that we're not capable of having healthy relationships.

"Billy?" I say. He doesn't look at me.

No, we can do this. I believe in us.

I open my mouth to say something, but Billy beats me to it: "I think we should take a break."

My heart stops. For a moment, I feel like I'm falling, like gravity has given up on me.

Where is the little girl? Why isn't she here?

"What are you talking about?" I say. My voice is small, birdlike.

"I just need some space to figure some things out."

"Wait, are you *breaking up* with me?" And then the vacuum inside me turns into a black hole. It is heavy and dense. It is violent and wants to suck me in and seize and destroy everything in its path.

"I think I need to be alone," Billy says.

"Are you fucking serious?" I say. There's the familiar feeling. There's the fire to cover up the hurt. "You're pushing *me* away?"

"I'm not pushing you away."

"That's exactly what you're doing and you know it. Can we talk about this?"

"I'm tired of talking."

"No, Billy. We need to talk about this."

"Please!" he says, finally looking at me. Something in his eyes tells me to stop arguing. I can't make him want to talk to me. I can't make him want to try.

"Can you take me home now?" he says.

"Fine," I say.

"Fine," he says.

I can't talk him into loving me.

Outside, caught in the middle of the ice storm, the little girl pounds on the window with her tiny fists, her mouth open in a silent scream.

BILLY

IT'S BEEN THREE DAYS SINCE THE ICE STORM, THREE DAYS since news broke about Caleb's ATM transactions and he moved to Lydia's and we decided to take a break. Or I guess I decided to take a break and she went along with it. I still don't really understand what happened. I stood there in Lydia's broken studio watching her lay down the law with Caleb and make all these rules, and all I could think about was that she's the strongest person I've ever met and why can't I be half as strong as her and how am I ever going to get my shit together if I just follow her around my whole life?

I could have told her all that. I think she would have understood. But I'm so tired of talking. I'm so tired of everything. I'm tired of living in Lydia's shadow, living in Caleb's shadow. I'm tired of being a shadow.

Lynn A. still hasn't come back to the meeting. Why is her trip taking so long? Doesn't she know I need her?

Most of the ice has melted. Rome is swarming with tourists and private investigators and newspeople from all over the world. There was no bomb after all, but school was canceled for one day to give everyone time to thaw out. I started eating lunch with Mrs. Ambrose again, and she spent Wednesday's lunch period telling me all about chakras and crystals and some kind of magic stone egg she bought from her spiritual life coach that she puts in her vagina, which I'm pretty sure is illegal for her to talk to me about. I wanted to tell Lydia about it so bad in Miscellaneous Science, but I didn't. She said hi and I said hi, then I looked out the window for the rest of class, and that was the extent of our conversation.

The crows were waiting for me outside of school yesterday. They followed me all the way home, and then about halfway there, one dive-bombed me. Then a few seconds later, another one did it. Then they all started squawking and wings started flapping and all of a sudden there were a million birds swarming around me, grabbing me with their talons and beaks, like they wanted to carry me away with them. I ran the rest of the way yelling and flapping my arms around trying to swat them off, and by the time I got home my hair was all over the place and I was covered with splatters of bird poop and feathers. And for a split second, I believed it really, truly couldn't get any worse, but then of course it did.

Because when I got home, there was a dump truck parked outside my house and a TV crew set up inside. A pink-clad woman with a clipboard was shouting orders at everyone, while a bunch of smelly large men in *Hoarder Heaven* T-shirts hauled Thrift Town bags out of the house and threw them into the truck. Grandma was just sitting on the porch under a blanket, rocking back and forth. I kept asking her what was going on, but she was catatonic. She didn't even say anything about me being covered in bird poop, so I knew something was really wrong. I finally got the lady with the clipboard to stop yelling at everyone for a second so she could tell me that Grandma got bumped to the top of the *Hoarder Heaven* waiting list when they found out she was Caleb Sloat's mom, and her episode will be put on the fast track to air.

"But is she *okay*?" I asked the bossy pink woman.

"I'm the professional organizer, not the counselor," she said.

"When's the counselor going to get here?"

She just rolled her eyes and started yelling at someone in the kitchen.

I wanted to call Lydia and tell her about it, but instead I sat by Grandma for the next hour or so, watching the men haul her years' worth of collections out of the house. The counselor finally showed up and was able to assure Grandma, with a TV camera in our faces the whole time and the help of a box of snack cakes, that all her things are going to a storage unit that she is free to visit anytime. That perked Grandma up, and for a split second, I had the strange feeling that everything was going to be okay. But of course that quickly passed.

The weird thing is, the house seems to have relaxed a little. It's still making the regular noises it always did, but it's not nearly as aggressive as it has been lately. Ever since Caleb left, it's like a spell was broken, like a huge weight was lifted. Lydia's painting is back to being beautiful instead of scary, and I even managed to sleep last night, for the first time in I don't know how long, and I'm feeling a little less like my brain's going to explode any minute. These are good things. I should feel better. But all my weird feelings are still swirling around inside of me, and I still don't know what to do with them, and now instead of feeling like I'm losing my mind, I just feel really, really sad.

The TV people have left for the day. I hear the front door open, then slam closed. "I want to make your room more of a historical exhibit," Grandma says as she scuttles into the living room, her arms heavy with new Thrift Town bags.

"I thought you were supposed to be getting rid of stuff," I say.

"Dammit, Billy!" she says. "This is for business. Did you even hear what I said? This is what I need you to do. Go up to your room, remove anything that screams, 'Billy,' and replace it with what's in these bags."

"What is all that stuff?"

"Things that look more like what Caleb would have had in his room. You know, like real boy stuff."

My guts twist. If Caleb was a real boy, what does that make me?

I do what Grandma says. I march up the stairs while she stays at the bottom, administering decorations. "Put that one on the wall next to the bed!" she yells up at me. I unroll a NASCAR poster.

Really? That's what Grandma thinks Caleb would have had in his room? I guess it doesn't really matter. None of Grandma's tour customers are going to care one way or another. No one wants to know who Caleb actually is.

I look around my room and realize there isn't much for me to remove to make space for the fake Caleb exhibit. I took most of my furniture to the attic, and in the almost ten years this has been my bedroom, I've never done much decorating. I heard on a show once that a person's home is a reflection of their soul. So what does my room say about me? That my soul is empty?

I hang up the NASCAR poster, a Seattle Mariners poster, and a poster of a Black Bart Simpson on a skateboard. I blow up an inflatable pink guitar and put a broken lava lamp on the floor next to the bed, scatter some books about guitars and a few pairs of sweatpants around the room, drop a mostly deflated soccer ball in the corner, though I'm almost positive Caleb has never kicked a soccer ball in his life.

"Are you done?" Grandma yells from the bottom of the stairs.

I inspect my work. This looks like the room of a total asshat.

"Yes," I say.

"Okay, I'm picking up a tour, then we're heading over here in twenty minutes. You better scram."

I know that's the closest I'm going to get to a thank-you.

After she leaves, I turn on the AA channel, but Lynn A. still isn't there. Right above her empty seat, there's a new poster of a picture of a river and text in Comic Sans font over it: DENIAL IS NOT A RIVER IN EGYPT. I've been hearing that saying in meetings for years, but I still don't know what it means. What does denial have to do with Egypt? I'm guessing they're saying denial is bad, but they also always say, "Fake It Till You Make It," and isn't that kind of like saying denial is good? I am so confused. How I am supposed to practice these principles and do what they tell me if I can't even figure out what they're telling me to do?

Then, sitting on the coffee table under some wadded-up napkins, I see Grandma's laptop that she brought home from work. She finally got Internet at home, but she still won't let me touch her computer, but she's not going to be here for at least ten minutes, and I'm sure I can do one simple Internet search before she comes around to smack my chin. Luckily, she's even worse at computers than I am and hasn't figured out how to lock it with a password.

I open up the Internet browser. I type: "Where is Lynn A.?"

The first thing that comes up is her obituary.

I slam the computer on the coffee table. I don't want to read what someone else says about her. I don't want to know the names of her family or where she was born or what jobs she's had. I don't want to read that version of her life. I want the one she talks about in meetings. I want the story of pain and redemption. I want the hopeless life with the happy ending. I want the miracle. I want her in her chair, in that room, on my screen, in my house, where she was supposed to stay forever and never ever leave me.

She was never on a trip. She was never on an airplane to visit her new grandchild. She was just dead. Gone. Forever. I will never see her again. She is in the same place as my mother—nowhere.

I go to my room. I look at Lydia's painting now, still and lifeless. I look at the hole in the wall with nothing coming out of it. I look around at my sad little room, full of other people's garbage, with nothing in it that's mine, and my heart feels like all those hundreds of crows are tearing it apart, and then I scream the loudest I've ever screamed in my life, so loud it makes my throat feel like it's bleeding, and then, just like that, it's over, and I feel almost exactly the same, and the silence settles, and nothing's changed, and the house says nothing in return, doesn't even shake in acknowledgment, and the crows have devoured everything inside me so all that's left is a deep black void and a few stray feathers. And now I'm numb. Now all I want to do is sleep.

I pack up my few belongings—mostly clothes from Thrift Town—in the now-empty Thrift Town bags. I place the shoebox full of money on top and haul everything upstairs to the attic.

Everything is still here from when Caleb left, in the same state of disarray. For some reason, the *Hoarder Heaven* people haven't come up here, like they have no idea it even exists, like the house is hiding it from them.

The toilet bucket has had some time to fester. After I throw it into the forest of dead weeds in the backyard, I begin my work. I build a little bed out of a stack of blankets. I set the bedside table right side up and put the box of money in the crooked drawer. I steal a light bulb from the downstairs hallway and replace the smashed one in the lamp. A couple of Caleb's dolls were abandoned during the hasty escape, so I set them on one of the lawn chairs and face it toward mine. And then I start the long and grueling, but strangely relaxing, task of refolding and stacking the dozens— maybe hundreds—of blankets scattered around the attic, and the two orphaned dolls watch silently as I build my own new walls.

LYDIA

I'M NOT SURE WHAT EXACTLY IS HAPPENING RIGHT NOW.
Natalie and I just finished Saturday morning classes, but instead
of each of us going our separate ways, Natalie invited me "to do
something," and I said yes even though I had no idea what that
even meant, because what are two dancers supposed to do together
if they're not dancing?

So now I'm sitting in the passenger seat of Natalie's car. I didn't
mention I drove to practice too. Larry's van is parked out of sight,
two blocks away.

"Are you hungry?" Natalie says.

"Always," I say. How many calories did we burn in the last three
hours? At least a thousand. And what did I have for breakfast? String
cheese, a mostly brown banana, and a cup of black coffee.

"Want to get drive-through and park at the beach?"

My stomach lurches in joy. "Oh my God, *yes*. But wait, aren't
you supposed to be on Mary's high protein and organic vegetable
diet?"

"At home, I am. But when my mom's not looking, I eat whatever I want. There's only so much grilled chicken and quinoa a
person can eat before they crack."

Natalie pulls up to the drive-through screen and places our order. Double cheeseburgers, fries, and chocolate milkshakes for both of us. A real dancer's diet.

Billy would love this meal. He would close his eyes when he drank the milkshake. He'd somehow get ice cream all around his mouth even though he was drinking with a straw.

I shake my head to dislodge the thought of him. We haven't hung out or really talked for five days, and I feel like a part of me is missing. The little girl's been moping around too. We both miss him.

But right now, I'm with Natalie. Right now, I want to try to be happy.

"What if you brought this home and ate it right in front of your mom's face?" I ask Natalie as we wait at the window for our order to be ready.

Natalie thinks about this like it's a very serious question. "She'd probably cry. Then she'd ask me what she did wrong. Then she'd send me to the youth pastor at our church to talk about it so she wouldn't have to deal with it anymore."

"Wow. That's a pretty serious reaction to a cheeseburger."

"Cheeseburgers are pretty serious."

Natalie pulls a card out of her wallet to pay when the order is ready. "Wait, how much is mine?" I say, rummaging through my backpack for my wallet.

"Don't worry about it," Natalie says. "It's on me."

"You don't have to pay for me."

"It's fine," Natalie says with a smile, and hands her card to the cashier in exchange for two greasy bags of food.

"No, I can pay for myself," I say as Natalie hands me a milk-shake. She doesn't get it. Billy would get it.

"I know. I just wanted to—"

I shove my money at Natalie. "Take it," I snap, immediately cringing at the sharpness in my voice.

"Fine," Natalie snaps back. The car behind us honks. Natalie puts her hands on the steering wheel and drives.

I am sliced down the middle. On one side is the angry girl who's used to fighting everyone; on the other is a girl looking at Natalie, feeling like shit for hurting her, a girl who knows Natalie was just trying to be nice, that she would offer to buy me lunch even if I was the richest person in the world. One girl desperately wants to say, "I'm sorry," but the other girl is holding my lips shut.

We drive the short distance to the closest public beach in silence. On the way, we pass two fire trucks battling an apartment building engulfed in flames; the homeless encampment near city hall, now eerily vacant and surrounded by police tape; the intercounty bus depot, its benches full of junkies; and the tornado pit, full of garbage and broken dreams. All of this decay behind the shiny new signs announcing the upcoming Unicorns vs. Dragons festival. This is not the part of Fog Harbor the tourists come here to see.

The beach is empty, desolate, streaked with the icy stripes of frozen freshwater streams trying to make their way to the ocean.

I remember exploring these beaches as a kid, how they seemed to go on forever, how they were full of endless treasures—shells, sand dollars, old barnacle-crusted buoys. I remember imagining all the faraway places the weathered driftwood could have come from, places where these logs were once trees with roots. I wondered if any of them came from the island across the ocean where my mother was born, an island in the Philippines whose name I never learned, a place where maybe I had uncles and aunts and cousins, maybe even a grandma and a grandpa. But Mom never wanted to talk about that. I learned it was better to keep those fantasies in my imagination, where they were safe.

We scarf down our food in silence and watch the world in grayish blue slow motion. Seagulls tease the waves out of habit, but it's obvious their hearts aren't in it.

"Do you feel ready for the big show next weekend?" Natalie finally says.

"As ready as I'll ever be," I reply. "It's cool you have your own car."

"Yeah. It's good for my parents, too, so they don't have to drive me to dance all the time."

"Yeah," I say.

Jesus. We might as well be talking about the weather.

Natalie turns her head and looks at me. Our eyes meet, and I feel part of me grow, the part that wants to do things like look Natalie in the eye and talk about stuff that matters.

She bites her lip and looks away for a moment, then looks back, like she wants to say something but she's not quite sure she has permission. "What?" I say. I force my voice to be gentle.

Natalie takes a deep breath. "Honestly," she says, looking at her lap, "I think more than anything, my mom was relieved I could finally drive myself to get my hair relaxed in Olympia every month and a half." She exhales what seems like five breaths' worth of air, like she had been holding those words in for a very long time. "I've been going there since I was eleven, right? And the appointments are, like, four hours long. And my mom's this little white church lady who's probably never really known a Black person her entire life except me."

I smile even though my heart is suddenly outside my body, beating between us.

"I remember her sitting there in the salon trying to look at her phone or whatever," Natalie continues. "But she's got this look on her face like she's being tortured, because she's never once been somewhere where she's the minority, you know? After two times like that, I was like, 'Mom, you should go run errands or something while I'm in here,' and she looked so relieved to get off the hook." Natalie pauses. "But do you know what she said? She was like, 'Honey, I don't know if you're safe here by yourself.'"

I can't think of anything to say except "I'm sorry." What's the deal with daughters being so responsible for their mothers' feelings? What's the deal with mothers constantly letting their daughters down?

Natalie smiles, but she also kind of looks like she's going to throw up.

"You want to hear something else sad?" I say. "I've never even met a Filipino person besides my mom. Not one. She never told me anything about where she came from. No stories, nothing about her family or growing up there. Like she erased it. She just decided it didn't exist as soon as she moved here. Like becoming American meant starting over from scratch and forgetting everything she used to be. Anything I know about the Philippines, I learned on my own online. I don't even know what island she came from. There's, like, over seven thousand of them."

"Maybe something bad happened back there," Natalie says. "Maybe she really needed to forget."

"Yeah, probably," I say. "But whatever happened, isn't it mine, too? Don't I have some sort of right to her history? And maybe forgetting isn't the best way to get over something. Because you never really can, you know? You can't force yourself to forget. I think that's part of why she was so depressed and miserable all the time. She ran halfway across the world, but whatever she was running from was still inside her, and she refused to look at it."

"Maybe we're all running from something," Natalie says.

I wonder where Billy is right now. I wonder if he knows what he's running from.

Do *I* know what I'm running from?

That's when I notice the little girl on the beach, chasing seagulls, as if it were a rare sunny day and not wet and cold. She reaches out her tiny hands, and the birds go flying. Why is she so happy all of a sudden? Why is she so free when my heart feels like it's breaking?

"Moms," Natalie says.

"Yeah, moms," I say.

"I love my mom," Natalie says, tears in her eyes. "But sometimes she breaks my heart."

I just nod, because I know if I speak, my words will turn into sobs. There's nothing I can say that will explain the feeling of my heart wanting to be inside hers, the feeling of wanting her heart inside mine, nothing to explain that these tears falling down my face are for both of us, that I want my tears to wash Natalie's away, that I want to cry so she will never have to cry again. But my lips are sealed. There are no words for any of this.

"Thank you for listening," Natalie says softly, sniffling.

"Anytime," I say.

"I'm kind of embarrassed."

"Don't be."

"You're crying."

"So are you."

And then Natalie laughs. And I laugh too. And our laughter calls all the birds back that the little girl chased away, and the deer hiding in the dune grass trot out to see what's going on, and a half dozen seals slide onto shore, and a pod of orcas jump in the distance, and a bald eagle screeches overhead into the infinite sky, and the little girl sits on the hood of Natalie's car, the afternoon wind whipping her hair around like flying snakes, while Natalie and I sit beside each other inside the car, laugh-crying like our lives depend on it.

BILLY

THE *HOARDER HEAVEN* CREW FINALLY CLOSED UP SHOP and did their exit interviews with Grandma this morning. She wouldn't let them interview me. I want to tell myself it's because she's protecting me from the toxic effects of fame, but most likely it's because she doesn't want to share the limelight.

School's out for four days for the King's birthday holiday weekend, and so far I've pretty much spent the whole time in the attic. At first I came down to use the bathroom and get food, but by the second night I stopped doing even that because I found a large bowl to use as a toilet and I decided eating wasn't really worth the trouble anymore. Without Caleb to shop for, I've lost the will to buy groceries, and Grandma usually forgets to get me anything when she brings home takeout.

I'm pretty sure loss of appetite is a sign of clinical depression.

I know this isn't good. I'm way too young to become a hermit, especially a clinically depressed one. But I honestly can't think of any other options. Until just a few hours ago, the house had been crawling with *Hoarder Heaven* people and that pink lady yelling at everyone, and tours keep going in and out, and all I want is some peace and quiet and the attic is the only place no one ever goes.

It's the first day in forever that it's not freezing cold, so I did manage to come outside and sit on the front stoop this afternoon, which hopefully means I'm not a total lost cause. The couple who's been camped outside the house for weeks is enjoying the nice weather too. The guy is looking in his side mirror shaving his beard, while the girl is sitting on a foldable chair painting her toenails. They offer me some soup they have warming on a camping stove, but I say no because it's important to have boundaries with these people.

I've been sitting here for a long time watching a crow pick at something dead and sticky on the pavement, trying not to wonder what Lydia and Caleb are doing without me. For someone who's supposedly taking space to be away from those two, I sure spend a lot of time with them in my head.

The stillness abruptly ends as a police car turns onto my street, and I'm too depressed to even be scared. I close my eyes and take a deep breath to prepare myself. If I don't fight, they'll hopefully be gentle with me. Maybe they'll have some mercy because I'm a kid. Maybe they'll place their hands on top of my head so I don't bump it when they put me in the back of the cop car. But when I open my eyes, they're pulling up in front of Cult Girl's house, not mine. Two police officers get out and walk to the front door. The stern-looking lady who must be Cult Girl's mom opens it. They tell her something. Her face is blank as she lets them in.

I watch the house as if it will give me some kind of clue about what's happening inside, but houses in general have stopped talking to me lately. But then all of a sudden, the door opens and Cult Girl walks out and sits on the stoop directly across from mine and looks right at me. I wave, and she waves back and then she actually says, "Hi," like, with her actual *voice*, and I can barely hear it because she's all the way across the street and she said it really quiet, like she's still practicing speaking and hasn't quite gotten the hang of it yet, and I'm so excited I can't help but shout, "HI!" really loud back, and it's so loud the crow flies away without finishing his dead thing, and Cult Girl smiles like maybe she's even thinking about laughing, but then she changes her mind and gets a scared look on her face and turns around like she expects someone to be there, and I guess I probably shouldn't have shouted so loud.

Then the door opens and Cult Mom comes out and gives me a dirty look while squeezing Cult Girl's shoulder what seems like way too hard, and then she flinches and looks down and follows her mom back into the house. But before the door closes behind her, Cult Girl turns around to smile at me one last time, and it's a smile like we're in on something together, just me and her, and for a split second I forget to miss Lydia and Caleb.

It's weird, but I swear the smell of old man breath is suddenly gone from the air. It's like a breeze blew in from the ocean and washed all the funk away.

What I see when I go back in is not the familiar mess of my home, but its professionally tidied-up evil twin. It feels wrong, like I don't belong here anymore. Why can't everything just go back to the way it used to be? I was fine before all this madness started, when it was just me and Grandma in our broken house in our broken town, before Lydia and Caleb arrived and mucked things up. I think I'd even be okay with being shoved in a locker again once or twice if it meant I'd get to walk through the door and see all the old Thrift Town bags and Grandma on the couch with nothing to do but watch TV and yell at me occasionally. Even her constant complaining and ordering me around sound better than this, whatever this is. I want to watch my old therapy talk shows and AA TV and believe I am actually learning something useful about life. I want to go back to the time I was not so aware of my own misery, back when the world was small, back to the time I didn't think I had the option of anything different, back before I had anything to lose.

People talk about hope like it's this great thing, but they're wrong. Because once you start hoping, you can't stop. It's like an addiction. Hope is as bad as heroin.

"Something's happening across the street," I tell Grandma, who's sitting on the couch with the TV on, glaring at the laptop balanced on her belly. "A cop car just pulled up to that weird family's house."

"That nutjob lost it at work," she explains, squinting her eyes at the screen. "Shaylene said the prison had to go on lockdown and he got hauled away in a straitjacket. He's going away for a long time. Guess that means the wife and kid won't be around much longer either. Not sure how that woman's going to pay a mortgage if she's not allowed to work and her husband's in the loony bin."

Cult Girl can't leave. We just started getting to know each other. I don't think I can handle losing anyone else right now.

"That's mean, Grandma," I say, but what I really want to say is, "I think you have narcissistic personality disorder." I watched a therapy talk show about it once. They had a checklist of symptoms, and Grandma got a perfect score.

Then Grandma says, "Your girlfriend's dad is bugging me," and it takes me a while to figure out who she's talking about, and when I do, it feels like someone punched me in the gut because it reminds me how much I miss Lydia. "He keeps e-mailing and calling me with some nonsense about partnering with him for some tour next weekend. Who in their right mind would want to tour *Carthage*? Something about unicorns and dinosaurs."

"Dragons," I say. "You know about the festival, don't you?"

Grandma just grunts. Of course she knows about it. But she's one of those stubborn old Romans who refuse to acknowledge the series because it's more Carthage's than Rome's.

I wonder if Larry knows Lydia's big dance show is at the same time as the festival. Knowing Lydia, she probably hasn't told him about it.

I haven't gotten my ticket yet. I don't know if I'm still invited. But I want to go. Of course I want to go. The show feels like it's part mine, too.

"Whatever," Grandma snorts, shaking the computer on her lap. "You know what this is, Billy? *Subterfuge*. He's going to be nice and try to win my trust so I tell him all my trade secrets, and then he's going to steal them."

"Maybe he just wants to be friends."

Grandma looks at me like I'm the stupidest piece of shit she's ever seen, and I feel a strange relief spread through me. For a moment, things feel normal again.

"Nobody just wants to be friends, Billy. Everyone wants something."

She's right. Everyone wants something. And when they stop wanting what you have to offer, they stop wanting you.

A sound like a creepy out-of-tune carnival song rings through the house like it's coming out of the walls, and it takes me a while to remember it's the sound of our doorbell. A chunk of ceiling the size of a baby's hand falls from above and smashes onto the coffee table. Even *Hoarder Heaven* can't fix everything.

"Goddamned tourists," Grandma says.

"I thought you loved tourists," I say.

"Not when I'm off the clock. Are you going to get the door or what?"

It's probably a weird fan. There's been a steady stream of them, especially since the ATM news broke. None of them had much to say when I opened the door. One of them simply asked, "Is Caleb here?" like she was a friend stopping by for a casual visit.

But that is not who is at the door this time. Standing before me, the gray sky softly glowing behind them, are two very large men in full police regalia, the same ones who were just across the street at Cult Girl's house.

"Hello, young man," one of the cops says.

"Uh, hello?" I say, staring at the gun on his belt. I am as tall as him but only about one-third his width. The shorter one is even wider. I feel myself shrink. Can they tell I've been harboring a fugitive just by looking at me?

"May I speak to Tammy Sloat, please?" says the shorter cop.

"Uh, Grandma," I say, my voice shaking. I am such a wuss. "Grandma!"

"What?" Grandma yells from the living room.

"Cops are here!" I yell back. Then I hear her stomping.

"What's this about?" she says as she approaches the door. The entryway is not big enough for both of us, especially with the board sticking out of the wall, so I fall back and plop down on the stairway. *It's over*, I think. *I'm going to jail. They're going to eat me alive.*

"We'd like to ask you some questions about the whereabouts of Caleb Sloat," the taller cop says.

"I already told those other detectives I don't know where he is," Grandma says. Is that fear I detect in her voice? "I haven't talked to him in years." Is that sadness?

"Mind if we come inside and look around?" says the wider cop.

Grandma is silent. From behind, all I can see is a glimpse of each cheek as she looks from cop to cop. I don't know what to feel if I can't read her face.

"Is this an official investigation?" Grandma says. "Do you have a warrant?" She's watched enough detective shows to know how this works.

The cops look at each other. "Well, um," says the tall one, looking at his shoes. "Not exactly."

"We just have a few questions, ma'am," says the wide cop, almost whining. "It won't take long, I promise."

"Are you even assigned to this case?" Grandma says.

The cops just look at each other. The wide one's face turns bright red.

"You need to leave," Grandma says. "Or do I need to call the cops and have you written up for trespassing and harassment?"

Sometimes Grandma can be a badass.

But her face does not match her voice. Her voice was angry and strong, but when she turns around, her forehead's all wrinkled and her lips are quivering. She takes a big gasp of air and clutches her neck as she scuttles away without closing the front door, and I see a big tear drip down her face as she turns the corner into the living room.

"Um, bye?" I say to the cops from my seat on the stairs.

The tall cop sighs.

"Yeah, okay," says the wide one, deflated.

"Dammit, Gene," the tall cop grumbles to his partner as they walk away.

"It was worth a try," whines the wide cop as I close the door behind them.

I find Grandma sitting on the couch with her face in her hands, her back heaving with sobs.

Grandma doesn't cry. I don't know what to do. I only know what to do with her anger, her hunger. Not this.

"Grandma?" I say. "Are you okay?"

She doesn't say anything.

I tiptoe closer. "Do you need anything?"

"He's my son," she moans. "My goddamned *son*."

I touch her back, lightly. This is what people in TV shows do when someone is like this. It is supposed to make them feel better.

Now is the time to tell her about Caleb. She needs to know that he's safe. That I know where he is. That she can see him again.

I feel her tense under my hand. She stops crying.

"Grandma?" I say. "I have something to tell you."

But then she spins around, whacks my arm, lunges, and even sitting on the couch she's strong enough to push me to the floor. My butt slams on the hard wood as my back smashes into a bookcase. I will have bruises tomorrow, but not anywhere anyone can see. The new one on my butt can join the old faded one from when Caleb pushed me.

"Get away from me," she growls.

I am numb. It doesn't even hurt. I barely feel my body as I stand up. I don't even remember what I was thinking a few seconds ago.

This is what we do. Grandma. Caleb. Me. I tried to be different, but who am I kidding? We push people away when we're hurting the most. We *literally* push them away. We're so dumb, it's not even a metaphor.

The house is silent as I climb the stairs to the attic. It has nothing to add to the conversation.

I feel immediate relief as I enter the structure I rebuilt out of blankets, more rounded and cavelike than Caleb's walled fortress. I find a loose sheet and hang it over the window, muting the already pale natural light. It's like the outside barely even exists anymore.

I think about the painting in my room downstairs. I wonder what it's doing. I guess I could hang it up here, but something tells me the attic wants to stay bare.

I sit in the dark. When you can't see anything, the world is so nice and small and manageable.

Maybe I should stay up here forever. Maybe becoming a hermit isn't such a bad idea. It could be so much worse.

LYDIA

IN LESS THAN A WEEK, I WILL HAVE QUITE POSSIBLY THE most important afternoon of my life. Except for maybe the afternoon I found out my mom was dead, but that's the opposite kind of important than this coming Saturday. Fog Harbor Dance Academy's annual Winter Showcase isn't just any old dance school recital. We perform at the biggest theater in town. Tickets sell out every year. People come who don't even have kids who go to the school. Dancers use the videos of their performances in their applications to college and dance companies. If this thing goes well, I might actually have a future besides working at Taco Hell for the rest of my life.

I dump the bag of groceries I picked up at BigMart on the kitchen counter, exhausted after three hours of practice at Natalie's house. We spent the first half on the modern and contemporary ensemble pieces, and the second half on our pas de deux, with a lunch break in the middle. Natalie's mom hovered around the kitchen without saying anything while we scarfed down the protein smoothies and fancy tuna salad she made us. The salad had some kind of French name I can't remember. Natalie's mom is one of those people who overpronounces "croissant" to sound fancy.

The whole time I was eating, I was terrified I was holding my fork wrong. I was terrified the little girl was going to do something to embarrass me. But she was surprisingly well behaved, like even she wanted to impress Natalie's mom.

Neither of us are quite ourselves when Natalie's mother is around, especially Natalie. Her shoulders tense as soon as her mom is near. She turns silent and almost surly. The smart and funny girl I've been getting to know just kind of evaporates in the presence of her mother, and she turns into a ballerina-shaped shell. I think about how jealous I used to be, how much I thought I hated her for having such a perfect life. I wonder how many people I've hated like this, for no good reason.

Now I'm in my kitchen, taking a few items from the grocery bag to deliver to Caleb. He's been here for almost a week, and every time I enter what used to be my studio, he's either reading or sitting cross-legged with his eyes closed. Once he was even doing what appeared to be yoga. He cleaned up all the broken glass. He's been polite. He says thank you every time I bring him something. He hasn't asked for drugs or anything weird. He even offered to help rebuild the studio. But I'm not getting my hopes up. I know how these things work. People don't really change. They may have a few good days, but they'll always return to the worst versions of themselves when things get tough.

I put my key in the dead bolt, but it's already unlocked.

I open the door and Caleb is gone.

"Hello?" I say. Nothing.

I look in the bathroom. Nothing.

I look in my room. Larry's room. The hallway closet. Nothing. The apartment is empty.

"Oh shit oh shit oh shit oh shit," I say out loud. Where is he? Would he just leave without telling anyone? Is he out looking for heroin? Did he keep a shard of mirror and take it somewhere he wouldn't make a mess? I remember hearing that it's common for people to seem to get better briefly before killing themselves. If something happens to Caleb on my watch, Billy will never forgive me.

I run outside because the apartment feels like it's crushing me. It is still so full of my mother, still so full of the kind of silence that has weight and mass. The little girl clings to my leg and won't let go.

Then suddenly I feel the grip on my leg loosen. I look down and see the girl distracted for a moment, sniffing the air. It's then that I notice the smell of something burning. Black smoke rises from behind the apartment. I run toward it, fearing I will see something I will never be able to unsee.

And there is Caleb, very much alive, sitting on a log, staring at a fire burning on the ground in front of him. He is freshly shaven, and his usually unkempt shoulder-length hair appears to have just been washed and is tucked behind his ears. A wave of relief almost pushes me to the ground, but the girl grabs my hand, steadying me just in time, and leads me to the fire.

We sit down on the log next to Caleb, facing the thick wall of evergreens that separate us from the river. He does not seem surprised at my arrival.

"Want some tea?" Caleb says, raising a steaming mug.

"No," I say.

"Did you know the worst part of a craving lasts just about as long as it takes to make a cup of tea? If you really concentrate and focus on every step of making the tea, by the time it's ready, the craving is over."

"That seems a little simplistic."

"Most of the time, the simplest answer is the best."

"Are you a philosopher now?"

Caleb shrugs. "I've just been thinking."

I look into the fire and watch as the remains of Caleb's weird dolls burn and melt and turn even more grotesque than they were to begin with. The little girl watches too, and she looks almost sad, like she knew those dolls. I wonder if she remembers how bizarre things got the last time we were here at this fire together.

"You killed your babies," I say.

"Better than them killing me."

"Did you use the pink razor to shave your face?"

"Yeah, sorry. I'll buy you a new one."

"The pink one's Larry's. He's convinced girls' razors are better because they're more expensive."

We sit in silence for a while. The little girl pokes the fire with a stick, making sparks fly, occasionally looking at me out of the side of her eye like she's checking on me. I'm starting to understand what her looks mean. She's calm right now. She seems to be the happiest when I feel the most uncomfortable, like my discomfort is exactly what she wants.

The mouth of one of the dolls melts open into a silent, burning scream.

"I thought you killed yourself," I say.

"I'm done doing that, I think."

The last thing I want is to care about this guy. But that doesn't mean I'm not curious. I want to know what changed, what it was that made him shave, made him stop asking for drugs, made him start saying "please" and "thank you." What made him want to stop dying? It couldn't have been something as simple as a change in location. But maybe there was another goodbye, something that happened in that attic that woke him up. Because maybe all those rehabs, all of Caleb's public humiliations and failures, even the overdoses and near-deaths—maybe none of those were ever going to be his bottom. Why fear death if you're the only thing you have to lose?

I feel the little girl's fingers thread through mine, and I don't pull my hand away. We sit there next to Caleb, holding hands for I don't know how long, watching the fire destroy the dolls he worked so hard to create.

"I'm tired," Caleb says. A doll makes one last gasp before crumpling in on itself. The little girl waves goodbye to the remnants in the fire.

"All you've been doing is sitting around doing nothing," I say. "How are you tired?"

Caleb smiles faintly. "The most exhausting place in the world is inside your own head."

"Okay, Yoda."

He takes a sip of his tea. With his face freshly shaven, he looks younger. Similar to the famous version of himself, but much healthier. Less pissed off, but a lot sadder. A lot more like Billy.

"How's Billy doing?" Caleb says.

"Not good."

"It's my fault."

"Yep."

The river rushes, out of sight. The fire crackles. As if we are camping—one of those Seattle couples in fleece jackets and fancy hiking boots who drive their Subaru out to this forgotten corner of the world on a holiday weekend to pretend they love nature and breathe the same air as a bunch of people they never think about.

"Billy hasn't been okay for a long time," I finally say. "Way before I met him. It just took your bullshit to make him see it." The girl stirs the bed of coals with her stick, making sparks fly. She has a smile on her face. She could be our daughter. "And now he sees it," I say.

And what about me? What is my part in his not being okay?

"I want to make it better," Caleb says, his voice raw. Is he crying? "How do I make it better?"

"How should I know? Stop being an asshole. Take care of your own shit. Those are probably the first steps." I sigh. The girl sighs too. She leans against me, so weary for such a little ghost. The weight of her body feels good against mine. She's not so bad when I don't fight her. Without thinking, I put my arm around her, and when I realize it's there I don't pull it away.

How does anyone make anything better? Billy's been trying to do that his whole life, but he's just been running in circles. Is there a way for people to be close without sucking each other dry?

But then I see Billy's face in the fire. Natalie's. Even a faint shadow of Larry's and my mom's. The fire suddenly burns hotter, but it is not the oven like the last fire, not painful. I am not scared. My heart fills with warmth despite the sadness, as if loneliness and love can coexist, as if they are meant to. The girl squeezes my hand so hard it almost hurts.

I stand up and shake her off. She looks at me with pleading eyes, like she's not ready to leave. "So are you going to get out of here now or what?" I say, but as the words come out of my mouth, I realize I'm not entirely sure what I'm asking. Caleb can't stay here; that's obvious. But there is also something accusatory in my question, something shaming him for leaving Billy years earlier, something daring him not to leave again.

"Soon. I just have to figure a couple things out first. I need to borrow a computer."

"What are you going to do with it?"

"Research my options."

I'm supposed to be suspicious. There's all kinds of trouble a person can get into with a computer. But I feel a strange, unexpected clarity: I trust him. "You can use Larry's," I say. "But only for, like, two hours. Then I'm taking it back."

"Okay."

"You know you can't stay here forever."

"I know."

"You have until Saturday. Then I kick you out."

"I know."

"What are you going to do?"

"I'm thinking about it."

"Don't think too hard."

"Trust me. I'm trying."

"I know," I say.

"Thank you," Caleb says softly, his eyes on the fire. "For everything. For being family to Billy."

And that's when I start crying. My tears are silent and thick. I am grateful to Caleb for not looking at me, for pretending not to notice.

Billy is my family. I can't let him drift away.

And all of a sudden, I can't see the little girl anywhere.

BILLY

I KNOW RAIN. I'VE LIVED HERE MY WHOLE LIFE. I KNOW the constant drizzle, like a sprinkler turned on half power that no one ever remembers to turn off, how it seeps into you, how your pant legs and ankles are always wet, how nothing ever completely dries, how you get so used to looking at the ground to keep the raindrops off your face that you forget to look up even when the sky clears.

But this is a different kind of rain. This is the sea falling from the sky. It's been raining bullet-size drops nonstop all day. Storm drains are overflowing all over town. People are making sandbags out of the beach to put in front of doors and garages. The few basements in Criminal Fields are now swimming pools.

In just a few days, Fog Harbor County went from record cold to record rain. In that time, someone cut down the five trees that have blocked Cult Girl's house since before I can remember, and even though it's raining, the windows are wide open, like the house needs to breathe after all its years of being shut tight. I'm sitting on my front stoop, watching the river that used to be my street carry things it's collected from upstream—a pizza box, a green plastic comb, a deflated bike tire, several beer cans, a dirty syringe, a baby shoe. Who knows how far these things have come. Who knows where they are going. Maybe they'll make it all the way to the ocean. Maybe they'll float all the way to the other side of the world and become someone else's trash.

I look up and see Cult Girl standing in her doorway across the street, looking straight at me. For someone whose dad was just committed to a mental institution, she doesn't look that upset. If anything, she looks happier than I've ever seen her.

I wave. She waves back, then runs inside the house. No surprise. Nothing ever really changes, even if it looks different on the outside. A dead, bloated pigeon floats by, followed by what appears to be a pair of boxer shorts.

But then the girl reappears, carrying an umbrella. She runs across the river, splashes punctuating her steps, and sits down beside me.

"I like your outfit," I say. She's wearing a black button-down shirt with ruffles around the collar, a black knee-length skirt, black tights, and black winter boots. Her long dark brown hair is hanging down around her pale face instead of being up in its usual tight bun. If I had to give her style a name, I'd call it "Goth librarian." It certainly is different from the shapeless floral-print sacks she usually wears.

"Thanks," she says. "I like black." Her voice is lower than I imagined it would be, like something inside her is older than she looks.

"My name's Billy."

"Ruth."

"It's funny we've lived across from each other our whole lives and never talked to each other," I say.

"'Funny' is not the word I'd use," Ruth says.

"I'm sorry about your dad."

Ruth looks me in the eye for a moment, saying nothing, but I see the answer in her eyes: *I'm not.*

"It's going to be a long time until he gets out," she finally says. "If he ever gets out."

I have no idea what to say to that. Usually things just come out of my mouth even if I don't know what to say, but this isn't a conversation I want to mess up.

"My mom says I can go to public school now if I want to," Ruth says.

"Do you want to?"

"I don't know."

"I'd show you around."

"Thanks," Ruth says, and smiles. She has a nice smile. I want to see more of it.

An actual boat floats by now, one of those plastic ones babies play with in the bath. It seems so sure of where it's going, like it has charted its course and is right on track.

"It's weird suddenly having to make a choice like that," Ruth says. "To make a choice at all. I never really had to make any choices before. But now I'm free or something, and I have no idea what to do. Like, what's the point of freedom if I don't even know what to do with it?"

I don't know if she wants me to answer, or if this is one of those questions people say out loud because they just want someone else to be confused with them.

I am confused. I don't know what my choices are. I don't even know what I want. I am frozen in place while everyone else is moving on.

"I think I'm having an identity crisis," I say.

"Me too," Ruth says. We sigh in unison.

This is a pretty deep conversation to be having with someone within the first two minutes of ever talking to them. But in some ways, Ruth is my oldest friend.

"I think maybe life is one big long identity crisis," I say.

"That would be disappointing."

I shrug. "You can't be disappointed if you never expect anything in the first place."

"That sounds like a sad way to live."

Even Ruth knows more about living than I do.

"Are you moving?" Ruth asks.

"No. Why?"

"Trucks kept taking loads of stuff out of your house."

"My Grandma got on that show *Hoarder Heaven*."

"What's that?"

"A show about hoarders."

"What's a hoarder?"

"Someone who can't throw anything away."

Except people. They can throw away people.

"Why do you always hide your eyes?" Ruth says.

I tuck the long curtains of hair covering my face behind my ears and immediately feel anxious.

"That's better," Ruth says. "Now people can see you."

"I'm not sure that's better."

"You have nice eyes."

I hide my face in my hands. I don't want anyone looking at my eyes, even if they think they're nice. The good news is Ruth doesn't seem alarmed by my behavior. She's been so sheltered she doesn't even know I'm abnormal.

"Do you know the story of Noah's Ark?" Ruth says.

"Sort of."

"I think this must have been the kind of rain that led to the great flood."

"Should we be worried?"

"Maybe we should start building a boat."

I look at her, not knowing how to react. For all I know, the only history she's ever been taught is stories from the Bible. She might think the Earth's still flat.

"I'm kidding," she finally says.

"Oh."

"My mom has taken me to the library twice a week for years. In case you don't know, they have a lot of books there. And Internet. And very kind and subversive librarians who take curious home-schooled kids under their wings and teach them stuff they're not supposed to know."

"How was that book?" I say. "The one you hid behind my house."

"Good," she says thoughtfully. "Very realistic. Do you think that town's close to here?"

"What town?"

"The town in that book."

"I don't know. I never read it."

"Oh."

"You're a lot different than I thought you'd be," I say.

"Thank you." Ruth smiles. "That's just about the nicest compliment you could give me."

We sit there for a long time, watching the downpour and the parade of garbage floating by. Maybe this is the great flood. Maybe the earth or God or whatever has finally had enough. Maybe it's time to get rid of the mess we've made and start over from scratch.

"My mom'll be home from the store soon," Ruth says. "I should go."

"Okay."

"It was good talking to you."

"You too."

I watch as Ruth splashes across the street back to her house. I wonder what it's like inside. I think it probably smells a little like my house before the *Hoarder Heaven* people came—a mix of mildew, disintegrating wallpaper, and despair. But maybe like my house, Ruth's has transformed in the last week. Someone chopped those trees down. They're airing it out. Her world is turned upside down too.

I walk into the house and upstairs to my bathroom, careful not to step near the edge of the remaining floor. My foot went straight through the rotten floorboards last night, and I nearly fell into the kitchen.

I push my hair out of my eyes—the same yellow-wheat color and shoulder length as Caleb's. Maybe Ruth is right. Maybe I do have nice eyes. They're bright blue like my uncle's. They're shaped like his, and so are my nose and mouth. We share the same sharp cheekbones, the same angular chin.

I feel my chin. Is that hair? Am I growing a *beard*?

When was the last time I even looked at myself in the mirror? What else has happened to me while I wasn't looking?

Maybe it's time for a change. Maybe it's time for all sorts of things.

Maybe I should cut my hair. But would that mean I'm copying Lydia? What if everything I do will only ever be a pale imitation of something somebody else has already done better?

Maybe I could wear a ponytail. Or pull it up like Natalie and all those ballet girls. But Lydia would probably kick my ass for wearing a man-bun. If we're still friends, that is. Are we still friends?

I have to put my hand on the counter to keep myself from falling over. I need to eat something.

I miss her so much.

What have I done?

LYDIA

WHEN I CHECKED ON CALEB LAST NIGHT, HE WAS SITTING cross-legged on a pile of pillows with his eyes closed and was so blissed out, he didn't even notice I was there. I left a microwaved burrito and an apple for him on the floor and walked right back out the door.

I called Billy all day yesterday, but I think the phone was off the hook. His grandma finally answered and said he lost his phone privileges, then hung up on me. I'm not counting on her telling him I called.

God, that family drives me crazy.

Technically, I don't think we're supposed to have class on holidays, but Mary scheduled rehearsals for all the advanced and preprofessional classes today, even though it's the King's birthday. "Mastery doesn't come to people on vacation," she scolded a ballerina who started crying because her family would have to cancel their ski trip.

The little girl stares at me from the mirrored wall of the studio, standing where my reflection should be. She's wearing her pink tights and leotard and ballet skirt, mimicking my movements during barre warm-up. When I accidentally meet her eyes, she sticks her tongue out. I stick my tongue out right back.

I feel a nudge in my back and shift my eyes to meet Natalie's in the mirror. Natalie mouths, "Are you okay?" with a playful glint in her eye, and I cringe in embarrassment and melt at the same time.

"Lydia!" Mary snaps from her stool in the corner. "Do you have somewhere you'd rather be?"

"No, ma'am."

"Then how about you stay here with us?"

"Yes, ma'am."

The little girl spins around and wags her butt at me.

This is supposed to be Luz's advanced contemporary rehearsal, but Mary's oppressive presence has taken over. Luz stands at the front of the room leading the warm-up, but her attention and everyone else's are on Mary on her throne in the corner.

I can't focus. The big show is in five days, and I can't remember the choreography. It keeps slipping out of my brain, bullied out by more aggressive thoughts. This show is supposed to be the highlight of my short pathetic life, and yet I can't bring myself to be excited.

It's all Billy's fault. I never wanted a friend, but he weaseled his way into my life and made me care about him. And now he's not holding up his end of the bargain. Because isn't that what friendship is in the end? A kind of bargain? An agreement? Friends agree to talk to each other. Friends agree to not shut each other out.

"Lydia!" Mary shouts from her stool. "Wake up."

Everyone is in position to start rehearsal, but I'm still standing by the barre, having a staring contest with a little girl only I can see.

"You okay, kid?" Luz says softly. I flinch when she puts her hand on my shoulder. Her warm brown eyes almost make me lose it. I remember this feeling from right after my mom died, when I was so fragile, so raw, that even the most tender act of kindness hurt.

"I'm fine," I say with a clenched jaw, and get into position. Luz is talking at the front of the room, but I can't hear her. My gaze shifts between Mary's weighty presence in the corner and the little girl thrashing around in the mirror. The girl is angry now, no longer playful. She is lonely and she is sick of being ignored. She wants Billy back too.

I dance, but my attention is on the figure turning the mirror into a tornado. The girl spins and throws her body as if it's a weapon. She smashes into walls, shoves the stereo system to the ground, pushes Mary's stool over, kicks and flails her arms like someone on fire, and the dancers in the mirror scatter until the only person standing is the little girl in the middle of the room, alone, furious, a storm unto herself.

"Goddammit, Lydia!" Mary bellows when the music stops. She glides off her stool and stands in front of me. I can't quite meet her stare, but I focus on the faint lines around her eyes that show even through her thick makeup. I am out of breath, but it is not from dancing.

"Sorry," I pant. My body aches, as if I've been beaten, as if it were me in the mirror throwing myself around, so desperate to make contact, even if it hurts.

"Your lack of focus is unacceptable," Mary snaps. The class is utterly silent.

"I'm sorry."

"Did I make a mistake starting you at the top?"

"No, ma'am," I say, but right now I don't believe it.

I hear giggles from the back of the studio. And then I am no longer human, no longer a girl or a dancer. I am reduced to a fire of shame and fury as I spin around and spit, "Shut the fuck up, you fucking bitches!"

A collective gasp. I feel the oxygen leave the room.

"Out!" Mary shouts.

"What?"

"Go and wait in the lobby until class is over. With the way you're behaving right now, you do not deserve to dance in this studio. And if you leave before I get a chance to talk to you, you can know right now that you will not dance in the Winter Showcase and you will never be welcome back."

The only thing I see as I stomp out of the studio is black. I can't see Mary's angry eyes, or Luz's sad ones; I can't see all the skinny white girls huddled together in whispers; I can't see the little girl curled into a ball, crying, in the wreckage on her side of the mirror; I can't even see Natalie, concern pouring out of her, as she moves to follow me out of the studio, as Mary stomps across the dance floor and grabs her arm to hold her back.

In the dressing room, I am alone. The buzzing in my ears drowns out the muted song I've heard a million times coming through the wall as the class dances without me. I am numb as I pull on my jeans and sweatshirt, as I move from the dressing room to the lobby, as I sit on the bench and wait.

I think about leaving. I think about walking out of here forever. But where would I go? Dancing is all I have. Dancing is my only way out of this town and out of this life that never wanted me in the first place.

For some reason, I think about Unicorns vs. Dragons. How it was me, at age eleven, who read the series first, before Larry. I've never told anyone, not even Billy, that I loved it. I was obsessed. I had notebooks full of drawings and fan fiction. I barely talked to Larry, even then, but when I did, it was about the series. So he decided to read it too. And for a short time, it was something we shared, something we could talk about that didn't hurt.

But then Kayla or Kaitlyn or Katelyn made fun of me for my Unicorns vs. Dragons T-shirt when I was twelve and said only babies still liked it. So I punched her to prove I wasn't a baby. During my three-day suspension, I tore up my notebooks and posters and stuffed them in the trash can along with my Unicorns vs. Dragons bedsheets, stuffed animals, and action figures.

I grew out of it, but Larry didn't. He fished everything out of the trash can that I threw away and kept it. There's something tragic in how much he loves the fantasy, something desperate in the way he holds on to it, and now, all alone and sitting on this bench, I wonder if maybe it's the only way Larry's ever known how to hold on to me.

I notice the tears falling down my face just as I notice the small hand patting me on the shoulder. My little doppelganger. My ghost. My tiny self. It's a good thing Belinda isn't at the front desk, or else she'd have me committed—this spiky-haired girl, weeping, rocking back and forth, arms wrapped around something only I can see.

By the time rehearsal is over, I have cried myself dry. The little girl is asleep with her head in my lap. I'm not relaxed exactly, but something like empty. My rage turned to sadness, then turned to tears, and now the tears are all gone. It's like something passed through me. I stopped fighting it, and it stopped fighting too.

I tense when I hear the beginning of chatter in the dressing room. In a few short moments, a parade of dancers will file through the lobby, eager to see if I am still here, to see how far I have cracked.

Natalie hurries out of the dressing room before anyone else has a chance. My body softens as she sits next to me, in the space where the little girl used to be. She places her hand in the same spot on my shoulder.

"Hey," she says.

That's all she needs to say. I put my hand on hers and rest my cheek there. For a moment, there is perfect stillness.

But then the dressing room door bursts open, and our hands immediately return to our own laps as we create a few more inches of space between us on the bench. I look at the floor as the dancers file by. "Ooh, Lydia's in trouble," someone teases, and even though I'm looking down, I can feel Natalie shooting dagger eyes at the girl to shut her up.

When all the girls have gone, Luz comes out and kneels in front of me. I can only meet her eyes for a second before I have to look away. "If something's going on, you can talk to me, okay?" she says.

I nod, but I don't really believe her. Luz is great and all, but she has her own life. She doesn't want to hear about mine.

"Don't mind Mary," Luz says. "She only knows how to play bad cop."

"Okay," I say.

"Thanks, Luz," Natalie says.

"You make me proud," Luz says. "Both of you."

I thought I had no tears left, but I was wrong. I turn my head and rub my eyes with my fists. I have nothing to hide behind. Where's my long hair when I need it?

"Ladies, will you give Lydia and me some privacy, please?" Mary says as she enters the lobby.

"Bye, y'all," Luz says as she stands up. "See you tomorrow."

"I'll wait for you outside," Natalie says softly.

"No, it's okay," I say.

"It's no problem."

I look Natalie in the eye. "Really. No. But thank you."

She nods. "Okay. But call me if you need to talk."

Mary sits next to me in silence after Luz and Natalie leave. She smells like baby powder. I hate the smell of baby powder.

"My father died the day before my very first *Nutcracker*," Mary finally says after everyone else is gone.

I look at her, too surprised by her statement to remember to sulk.

"But I had to forget about him—I had to forget about my

feelings—as soon as I stepped on that stage. Whatever's bothering you right now, it must cease to exist when you enter this studio."

"Fine," I say. I just want this conversation to end. I just want to get out of here.

"Tell me something," Mary says. "Do you think you deserve to be here?"

I suddenly feel sick. Desperation and fear swirl inside me, heating up, transforming into what's familiar: anger.

"Are you threatening me?" I say.

"Excuse me?" Mary says, looking genuinely surprised.

"You think you can treat me like shit because I'm a scholarship student," I say. "You think all those other girls are better than I am because they can afford their pink overpriced shoes and ballet bullshit? Why even have a scholarship if you think I'm not worth your time?"

I am the twelve-year-old girl who punched Kayla or Kaitlyn or Katelyn. I am the girl attacking the person threatening to take away the thing I love.

"Scholarship?" Mary says. Then she laughs. A sharp, humiliating cackle. "Is that what you think happened? Oh, honey, I don't know what that strange little friend of yours told you. There's no scholarship. There's never been a scholarship. That boy is paying for all your classes. He asked me not to tell you, and I'm not sure why. I agreed to see you dance because quite frankly the whole situation was odd and I was curious. To be honest, I wasn't planning on taking you on as a student. I thought the whole thing was a joke."

I don't know if I'm breathing. I don't know if my blood is even pumping. My heart has stopped.

I'm a joke. That's all I've ever been.

"I changed my mind when I saw you dance," Mary says, her voice softening. "I felt uneasy about the whole secret payment thing, but I thought, if that's what it was going to take for you to dance here, I was willing to do it." Mary tilts her head to make eye contact, but I can't do it. I already feel too seen.

"Because you deserve to be here," Mary says. "You have the kind of raw talent I've frankly never seen before. And when I'm hard on you, it's not because I don't believe in you. Just the opposite. It's because I want you to be prepared. You haven't had the years of classes these girls have. You don't know the culture. It's vicious out there. You need to know how to maintain control even when it's vicious. That's why I'm vicious."

"Can I go now?" I say.

"Are you hearing what I'm saying?"

"Yes." I stand up.

"I'll see you tomorrow," Mary says. "Remember, leave everything else outside. All you are in here is a dancer."

"Okay." I start walking toward the door.

"I want you to make it," Mary says. "I think you can make it."

But I don't look back or stop walking. I don't hear the "I think you can make it." All I can hear is Billy's lie.

BILLY

GRANDMA'S BUSY GIVING TOURS ALL DAY, SO I STEAL HER computer and spend the rest of the afternoon watching old videos of Caleb. Not the ones I used to watch when I missed him the most, not of him young and mostly sober. I'm watching the bad ones, the ones right before he was sent to his many rehabs, when his skin was gray and his words were unintelligible, when he was angry and mean, when he seemed half dead. I'm done looking to be soothed by some nonexistent, fantasy version of my uncle. I don't know what I'm looking for, but whatever it is, it's not coming.

I'm numb as I watch Caleb nod off during an interview, as I watch Caleb fall down a short flight of stairs and just lie at the bottom without even trying to get up. I don't feel that familiar tug inside me, the one I'm realizing has made so many of my decisions. Maybe that feeling is some weird version of love. Maybe it's pity. Whatever it is, it makes even someone as pathetic as me feel like I have some kind of power.

It takes me several moments to figure out what I'm seeing when I walk downstairs to get some food. My house and everything in it keep changing. At first, I panic because I think Grandma's going to kill me because her computer's gone, but she doesn't even seem to have noticed. She's in her usual spot on the couch, but something is very wrong. The TV's not on. She doesn't even notice me standing there staring at her because she's so immersed in the thing she's holding in her lap.

I look closer. It's the first book in the Unicorns vs. Dragons series.

"Grandma?" I say. I can't remember ever seeing Grandma read a book, or, for that matter, ever seeing her in the living room with the TV off.

"Just a minute," she says. "I'm almost done with this chapter."

"What do you want to do for dinner?"

"I said just a minute!"

So I climb the stairs back into the attic. I burrow into my blanket cave and look out at the milky sky beyond the window. Of course I have homework to do, but of course I won't do it. What's the point of even trying at school when everyone's been telling me I'm dumb my whole life?

When Grandma decides she finally needs me, she'll be out of luck. Even her shouts won't make it up here. Either she'll have to get over her fear of heights, or she'll have to figure out how to take care of herself. I notice a tiny, familiar voice telling me to go downstairs, to be ready for her orders. But I don't listen to that voice anymore.

As soon as I hear the footsteps on the stairs, I know they're not Grandma's. They're too fast, too light. I'm not surprised when Lydia bursts through the door. And I'm not surprised by the words that come out of her mouth. I've been waiting for this moment. In some way, I'm relieved. When the inevitable finally happens, it means you don't have to wait anymore.

"You paid for my dance classes?" she shouts, stomping across the floor. "Why did you lie to me? That's fucking twisted, Billy."

"I was trying to help," I say weakly. "I thought that's what you wanted."

"But you didn't even ask me."

"I knew you'd say no."

"Of course I'd say no."

Lydia's sigh seems to deflate her, and she falls into the side of my cave, making the whole structure shudder.

"You can't just go around making decisions for people without their permission," Lydia says.

"But aren't you happier now?"

"That's not the point."

"What *is* the point?" I say. "You think there's something noble about not letting people help you? You think you deserve a trophy for your suffering?"

This whole town, this whole county, is full of a bunch of miserable people who think they're martyrs. Grandma. Caleb. Lydia. Everyone I've ever loved, victims of their own bad attitudes. And now I'm just as bad as them.

"That doesn't change the fact that you lied to me," Lydia says.

"I just wanted you to be happy."

"*You* wanted to be the one to *make* me happy."

"What's wrong with that?"

"Billy, you can't manipulate people into loving you."

"But I don't know how else to make them do it."

This is it. This is how friendship ends. This is how love dies. When the lies and secrets that kept it alive are revealed.

The house groans and shudders in the wind. I can see Lydia's body swaying slightly, like we are on a boat. Maybe the clouds have turned to water and we are floating out to sea.

Then something surprising happens. Lydia doesn't spit out some biting last words. She doesn't throw or kick anything. She doesn't stomp away. What she does is kneel down to where I'm sitting in my broken lawn chair, wedge her skinny butt next to mine, throw her arms around me, and cry.

I cannot tell my tears from hers, cannot tell the rocking of our bodies from the rocking of the tired old house, cannot tell the sea rising inside me from the explosion of the clouds outside, the raindrops so dense the wind pushes them around like waves, and the waves lap at the side of the house, make whitecaps in the streets, rapids in roadside ditches, until everything is drenched, the wet so deep nothing can escape it, nothing is untouched, nothing is dry, and Lydia and I make a raft out of each other, and our lies and secrets are washed away.

"Whatever it is you're doing up here," Lydia finally says, "it's not working."

"I know," I say.

"You need to get your head out of your ass."

"I know."

"You're my best friend and I fucking love you."

"I know."

We sit like that until the sky grows dark, the two of us squeezed into a broken lawn chair in the attic, watching the rain pour out of the formerly frozen sky, and it feels like the whole world is thawing.

LYDIA

TODAY IS THURSDAY, AND CALEB HAS UNTIL SATURDAY, when I kick him out. I've been reminding him every time I bring him food, and he just smiles and says he knows and then goes back to reading or meditating or yoga or whatever weird thing he's been up to.

The little girl has been pretty well behaved all week since Billy and I made up, but now I'm sitting at the kitchen table with Larry, who looks sadder than I've seen him in a long time, and she's kicking me in the shins.

"What's wrong?" I say, flinching as the words come out of my mouth. The girl stops kicking. She's trained me well.

He looks up from his laptop, as surprised by my words as I am. Our schedules are so opposite, I rarely see him outside the bar. I can't remember the last time I even saw him awake before school.

"Why are you up so early?" I say.

The radio is playing a local news show in the background. Something about how investigators into Caleb's disappearance are reviewing security camera footage from local ATMs. Any minute now, Billy's grainy security-camera face will be plastered on TVs all over the world. And only two people on the entire planet know

Caleb is sleeping on the floor on the other side of a door just a few yards from where I'm sitting.

Larry sighs. "I'm trying to get everything ready for the festival." He closes the laptop screen and reaches to turn the radio off. "But it's a disaster. All the holes I dug for my attraction keep filling up with water. The rain is going to ruin everything."

It takes all my strength to not mention how it was maybe not the greatest idea to have a festival in the rain capital of the country in late January.

"There's not really anything you can do about the weather. You can do the attraction next year."

"Yeah, I know," Larry says. "I just feel bad because this is a stop on the self-guided tour, and everyone's going to get here and expect something great. And all they're going to get are a few really deep mud puddles with broken lights at the bottom."

It's impossible to ignore the girl tugging on my arm. I try to be stealthy as I shake her off, but Larry looks up and says, "Are you okay?"

"My arm fell asleep."

I know what the girl wants me to do. But no way am I about to get up and give Larry a hug. Instead I say, "What if you moved your attraction inside? You have all your posters and those dolls and stuff you keep in the storage shed."

"Those are collectible figurines," he says. "And they're very valuable."

"Exactly. Didn't you say you have one of the most complete Unicorns vs. Dragons collections in the world? You can display that, and decorate the bar like crazy. Don't you still have that giant inflatable dragon and the life-size cardboard unicorn? Create a signature drink or something, maybe project the movies on the wall and play the soundtrack on the jukebox. That can be your attraction."

Larry looks like he's going to cry. There has been far too much crying lately.

"That's a really good idea," Larry says. "Thank you, honey."

I don't look him in the eye. I don't know what will happen if I do. I try not to look at the little girl as she wanders through the kitchen and disappears behind the fridge, like she's decided she has better things to do.

What is this weird feeling? Do I actually want her to come back?

What am I supposed to do with this silence now? What do normal people do when they sit across from each other at a breakfast table?

"Why didn't you tell me about your dance performance?" Larry says suddenly.

I tense. "How do you know about that?" The little girl hops out from behind the fridge and does a pirouette in the kitchen.

Larry looks down at his lap. "Billy called and told me. He said he knew you wouldn't tell me yourself."

Of course he did.

"So I looked it up online, and there you were on the schedule as a featured dancer." Larry looks up at me now. "Honey, why didn't you tell me?"

What's happening inside me is like when all the paints in a cheap set of watercolors get mixed up and become indistinguishable and brown. They're swirling together and making a huge mess that simultaneously feels like fire and nausea and chest pains and being full of helium. My ears are buzzing.

"I didn't think you'd care," I say, unable to look at him. These are not the kind of conversations Larry and I know how to have.

"Of course I care, honey," he says.

My muddled mess of emotions clears away as if being washed down a drain, leaving only one.

"You've never cared," I say. "You didn't care anything about my dancing when you made me stop taking classes."

"Money was tight for a while," Larry says. "You know that. Your mom left a lot of debt."

"Yeah, but then things got better, right? You could afford to get the van painted. You could afford all those precious collectibles you ordered online."

"I didn't know you still wanted classes. You never told me." He tries to reach across the table to touch my hand, but I pull away. "I thought you were happy with your studio. I thought you wanted to dance alone."

I feel the quick fire of my anger lose its heat, like the oxygen has been sucked from the air and the flame suddenly has nothing to feed on.

"If you would have said something," Larry says, "if you would have just told me, I would have helped you. Don't you know that?"

The fire is gone. I am left with a cold emptiness inside. I know Larry's telling the truth, and maybe part of me always knew returning to dance classes was an option, if only I said I wanted it. But I got used to Larry telling me we couldn't afford things. I learned not to ask because I knew the answer would be no. "No" became a part of my system, something I knew at my core, that asking for things—asking for help of any kind, wanting something from someone else—was not an option. So I got a job. I took care of myself so I'd never have to ask Larry for anything ever again.

But part of it was about more than money. Even if Larry couldn't afford to pay for all the classes and clothes and shoes, he would have at least helped me. And even if he didn't, I probably could have paid for at least a class or two per season myself with the money I made working at Taco Hell. So what stopped me? What kept me from doing what I wanted?

It took Billy to make it happen, and not just his money. Even if the scholarship had been real, even if I had seen the ad for it with my own eyes, I know I never would have tried out on my own. His belief in me changed something. It wasn't that I was afraid of letting him down, but more like that his hope was contagious. Yes, he lied to me. And yes, his motives weren't completely pure. But I know I never would have believed I was worthy of my dream without Billy believing it first.

"I'm sorry, Lydia," Larry says. "I haven't been a great dad."

"I haven't been a great daughter either," I say.

"But we're doing our best, right?" Larry says.

"I don't know," I say. "I hope so."

I look up for a moment and notice a thick line of gray at Larry's roots. "Your hair's growing out," I say. "I can help you dye it if you want."

"I'd appreciate that," he says.

"Can I ask you something?"

"Shoot."

"Did Mom ever tell you anything about her life before she met you?"

He winces, as if stung by my words. Then he sighs. "Your mother had a lot of secrets, honey. She kept all of that to herself."

"But you were married for ten years," I say. "How was that okay with you?"

"What choice did I have?" he says sadly. "She didn't want to tell me. I couldn't make her. I couldn't change her feelings."

"But did she have any idea how you felt?"

"I don't know."

"Did *you* have any idea how you felt?"

Larry stares into his coffee cup. I wonder how long it's been since someone asked him how he felt.

"There are things I will never understand about your mother," he finally says. "Things neither of us will ever have the chance to know. But I can't spend the rest of my life being mad at her. I just can't."

I've been doing the work of being mad for both of us.

But what if anger has never been the real feeling? What if it's been covering up something way scarier?

What if I'm just sad? What if I just miss her?

"I'm sorry about the dance classes," Larry says. "I should have known they were important to you."

"I should have told you," I say. "It's not your job to read my mind."

"As your dad, maybe it kind of is."

I'll never understand the demons my mom was battling, or why she wasn't able to be the mother I needed. Maybe sometimes people do their best and their best just isn't enough. And maybe there's a way to forgive someone that doesn't change the wrongness of what they did.

Maybe it's not my job to punish her. She's gone anyway. Who is there left to punish but myself?

I don't know where the little girl is right now, but I think she can see me, and I think she's some weird kind of happy, because this fucking hurts and I'm feeling it and I'm not trying to run away.

"I bought tickets to the show," Larry says. "Paul's coming in to watch the bar."

"What about the festival? What about your attraction on the self-guided tour?"

"They won't miss me if I'm gone for a couple of hours, and the main event isn't until later that night." He looks at me and smiles. "But I'd even miss that if I had to."

He's so corny, but I say thank you anyway. Then something catches in my throat, and my lips start to tremble. Am I going to lose it? In front of Larry, at the breakfast table before school on a Thursday?

But then a noise comes from behind the door to my studio. It's a small sound, like a book falling over, but it's amplified in the thick, awkward silence of the kitchen.

"What's that?" Larry says. "It sounded like it was coming from your studio."

"I didn't hear anything," I lie, simultaneously grateful for the interruption, but also terrified that I'm about to have some serious explaining to do. It's way too early in the morning to deal with Caleb.

"I'm going to go check it out," Larry says, scooting his chair back.

"It's probably just a raccoon or something."

"It might be rabid."

"Don't worry about it," I say, contorting my face into the shape of a smile to hide the fact that I can't breathe. Larry discovering Caleb hiding in my broken dance studio is the last thing I need right now. Just two more days until he promised he'd leave. We can make it two days without a catastrophe, can't we? "Go work on getting the bar ready. I'll check the studio."

Larry looks relieved at the prospect of escaping to the bar. "Are you sure?" he says. I nod. "Come get me if you need any help." Even Larry has reached his limit on this father/daughter heart-to-heart.

"I can swat a raccoon with a broom just as good as you, Dad," I say, and then my hand immediately flies in front of my mouth, as if I can catch the word that just came out of it.

Larry blinks at the sudden wetness in his eyes. His bushy eyebrows are bent in deep emotion.

I can't take it. "Get out of here, Larry."

"You haven't called me Dad in years," he sniffles.

"Jesus, man. Get ahold of yourself."

Larry smiles. He wipes his nose with a crumpled paper towel. "Guess I should get busy," he says as he stands up.

"Good luck," I say.

"I love you, honey." Larry doesn't wait for a response or, God forbid, try to hug me. He may not know me well, but he knows enough.

I sit alone in the kitchen after he leaves. The little girl is nowhere to be seen. I'm not sure how I know this, but I'm suddenly aware that she isn't going to be around for much longer. And I'm not quite sure how I feel about that.

BILLY

"NICE DUDS," LARRY SAYS WHEN I OPEN THE FRONT DOOR.

"Thanks," I say. I decided not to do anything new with my hair quite yet, but I did spruce up my wardrobe with a mini shopping spree at Thrift Town, where I spent a whopping forty-three dollars.

I've always chosen clothes that would make me as invisible as possible—jeans and plain T-shirts and hoodies, mostly. But no matter how normal I've tried to look, there's the fact that I'm way too tall and have a bunch of yellow hair sticking out all over my head, and I look like the way less handsome and much more awkward version of the most famous rock star in the world.

Now I think maybe I'll just roll with it. I'm pretty sure I will never not be weird. Maybe it's time to embrace it.

"I'm trying to develop my own signature style," I tell Larry. I'm wearing a pair of vintage brown-and-green-plaid polyester pants and a matching suit jacket, with blue Converse low-tops and a yellow T-shirt advertising some diner called Lulu's Luncheon in Idaho.

"I think you're off to a good start," Larry says. "You're a cool guy, Bill." I have never been called cool in my life. So far, I think my new signature style is working out pretty well.

"You look nice too," I tell Larry.

I've been trying to remember some of my old ways—the good ones, not the weird delusional ones that get me into trouble. The trick is figuring out how to be nice to people without lying and without being an asshole to yourself. Larry's dressed in a cheap blue suit and a Unicorns vs. Dragons tie, so I may be lying a little bit, but he's also got a big smile on his face, which makes a person look good no matter what they're wearing, so mostly I'm telling the truth.

We don't talk much on the way to the show. Larry's driving extra slow because even with the wipers on full blast, it's nearly impossible to see through the window. There are puddles in some places several inches deep that spray huge waves when we drive through them. The whole world looks like it's melting, with occasional bursts of white light followed by the deep rumbling of thunder. It's like the sky is at war with itself—half crying, half furious with anger.

"This is exactly what the weather was like in the battle in Book Three of Unicorns vs. Dragons," Larry says.

"Oh yeah?" I say. "Who won?"

"That's the thing, Bill. Luckily before too many died, they realized they were fighting the wrong enemy, that they'd both been getting played by their *real* enemy for generations."

"So they became friends?"

"They became allies, yes. They were too different to ever really like each other. But you don't have to like someone to be their ally."

"So who was their real enemy?"

"You have to read Book Four to find out."

"Are you kidding me? You just gave away Book Three."

Larry laughs. I have no idea why Lydia acts like she doesn't like him. Larry is awesome. "Humans, Bill," he says. "It's always humans. They ruin everything."

The lobby of the theater is a crowded mess of wet hair, dripping raincoats, and gnarled umbrellas. Half of Fog Harbor County seems to be here, dressed up like they're going to either church or a funeral.

"Were we supposed to buy Lydia flowers?" I say. "Everyone else has flowers."

"Oh," Larry says, looking around. There's a world of people who know things like you're supposed to buy people flowers when they're in shows. Larry and I are not part of that world.

"Do you think she's going to be mad at us?" Larry says.

"She'd be mad at us if we brought flowers too," I say.

"Good point."

We take our programs from the white-haired woman at the entrance to the theater and find seats in the middle. My eyes glaze over as I read what seem like a million different levels of ballet, tap, modern, and something called contemporary/lyrical/jazz. Lydia said after the intermission is when all the advanced classes perform and the real show starts. I honestly don't know if I'm going to make it that far.

"I think your grandma's coming around," Larry says as we wait for the show to start. "She actually answers the phone when I call now."

"You guys talk on the phone?" I say.

"A little."

I'm not sure how I feel about this. I wonder how Grandma is even capable of holding a conversation with someone like Larry.

I look around at all the people in the audience, all the parents holding programs in one hand and phones in the other, getting ready to take pictures. A few fancy video cameras are set up around the auditorium with cool-looking guys behind them. Lydia said they hire professional videographers that come all the way from Seattle.

Most of these parents probably go to things like this all the time, stuff like plays and soccer games and spelling bees and beauty pageants, and whatever else kids do that parents are proud of. I wonder if they can tell Larry and I don't belong here. Or maybe they assume I'm his son and we're here to see my sister dance.

I look at Larry, and he's holding his program so tight he's crushing it, staring at the stage like this is the most exciting thing he's ever done.

I wonder if Lydia even realizes how much he loves her. If she doesn't want Larry as her dad, I'll take him.

LYDIA

WHEN I WENT TO CHECK ON CALEB THIS MORNING, HE
was gone. A note and eight hundred dollars in cash sat on top of the
neatly folded pile of blankets and pillows.

> *As promised, I am leaving today. Money is the cheapest*
> *form of gratitude, but it is all I have. I'm not sure I*
> *deserved your hospitality, but I am determined to earn it,*
> *at least retroactively. Thank you for being so good to my*
> *nephew. He is the person I love most in this world, and if*
> *I am shitty at showing it, I am comforted knowing he has*
> *you. I hope to one day be worthy of his admiration. Thank*
> *you for everything.*
>   *Caleb*
>   *PS: Tell your dad his ATM is out of cash.*

I try not to think about it as I warm up. As much as I hate to
admit it, maybe Mary was a little bit right about needing to leave
everything behind when I dance. But I know it will still be there
waiting for me when the show is over.

Everything's running late because of the rain and a new mudslide on the highway south of town, and Mary is frantic. We were supposed to have more time to go through final blocking, but the teachers couldn't hold the doors closed anymore to keep the dance moms out, so all the dancers getting ready in the aisles had to run onto the stage before the stampede of people trying to get good seats burst in. Now we're all huddled behind the curtain, listening to the growing crowd on the other side and the torrential rain pounding on the roof. It feels like we're in a cave. Underground, but surrounded.

"Doors are open, people!" Mary bellows as she runs across the stage. "Everyone, finish warming up and do makeup touch-ups!"

I am lying on my back, one leg flat on the floor, while Natalie pushes the other toward my nose in splits. "Harder," I say.

"Are you sure?" she says.

"Yes." I grimace.

"Eight minutes!" Mary screams as she rushes across the stage in the other direction. "Teachers, get all dancers backstage."

Natalie looks down at me, her face haloed by the stage light overhead. I lift my hand and place it on hers where it is wrapped around my foot. She releases the pressure, takes my hand, and helps me off the ground. We stand there, eyes locked, holding hands for one brief moment, until Mary screams, "Everyone, backstage NOW!" Then we fly together behind the curtain, feet barely brushing the stage floor, just as thunder shakes the whole building and the houselights flicker.

As the show starts with the little girls' routines, Natalie and I continue stretching with the other dancers backstage in the greenroom, but we stay silent as they titter and gossip. As soon as I start feeling nervous, I look at her, and her eyes are always ready to meet mine.

"Just breathe," she whispers. And I do, but it is hard with her sitting so close to me, for entirely different reasons than this show being the event that will potentially set the course for the rest of my life.

I know Billy is out there, and Larry, too. Natalie's parents. Assholes from school. Random people I've served at Taco Hell. People from Carthage and Rome and all over Fog Harbor County. All these people I've spent my life trying to avoid, and in just a few minutes I'll be onstage in front of all of them.

Is this what I've always wanted? To have their undivided attention so they have no choice but to look at me, to see me as someone besides the sad little girl with the dead mom, as someone besides the poor loner with the chip on her shoulder? Is this my chance to finally show people who I am?

But is this who I am? Am I this thing I do? Am I my obsession and hard work? Am I my sweat and sore muscles and shin splints and calluses and blood blisters? Am I my talent? If I am the best dancer on the stage, the best dancer in Fog Harbor, the best dancer in the world, will it make the people out there love me?

Billy loves me. Larry loves me. But it is not because of this.

I look at Natalie again. She just keeps getting more beautiful. I still haven't figured out why she likes having me around.

Then Mary runs into the room and screams, "Have all the advanced dancers peed?!" and we collapse into giggles. Maybe Mary isn't so bad after all.

"Well, here I go," I say, standing up. Advanced ballet is the first act after intermission.

"Lydia, come on!" Mary shouts. The rest of the class is already filing out of the greenroom.

"Break a leg," Natalie says, her eyes smiling all kinds of things words could never say, and I run to the wings.

The advanced ballet routine is nothing special. It feels weird that my first time onstage in nearly a decade is for something I'm not particularly proud of. I dance as well as I can, then tear my skirt off as soon as I leave the stage. If I'm lucky, I'll never have to perform classical ballet ever again.

Advanced tap is next, with a patriotic number involving a lot of American flags as props. The preprofessional ballet class follows with the first of their ensemble pieces, a melodramatic Wagner opera. Thunder booms outside like cannons along with the music, like the dancers are graceful little soldiers in the middle of a war zone. The King would love this patriotic garbage.

Luckily, Luz's advanced contemporary/lyrical/jazz ensemble keeps things real. I finally start to feel comfortable, even if the pop song we're dancing to is a little cheesy. The houselights are dark, so

I can't see any faces, but I can feel their stares, their attention, and it fills me like fuel.

The preprofessional modern routine is when I finally arrive. My feet are bare, and all I'm wearing is a tiny black top and shorts that feel like an extension of my skin. I leap and spin across the stage with the other dancers to the wild, bass-heavy music. When we're done, the applause is louder than any thunder. I have never had this many people see me, *really* see me. Even if I'm in an ensemble. Even if part of what I'm doing is trying not to shine too much, trying to match the other dancers. Maybe there's something not horrible about being part of something bigger than myself. Maybe it feels okay to not fight it all the time.

I just wish I could watch Natalie's ballet solo. I've seen her dance it numerous times at the studio and in her home, but I've never seen her onstage, lit up, in full makeup and costume. I want to be in the audience with those hundreds of mesmerized people as they fall in love with her.

But how many of them will ever be close enough to see the way beads of sweat collect in the hollow above Natalie's collarbone, will ever get to wrap their fingers around her waist, will ever get to cradle her in a backbend, will ever get to eat junk food with her after four hours of practice?

Natalie only has a couple minutes to get ready for our duet while Simone the tap star does her solo. I don't look as she quickly changes out of her ballet costume, but I feel the heat of her body a few feet behind me. The tiny hairs on the back of my neck are electrified.

"Lydia and Natalie!" Mary screams in her muted backstage voice. "To your places!" Natalie comes up behind me and squeezes my hand for one brief second, and then we run to our opposite sides of the stage for the grand finale. We stand alone in the perfectly silent pitch-black moment before the music for our last, and best, dance starts.

I feel my deep breaths press against my ribs, and I know Natalie is feeling the exact same thing on the other side of the stage. The floor is solid under our strong, bare feet. The music starts with one otherworldly pluck of a distorted string instrument. Two sharp intakes of breath. Two pointed toes. Two lifted chins. And then two bodies in spotlight, moving toward each other like the rest of the world doesn't exist.

We have danced this choreography more times than we can count, but never exposed like this, never with so many eyes witnessing our chemistry as we pull and push each other away, as we touch and break apart, as we bend and twist, as our limbs get lost and merge into one another, as we become a single body. We become the music. The rest of our senses fall away.

I am only vaguely aware of the increasing thunder, the flickering lights. We twirl across the stage in tandem, fire and ice swirling together. We have no idea what we look like from the audience. Do they know we are conjuring our own weather, that the lights are throbbing with our movements, that we are whipping the shadows around us, that the theater itself is expanding and contracting like the lungs straining inside our ribs?

I flip Natalie in a roll across my back, and then we pop up and I spring into her arms. We lower to the floor in controlled splits, our faces tucked into each other's necks, breathing each other's heat, then wrapping into a single fetal ball until we are a naked heart beating onstage.

BILLY

THE AUDIENCE EXPLODES WITH APPLAUSE WHEN THE lights come back on and Lydia and Natalie get up to bow. They are holding hands, chests rising and falling together, beaming at each other, as if the hundreds of people giving them a standing ovation aren't even here.

All of a sudden I get it. Natalie was never meant to replace me. She is something else entirely.

My heart swells as I watch them gracefully walk offstage together. I am vaguely aware of Larry's quiet sobs next to me. Upbeat, triumphant music starts playing as pink toddlers run onstage, bumping into each other as they attempt to stand in a straight line and bow in tandem. Then the little blue dancers. Then slightly bigger ones in black leotards and white tights. Then they all scatter to the back of the stage while the big girls prance to the front.

Thunder punctuates the music with rhythmic booms. The lights continue to flicker. Phones start lighting up around the audience with emergency alerts. Larry pulls out his phone and joins the growing murmurs of "Oh shit." I am suddenly aware that my feet are cold and wet and I look down to find them immersed in two inches of water.

"Oh shit," I say too, then the thunder booms and the lights flare before going out completely. For a moment everything is quiet in the darkness. Then the coast guard emergency siren sounds in the distance, someone screams, and all hell breaks loose.

We are trapped in a dark cavern of screams and shouting. People push each other in the aisles and climb over each other to get to the doors. The black is punctuated with the eerie, bouncing, disembodied glows of cell phone flashlights.

"Over here!" Larry says, and pulls me to an emergency exit door near our seats that no one else seemed to notice. I am blinded by white light when he opens the door, and for a moment I think the world has disappeared and we are about to walk out into a cloud of glowing nothing.

It's a miracle no one gets trampled to death on their way out of the theater. People spill out into the street, five hundred plus people dressed in their Sunday best and several dozen dancers still in leotards and tights, all in various states of distress, many splashing as they run to their cars, some standing comatose as they stare at their phones. Parents try to comfort frightened, crying children. Others nurse those beaten and bruised while trying to escape the theater. A few just stand in the rain looking up at the sky like they've never seen rain before. Water pours down from above and splashes from every other direction. The emergency siren wails in the distance.

Larry pulls me through the crowd, and I only catch half of what he's saying over the sounds of the siren and the rain and everyone else's voices. Something about the King dropping a nuclear bomb on an island in the Pacific. Something about how the real flooding hasn't even begun. Something about World War III. Something about how this is about to get way more intense than weather. He keeps repeating one word over and over again: *tsunami*.

Larry climbs on top of a car and starts yelling. "Everyone, go to higher ground!" he shouts, but no one's listening. "Get your heads out of your goddamned asses and get out of here!"

A pack of dogs runs by. A couple of goats. Then a stampede of deer, a gang of raccoons, flocks of pigeons and seagulls. Rats as far as the eye can see, all heading toward the hills. They don't need news alerts to know when the sea is coming to swallow them up.

"Lydia!" Larry yells. He starts waving his arms wildly. I see Lydia weaving her way through the mob toward us, still in her tiny dance costume. She elbows a guy in the gut who's standing in her way trying to video the whole thing, then wraps her arms around me and squeezes so tight I cough. "You came!" she says.

"Of course I did," I say. "But I didn't bring any flowers."

Everything is soaked. Our skin is waterlogged, turning puffy. The emergency siren continues to sound. The animals continue to run. The humans continue to splash and bump into each other while Larry continues yelling on top of the car, waving his arms in the air, but no one ever listens to the guy who says the sky is falling.

"Where's Natalie?" I say.

"She went home with her family. I told her I had my own family to find."

I don't have time to get emotional. I'll save that for later. If there is a later.

"Larry, come on!" Lydia yells, and pulls on his pant leg. "Dad, we have to go!" She climbs onto the car and wraps him in a hug, and for a split second it does not feel like the end of the world at all.

But then we get back to the business of surviving. Fighting our way out of the crowd is like trying to swim upstream.

"Hey, wait!" a familiar voice yells, just as we break out of the main horde of people, just as a coyote rushes by in front of us.

"Who's that creepy guy in the sunglasses?" Larry says.

"Hey!" someone yells. "That's Caleb Sloat!"

"Larry," Lydia says, "where's the van? We have to get out of here."

"Are those my sunglasses?" Larry says.

Caleb pulls the sunglasses off his face and hands them to Larry as he says, "We have to save Ma."

Everything's going so fast, I don't have time to think about how incredibly weird this all is. Luckily, Larry's van is nearby, so we're able to get a head start on all the people chasing Caleb. The van door almost chops a woman's arm off as she grabs for Caleb's leg, but she tears off his shoe and flies backward just in time.

"Was that my shoe?" Larry says as he starts the car.

"Sorry, man," Caleb says. "I'll buy you new ones."

As we make our way to my house through the river that's replaced the road, I see more animals running for the hills, and among them are confused people in drenched Unicorns vs. Dragons costumes, elaborate makeup melting down their faces.

"That was one of the stops on the tour," Larry says sadly. "That corner is where Prince Drogon and Moonracer first kissed."

"No," Lydia says. "It's where they first had meaningful eye contact."

"Oh, I think you're right," Larry says. "I can't believe you remember. I loved when we used to talk about that."

"Now's not the time to get sappy, Larry. We have people to save."

Just then, what looks like a dragon and two unicorns run by, way larger and way faster than anyone in costume could possibly be.

"Those were really good costumes," I say.

I look at Larry. He's bug-eyed and pale. "I don't think those were costumes," he chokes out.

"Jesus Christ," Lydia says. "Focus, people."

"Grandma!" I yell when I burst through the front door. The first floor is already under a few inches of water. All that *Hoarder Heaven* cleanup was for nothing.

I splash into the living room, her bedroom, her bathroom. She's nowhere to be found.

"Did you find her?" Caleb says as he comes out of the kitchen.

"No," I say. "Maybe she was at the office. Maybe she got a ride to higher ground with one of her friends."

"But her van's outside," Caleb says. "I'm going to look upstairs."

"She won't be up there," I say. "She stopped going up there after you pushed her down the stairs."

Caleb flinches. The sky booms directly overhead, and the house shudders so hard a window in the living room cracks. And then another window cracks. And then another. And the house keeps shaking, and things keep cracking, the wallpaper starts peeling off, the ceiling starts crumbling, and plaster rains down on our heads.

"We have to get out of here!" I yell above the sounds of the dying house.

"I'm getting Ma," Caleb says, and bounds up the stairs, and of course I follow.

The floor of my bathroom has completely caved in. The toilet fell through to the kitchen and is now lying on its side on top of the smashed stove, and water is spraying everywhere. Caleb goes to check the other rooms. I find him in our old bedroom, looking at Grandma's exhibit of the son she never had.

"This is nuts," Caleb says. For a moment I forget that we're in the middle of trying to outrun the apocalypse, and I just now notice how drenched we both are, how our clothes are sticking to our skinny, shivering frames, how we look a lot like wet cats.

"People eat it up," I say.

"People are fools."

"Yeah."

The house groans. The floor tilts a couple extra feet in the direction it's always tilted, enough to make me stumble. "Come on,"

Caleb says, and he rushes out the door and starts climbing the stairs to the attic.

My cave is still there. And inside it, bundled up in the decade's worth of mismatched secondhand blankets she bought and hoarded like her life depended on it, even sometimes when we could barely afford food, Grandma is curled up in a big, soft ball.

"Grandma, you went upstairs!" I say.

Even though I should be busy worrying about dying, I can't help being proud of her.

"What choice did I have?" she whimpers.

It's amazing what survival instincts can make a person do.

Caleb steps out of where he was hiding in the shadows. "Hi, Ma," he says.

And then Grandma faints.

The house sinks even farther. I can hear beams snapping inside the walls. The floor buckles. The ceiling crumbles.

Caleb kneels next to Grandma and gently shakes her shoulder. "Ma," he says. "Wake up. We gotta go." He starts pulling the layers of blankets off of her.

Grandma's eyes flutter open and slowly focus on Caleb. "Are you a ghost?" she says.

"That's a complicated question to answer," he says.

"You came back," she says.

"It's time to go, Ma." Caleb stands and reaches out his hand to help her up. "I'm sorry I pushed you," he says. Grandma just sits there staring at him. I have no idea what she's going to do. I don't think she does either. It's like she hasn't woken up all the way yet.

She doesn't get angry. She doesn't start laying into him. She doesn't start complaining or blaming or any of the other things she usually does. Instead she says, very softly, "Can you ever forgive me?"

The house shudders again. Something big smashes downstairs. The one attic window shatters. "You guys, we have to go," I say. As much as I'm enjoying this tender family reunion, I'm really not ready to die.

"I'm trying to forgive you," Caleb says, and Grandma starts crying.

"Thank you," she says.

Caleb's face is blank, emotionless. "It's not for you," he says. "It's for me. I don't want you taking up space in my head anymore."

She sniffles, looks at him in confusion.

"It's my intention to forgive you," Caleb says. "But that doesn't mean I'm ever going to trust you again."

He reaches out his hand again. This time Grandma takes it and lets him help her to her feet. The floorboards crack under her weight.

"Let's go," I say, and Grandma and Caleb follow me to safety.

They follow *me*.

LYDIA

LARRY AND I ARE SITTING OUT HERE IN THE VAN, STARING at Billy's house, pretending like this isn't the most awkward silence in the history of our awkward silences. I'm still in my modern costume, which is basically just a bra and underwear, and even though I'm wrapped in a musty moving blanket, I'm pretty sure I'm going to freeze to death. The emergency siren blares in the distance, but the street is eerily silent and empty. Even the die-hard fans who have been camped out here for weeks have given up and moved on to higher ground. All that waiting, and they missed Caleb by a few minutes. I almost feel sorry for them.

"I'm proud of you, honey," Larry says from the front seat, looking at me in the rearview mirror. "You're a wonderful dancer."

"Now's not the time, Larry," I say. "The world's about to end."

"Seems like the perfect time, if you ask me."

Maybe I'm crazy, but it looks like Billy's house just tipped several feet to the left.

"I'm sorry you missed the festival," I say.

Larry shrugs. "There will be more festivals. Looks like I didn't miss much, really. But it's a shame about the bar. It really looked nice. Paul texted and said he had to close down because the river crested and the whole place is under two feet of water. Once the tsunami comes, goodbye, everything."

"I'm sorry."

I watch the reflection of Larry's eyes in the rearview mirror. He looks sad for a moment, but then his eyes crinkle in a smile. "You know what?" he says. "I think this may be exactly what I needed. I can use the insurance money to start something new. It might be nice to do something a little more life-affirming than serving beer to drunks."

"I feel the same way about tacos," I say.

It suddenly hits me that the only clothes I own are the glorified underwear I'm wearing right now. My phone and coat are still at the theater, which will soon be underwater. I have nothing.

Just then, there's a knock on the van door. I slide it open to find a small, pale girl around my age, dressed head to toe in black under an umbrella, rushing water up to the middle of her shins.

"If you're looking for Caleb," I say, "scram."

"Who's Caleb?" the girl says.

"Never mind."

"Are you friends with Billy?"

"Yeah. Who are you?"

"I'm Ruth."

"Are *you* friends with Billy?"

"Yes. Are you waiting for him?"

"Why?"

"Can I come with you?" She lifts an old suitcase into the van.

"Don't you have your own family?"

"My dad's on his way to the state forensic psychiatric hospital. My mom ran off to join a new cult in southern Oregon."

I sigh. Can this day get any weirder?

"Sure," I say. "You'll fit right in."

The girl climbs into the van and sits quietly in the backseat with her hands folded on her lap. Billy sure knows how to pick friends.

I can see cars stalled up the street where there's a dip in the road full of water that must have flooded their engines. People pour out of the vehicles, walking this way like slow, awkward zombies as they move through the brown river rushing down the street. Billy and company better get their butts out here soon, or I'm pretty sure we're going to get pummeled to death by the tsunami while Caleb signs autographs.

"The water's gotten higher," I say. "Will the van still run?"

"We've got some height on those guys," Larry says, turning on the ignition. I never thought I'd be grateful that he spent what could have been my dance class money to put a suspension lift system on his van and giant off-road tires that he never uses for off-roading.

"I'm going to go in and get them," I say. But just then, a news van pulls up. "Oh shit."

A burly guy hops out of the driver's seat and splashes around to the other side with an umbrella. That Seattle news lady Ronda Rash jumps into his arms, and he carries her to Billy's front porch.

"I have an idea," the girl named Ruth says. She hops out of the van with a splash and goes back into her house while I basically swim to Billy's front door in my underwear.

"Hey!" I shout to Ronda Rash, who's standing on Billy's front porch while the big guy goes back to the van. "You're trespassing."

"Is this your house?" she asks me. How is she still so dry? How is her hair so fluffy?

"No, but—"

"Then I really don't think it's any of your business." Her smile is sickly sweet. "Brian, hurry up!" she shouts to the guy in the van.

The zombies are getting closer. Their sweatpants are drenched with dirty floodwater. Larry starts honking, as if that's going to scare them away. If anything, it makes them go faster.

Then a door bursts open across the street, and Ruth emerges carrying a shotgun that is almost as big as she is.

"What the fuck?" Ronda Rash and I say at the same time.

Ruth climbs on top of Larry's van and aims the shotgun at the zombie fans, who have now reached the intersection just a few doors down from Billy's house. "Stop right there or I'll shoot!" Ruth yells, and they stop, stunned. Ruth keeps the gun pointed at them as she slides down the front window and hops onto the street like a goddamned superhero.

"Wow," Ronda Rash and I say in tandem.

Ruth slinks through the street-river, pointing the shotgun at the crowd the whole time. She sidesteps to the porch and says, without even looking, "You too, lady. Scram."

"I don't know what you think you're doing, young lady, but I think you need to put the weapon down. It's not civilized to—"

Ruth turns around and points the muzzle of the gun in Ronda Rash's face, just inches away from her nose.

"My God," she gasps, her eyes crossed as she stares into the barrel of the gun. "You people are crazy."

Then the front door flies open, and out come the Sloats.

"There he is!" the cameraman says as he hoists a giant camera onto his shoulder. The mob at the intersection starts screaming and splashing toward us. A few people fall and start floating downstream.

"Go! Go! Go!" Ruth orders as she spins around and shoots into the water just in front of the crowd, and water sprays everywhere like a fountain, confusing everyone for a few seconds while she guards us all the way to Larry's van.

"Ruth!" Billy says as soon as we're all safely in the van. "You're a badass!"

"Thanks," she says calmly as she wrings the water out of her hair.

"You're, like, really good with that thing."

"I got it for my tenth birthday. You never know when you're going to need to hunt your own food."

"Your dad's gun was different."

"My gun's a tool. My dad's gun's got no use but killing people."

"You *saved* us," Billy says, his eyes beaming, awestruck, and Ruth looks at him and smiles and maybe even blushes a little, and

I feel my heart burst into a million tiny warm stars. Billy's a goner.

"Hey, do you want some clothes?" Ruth says to me, and only now do I realize I'm shivering and my nipples are poking through the thin fabric of my top.

"Sure," I say, folding my arms across my chest. Ruth starts pulling some stuff out of a suitcase.

Caleb still hasn't sat down. He's crouching by the van door like he's thinking of opening it back up again. "Ma," he says, "where are your car keys?"

Billy's grandma is sitting in the front seat next to Larry, crying, and he's patting her knee, and I think that's probably the most action she's gotten in a couple of decades.

"Ma!" Caleb says. "Keys!"

She whimpers as she fishes them out of the pocket of her sweater. Caleb slides the van door open and throws the keys in the direction of the fans. "Take that white van and get to higher ground!" he yells at them.

A girl cries, "Oh my God, he talked to me!" and everyone starts screaming and stumbling toward us. But then Ruth aims her shotgun through a slit in the window and shoots just above the crowd, and they all stop in their tracks.

"Say goodbye to our home," Caleb says as he slams the van door closed, and the house shudders one last time. Billy's grandma emits a strangled sound as the roof caves in, the remaining windows all shatter, and glass rains into the street, some of it getting in Ronda

Rash's hair before the cameraman whisks her to safety inside the news van, and then the whole house crumbles to the ground in a cloud of dust that mixes with rain and instantly turns to mud.

The crowd surges forward into the ruins and starts tearing apart the wreckage, looking for artifacts. Even the zombies climbing on the van get distracted and change course.

"Vultures," Ruth says, her gun still pointed out the window. I think I like this girl.

"I guess we're officially homeless now," Billy says.

"Is that *Pete*?" Larry says.

I look where he's staring, and there's the soft, green lump of Old Pete, more moss than human at this point, in a rowboat in the middle of the street, rowing in the direction of the ocean. And there, sitting in the back of the boat, is the nine-year-old version of myself, in her little pink ballet outfit, finally ready to leave.

"He's going the wrong way," Billy says.

"No, he's not," I say.

"Why are you crying?" Billy says.

"I'm not," I say. But who am I kidding? I'm someone who cries now.

The little girl's work is done.

BILLY

HAS THE EMERGENCY SIREN BEEN BLARING THIS WHOLE
time? It fills the air as we drive to the hills. Seals and otters try to
race us there. I see a bald eagle catch a fish at the gas station.

Larry has the radio on full blast, and we've got all the windows
down so people can hear it. "This is the Emergency Alert System," a
calm voice keeps repeating, followed by instructions to get to higher
ground. Between that and the siren, I'm pretty sure I'll be deaf by
the end of the day, if I survive that long.

Fans still in costume from the Unicorns vs. Dragons festival are
helping people out of stranded cars. A small dragon paddles a kayak
full of pet cats and dogs.

"Wait!" Caleb shouts. "Stop the car."

"We have to get to higher ground," Larry says.

"What is that dummy doing on the roof?" Grandma says. Larry
found her some beef jerky and trail mix in the glove box, so she's
feeling much better and started talking again.

I look out the window, and there's One-Armed Gordon sitting
on the roof of his house, clutching an old soggy teddy bear to his
chest with his good arm. Caleb opens the van door even though
we're still moving and jumps out. Larry stops the van.

"If we drown because of that loser, I'm going to smack some chins," Grandma mutters.

We all look out the window as Caleb climbs a ladder leaning against the house and crawls across the roof to where Gordon is sitting in the pouring rain. Gordon's face when he sees Caleb is pure joy, like he was waiting there for him all this time, waiting for his one and only true friend to save him.

"That's sweet and all," Lydia says as they embrace, "but we *so* don't have time for this right now." She's wearing a polyester skirt and a button-down shirt that Ruth gave her, and she kind of looks like she should work at a funeral home. "What could they possibly be talking about?" Caleb and Gordon seem to be having some kind of serious discussion on the roof.

After a couple of minutes, they finally start climbing down the ladder, but then Gordon splashes next door and starts knocking on the neighbor's door, and Caleb makes his way to the van through the river of the street, his eyes clear and full of determination, his drenched T-shirt revealing all kinds of new muscles I never noticed, all heroic and puffed up like a soldier in one of those old war movies.

"Gordon's taking that side of the street," he says when he gets to the car. "I'll take the other. You guys take the side streets. Knock on every house with a light on or a car still in front. We'll make our way toward the hills while Larry keeps broadcasting the emergency message."

Nobody questions his orders. We get to work.

I have never been so focused in my life.

We go door-to-door and tell the few remaining people what's going on. How they heard the siren and did not think to check the news, I have no idea. Caleb has to give a few autographs along the way. Lydia stops a passing car that still has room in it and shames them into letting a homeless guy ride with them. Gordon throws a stray chicken into the back of a passing truck. Ruth has her own strategy involving intimidation tactics and sticking her shotgun in people's faces when they open the door and ordering them to vacate.

We run into a few old folks who try to refuse to leave, but Ruth convinces them with her gun. Caleb has to throw one guy over his shoulder who kicks and screams and hits him with his cane and calls him a commie while Caleb carries him over to a car that's just about to take off and opens the door, getting pummeled the whole time.

"What are you doing?" screams Kayla or Kaitlyn or Katelyn from school, who's sitting in the passenger seat half naked holding a guinea pig in a cage on her lap. Then Graylon or Grayson or Braydon, who is shirtless in the driver's seat, is like, "Hey, aren't you Caleb Sloat?" and then he squeals in a high-pitched voice, "Ohmygod ohmygod ohmygod, I am your biggest fan!" and Caleb just puts the thrashing old man in their backseat and closes the door and runs to the next house.

It's slow going with all the traffic trying to get away from the coast and having to dodge the abandoned cars and their passengers stranded next to them in a foot of water with hopeless looks on their faces. Ruth starts knocking on the windows of trucks that still have empty beds. "You better fill up with people and bring them to higher ground," she commands, pointing the gun between the drivers' eyes, her voice low and growling, surprisingly intimidating for someone who's barely tall enough to see into the windows. "And when you're done, you come back and you keep coming back until you can't come back no more. If you don't, God will know, and I will know, and I will find you, and you'll be sorry."

I simultaneously want to cry and hug her and kiss her and run away and throw up.

I'm pretty sure this is what falling in love feels like.

We are exhausted by the time the road finally starts going uphill. We climb into the van and Larry turns off the radio, but I think the announcer guy's voice has left a permanent scar on my brain because I can still hear it, along with the blaring siren and the ringing in my ears.

I stand on my knees in the backseat, looking out the rear window at the view of all the people behind us. By now the trail following us is blocks long, a combination of cars, trucks, bicycles, kayaks, animals, people, someone in a cape riding a white horse with a unicorn horn strapped to its head, hundreds, maybe even thousands, of Fog Harbor residents and fans of Unicorns vs. Dragons and Rainy Day Knife Fight, following a van full of weirdos with a giant dragon head painted on the side to safety.

Lydia puts her arm around me and looks out the window too. It may be the end of the world, but it feels good to have my best friend back.

"I love parades," I say.

"I know you do," she says, and squeezes.

LYDIA

"WHAT HAPPENED AFTER THE GREAT FLOOD?" BILLY ASKS Ruth as we make the slow ascent into Rome Hills. "Was everyone okay? Did they rebuild and stuff?"

"The waters took a while to recede," Ruth says. "But then there was a brave new world to conquer, so all the people and animals spread out and made more people and animals. Then God invented rainbows."

"That's a nice story," Billy says.

"I guess," Ruth says. "But it's just a story. God also said He'd never make it flood again. But He lied."

"But the King did this," Billy says, "not God."

"What are you idiots talking about back there?" Billy's grandma says. For once, we're probably on the same side.

"God made it flood because He realized He made a mistake and humans were evil and needed to be destroyed," Ruth says matter-of-factly.

We're all quiet. No one can really argue with that.

The van smells a little like wet cat, but things could definitely be worse. Gordon keeps blubbering in the backseat about how good it is to see Caleb, and Caleb's just nodding calmly like some monk.

Ruth has finally put the shotgun down. I can tell Billy's trying really hard not to stare at her, but he sneaks little glances, and each one looks like he's getting ready to propose marriage. Larry's keeping his eyes on the road while Billy's grandma munches on the last of the glove compartment snacks.

What a bunch of amazing, wonderful losers we are.

What if we're the only ones who make it? What if Larry's van is the ark?

The thought makes me shudder.

Traffic starts thinning the higher we get as people pull off on side roads, taking over the quiet streets full of perfect views of whatever's coming. But we're not taking any chances. We're going straight to the top.

"Natalie lives down that street," I say. "I bet she's all safe and warm in her house with her family, drinking tea and watching all this on TV."

"Do you want us to drop you off at her house?" Billy says. He looks at me hopefully, holding his breath.

I smile. "Nah," I say. "If I'm going to drown in the great flood, I want to do it with you."

When we get to the top of the hill, there are already a few cars lined up and pointed toward the ocean, like they're getting ready to watch Fourth of July fireworks instead of their whole lives getting washed away.

"Park the van right under that ladder," I tell Larry. "And give me your phone." I quickly text Natalie where we are.

"Are we going up there?" Ruth says.

"Just like old times," Gordon blubbers.

"No one's making me go up there," Grandma says. "You all can fall to your deaths. That's fine with me."

"I'll stay in the van with you," says Larry.

"I never said I needed company."

"Larry just saved your life, Grandma," Billy says. "Stop being an asshole."

I've never been so proud of him.

His grandma just looks at him in shock, and Caleb starts laughing like a maniac. And then Gordon starts laughing. And then Ruth. And for a tiny split second, I almost feel sorry for the nasty old woman, but then she smiles and starts laughing too.

I guess something about the world ending makes people act a little out of character.

Maybe the world should end more often.

BILLY

HERE WE ARE SITTING ON THE WATER TOWER, WAITING
for a tsunami. It stopped raining as soon as we got here. Maybe
the weather decided to give us a little break before things get
really wet.

"Do you think it's going to get us up here?" Gordon says, still
holding on to his teddy bear.

"Who knows," Lydia says. "None of us are tsunami experts."

Birds keep flying overhead, and a bunch of deer and raccoons
run by under us. There are mice and rats everywhere. More people
keep coming, some in cars, many on foot.

"Does anyone have any snacks?" Lydia says. "I'm starving."

"Billy's grandma ate them all," says Ruth. Somehow, she managed to climb the ladder while holding the shotgun. Good thing
I'm so cold, or I might have to deal with hiding a boner, and I really
don't think I could handle that right now.

"Caleb, man," Gordon says, staring at the graffiti on the side of
the water tower, "did you see all this stuff?"

Caleb nods quietly without turning to look. He's staring out
at the sea. Besides his laughing outburst in the van, he hasn't said
anything in a long time.

We could die any minute. Maybe now is a good time to talk about stuff.

"Hey, Caleb?" I say. I'm sitting next to him on the narrow platform. We're all in a row—Gordon, Caleb, then me in the middle, then Lydia and Ruth.

"What's up?" he says, still staring out at the horizon, like he doesn't want to miss the first sign of the wave.

The sky has almost completely cleared in the few minutes we've been up here. Just a few wispy clouds remain, and the rest is dazzling blue. It's so different from the last time Lydia and I were up here, when we were swallowed up by white, when we couldn't see anything. We were weightless then, floating. Today, even though I'm a hundred feet in the air, I feel closer to the ground than I've felt in a long time.

"I've been wondering something for a long time," I say. "In all the interviews you've done, how come you never mentioned me?"

Caleb turns to me now. His blue eyes look into mine with surprise.

"I guess I was just wondering why," I say. "Because it kind of hurt my feelings. You pretending I didn't exist."

After a pause, Caleb says, "That wasn't it." He shakes his head, like he's trying to dislodge something in there. "That wasn't it at all. I was trying to protect you."

Suddenly, everything is silent. Birds stop chirping. The world is holding its breath, waiting for something.

"I gave them everything," Caleb says, "but I was never going to give them you. You weren't a part of those stories. You were the one good thing."

A single tear falls down his cheek, and I hear a sound like the whole earth roaring.

LYDIA

THE OCEAN TRANSFORMS. FIRST THE SEA GOES OUT,
sucking water away from the shore, revealing the rocky ocean floor.
Then the sea rises in smooth, undulating waves out to the horizon.

"Holy shit!" Natalie says, suddenly with us. Ruth scoots over to
make room beside me.

"You came," I say as Natalie sits next to me on the platform,
warm relief dissolving my fear. For a moment, I forget why we are
here. For a moment, Natalie is the reason for everything.

"Of course I did," she says. "My parents kept *praying*. It was
driving me crazy."

"Tell me about it," Ruth says, cradling the shotgun in her lap
with something like affection.

Then the waves start.

The first waves obliterate the shoreline, sending water inland,
smashing the lines of beachfront vacation cabins and hotels. The
already full river spills water everywhere, and the harbor swells and
explodes all over downtown Rome. The waves keep coming, water
quickly creeping further and further inland, adding inches, then
feet, to the already flooded streets.

But those waves were just practice.

Natalie grabs my hand as we watch what's coming—a wall of water at least twice as tall as the tallest building in Rome, barreling toward the shore in slow motion, getting taller and taller the closer it gets. A sound like a freight train drowns out the emergency siren.

And then the beach is gone. Completely gone. Docks and buildings are smashed into kindling. Cars float inland like boats. The ocean swallows Rome and Carthage block by block, erasing entire neighborhoods, pulling down the wooden houses in Criminal Fields as if they were built with toothpicks.

"There goes my house," Billy says.

"Mine, too," says Ruth.

"I'm so sorry," says Natalie.

"I never liked it that much anyway," Ruth says.

"There goes Larry's bar," I say. Natalie wraps me inside her arms.

Caleb has his arm around Gordon, who is weeping, inconsolable. Ruth stares out at the scene blankly. Natalie is pressed up against me, silent tears running down her face, holding on to me so tightly, I am almost not cold.

The water comes and comes. Cars bob around like they're weightless. Even up here, I can hear the sound of all the debris smashing into itself. All those homes, turned into driftwood that will get sucked out to sea and wash up on someone else's shore.

I don't see any people, but who knows how many are hidden, still stuck inside houses and cars? Who knows how many we didn't save? Who knows how many lives are being lost at this very moment, how many people did not hear the siren, did not have smartphones to tell them what to do, did not turn on their TVs or radios for the emergency broadcast? How many did not have vehicles to get away, did not have friends or family who thought to save them? How many were simply forgotten?

And how many knew perfectly well what was happening but chose to stay anyway? How many thought going down with the only world they've ever known was better than trying to start a new one?

As far as I can see, Fog Harbor County is covered with water. The sturdiest buildings poke out. Fog Harbor High is, unfortunately, still standing. The prison. BigMart. Even a tsunami can't destroy those.

The waves keep pulsing through the flatlands of Criminal Fields, crashing into the base of the hill. We are safe up here on our island. How'd we get so lucky? What gives us the right to survive when so many will not?

I look at Natalie. She is so beautiful when she's crying. She's so beautiful, always.

Why do I even get to think that right now? Why do I get the privilege of loving her?

And even though this is probably one of the least romantic moments in history, even though so many lives are being ruined and lost, even though we're surrounded by weirdos on top of a water tower and I don't know what's going to happen and I feel scared about everything, I figure, what the hell? You only live through the end of the world once.

I look into Natalie's deep brown eyes. I see them crinkle at the sides in a smile. I lean in and feel the world expanding as my lips touch hers. I feel everything pulse open and wash clean, and I think, this is what it feels like to be limitless and on top of the world.

Then I hear crying. Natalie pulls away gently, and we both look down to see a girl in soaking wet sweatpants, a Rainy Day Knife Fight T-shirt, no shoes, thick black eye makeup running down her face. She must have swum to get here. She must have hiked barefoot up the entire hill. And now she's just standing there, her entire body shaking with sobs.

"Hey!" I call down to her. "It's going to be okay." And I think I actually believe it, because here we are, safe, and the world did not end today. The sky is blue and the sun is shining. I hear some birds starting to sing again. I just kissed the girl of my dreams, Billy's been in love for at least half an hour, and Caleb's alive and healthy. Maybe I've stopped needing to hate my mom so much, Larry's turning out to be a pretty good dad, and I kicked the Winter Showcase's ass. Sure, Criminal Fields has been sucked out to sea, but no one liked it much anyway, and what are we in Carthage and Rome but a bunch of survivors?

The girl on the ground shakes her head. "You don't understand," she says. Her smile is so big, it makes the sun shine brighter. She's staring straight at Caleb. "This is the best day of my life!" she cries. I guess it's all about perspective.

Then Gordon says, "Now what?" and nobody knows how to answer.

EPILOGUE

BILLY

A LOT HAS HAPPENED SINCE THE TSUNAMI.

First of all, the King died. Around the same time the tsunami was obliterating the entire west coast, he was killed instantly in a freak accident at one of his ski resorts involving a falling icicle straight through the heart. Larry's convinced unicorns had something to do with it. Grandma thinks it was the Canadians.

The good news is his bomb missed the island target by several hundred miles. The guy flying the plane claims it was an accident, but no one believes him. No one accidentally bombs the exact spot in the ocean that'll do the least amount of harm. The United Nations wants to give him some kind of big medal. They might even let the US back in as a member soon.

It's July now, and the population of Fog Harbor has already decreased by 37 percent. The majority of those who left were people who had been threatening it for years but never quite got their acts together. Nothing like having everything you own wash out to sea to motivate you to start over somewhere else. Gordon went to Tacoma to start a video game store with his insurance money, which, according to Caleb, is something he'd been talking about doing since they were eight years old.

Some environmentally conscious building company bought a big chunk of Criminal Fields and started construction on a bunch of little communities made out of recycled materials, with organic gardens and free bicycles and solar panels and electric vehicle charging stations, and all these artists and people who can't afford to live in Seattle anymore are buying them up, sight unseen. Everyone keeps talking about how Fog Harbor is going to be a big new tech hub, and I'm not really sure what that means, but it's probably better than a bunch of unemployed people sitting around being grumpy waiting for trees to grow back.

FEMA bought all the foreclosed mansions on the hill for cheap and put all the displaced people in them because it was less expensive than bringing in trailers. Grandma and I are sharing one with Lydia and Larry and a doomsday-prepper family who immediately turned the wine cellar into a panic room. They've been surprisingly good housemates. Ruth is staying with us too. The paperwork to make her an emancipated minor went through pretty quickly. People tend to expedite those things when one of your parents has been deemed criminally insane by a federal judge and the other one ran off to join a cult. The only bummer is that Grandma said Ruth has to sleep on the other side of the house because hanky-panky will not be tolerated, which is ridiculous because walking down the hall at night is hardly a deterrent when you're highly motivated, which we are. It's not even like we spend all our time doing hanky-panky (though that is a large percentage of what we do). It's like we're making up for lost time after a whole lifetime of never being touched or listened to. So we do a lot of both of those things.

Ruth and I are making plans to move to Olympia together in the fall. She insists on bringing the shotgun, and I am totally okay with that. Maybe I'll even learn how to use it. Neither of us really knows what we want to do with our lives, but that's not something either of us have ever really thought about, so I don't know, we're just going to spend some time thinking about it. We're not in too much of a hurry.

Caleb's at some silent meditation retreat in Thailand. He's deciding if he wants to be a monk or a folk singer. He said the best way to stop running from himself was to be forced to sit still for a while, and Lydia rolled her eyes and told him to save the poetry for song lyrics.

Larry and Grandma joined forces and are starting a company together that will focus on Unicorns vs. Dragons–related stuff, because apparently Grandma's been converted into a superfan and has lost interest in exploiting her son's fame. They just signed a lease for a small building that was miraculously unharmed in the floods, and Larry got a no-interest loan from Caleb to buy a bunch of Unicorns vs. Dragons–themed merchandise wholesale, so they're going to run a combination gift shop/tour company. They're also thinking of staying in the big house together after we all leave. I like to joke to Lydia that we might be siblings soon, but that always makes her punch me.

Natalie's getting ready to go to some fancy ballet college in New York called Juilliard. Lydia's going to another fancy school called Alvin Ailey, where usually they require several years of training and an in-person audition, but her teacher pulled some strings and they accepted Lydia's Winter Showcase video as her audition because of extenuating circumstances, i.e., her whole town being wiped out by a tsunami. Caleb wanted to pay for everything, but Lydia wouldn't let him. I will never understand why she would choose waitressing and thousands of dollars of financial aid debt over getting a free ride, but that's Lydia for you.

I'm going to miss her, but I'm trying not to think about that. Maybe I'm in denial. I keep thinking about the AA slogan "Denial is Not a River in Egypt" on the sign above Lynn A.'s empty chair, and I like to think it's a message she left especially for me. And even though I still don't know what it means, I'm assuming AA agrees with the therapy talk shows I used to watch that said denial is a big no-no, but they also weren't too into negative thinking, and now that I think about it both AA and those shows were full of contradictions. The way I figure it, why should I spend these last couple months I have with Lydia thinking about how much I'm going to miss her? I can save those feelings for after she's gone, when they'll actually be relevant. That's not denial; it's common sense.

Before Caleb left, he taught me a lot about living in the moment. Apparently that Buddha guy he likes came up with the idea way before therapists did.

The days after the tsunami and the King's death were a weird time for TV. Footage of devastation from the bomb and tsunami was followed by videos of people all over the planet dancing in the streets because they didn't have to worry about being bombed anymore. Countless lives were destroyed while countless others were liberated, and all of these things were happening simultaneously, on the same planet, and there was room for all of it. One of the weirdest things was that a lot of the places that were hit the worst by the tsunami were also celebrating. People in San Francisco and Hawaii and Japan were dancing on top of flooded houses and cars while they were waiting to be rescued, like their loss wasn't as important as the fact that the whole world was suddenly a lot less scared. And I think I sort of know how they felt. Because my house is gone and my town is gone and Caleb is gone (again) and Lydia's going to be gone soon, and I have no idea what I'm going to do with my life, but I also have a girlfriend and a best friend, and I actually managed to graduate high school, and the world is way bigger than I ever realized, and I have a whole lot of unknown ahead of me, and it's scary at the same time that it's exciting, and all of those things can coexist, because I am not one thing. Nobody is.

Today is the Fourth of July, and I guess I'm feeling pretty patriotic. Lydia, Natalie, Ruth, and I are sitting on top of the water tower facing the sea. The sun is halfway in the ocean, and the sky is an explosion of the kind of fluorescent colors people always say you don't see in nature, but here they are, and what's more natural than a sunset? We're waiting for the annual Fog Harbor fireworks show to start, but I'm pretty sure it won't compare to this—just sitting here together, in the quiet at the end of the earth, waiting for night to fall. We survived a tsunami and the worst winter in history, and now the sea is calm, the sky is clear, the air is warm, and here we are, with a perfect view of infinity.

ACKNOWLEDGMENTS

It's a strange thing when a place you know becomes famous for all kinds of strange reasons, like rock stars and YA fantasy series. Before that, it was just where my family was from. I grew up listening to my dad and uncles' and aunt's stories and visiting that wild coast and those decaying towns. The fog and rain and tangy smell of pine needles and creosote are in my blood. So is the legacy of doing what it takes to survive. We are a family of survivors.

Thank you to my father, for proving everybody wrong. Thank you for teaching me about hard work and not taking anything for granted.

Thanks to my uncle Dave, for the tour, and to my cousins, for opening your home and family to that lost blue-eyed genius so many years ago. Maybe nobody could have saved him, but you were part of building the music that changed the world, and maybe your love helped him stay with us a little bit longer.

Maybe we can't all go home again, but we can make new homes wherever we end up, and maybe the new ones can be better than we ever imagined possible.

Photo by Ed Glazar

My deepest gratitude to the following:

Amy Tipton, for a whole decade(!) of support and cheerleading. And to Michael Bourret, for many new adventures to come.

My soul mate editor, Liesa Abrams, who understands me, not just as a writer, but as a woman and human being. Thank you for your wisdom and insight, your big-picture brilliance, and your friendship.

Thank you to everyone at Simon Pulse who makes the book magic happen—Michelle Leo, Mara Anastas, Nicole Russo, Jessica Smith, everyone behind the scenes whose names I've never learned, and the tons of people I know I'm forgetting. I couldn't do this without you. Also, how is possible that you're all so *cool*? I want to come to the office and just hang out sometime.

Thank you to all the librarians, teachers, booksellers, and bloggers who champion my work and help lead young readers to the books they need to read.

I am not exaggerating when I say this book would be an unreadable garbage pile of clichés and half-baked ideas if it weren't for these people and their generosity of time and brilliant feedback: Frankie Bolt, Jaye Robin Brown, Stefanie Kalem, Alison Knowles, Mark Oshiro, Brenda Rufener, and Amber Smith. I did not write this book alone. You are all on every page. Thank you for opening your hearts to my weird little world.

Shout-out to my Nebo gals, for three years and counting of refuge and solidarity.

Shout-out to my husband, Brian, for being my home. To my daughter, Elouise, for being my heart and greatest work.

Shout-out to everyone who continues to do the brave work of love even when the world is breaking. We are the ones who will rebuild it.

ABOUT THE AUTHOR

AMY REED is the author of several novels for young adults, including *The Boy and Girl Who Broke the World*, *The Nowhere Girls*, *Beautiful*, and *Clean*. She also edited the anthology *Our Stories, Our Voices: 21 YA Authors Get Real About Injustice, Empowerment, and Growing Up Female in America*. Amy is a feminist, mother, and quadruple Virgo who enjoys running, making lists, and wandering around the mountains of western North Carolina, where she lives. You can find her online at www.amyreedfiction.com.